Dead Philadelphians

Dead Philadelphians

Frank Frost

CAPRA PRESS
SANTA BARBARA

Cover and book design by Frank Goad, Santa Barbara

This is a work of fiction. All characters herein are fictitious and any resemblance
to persons living or dead is entirely coincidental.
Kali Vrisi is an imaginary village.

LIBRARY OF CONGRESS CATALOGUING-IN-PUBLICATION DATA

Frost, Frank J., 1929-

Dead Philadelphians : a novel / Frank Frost.

p.   cm.

ISBN 0-88496-438-8 (pbk. alk. paper)

I. Title.

PS3556.R975D42   1999

813′ .54—dc21   98-54916

CIP

Capra Press
P.O. Box 2068
Santa Barbara, CA 93120

To Victoria, for her long hours
and Molly, for always being there
and Mandy, who fixed it.

Prologue
South Dakota

At ten that morning, 300 miles into South Dakota, Danny Castle made his first mistake. He'd gotten up before dawn in Buffalo, Wyoming and had kept the needle between 75 and 80 for the last six hours. The old maroon Mercury he'd bought for cash in Reno had a faded, patchy paint job and the beginnings of body rot but the tires were fairly new and the motor was still smooth and robust. Even at eighty, which he thought was pretty fast, some of the few cars on the road had actually passed him, and not slowly.

So he'd gotten impatient in that desolate flat wasteland and let the car creep up close to ninety. He went under an underpass on the I-90 and a second later there was a flashing roof rack in his rear view mirror. He didn't even swear, although he felt like it, just let his breath out in a long sigh, took his foot off the pedal and let the Merc cruise over to the shoulder. Speeding. If he was lucky the guy would take cash.

The trooper took his time, sitting there in his patrol car. *Calling in the license,* Danny thought. *But it's clean, completely legal.* Now the guy was getting out, tall, lanky, putting on his trooper hat that looked funny with his long hair under it, dark hair, hanging down to his shoulders. He had a long face too, and a Fu Manchu mustache hanging down either side of a mean mouth. Dark, dark sunglasses, of course.

"Show some ID, license, registration?"

"Got it right here officer." Danny gave him the registration, the Nevada driver's license with the name Frederick James on it. The trooper looked at the papers long enough to translate them into another language. Then he pursed his lips and lines of heavy thought crossed his forehead.

"Going a bit fast, weren't you?"

Danny gave him a rueful chuckle. "Yeah, I guess. It's a long straight road. Just wasn't thinking about it, no traffic or anything."

The mean mouth got meaner. "Supposed to keep your mind on your driving all the time. You wouldn't been havin' a little drink, would you?"

"A bit early for me, officer." Danny was thinking fast now. *What did this asshole want? What did he hear over the radio? Was it just the boredom factor, stop one of the six cars that went by here every hour and hassle the driver, play nazi?*

"Okay, pal. Outta the car. Let's see how you do on the field test."

Danny kept his face expressionless. But he took the keys out of the ignition and locked the car before he got out.

"Why'd you lock the car? Whatcha got in there?"

"Officer, you want to give me a ticket, give me a drunk test, let's get with it, okay?"

The effect was immediate. The trooper straightened up, his face reddening. He put one big knuckled hand on his revolver.

"I'm asking you once. Open the car."

"I don't have to. You can't search my car unless you arrest me and you got no cause to arrest me, only cite me for speeding."

Now the trooper put on an ugly smile. Danny thought, *why did I run into the dumbest chump in South Dakota, for Chrissakes!*

"Well, pal, you just got arrested. You flunked the sobriety test, being a smartass. Drop your keys on the ground, turn around, put your hands behind your back."

Danny could now see the clenched teeth, the widened nostrils, could hear the high tremor in the voice, the unmistakable signs of an amphetamine high. *A goddamn crankhead*, he thought. *How did I get so lucky.* But he turned around obediently, knowing that this speed freak was on the edge, might shoot him just for kicks.

The trooper cuffed him, dragged him roughly by the arm to the rear door of the cruiser. He opened the door and as Danny started to get in he said, "Watch your head," and slammed Danny's head against the door frame. Danny felt the skin on his forehead split and quickly rolled into the back seat. The trooper was holding the door open and watching the trickle of blood start to dribble into Danny's eyes. For the first time there was a bit of uncertainty in his manner.

Now he's thinking, did I go too far? was Danny's first reaction. Then the trooper slammed the door, went back and picked up the keys to the Merc. He opened the driver's door, looked all around, seeing nothing, no bags, just an empty cardboard coffee cup on the floor. He came around to the trunk, opened it, found the suitcase, the black canvas carry-on with wheels He closed the trunk, set the suitcase on top and looked back at Danny with a nasty grin on his face. He unzipped the suitcase. Hmm. Clothes, no drugs, no weapons, gotta dig deeper. He pushed the layer of clothes aside, the toilet kit...and stopped dead. Danny knew what he was looking at. About a hundred and fifty thousand dollars in hundreds, neatly banded and stacked.

*

The Sheriff's substation was in Biscuit, county seat of Biscuit county. The trooper called a gas station in town to get a tow truck out there to bring in the Merc. They passed him coming out on the way into town. At the Sheriff's modest headquarters, a one-story frame building, the trooper, carrying the suitcase, pushed Danny through the door. A bulky woman wearing a khaki uniform looked up from behind her desk. She looked at Danny, then to the trooper, then back to Danny, who now had blood in his eyes, and drooling down one cheek.

"Jesus, Cecil," she expostulated, "I didn't have enough to do today you gotta bring in another beat-up prisoner? What the hell did this guy do?"

"Hell, Marie..." the trooper started.

"It's 'Sheriff,' to you, Cecil." Cecil stopped in his tracks, then took a long breath. Turned and gave Danny a big sarcastic smile. He was going to show off for Danny now, in front of this dumb broad.

"You got it, Sheriff. Pardon me, I forgot myself. This guy, this *perpetrator*, flunked the sobriety test, gave me a hard time, I had to force him into the unit."

"You breathalyze him?"

Cecil smiled at Danny again. "Guy refused to be breathalyzed. I..."

The Sheriff came right over and looked into Danny's eyes. "Did you refuse to be breathalyzed?"

"He never asked," said Danny. "And he never gave me a field sobriety test. I haven't had even a beer since yesterday afternoon."

"Hell, they all lie," said Cecil. "Probably's worn off by now." But the Sheriff was back at a cabinet, came out with a big plug-in contraption that had a mouthpiece covered by a disposable piece of plastic. She set it on a formica counter next to a coffee maker, then had to unplug the coffee maker so she could plug in the machine.

"What's your name, son?"

Danny had to think a minute. "Frederick James, Sheriff. I gave him my license, registration. Everything's legal, I don't know why..."

She cut in. "Mr. James, do you consent to a breathalyzer test? If you don't you will be taken to the county clinic and have a blood sample taken." She now spoke in a confidential tone. "Son, sometimes your blood alcohol will wear off on the breathalyzer, but that blood sample will nail even the martini you had before dinner last night. What'll it be?"

"I'll take the breathalyzer, Sheriff. Don't make any difference. I don't have any alcohol in my system."

She put the mouthpiece in his mouth. "Now breathe out steadily while I count to five. Don't try to breathe too slow. Machine doesn't work that way."

He breathed steadily for a five count into the mouthpiece. The Sheriff pushed a button, consulted a gauge. A green bulb lit up on the display. Then she turned and looked at Cecil, who seemed unduly relaxed.

"Cecil! Blood alcohol is zero. ZERO! You hear that?"

Cecil had a smug smile on his face. Without saying a word he opened the suitcase, turned it upside down on the Sheriff's desk so that the piles of hundred dollar bills spilled down in a heap.

"So. What the hell you think of that, *Sheriff*! Why don't you breathalyze that?" He was wearing a triumphant, shit-eating grin.

"Jesus, Mary and all the angels!" The big woman couldn't stop staring at the pile of bills. Then she narrowed her eyes at Danny.

"Where'd this money come from, *Mister* James?"

Danny was thinking quickly. "Sheriff, I'd like a lawyer. And I can pay for a lawyer, although Cecil here never bothered to read me the Miranda. Otherwise, I'm not saying anything."

"Let's lock him up, Marie," Cecil was urging. "Son of a bitch musta knocked over a bank or something."

"Wait," said Danny quickly. "If the courts are open here, I have the right to be taken before a magistrate. That's the law."

"See!" yelled Cecil. "Sonofabitch is a jailhouse lawyer. We're gonna nail his ass." But the Sheriff was not that sure. She picked up a phone and spent a minute in conversation. Then she hung up, looked back and forth at the trooper and Danny.

"Guy's right. Court is in session. Al's bailiff says there's a recess coming up. Sure you want to go up in this court, Mr. James? They call him 'Maximum Al.' His honor Albertus Uxkull. And I know he's got a hell of a hangover this morning."

*

The "courtroom" was just a conference room attached to City Hall. On court days they moved the big table up to the front of the room and let the judge sit behind it. Everything else was just folding chairs. The young prosecutor from Pierre saw the procession come in. She saw a nice looking young guy in handcuffs with a bandaid on his forehead. Dark brown hair, interesting hazel eyes. Big old Sheriff. Marie Bacon, been in office twenty-two years and not slowing down a bit. Then the tall trooper with the crazy eyes you could only see when he took off his sunglasses.

She'd had four cases that morning, one of the two mornings

a week she came over to Biscuit. Couple of drunk drivers, a teenager caught smoking dope, migrant farm worker who tried to hold up a convenience store with a water pistol. She had four out of four convictions. Crime capital of south central South Dakota, she was thinking. The dweeby looking court reporter, she knew, was dying to get outside for a few of his forty cigarettes a day. Then Cecil sat down next to her and opened this suitcase full of hundred dollar bills.

"And I was the guy who nailed him," he was saying triumphantly, trying to look down her blouse on the sly. His breath was sweet with ketones and almost made her gag but she pulled herself together, asked him, "What's the charge?"

"He was driving weird, I pulled him over, he was drunk and attacked me. When I subdued him I found this suitcase in the trunk of his car..."

He was interrupted by an ancient bailiff hollering, "All rise, the honorable Albertus Uxkull."

A portly, elderly man in a black robe came out of a back room, looking around with hatred. Behind his glasses Danny could see little red eyes. The Sheriff had now talked to the clerk of the court, a withered man in an ancient tweed suit. The clerk stood up.

"In the matter of the arraignment of Frederick James. Charged with driving under the influence, assaulting a peace officer, possession of stolen money."

Everyone in the court now stared at Danny Castle. Hardly anyone had ever heard of anyone charged with three crimes all at once. His honor cleared his throat, just getting ready to ordering Danny jailed till further notice. So Danny spoke up.

"Your honor, I can afford to pay for a lawyer, and I want a lawyer."

A look of pain crossed the judge's face. He called up the

young prosecutor and talked with her for a minute in muted tones no one could hear. Then he asked his bailiff, "You think Freddy is down at Rosie's having breakfast?"

The bailiff looked at his watch. "It's a little late, your honor, but it's a good bet."

"That sonofabitch was with me down at Elks last night. I left at two and he was just getting up a good head of steam. If I gotta sit here through all this dismal crime wave he's gotta be here too. Jim, go the hell down to Rosie's and don't come back without Freddy." He whacked the table with his gavel and said, "Court's in recess. Ten minutes." Then he looked at the Sheriff. "Marie, come on here in chambers. I need some background on what the hell is going on here."

*

It was at least a half an hour before Danny saw a disreputable old man being guided into the courtroom. He had gray hair going everywhere on his head. He was shrugging his way out of an old raincoat, under which he was wearing a tattered wool cardigan sweater, buttoned erratically, and shapeless black cords. The old man paused a moment, surveyed the courtroom. Then he zeroed in on Danny, moved right to the chair next to him and slumped down with a vast sigh. His bleary eyes matched those of the judge.

"Son, you're wearing handcuffs. You must be the defendant."

Danny took his time answering. He'd been thinking, *you're trapped in some sitcom from hell, all these characters. Who is going to walk in next, Andy Griffith? One of those Gomers or Gilligans? Maybe I'll wake up still back in bed in Wyoming. But* he didn't. He was still looking at the ravaged face of the man who was going to keep $150,000 and everything else in his car from going up in smoke. So he played it straight.

"Sir, my name is Fred James. I was just driving on my way from Reno and I got caught a little over the speed limit by that nazi over there." He indicated trooper Cecil, who was still staring at the young prosecutor from Pierre. Then he proceeded to tell the old man the events of the morning. His lawyer listened carefully, even intelligently, then laid a hand on his arm.

"Son, You're going to be out of here by lunch. Call me Freddy. Fred Lindquist. I"m retired but they make me earn my Social Security here now and then." Danny was about to tell him he could pay any fee he charged but Freddy just settled back in his chair with a broad smile on his face and burped softly.

A minute later Judge Uxkull came back in, followed by the Sheriff. He paused at his table and took a long drink of water, looking out over the handful of people with no great interest. Then he looked at the prosecutor.

"Ms Fisher, you're ready to arraign this, uh, Mr. James?"

"Yes, your honor. Arresting officer will testify to driving under the influence and assaulting a peace officer. And this..." She pointed to the pile of money, "Is obviously evidence of a robbery."

The judge consulted his watch. "Ms Fisher, in forty minutes we're going to adjourn. Would you mind if I deposed the witnesses?"

Ms Fisher looked around wildly, as if trying to locate supporters dying to hear her strong performance as a prosecutor. But since almost no one was in the room except the principals, she nodded, reluctantly. "No sir, please go ahead."

Judge Uxkull then looked kindly, benevolently over at

trooper Cecil. "Cecil, would you please share with us your version of the arrest of Mr. James."

Cecil obliged, he'd seen this car weaving around at a hundred miles an hour. He'd pulled him over, gave him a sobriety test, which he flunked. The perpetrator then attacked him and he was obliged to defend himself, inflicting a small cut on the perp's head. He then searched the car, finding the results of an obvious robbery.

The judge then asked the Sheriff, "Marie, you give this young man a breathalyzer test?"

"Yes, your honor. It was zero."

"*Zero*? Flat out zero? Not just a little bit over?"

"No, your honor. Zero."

Judge Uxkull looked at Cecil, then at the money, then at Danny.

"Young man, you want to tell us all what the hell is going on?"

"Objection!" Danny was startled by the powerful voice of the aged, hungover man at his side. His lawyer was now standing up, actually staggering to his feet.

"Al! Uh, scuse me, I mean your honor? Dammit, you know well as I do you gotta let this young man take his money and walk out of here! Wait a minute." He leaned down and asked Danny quietly, "Were you speeding?"

"Yeah, about ninety," Danny said.

"My client admits to speeding. About ninety. I take that back. You fine him the standard $10 for every mile over the limit, he gives you two hundred dollars, *then* he walks out of here. You got a problem with that?"

Cecil sat bolt upright. But the judge was looking at the prosecutor. "Ms Fisher? You have an argument?"

The young Ms Fisher was deep in thought. She was looking strenuously down at a yellow lined pad on which she had scribbled some notes, hoping to find some answer there. Then she looked up.

"People agree there was no DUI."

"Good, good." The judge and Danny's counsel were nodding in unison.

"But there is the assault on a peace officer."

"Officer's word, unsupported," answered Freddy. "And is this the place to go into the arresting officer's record on matters of this sort? I remember a judgment the county had to pay about four months ago..."

"Strike that last statement," the judge told the court reporter. "And you shut up!" This was directed at Cecil, who was half way to his feet, protesting. "Go on, Ms Fisher."

"Yes, your honor. People will drop the assault charge on the arresting officer." In her heart she was hoping that someone *would* attack the moron with the lethal breath and rapist eyes some day and hurt him badly.

"But," she said. "There is the matter of the money. If Mr. James can explain to us where he..." She got no further. Freddy Lindquist was on his wobbly feet again.

"Counselor, with all due respect, and I know you went to law school maybe forty years after I did, and I haven't been keeping up with all the latest stuff, but the way I learned it, Mr. James was stopped for speeding, for which he has agreed to post bail, the arresting officer by his own admission had no probable cause to search the car, the money is therefore fruit of the poisoned tree and is not admissible evidence in this case!"

She was protesting, now on her feet too. "But there may have been a crime! If the money was stolen, if Mr. James is wanted somewhere, we can at least hold him as a material witness, without charging him!"

Now everyone was looking at the Sheriff. She was sitting there slowly shaking her head, no. "Got on the wire first thing. Not a single big robbery in the eleven western states last forty-eight hours. A gas station, couple of convenience stores west of here. That's it. And no description out that fits Mr. James."

The judge was looking at Lindquist. "Hell, Freddy, I think you won. Your client going to tell us anything about that money?"

"I don't think so, Al. Maybe he saved his lunch money, or getting ready for a big shopping trip, whatever. The whole point is, you can walk around with as much money as you want, no one can ask you where you got it. Every person I know in this courtroom is a Republican. You gonna argue with that?"

Wham! Judge Uxkull brought down his gavel. "Court's adjourned. Defendant's charged with twenty miles over the speed limit. Mr. James, don't forget to leave two hundred dollars with the bailiff. We meet again next Tuesday. Mr. James, you may pick up your property and your car and be on your way. Marie, Cecil, join me in chambers a minute." But Cecil had already walked out of the room.

*

Art Mangorff was a town cop in Thistle, about a hundred miles east of Biscuit, on the I-90. He was talking to his pal Cecil on the phone. Cecil sounded crazy mad. He was on his car phone in his own car, barreling down the I-90 at close to 100 miles an hour.

"Art! You know that big Wall Drug billboard just east of Thistle, you get your ass out there with your cruiser, wait for me to join you. We got some son of a bitch with a hundred fifty thousand in a suitcase coming your way!"

"Damn, Cece! We going to book this guy?"

"Book him, hell! The bastard talked those old assholes in Biscuit into letting him skate. All that lawyer bullshit! We're just plain going to hijack him!"

Art took his time replying. He was an old shakedown artist, himself, pulling down tourists in rich cars for speeding, but always safely, knowing that a New Yorker heading west, or a Californian heading east would be perfectly happy dropping a hundred, even two hundred on a cop to avoid driving back twenty miles to sit in a South Dakota police station. People didn't even stop to *eat* in South Dakota. So Art was sorting out the idea of hijacking someone with big money.

"Okay, Cece. Suppose the guy has the money. And we pull him over, take his money, then what?"

"Art! This guy is a fucking crook! He prolly killed someone to get this big a haul! We pull him over, we go, 'Show some ID,' somewhere along the line he's going to make a move. I'll be ready, blow the fucker away, we put him in the trunk of his car and run it down into one of those gullies going down into the river, you know, full of brush. No one'll find it for months, if ever. Art! You with me on this?"

"I dunno, Cece, I never killed anyone..."

"Hey! A scumbag like this, they'd prolly give us a medal. Jesus, Arty! Hundred and fifty thousand dollars! Shit, you could buy half the state with that kind of dough!"

Art considered the argument, found it motivating, if not completely convincing. "Okay, Cece. I'll meet you at the billboard. But let's play it by ear, maybe just take the guy's money. What's he going to do? Sue us?"

*

Danny had taken Freddy Lindquist's word that Rosie's cafe had the best chicken fried steak north of the Platte river, wherever that was. He hadn't eaten since leaving Wyoming, he was hungry and he found his steak crisp on the outside, juicy inside, and the cream gravy light and tasty. He finished his coleslaw, drained his coffee, paid the bill, and headed the old Merc east once more. He was figuring on continuing on the I-90 through Minnesota, then down through Wisconsin, where he had a bank account in a small town, clean it out, and then New York as fast as he could make it, before anyone could figure where he was. But first he had to get through the rest of South Dakota. He had a bad feeling about Cecil. He'd looked at his road map but nothing went through the state like the I-90 and he'd figured he'd outrun him.

Near a little town named Thistle he had to pull off to fill up. The old Mercury could go eighty miles an hour for days on end but you had to pay for it—about fourteen miles to the gallon, as far as he could figure it. He pulled out of the Mobil station, went by the Thistle offramp and decided to put his foot on the floor for a bit, flat country, no cars, no cops showing. When he saw the flashing gumballs in the rear view mirror this time, he decided to see what kind of speed the Merc had, so he went up to ninety, ninety-five, ninety-eight, and they weren't catching up but he wasn't running away either and he didn't want them to radio ahead for a road block so he coasted off to the shoulder again.

The countryside here was more populated, a few more trees, waves of green wheat out in the fields in the springtime, but at three in the afternoon there was still almost no traffic on the I-90. He felt under the seat where he'd put the .357, had gotten it out of the door panel after the Biscuit fiasco. At the last moment he saw an offramp coming up so he speeded up, went up the offramp, then took the left onto a country road leading nowhere, as far as he could see. The cop car hit the siren when it saw him take off but it was right behind him now and he parked on the side of the road, middle of nowhere, cows eating off to the west, something green coming up strong on the east. When the two guys got out of the cop car right away he knew something wasn't right. They hadn't radioed in his license. And then he recognized the rangy trooper, although he now had a sweatshirt on and a baseball cap on backward. He was backing up a stocky man in uniform. Both of them held shotguns. Danny Castle thought to himself. This is not an arrest. They are going to kill me for the money. Period.

He knew that he could lean out the window with the .357 and take them both out. But he'd never ever killed anyone and he didn't want to. Instead he slipped the Merc into reverse and began revving up the motor, looking in the rear view mirror all the way. Then he turned the wheel a bit so he had a trajectory out into the middle of the road, then opened the door and looked back, as if he was about to get out. The two men were right behind his left rear wheel when he popped the clutch and hit the accelerator. *Bam!* His rear bumper caught the first man, threw him back into the trooper. They both went down into a heap and he could feel the car go over them. There was complete silence. Then he could hear a shrill wailing from in front of his car.

Danny got out of his car, pistol in his hand. Both the cop and the trooper were sprawled in the road. His car had passed over both of them without lethal damage but he had run over the cop's arm and the trooper's leg. Somewhere along the line the undercarriage of the car had smacked both men on the head and there was a lot of blood. The shotguns were lying in the middle of the road so he picked them up and threw them into the ditch down off the shoulder. Then he stood over the two men, pointing the .357. He was so mad he could feel the blood pounding behind his eyeballs.

Two agonized faces were focused on him. "I could kill both of you right now and get away with it," he said. "I know you're outside the law. Maybe I should get in your car and run you over again, finish this off."

The cop managed to croak. "No, no, didn't mean to..." He was trying to scrabble away, off the road. Danny put his foot on his chest.

"I don't care how you explain this, but if I get stopped again before I hit Canada I'm going to make some phone calls and you guys are going to die slowly. You understand?"

The cop nodded vigorously. The trooper was being a tough guy, and spat contemptuously so Danny went over and jumped on the leg that he'd run over. Then he walked over and looked in the police cruiser. As he had thought, the radio was off, so he ripped out the mike and made sure it stayed that way. Then he got back in his car, reversed and got back on the I-90. This time he turned south at Sioux Falls and started taking small roads. If, against all probability, those assholes thought he was going to Canada and actually called in law enforcement, they'd be looking in the wrong direction.

*

Two days later Danny was in New York City. He drove around the town in wonderment for about three hours. He'd never been in New York in his life but he'd heard about the place so much, he had to see it. Finally, after he'd had his windshield washed about fourteen times by bums at stoplights, the windshield getting dirtier each time, he decided to bail out. Down on the lower west side he left the car on the side of a street that would be illegal for parking six days from now. When he got out, he looked around, then unscrewed the license plates. He shouldered his pack, picked up the suitcase and walked out of there. About three blocks away he threw the license plates and the .357 into a dumpster. When the cops found the old Mercury, no plates, they'd gingerly pop the trunk, hoping against hope there were no ancient dead bodies in there. When they found it completely empty they'd never bother to check the chassis number, old car like that, just have it towed and trashed. He wouldn't leave a trail here in New York.

The cab took him out to Kennedy, to an airport hotel, and he phoned around until he got a flight to London. He could have gotten a direct flight to Zurich but just in case, he was going to buy that ticket after he got to Heathrow, not leave a direct trail. He'd never flown first class before and it was a stunning revelation. Mr. James wanted to bring on board as carry-on luggage one black rolling suitcase and one big backpack. No problem, Mr. James. Mr. James was wearing jeans and a nice leather jacket. But on his feet he had soft brown tassel loafers that looked like you could eat them, they looked so soft. Now the first class attendants knew he was someone important, somebody in media, entertainment, maybe a director? Only boring businessmen wore crumpled pinstripe suits. Mr. James was polite, pleasant, asking the names of the attendants. "Sandy? Thank you Sandy! Yes, I'll have the champagne. No, I won't want to eat for a while, Fiona, was it? Look, I need to sleep for a bit, had a hard trip. If I wake up in about four, five hours, could I get a meal then? I could? Hey,

Fiona, you're great! The cabin staff decided that Mr. James was a keeper—he was obviously someone big, but he was so nice, it was unbelievable. And he had interesting hazel eyes. Fiona made up her mind to find out if he wanted company in London.

He had a glass of champagne. Then, up in the air over the west Atlantic he needed something stronger. For the first time in four years he could really relax. He got a double Tanqueray on the rocks, sipped it, thought *that's it. That's what I needed.* And he leaned back and thought about those years.

PART 1

Chapter One
Santa Monica, Four Years Ago

THERE WERE FOUR OF THEM hanging around the Club
Athena, there on Lincoln, in Santa Monica, good looking
young guys, three Greek-American kids and one goomba.
The goomba was Antonio Scarlatta and he was six foot
three and around two-eighty, depending on what he'd had
to eat the last day, it could make a difference. Nobody
called him Antonio, he was just Goomba. At the age of
twenty-seven he was still going to West Bay City College
and they were glad to have him there on the football team.
Goomba'd played with a community college down in
Orange County four years ago, then had one year at San
Diego State and parlayed that into a tryout with the
Chargers. He was big and tough and willing but he wasn't
fast enough for the pros so after a couple weeks and an
exhibition game they let him go and he drifted back to his
home town and told West Bay he was only twenty-two and
cherry. First day the coach saw him knocking defensive
linemen on their ass he told him, don't worry, you can play
here for the next five years, here's a list of classes you don't
have to go to, just swear to me, you don't have a record.

Goomba didn't have a record, but he drove for people
he knew were crooks. His main man was Ottie Shamus.

The guy had been on county commissions, had been on the city council, always in trouble, taking bribes, drunk driving, beating up women...but that was a while ago and Ottie was now a big shot lawyer and lobbyist for developers, movie people, industry, anyone who needed a permit from a public agency, because he knew the ropes, knew how to grease the wheels of commerce, keep them turning.

Ottie was a huge bag of guts and he liked Goomba because he was huge too but hard and he looked good driving Ottie's car around town. Any problem, Goomba would get out, stand up, and people would turn reasonable. Goomba had been a car parker at a restaurant a year ago when Ottie came out and had a difference of opinion with his dinner partners. Goomba had rolled up in Ottie's Mercedes just in time to see this guy grab Ottie's throat and start slapping him around. Goomba took the guy and threw him into the ice plant and just looked at the other guy until he left. "Sorry about the disturbance, Mr. Shamus," he'd said and after that Ottie had started calling him to drive him around.

"Guess what Ottie's into now," said Goomba to his friends. "He's going to take a big bag of dough from the mob, supposed to spread it around to get some project passed, I don't know what."

"What kinda money we talking about here?" asked Costa, the squirt, the youngest guy, had just started at West Bay, thinking of business econ as a major, but having trouble with the math.

"Six hundred grand and some extra stuff," said Goomba.

"Jesus!" They were all impressed.

"How the hell you find that out?" asked Costa. "Those guys don't blab about shit like that!"

"Hell, they been trying to nail Ottie for years, tie him to the mob," said Danny Castle. He was a big rangy kid, had finished junior college and was working maintenance over at the studios, nothing regular, trying to decide what he was going to do with his life, keep his mother from driving him nuts about the great jobs her friends' sons all had, working at the restaurant when his mother needed him. "Maybe we could help the cops nail him and maybe pick up some reward money."

"Or better, maybe we should just take the money." This from Johnny Z.

"Sure!" "Right!" "Duh!" There was a chorus of sarcasm at the idea of stealing from the mob.

"What kind of name is that, Ottie, anyway," asked Costa. "And Shamus. Is that Jewish?"

Goomba smiled tolerantly. "Complete and total Irish, numbnuts! His name is Arthur and he came out from Boston about thirty years ago. 'Artie,' you know, but in Boston they say 'Ottie.'"

"Ottie, Artic, whatever. Okay, so it's a big risk, but maybe it could be done!" said Johnnie.

Actually, as they all knew, Johnnie Z had stolen things. He didn't brag about it or anything but they'd all heard this and that. And he'd been shot once. They had missed seeing him around for a while and Johnnie's sister Katie told Danny that her brother had to go to Phoenix and stay with an aunt for a few weeks. When he came back he was still holding his left arm funny. And you couldn't talk to him about it. He'd blow up if you pestered him, tell you that everyone would get in trouble if you didn't keep your mouth shut.

This was the first time anyone could remember that Johnnie Z had offered to share any wisdom about stealing, so they all listened.

"First of all, lemme ask Goomba. How the hell did you find out anything about Ottie and the mob?"

Goomba did a studied, Hollywood look around the bar, make sure no one's listening in. Then he frowned.

"I dunno. I shouldn't have mentioned it. Word gets around, I'll be the one gets blamed."

"Hey!" said Costa. "Are we all buddies, or what? We all been tight for years! Do we talk about each other? Anybody tell your coach that you played in the pros, Goom?"

"Well. No, but I still dunno."

"Why'd you bring it up then, you weenie!" Danny smacked him on the back of the head and they all laughed.

"Well, okay. But you gotta realize, if the word gets out I'll probably wind up hanging on a meathook and I'll let 'em know you guys know too." His tone got conspiratorial. "You know all that stuff I been ordering, last few years?"

They all knew. Goomba was a nut about gimmicks, all the stuff you could order from the ads in *Soldier of Fortune* and the survivalist magazines. He'd started with an old AK-47 he'd bought at a swap meet for a couple of hundred. It had been made legal so you couldn't fire it full automatic but you could buy this conversion kit mail order and restore it, and he did. They'd taken it up the Angeles Crest highway and taken turns firing it automatic, spraying cans and bottles like Stallone, Schwarzenegger, one of those guys. Then he got lock picks and a gadget, looked sort of like a pistol, you could stick in a car ignition or door lock and open it in eight seconds, flat—only not now with the new models, Lexus, BMW, those good cars. Goomba had a used infrared night scope. You could sit down at the beach at night and watch what couples were doing in their cars, or check out the junkies shooting up in the park down the street. Sounded like fun but it got old real quick. Goomba had sent away for instructions on getting a false passport and he'd put together three of them, with a space where you could laminate in a photo. "You can't get back *in* to this country with 'em," he explained, "'Cause they don't have the magnetic bar code when the customs guy sticks it in the slot. But you can get out of the country 'cause the only person who checks it is the agent at the check-in counter."

Now Goomba was into electronic surveillance. He had phone taps you could screw into someone's phone, then sit in a car a block away and hear their conversations. And then he got a parabolic mike.

"See, you just aim this thing like a gun, up to a hundred yards away and you hear people talking, like they were a foot away, listen through the headset. Even plug it into a tape deck, you got a record of the whole thing."

"So what're you gonna do with all this shit?" asked Danny. "You musta spent a thousand bucks already this year."

"I'm thinking of being a private detective. But you wanna hear about Ottie, or what?"

"Yeah, yeah, go on!" "Shut the fuck up, Danny!"

"So the other day, Ottie calls me up and says he's having a meeting with a guy who doesn't want to be seen with him. What we gotta do is drive around while somebody else is tailing us, make sure we're not being followed. When they're sure, someone calls on the car phone and just says one word, the name of a restaurant. So we drive over to Glendale and I drop Ottie at the door. 'Wait a second,' he says, 'I want you to drive around the block. I'm meeting a guy in the garden out in back, they got a few tables there. You park on the street down there and you'll see a big high hedge. You can't see through it but the garden's there behind it. My friend doesn't think he's being followed but if any other cars come down that street, slow like, or park there, tap the horn a couple times.' So I go, 'You want me to move 'em on, anyone comes along?' and he goes, 'Jesus Christ no! Less attention you get the better. Just stay in the car, read a magazine.'"

"Is this an Italian restaurant," asked Johnnie Z, with professional curiosity.

"I don't think there're any Italian restaurants in Glendale," said Costa. "Well, maybe one. I think one time I was—" Everyone yelled for him to shut up and for Goomba to go on.

"So. I'm sitting around the block watching the hedge and I thought, what the hell, maybe I can hear what Ottie and this dude's talking about. I had my mike in my case I carry around. It folds up small. So I put it together, put on the head phones and point it at the hedge. No shit, it's like the hedge wasn't there at all! First thing I hear is a couple broads talking, la-de-da, la-de-da, so I move it a bit, here's a guy bullshitting his girlfriend, then suddenly Ottie is talking in a low voice. Then this other low voice says, 'Okay. Six-fifty ought to do it. And the other stuff, that's for the big one, we straight?' or something like that. And Ottie says, yeah, and the other voice says. 'The problem is getting the suitcase to you.' and Ottie says, 'Just send a courier over with it.' and they both laugh like it was a dumb idea."

"It would be dumb," said Johnnie Z. "If this guy is the mob the feds are probably all over him all the time. Somebody hands Ottie this case and suddenly there are suits all over the place, 'Scuse me, Mr. Shamus, sir, could we have a look at that suitcase?'"

"Yeah," said Goomba. "I was thinking something like

that. Anyway, the other guy goes, 'I'm going to put the shit in the suitcase and someone I really trust is not going to let go of it until they see it in your hand. It's too fucking valuable just to screw around with.' So Ottie goes, 'I got this driver I trust, sitting right out there in the car now, he can break people in little pieces, if we pick the case up, it's going to be safe until I can get it in my office.'"

"Well that screws it up, Goom," said Danny. "They know you're the driver and something happens to the case, they'll be all over you!"

"No, wait!" said Goomba. "This guy tells Ottie, I don't want your fucking driver. I'll send a guy to be your driver that day. Guy I know, maybe he can't break guys in pieces but he loves to shoot people more than anyone else I know. You'll get to your office okay."

"Anyway, how they going to make the transfer?" asked Johnnie Z.

The way it happened, the way Goomba explained, these two guys had talked it over and finally the mob guy said, here's a way we did it before. Everyone around LAX has baggage, right? Drive to the Mar Vista Plaza hotel there near the airport. Bring a black canvas carry-on suitcase with the wheels, the kind everyone in the world has these days, pack it with old newspapers, any dumb thing. You get a ticket at the hotel's parking kiosk where you see the big sign, AIRPORT PARKING, $7.95 PER DAY, then drive around the building, park out in back, walk through the hotel to the front, ten o'clock sharp, and get in the airport shuttle out in front. Someone'll be across the street watching and our carrier will be in the shuttle already with a suitcase just like it in the luggage rack there, up front, got a little piece of orange tape around the handle. Put your suitcase next to mine, and when you get to the airport, take the one with the orange tape, get out, wait for your car to show up again and you're all set. We got a car following you there and back to your office again, four guys, would rather kill than eat, so don't worry.

"So, Ottie went for that?" asked Danny.

"Hell yeah," said Goomba. "Everybody knows Ottie totally hates to fly. In case anyone was tailing him, which would be weird, and they would ask him, how come you went out to LAX and then never took a plane, he'd just say, I couldn't do it, I chickened out. It's happened, believe me. I think they made up a good safe plan."

"Now, if someone could pick off that suitcase in the shuttle bus," suggested Johnnie Z and that got them all talking, laughing, thinking up crazy ideas, and then Danny got the floor.

"Hey guys, it's not that impossible. Let me check something out."

What Danny did the next day was hang around the Mar Vista Plaza and see what was going on. He got a ticket at the kiosk in front, then drove around in back and parked his car. He was wearing jeans and a warmup jacket, carrying a light canvas bag. He walked through the hotel to the front, seeing about twenty people who looked just like him, waiting for the shuttle. No one in the hotel paid him the slightest attention. When the bus arrived he got on, a little before ten o'clock. He had to wait about five minutes, then six other people got on, then suddenly a flurry of cabin attendants all speaking Spanish rapid fire to each other. They were jamming their bags into the luggage rack in front all helter skelter. Almost half of them had black canvas carry-ons with wheels. On the ten o'clock run the shuttle driver obviously waited for the crews before he left. When Danny went back in the lobby he mentioned to the clerk at the desk that all the flight crews coming out of the Mar Vista Plaza seemed to be speaking a foreign language. The guy told him, hey, we call this the Hotel Spic and Span. All the Mexican and Latin American airlines people stay at this hotel, they get a good deal on the rooms, some arrangement the management worked out with the airlines. They're great, lots of fun, they dance all night in the bar.

Danny reported back to the guys and they talked about it, seriously this time, sitting down on the beach with no one listening in.

*

It was three days later. Los Angeles is not really much of a mob town. There is not even a Little Italy. The guy who was running most of the mob business was Herschel Jolly, who was not Italian even, but married into the New Orleans families. He was trying to get out of the hooker and narcotics rackets. Some of his people ran a sports book that was worth a million or so on a good NFL weekend. He had a great hijacking operation down on the docks. But this being southern California the big money was in shady land development and that was occupying more and more of his time. Herschel was in his fifties, a big guy who looked like a slob, who joked a lot, but dangerous. Many people had disappeared after little arguments with Herschel Jolly.

Herschel was on the phone to his mother.

"Ma, I need a favor."

"What! You want me to come over, start your car or something? Why don't you get that dumb *lukshe* you married to start the car, get blown up?"

Herschel chuckled with resignation. "Very funny, Mama. We got ten thousand feds listening to my phone and they're listening to a sitcom about a mobster and his mother. Listen, I promised, first thing I'm going to get you an agent, so you can promote your routine. But now, I promised you a trip to San Francisco, remember?"

"So? Maybe six months ago? And now you get around to it? Herschel! What's the problem? Listen! I don't carry drugs!"

Herschel chuckled again. "Mom, I can get you on with Rodney Dangerfield at Caesar's, maybe next May, you work on your delivery a bit. But here's the thing. Your cousin Julie phoned and asked me if you could come up to San Francisco. She tried to phone you three days and the phone was busy. Were you on the web again and forget to sign off?"

She was indignant. "I never forget to sign off! The prices they charge? And what does Julia want?"

"Ma, what do you know about prices? I pay your Internet bill. Anyway, Julia just said she wanted to see you. And she wanted the photos from our dinner down here last June. So if you could come over tomorrow morning I'll give you a first class ticket to San Fran and a packet of photos for Julia. You want to do some shopping up there, just put it on your card, no problem."

Three days later Ottie Shamus left his office in downtown Los Angeles wheeling a black carry-on suitcase. Down in front of his building his black Mercedes was waiting with an unfamiliar dark man behind the wheel. He got in and without saying a word the driver pulled out, took the nearest onramp to the Harbor freeway, then right on the Santa Monica.

"I always stay on the Harbor down to the Century," said Ottie, just making conversation. The look he got in the rearview mirror shut him up and he just slumped in the back seat while the driver drove west, took the interchange on the 405 south, then got off on La Tijera and finally turned down Airport. They turned into the driveway of the Mar Vista Plaza hotel, swung around the building into the parking area in back and Ottie got out at exactly ten o'clock. He walked through the hotel and there was the shuttle in front, only a couple of people in it so far, a bandy-legged, elderly lady with a cheap chocolate-colored wig who was fussing about her coat getting wrinkles, and an Oriental man who looked like the shot put champion of whatever fucking country he came from. Ottie got on and put his bag in the luggage rack, noticing with pleasure that there was a black bag there with a little piece of orange tape on the handle. Then he sat down as far from the big Oriental man in back as he could. Everyone waited silently for about five minutes. Then suddenly there was this big rush, all these men and women in black or navy blue uniforms, laughing, cackling, all babbling away in Spanish. Also a couple of tourist guys, one with a Knotts Berry Farm T shirt. Another wearing fake gang clothes, the shorts halfway down the calf and what looked like size 18 Reeboks with the laces untied. Oh yeah, and the cap on backwards. Ottie tried to keep an eye on the suitcase with the orange tape as the crowd milled around the luggage rack, talking, smiling, apologizing to each other as they swung their bags up onto the rack. The asshole kid with his cap on backward came walking to the rear, tripped on his laces and almost fell on Ottie's lap. The big Oriental was on his feet in back, eagle eyes on the black bag. Then this senorita yelled to the driver, "Hey Juan, I forget my ozzer bag, I take thee next boss, hokay?" and she got off with her black bag. Both Ottie and the Oriental were on their feet now, shoving toward the luggage rack but they could see the bag with the orange tape and the lady was on the side-walk, waving to someone on the bus, holding her own bag, which had a big green ribbon around it. Ottie and the Oriental relaxed.

On the way to the airport Ottie looked out and back a couple of times. Sure enough, there were cars out there with bad people in them, cruising alongside the shuttle bus, probably the safest vehicle in Los Angeles to be in at that exact time. At the international terminal all the Latinos got off and Ottie was there almost alone, with the big Oriental, two tourists with funny caps, and a couple of elderly ladies. At the United terminal, the last one on the loop, Ottie got up, took the bag with the orange tape and got off. He waited at the curb until his Mercedes pulled up with Jolly's driver keeping an eye on the rear view mirror. The Oriental exchanged a look with the driver, looked at the traffic behind the car, and then said, "Okay, get going." The big man watched Ottie get into the Merc, then abrupt-ly turned and walked into the terminal as if he was actual-ly going to take a plane.

Ottie wanted to take a peek in the suitcase in the car but there was a small brass combination lock on the zipper and he'd forgotten the combination so he waited until he got back to his office. He broke his nineteenth-century Burmese letter opener trying unsuccessfully to pry the lock open, then, sweating and cursing, he got a pair of scissors out of his desk drawer and laboriously cut a slit the length of the suitcase. There was a lot of crumpled newspaper in there. *The money wouldn't take up that much space, or the rest of the stuff. Must be underneath,* he was thinking, and pulled all the wadded newsprint out, every bit of it, realized the suitcase was empty, savagely attacked the outer compartments, hurling the balls of newsprint into the middle of his office, stared unbelievingly at the orange tape around the handle of the suitcase, and then, not being a stupid man at all, tried to remember every detail of the young woman who had gotten off the shuttle with the other black suitcase.

*

The FBI agent called his boss. "We picked up Jolly's mother going into Jolly's building there on Sunset. She comes out with a huge Oriental-looking guy carrying her suitcase. They drive to the Mar Vista Plaza Hotel on Airport and they both get on the shuttle. We got two cars watching the shuttle and our usual guy up in the KWAX traffic-watch helicopter. The shuttle goes to LAX and she gets out with her suitcase at American, actually checks it in at the curb. We rush down to baggage and grab her bag. It's full of wadded newspapers."

"Shit! What about the Oriental guy?"

"He didn't get off there. We figured him strictly for security."

"So where did he get off?"

"Well, our cars dropped the shuttle when Mama Jolly got out but the helicopter guy says he thinks the Oriental guy got out at United. He's got photos of everything but we'll have to wait until we get some blowups. Something's going on but I don't know what right now!"

*

Costa threw the wig across the room and started struggling with the brassiere stuffed with kleenex.

"How the fuck you take one of these things off?" he yelled, but he couldn't help laughing. Nor could anyone else.

"Come on man! You never took a bra off before! Get out!" There was a great roar, great hilarity. They were all in Goomba's mom's garage, that he'd fixed up as a weight room. Now Costa was taking off the slacks.

"Shit! I had to take a leak in the hotel and I started to go in the men's room! Then just in time I remembered, so I go in the women's room. Hey, man, it's weird in there! I go in one of those stalls and then I remember there's no zipper on ladies' pants, so I had to pull 'em down and sit on the pot."

"Okay, okay," everyone was saying. "Anyway, it worked out. So what we got here?"

There was a little lock on the zipper of the suitcase. Goomba put a pair of pliers on it, crunched down hard, and it fell apart. The four young men leaned forward as Danny pulled the zipper all the way around, then lifted the top of the black bag. It was full of wadded newspapers.

There was a big sigh as lungs deflated.

"Well, shit!" "Good try anyway, Costa!" "So what the hell was going on?"

"Wait a minute," said Danny. "That's just the top layer." He dug down into the suitcase, threw the wadded papers onto the floor. There on the bottom of the bag was a layer of neatly banded hundred dollar bills. There was complete silence for a moment.

"Holy Mother of God!" said Johnny Z.

"*Panayía mou!*" said Danny, reverting to the Greek his mother spoke when she was excited.

There was a rush to count the money, which Goomba won simply by pushing everyone out of the way. So they watched him count the parcels of one hundred hundreds, ten thousand dollars each, until the last one fell on top of the pile and they all breathed in unison, "Six hundred and fifty thousand dollars!"

"Man, look at them dead Presidents!" said Costa.

"Makes me want to study U. S. History," laughed Johnnie Z.

"You better," said Danny, "'cause that's Ben Franklin on the hundreds and he was never President."

"Ben Franklin wasn't President? Bullshit!" "Get outta here, Danny!" yelled Johnnie and Costa.

"No. He's right," said Goomba. "And you know who else? On the ten—Alexander Hamilton—was never President. I told you guys, you should watch *Jeopardy* more often instead of jerking off so much. You learn something!"

"And you know what?" said Danny, who had been feeling the suitcase. "There's something else in here. Here in the outside pocket." He took out a large, thick manila envelope thoroughly sealed with packing tape.

"I don't fucking believe this! More money?" cried Johnnie.

Danny tried to rip the tape but there were three layers wound around it. He pulled out a little pocket knife and slit the bottom instead. Into his hand slid a pile of financial documents two and a half inches thick, with two stout rubber bands around them. Everyone gazed at a masterpiece of engraving, with eagles, Minute Men, curlicues, ancient looking courthouses set in oval frames, floral borders, all in a brownish-purple ink, and Old English text. In the very middle of this jungle of floral engraving was the portrait of a stern man with a high collar. He was faced firmly to the left, looking backward into a distant past he obviously prefered. A very thin pennant waving under his portrait identified him as Matthias Wingerden, 1837-1918. What they all saw next in the text was the denomination in the corners: $100,000.00. And there were one hundred and twenty of them.

'Well, shit!" said Johnnie. It's just some stocks and bonds. Completely fucking unnegotiable unless you can prove you own them."

"Now wait a second," said Danny, who was trying to read the small print. "It says here, 'Will pay to bearer...' whatever that means. I think we ought to do a little research on this."

"Research, hell!" said Costa. "Let's split the cash first, have a party, get drunk, get laid, then we'll do the research."

Danny held up a hand. "Remember? We agreed to sit on the money for two weeks, not go around like assholes throwing it around? We agreed Goomba would keep it here in his safe, right Goom?"

Goomba nodded seriously. "Absolutely. Mob guys are probably out all over town right now asking, 'Who's throwing money around?' And you know what? They find somebody with a big wad of cash, they'll ask him, where'd you get it. And if they don't like the answers, the guy'll wind up in Mr. Jolly's basement, hanging naked on a meathook stuck under his shoulder blade. Then they hose you down and fry your balls with a cattle prod. And then you know what...?"

But he was drowned out by a chorus of protest. "Okay, okay, Goomba, we get the message...Yeah, we all agreed!"

There was quite a long discussion but eventually they decided to let Danny and Costa, the Bus. Econ. major, find out what kind of financial instruments they had stumbled on and whether they were worth anything.

*

In the Silverlake district there was a Thai restaurant Herschel Jolly had never visited. He was fairly certain there were no federal bugs in place in the soy bottle, or wherever. So he was meeting there with a lawyer Ottie Shamus had sent to talk to him. Mr. Jolly had some of his guys with him, including the big Korean and a muscle man named Tony and another named Manny. The lawyer's name was Marvin Nelson. He was an Anglo, weighed maybe 190, but pudgy, only five eight. Since they'd started talking he'd had to go to the bathroom three times. His face was a sheet of sweat, in fact the Thai waitress had told him, giggling, don't eat so much of the hot stuff, eat more rice. That wasn't his problem. In fact he couldn't have eaten one grain of rice, he was so terrified.

What Mr. Jolly had just said to him was, "You realize I can't grab Ottie and ask him questions, the fucking feds watching everything I do, sneeze, take a shit, whatever! But we can pick you up sometime, you're not watching, and take you to a garage down in Hawthorne. Tie your feet to the floor, tie your hands to the lube racks then raise 'em all the way real slow. Shit, you'll be as tall as that Kareem guy, be the first fat white basketball player. You could probably buy and sell me, what they pay those assholes!"

Jolly was just pretending to be a funny guy. Inside he felt like death. He was thinking, if he could find anyone involved with this double cross they'd be on the lube racks for a long time. And then store them for a while on the meat hooks. Mr. Jolly's guys sitting there were laughing their asses off but the lawyer, Nelson, just started crying softly. Jolly let him go on for a bit, then signaled for his hard guys to shut up a minute.

"Okay, pal. Let's lighten up a bit. I'm willing to agree that Ottie didn't steal my money, okay? But he knows what's going to happen if I ever find out he was involved. So. Now what?"

This was in response to the lawyer trying to get out of his seat in the maroon vinyl booth.

"I've got to go to the bathroom again."

"Okay, okay. Tony, go with him, make sure he doesn't flush himself down." The tall guy with the weightlifter's build and a Hawaiian shirt got up dutifully and followed Nelson down a narrow hall.

When Nelson got back from the bathroom safely they got down to real business. Nelson had brought a tape recording from Ottie, a studied recital of everything he had observed.

"I got to the hotel about nine, uh, let's say nine fifty-five," Ottie's voice was saying. "Got on the shuttle and put my black bag right next to the bag with the orange tape. I sat in back. There was this humongous Asian guy I figured for your muscle and an old lady now I hear was your mother. We all sit there nobody saying shit until at ten the shuttle driver gets in and then all these Latino cabin crews come running out and get in the bus. They're all throwing bags around so I get up to watch, your guy Odd Job, or whatever, he gets up, then this idiot in shorts, his finger up his nose, trips over his shoes and pushes me back into the seat. When I get up again the only thing I see is this Mexican bitch, walking away with a black bag. The bag with the orange tape is still there on the rack, she's wheeling a black bag with a green band around it. I didn't take my hand off the bag with the orange tape until I got back to the office, I find out it's a switch, is all I can figure out, and I got the message to you. What I can't figure out is how anyone found out about the way we were going to switch the bags. No one could have known we were going to that restaurant in Glendale the other day and even if they did how could they have overheard us. They'd a had to stick a mike in the hedge there and my driver was sitting right across the street just to make sure no feds were going to sneak up on us."

The tape stopped. Mr. Jolly sighed. "I gotta talk directly to Ottie somehow. We'll figure out something. In the meantime, tell me, Mister Nelson, what about this driver? Who is he and would he try to listen in on what your boss was talking about?"

"His name is Antonio Scarlatta," said the lawyer, sounded relieved now the heat seemed to be off him. "But everyone calls him Goomba."

"A goomba and they call him Goomba! What do you think of that, Tony?" asked Mr. Jolly.

Tony shrugged his shoulders. "I prefer guys to call me by my name, you know what I'm saying? 'Goomba'? I dunno. Depends on the tone of voice. Now 'wop' or 'guinea' you'd have to be close, would be my guess."

"So does this guy sneak around listening to people?" Mr Jolly asked the lawyer.

"I would say no," said Nelson, "His size, he doesn't really sneak anywhere. He's this huge guy Ottie uses for security. I don't see him eavesdropping or planning heists this intricate. And that morning, you sent your own driver, and we found out Scarlatta took his mother to Mass."

"We'll probably get around to checking him out anyway," said Mr. Jolly. "Hey Moon!" he called across the room. The big Korean got up from the table where he was watching the door and came over to the booth.

"Listen to the tape and tell me what you think."

Moon listened impassively, then nodded his head. "That's what happened. Ottie was on his feet and so was I, watching the bag, with all the people around the luggage rack. There's a flight crew, four guys and a stew, then like two tourists, asshole looking guys., one of 'em trips and falls on Ottie. Last moment the stew gets off with her bag.

I was going after her but Ottie points at the bag with the tape and I see the stew has a bag with a green band around it. We get to the Bradley terminal, the flight crew gets off and I'm watching hard. But they all check out their bags, you know, 'let's see——is this one mine? oh yeah it is,' before they get off. So they all have the right bags. All the way to United after your mother got off there's just the one bag, the one with the orange tape. Ottie takes it, gets off and waits for his car. Your driver there, Freddo, he gives me the nod—nobody following he could spot."

Mr. Jolly was just sitting there, shaking his head, I dunno, I dunno. Finally he looked at the lawyer, then looked at big Moon.

"You know, back when old Montesi was running things here he would've whacked everyone involved, just on general principles. You first, Moon, 'cause you were on the scene and fucked it up, then Ottie, his driver, then about a dozen people just because he was pissed. But times are different. The deal is much bigger than the heist. Somebody's going to make six hundred million off this deal and we're still in for a third. Mister Nelson, tell Ottie we'll have to talk, soon as I figure out a way nobody can see us together, which might kill the whole deal. Everyone else, I want you out on the street with everyone you know. Who's spending money? And who is asking questions, trying to peddle old bonds?

*

"The hardest thing was getting the green band on the bag," said Costa. "I got the one that slips on, elastic, you know? Instead of the one you have to buckle on. Still, I had to do three things, put the black tape over the orange tape on the money bag, then slip the green band around it, then put my bag that I put some orange tape on right there in the same spot. And the whole time one of those fucking Mexican pilots or whatever was trying to feel my ass. At least he was standing in the way, Ottie couldn't see me. When I got off the bus I swear to God I thought I was going to have gangsters chasing me all the way to the parking lot!"

"Tell me about it!" said Danny. When I tripped and fell on the fat guy, Ottie, it was like some bad movie, you know, you see a real fake move like that and everyone in the audience is like, 'Right! Like no one can figure that one out, give me a break!' And then I had to ride the whole way to the international terminal with this huge Chinese guy staring at me. But you did good, Costa. No doubt about it, you had the hardest job. But you always had the quick hands."

They were walking away from the Santa Monica Public Library, after spending a couple of hours looking up anything they could find about bearer bonds. They were both in a good mood because what they had found was good news.

"I'll meet you at Goomba's after ten," said Danny. "I gotta help my mother at the restaurant tonight. One of the guys is out sick."

*

Danny had to make a new batch of *tzatziki*, peel the cucumbers, then slice the white part and salt it to get a lot of the water out. You had to squeeze it, it was labor intensive. He mixed the cukes into the yogurt and added a dozen minced cloves of garlic. While his mom wasn't looking he put in the good olive oil, the extra virgin. His mom always used the cheap stuff, trying to save money and wouldn't believe anyone could tell the difference. He could, and anyone could see the difference, the good olive oil beaded green on top instead of dirty yellow. He put in an extra dollop and smelling it could imagine the cool shade of an olive grove there in Greece where he'd never been, some island, maybe. Smelling it, not paying attention, and his mother caught him.

"Thanassi! I told you, not the good oil. You want us to go broke?"

"Oh, Ma! I keep telling you, one batch of *tzatziki*, it's like fifty cents more! And the locals notice. I swear!" He put his arm around her and kissed her. She'd been raised in the time of poverty, working sixteen hours a day and cutting every corner just to make the payments, especially after Danny's father died. It was a successful restaurant now, even in the *Times* restaurant review once, but she couldn't get over old habits. She kissed him back and went away, half pacified.

Now Danny set out all the *mezedes* ready to dish out— the *tzatziki*, eggplant salad, tarama salad, the *dolmadakia*— the stuffed vine leaves—feta cheese, olives, the little *saganaki* dishes with kasseri cheese and butter, ready to go under the broiler. He chopped two dozen tomatoes, some more cucumbers, green peppers, purple onions and put them in plastic tubs next to the feta and olives so they could make the Greek salads in a hurry. Then he lit the charcoal and got the grill ready.

The house specialty was *kotópoulo tis skháras*—barbecued chicken. Danny cut up eighteen chickens into small pieces and rubbed them all with the marinade his father had invented: pureed garlic, anchovy paste, mustard, lemon, and mixed herbs, salt, pepper, and oil. Then he got a dozen folding grills out and loaded them with the chicken pieces. When an order came in, the little eight inch-square grills with the chicken folded inside would take about six minutes on one side over the charcoal, three on the other and be done, so they could move a lot of chicken. That was the reason for the small pieces. The stuff was addictive and Goomba could eat three of the grills without even trying hard on those days when he'd been paid and could afford the $9.50 an order, supposed to feed two people.

The chicano guy, Chuy, came in and started the fryer going for the potatoes. Meanwhile Danny's mom and his cousin Katina were setting the tables and organizing the rest of the kitchen. They opened the doors at six and trade was slow at first, tourists in shorts with white legs peeking in nervously and Katina telling them, come on in, look in the kitchen, see what looks good, I'll translate everything. Danny usually put an order of chicken on to grill just to get the place full of barbecued chicken perfume. They had a full house by 7:30 which lasted for an hour. Then, closer to nine, the local Greeks came in, still keeping Greek hours for meals. Saying hello to Danny's mom, joking with Katina, some of the older ones calling him Thanassi the way his mom still did. They were the ones who drank most of the retsina the restaurant served. Most of them were fed by ten and Danny managed to get away, leaving the cleanup for Chuy and Katina, because they actually got paid. He didn't really mind cooking and serving because it was a family thing and he had grown up doing it, since he was six, helping to clear tables, bringing water and silverware at first, then as soon as he could carry a tray, bringing the food orders. What he really hated was Friday and Saturday nights, when they put on the *bouzouki* records and he and the two other Greek waiters had to dance the *syrtaki* and other dances for the patrons. He always felt like an idiot twirling around and slapping his shoes even though everyone said he was the best dancer and sometimes they would put him on alone to do the Zorba dance that got faster and faster as he leapt and plunged and whirled, ending triumphantly sweating and grinning ear-to-ear, pretending that he had done something hard and enjoyed it tremendously. He complained to his mom that it was Disneyland Greek stuff but she said it brought the customers in. Why not have some stupid belly dancers then, he said, like they have at all the other Greek restaurants in town? Because it's not really Greek, his mom said, it's really a Turkish or Egyptian thing. In Greece the women don't even allow it except in tourist nightclubs.

The guys were waiting for him there at Goomba's weight room. Costa had agreed to let Danny tell the story and he'd jump in with details if he thought of them.

Danny held up one of the bonds. "This was just another way for cities to borrow money," he started. "Usually for a specific purpose. You can see here the small print says, 'Lower Schuylkill regional sanitation modernization, plant construction, and storm flood control.' Let's say it's a project that'll cost maybe seventy million bucks. We looked it up on the map; this is most of Philadelphia we're talking about. A big city. So they print the bonds and sell them to people who want tax-free income from the interest."

"And 1973, when they were issued, interest rates were pretty good," put in Costa.

"They also used to sell them to people who wanted to transfer big sums of money without any paper record. That's why they were called 'bearer bonds.' You own one of these, you can take it to your bank and cash it in just like money. Or you can leave it to your kids and they can skip the inheritance taxes."

"Or the mob can use them for payoffs," added Costa.

"You said 'used to,'" said Goomba. "What happened, they're no good now?"

"Well, that's a gray area," said Danny. "And we're going to have to find out. But here's what happened." He looked down at some notes. "The Tax Equity and Fiscal Responsibility Act of 1982—they call that TEFRA— said bearer bonds were now going to be required to be registered to an owner and all transfers would have to be recorded. So that was the end of bearer bonds." Seeing the confused expressions on several faces, Danny went on. "See, the only real advantage of bearer bonds was that they were untraceable. Once they had to be registered nobody bothered issuing them anymore."

"But these, if they were issued in '73, they'd still be like legal?" asked Johnny.

"Well, we're sure they're legal, and probably worth their face value," said Danny. "So you go to your bank and you go, 'Hey man, I was going through my attic and I found these in my grandfather's stuff. Can I put them in my account?'"

Costa went on. "And the banker is like, 'Well, we'll have to check them out to make sure they're still negotiable.' So the word gets out and pretty soon we're all hanging on meat hooks."

"Yeah," said Danny. "You can see the problems."

"Hey!" said Goomba, looking at the glum faces. "What the fuck, we got six-fifty K to split up, and you guys are worried about some paper, may not be worth wiping your ass on! I say we just burn them!"

But he was outvoted. They wound up splitting the cash, one hundred sixty-two thousand dollars apiece in hundreds. Then they decided to let one of them put the stack of bearer bonds in a safe deposit box for a while, maybe even a year or two, until they could figure out how to cash them in safely. For some reason everyone was looking at Danny.

"If only," Goomba was saying, "Because you own a house and a restaurant and we know how to find you if you decide to fuck your old buddies." Everybody was nodding except Johnnie Z. And he didn't look happy.

"Not that I don't trust Danny," he said. "We all do. But I travel a lot, I even know some crooks. Let me take just one a them bonds. I promise I won't flash it anywhere near L.A. But maybe I can find some way we can discount them somewhere else, Chicago, who knows? Then we got a real financial background. I mean, a hundred sixty thousand bucks sounds like a lot of money, but like, can you buy a place to live around here, even a piece of shit in the black district of Santa Monica? And to invest in something that'll keep paying off—forget it!"

They were all nodding. "You're right, Johnnie," said Goomba. "We're not cheap crooks. I'm not just thinking how much drugs I could buy. In fact, I never bought any drugs!"

"You bought a hundred dollar bag of Humboldt from me," said Costa. "All buds, too."

"Yeah. Well. You know what I mean. Nobody here is actually dealing drugs for a living. We're capitalists, man. We'd all like to buy some real estate, some kind of investment we could live off the rest of our lives."

"And a share of them bearer bonds, that could do it!" said Johnnie.

"Yeah but what's the hurry!" This from Costa. And everyone agreed. Johnnie was still unhappy so Danny said he'd let him have one of the bonds, but he'd have to put up some security, something major, so they could trust him not to go do anything stupid.

The next day Danny had packed, said goodby to his mother and told her he had to go check out a scholarship at the University of Nevada up there in Reno, where he might get a economics degree. She was so crazy for him to get a college degree and a real job that she didn't even complain.

"Thanassi, you go. I get your other cousin, Pavlo, he can learn the business. It's time for him to work. He's sixteen and hanging around those gang guys with the dumb pants on. His mother is complaining to me. You go, get your college degree, father would be proud!"

But he didn't get the college degree. He got four years in the slammer.

*

Johnnie came over just before he left and gave him a big envelope.

"It's some kind of securities from Arizona. Worth sixty K they told me. I can't cash them in yet, just like your Philadelphians there."

"Yeah," said Danny. "That's what we got, dead Philadelphians. Ben Franklin, and that guy Matthias Wingerden, on the bonds. I looked him up too. He was some old crook, owned everything south of Philly down to where the Duponts took over."

"Who're the Du Ponts?" asked Johnnie Z.

"Never mind, Johnnie. Here's your bond. Be careful."

"Yeah. You too."

*

Danny stopped at Santa Barbara on the way north and rented a safe deposit box at the San Roque Savings and

Loan. It was the first bank he hit taking the offramp from the freeway. He also opened a small money market account and arranged for the box rent to be paid automatically from it. He got into Reno about eight that night, had a good sleep in a motel and then the next few days went from bank to bank, depositing something over nine thousand dollars in cash in each one. Goomba had worked out the system from the paranoid survivalist literature he kept ordering. The banks have to report any transaction over $10,000, especially in cash. So just put in something a little less. Reno is a big gambling town, no one will question the deposits. And it's less obvious than Las Vegas, if the mob is looking for people socking money away.

Danny hit the whole area, not just Reno, but Carson City, Incline Village, anywhere there was a bank. He wound up going to eighteen different banks, and then sat in his motel at night memorizing the banks rather than keeping a written record. Goomba had read a spy novel and said it was simple. It wasn't simple, but he found he could do it, even sing the names in a little song.

He kept ten thousand in cash and headed back home. He parked outside the restaurant and the next thing he knew he was smashed up against the car and was handcuffed behind his back.

"Federal officers, Mr. Castle," said the tall blond guy. "Mind if we look in your bag?" And there was Johnny Z's envelope full of securities, which Danny had never even looked at. Turned out it was part of a robbery from a mail truck in Phoenix.

Long afterwards he wondered how Johnnie could have been so stupid. He'd gone directly to the Bank of America in downtown Los Angeles and tried to cash in the bearer bond. He'd been detained by the guards in the bank and when the higher authorities searched him and his car they found part of the mail truck heist from Phoenix. That brought in the FBI. Johnnie's lawyer told the feds that the evidence was dirty, that they'd had no cause to arrest his client. The feds replied that it was hard to predict what a court would do but that if Mr. Zafiropoulos could give them someone else from the robbery he might skate on this one. So Johnnie Z. gave them Danny, figuring that no one could put Danny at the scene of the crime. And Johnnie skated right back to Phoenix, where he copped to lesser charges and went up for sixteen months.

But he forgot that Danny was in possession of stolen property, a serious federal felony. It was true that they couldn't put him at the scene of the crime. But since Danny resolutely refused to say where he'd gotten the Phoenix securities or the ten thousand cash, and since the jury had seen two wealthy celebrity defendants from Hollywood walk away not guilty just the last two months in highly publicized trials, they were not in the mood for leniency. The judge, before sentencing, asked Danny if he wanted to reconsider explaining his connection to Mr. John Zafiropoulos and where he had gotten the stolen property, but Danny pleaded complete ignorance and therefore got the whole shot, five to ten up at the federal prison camp west of San Luis Obispo, there on the central coast.

Chapter Two
The Joint

First thing they asked him was what did he work at, if he'd ever worked. He thought about his maintenance jobs for a second but then he told them he was a cook and they said, great, and we hope you're better than the other shitheads there in the kitchen. Danny figured he'd at least eat well, have regular hours. Later, one of the other cooks told him it was a smart move because nobody would mess with a cook——there were too many opportunities to get something unpleasant in your food.

Nobody messed with Danny anyway. First, he was a big kid and looked tough. Second, this was a federal prison and had more white collar crooks than killers, rapists, and random violent psychopaths. Finally, Danny had always gotten along with people, had good vibes and good attitude so he was considered a cool dude there at San Luis Obispo too.

He got into a routine right away. Cooking took about two hours each meal, three times a day, sometimes a little more, depending on the prep. In between, because this was a low security joint, he could go out on the playing fields, play some ball, lift weights, jog around the perimeter. Once a week at first his mother would come up, sometimes with

Goomba, and she would try not to cry, ask him how he was eating, if he couldn't get an appeal. She swore she'd mortgage the restaurant to pay for an appeal, convinced that Danny had been set up and framed. She railed on about Johnnie Z, the lowlife, and how could a Greek kid do this to another Greek boy, his best friend. When Goomba could get a word in he'd report on the gang, how Costa moved out of town, didn't know where, tell about how other friends of theirs were doing. He couldn't say anything about the heist because everything they said over the phones, with that glass window in between, was recorded. And of course Danny's mother didn't know the first thing about it.

After about two months Danny had a good tan, he could run ten miles without breathing hard and he could bench press his weight about twenty times. Hundred and seventy pounds, down ten pounds from when he was sitting around at the Club Athena. He liked to box now and then too, even though he got his ass whipped, mostly by Mexicans, in there for dealing drugs mostly, guys'd been fighting in the streets since they were little kids, and now, doing heavy federal time, they just wanted to hurt people. Also, Danny was going crazy, wondering if he could make it, or go out over the wire and be a fugitive the rest of his life, or maybe start in on the booze and drugs, available everywhere if you could pay for them. So in September, when the local college sent over applications for anyone who wanted to get a degree there in the prison camp Danny put in his name. Under "fields of study" he put Business Economics, because one of the things that kept him sane was thinking about all those millions of dead Philadephians out there and how they could be invested. Then he had to put down a second field and he couldn't think of anything so he put down "independent research." The first day he met with a counselor from the college he couldn't believe it. He'd expected some nerdy guy who had signed on to the prison extension program to make some extra dough, maybe to support a wife and six kids in San Luis Obispo or Santa Maria. Instead he got Barbara Johnson.

Barbara saw this good looking young guy come in the conference room. He had a good tan, good build, interesting hazel eyes, and she wondered if he was just another con man trying to set something up outside. That had happened a couple of times with their college program, but not to her. Barbara was a big sweet woman, about forty, teaching English Lit there at the college. She was maybe just a bit overweight, but she had a beautiful serene face that got animated when she talked to anyone she thought might have some underdeveloped intelligence, something she could bring out. She'd been teaching extension at the prison for four years and her colleagues couldn't figure it out, why she would waste her time with those losers. Her long-time boyfriend Henry, who taught computer science, sometimes wanted to ask her how many of those cons who took the courses had actually gotten a degree and gone on to do anything worthwhile. But he knew the answer so he never asked. He was hoping that someday she'd agree to move in with him. Being a scientist he had figured out how much money they'd save, just sharing expenses. Being a literature professor she knew that two people living together was not just mathematics.

"Hello, Mr. Castle. Uh, your first name is Athanassios?"

Danny was impressed right away, that she knew how to pronounce it. "Yeah. I mean yes, ma'm. I never use the name, actually. My mom calls me 'Thanassi' but when I was in grade school kids started calling me 'Nazi' so I said, call me Danny, that's what one of my cousins is called, another Athanassios."

"So you're Greek-American, is that right?"

"Yes ma'm. My people came over two generations ago."

"I shouldn't be asking all these personal questions, but why is your last name Castle?"

Danny chuckled. "It's an old immigrant story. You got a long foreign name back in the old days, the guys at Ellis Island didn't want to bother with it and they'd ask the old guys where they were from, maybe get a name with fewer syllables. My grandfather came from Kastelli, that's in Crete, so he said 'Kastelli' and the immigration guy said, 'How about 'Castle', close enough—sounds American?' Everyone wanted to be American, so Grandpa said, OK, Castle. Sounds fine."

Barbara laughed, a warm laugh, really enjoying the old story. From there on everything was great between Barbara Johnson and Danny Castle. She wanted to know, why Business Econ.? and he said that he and his mother jointly owned this restaurant, that it was making money and he thought he should know more about investing, once he got back out again. She said, fine, I'll get the correspondence courses for you and there'll be an Econ. prof. who can come out and answer questions maybe once a week. Now, what's this 'independent research'?

He'd been thinking about that since he'd filled out the application.

"You know? I'm Greek, and my family always talked about how great the Greeks were, but I never read any Greek history or literature, and I don't think my mom and my pop did either, they'd just go on about Constantine, and how he made everyone Christian, or Alexander the Great and how he conquered the whole world, but nothing in between, or how the Greeks just happened to be so, uh, uh..."

"Maybe just at the right time and the right place in history, and with the right attitude?" asked Barbara.

"You're right. But from the little I read, they were running everything, even when the Romans took over, for what—more than a thousand years? And even today, Greek Americans, lowest rates of all immigrants when you're talking about welfare, unemployment, highest rates for small business owners, lowest rates for crime—until me," he added sheepishly.

"Look, Danny." said Barbara Johnson. "We've got one main rule here. We don't talk about why you're here, what you did, whether you're guilty, anything like that. Okay?" He nodded, yes.

"But I will agree with you, you don't hear about many Greek people in prison."

But the next week he met one of those, too.

The old man sat down at the picnic table outside the messhall where Danny was taking a break in the shade of a big oak tree. He was drinking a cup of coffee and thinking, watching guys playing touch football, others jogging, even throwing frisbees, that you could almost fool yourself that you were at camp, in fact they called it a Prison "Camp," or on a college campus, if you could forget about the fourteen foot chainlink fences in the distances across the playing fields and the gun towers spaced along the fences. There were guards up there who *would* shoot you, everyone was told, if you tried to climb the fence and didn't mind the high voltage.

"You're a Greek," said the old man. A statement, not a question. Danny took his time answering. He'd learned not to make friends too fast, then find out guys wanted to sell you dope, wanted sex, wanted to find out how tough you were. But the old guy looked harmless.

"Yeah. How'd you know?"

"I'm Greek. I can always tell. Sam Papadakis." He stretched out a big hand. "And you? How'd you get the name Castle, which I asked the other cook this morning?"

Danny went through the story once again and Sam Papadakis nodded. It was a familiar story, he said. Greeks, Jews, Polacks, we all run into some idiot at immigration who even has a hard time even spelling "Jones, Brown," whatever, let alone foreign names.

"I can see dropping the Athanassios," he said. "But Kastelli, that's a good name. I even know the town." Danny felt a little startled. The name of the town had always been there in his mind like some abstract scrap of myth, so familiar he'd never had to think about it. Now here was a guy who'd seen people walking down the streets, going into shops, talking to each other, and the town took on a reality he wasn't used to.

"Nothing like a tourist town, you know. Just a regional market town, farmers, shopkeepers, the local high school."

"Are your people from Crete, too?" asked Danny, still trying to imagine what a town on Crete would look like.

"Always have been until I left after the war. We lived in a valley there in the middle of the west part. The Germans were on the island for over three years when I was young. My father actually made money in the war, smuggling mostly. But he made enemies too."

Sam Papadakis described his life as a teenager, with the German soldiers always around, patrolling the main north-south road that ran through their town. His father would leave for a couple of weeks at a time and wait for a British sub on the south coast. He'd come back with a shortwave radio on his back to be delivered somewhere, he never said where, or guiding shadowy figures who disappeared up into the mountains. And the British kept sending the little bags of sovereigns, the gold coins, to keep the underground networks happy and working hard. But after the occupation there was a feeling in his valley that some people had been too lucky, had done too well in the war when other fathers and uncles and brothers had been shot by the Germans, or worse, tortured to death to make them tell secrets.

"One day my father sold all his sheep, sold his land to his brother, and we got in the back of a truck and drove north to Souda Bay, me, my mother, two sisters. We took a boat to Athens and some English people there put us on another boat to Canada. It was some kind of final payoff to my father. He was one smart cookie, always could see where the wind was blowing. Took him about six months to see it wasn't blowing in Canada so we moved to Chicago and I been there ever since, except now at this country club."

Danny wasn't going to ask him why he was there, you didn't. You waited until they volunteered. But Sam went right on.

"Then I made a mistake about what you could and couldn't get away with in the banking business. So I'm here looking at a little R&R for the next three years. You?"

So Danny told him about the securities he'd been holding for Johnny Z, but none of the rest of it. Sam Papadakis nodded his head.

"That's a tough break, kiddo. Maybe there's something you're not telling me but that's okay. Anyway, we can probably help each other out now and then."

Danny asked him how that could work and Sam explained. The feds still wanted to know more details about his banking scheme, where some of the money went. So he assumed that they recorded everything he said when his lawyer came to visit. He proposed that Danny could pass along information instead, get it to the right people.

"I wouldn't just ask as a favor, you know what I mean?. I'll set up a payment plan, you could collect when you get out."

Danny told him, forget about the money. Two Greeks should help each other. And he was thinking, Papadakis could do the same for him, write some letters to people like Goomba that wouldn't ring alarm bells if someone was reading all his mail.

*

When Danny started working on his courses and hanging out with Sam Papadakis most days the time started to go faster. And he looked forward to seeing Barbara Johnson every week. She'd started him writing an essay about each reading assignment. He started with Homer's *Iliad*, which Barbara said was not only the greatest Greek epic poem but also the very first piece of European literature. So he wrote about Achilles and his silly pride and how he'd known Greeks just like that, his father's cousin who got mad at his father one day playing cards and didn't talk to him the next twenty years. But when he started reading the *Odyssey* he liked it a lot better. He explained that the *Iliad* was mostly about pride, and anger, and fighting, but Odysseus was the thinking man's Greek and that the plot of the *Odyssey* was so familiar, like a Western, where the stranger comes quietly into town, scouts out the territory, sees what's going on—that the neighboring cattlemen are trying to take over—and then finally reveals who he really is and kills all the bad guys in a big shootout and goes to bed with his wife, after being away for twenty years.

Barbara was delighted with his essay, the longest he'd written, more than ten pages and she said he was a natural critic, that he was one of the few students who'd ever figured out that the *Odyssey* was actually about revenge instead of fabulous travel stories. She was also thinking about Odysseus gathering up his wife and taking her to bed after all the excitement, a big, hardbodied man, needing release after so much tension. And then Danny said he'd gotten a kick out of Athena holding up the dawn so that Odysseus and Penelope could enjoy all the pleasures of love as long as they wanted. He'd been thinking too, about a well-rounded woman, with soft skin, without a man for a long time, and how long it might take to pleasure her to perfection. And so imperceptibly an idea was born that could return and return in the night to both of them.

One day Sam sat down there at the table under the oak where Danny was waiting and said *"Ti káneis, moré?"* And Danny answered without even thinking, *"Kalá, polí kalá, ke si?"*

Then Sam came out with a long, fast babble of Greek. Danny just shook his head so Sam asked, "How much Greek do you know, anyway?

Danny had to admit he only knew kitchen Greek, the things his mother said now and then, how are you, how did you sleep? Or things like, *"Grígora, kópse ta kotópoula!"* meaning, quick, cut up the chickens.

Sam started asking him questions then in Greek, but slowly and pronounced clearly and Danny was amazed how much he actually knew and had stored there in the back of his brain.

"There's probably a lot there," said Sam. "It's in your genes. And since we got no appointments we can't break the next three years, what do you say we brush you up on your Greek?"

It only took Danny a couple of weeks, getting better all the time speaking and understanding Greek, to realize in a sudden burst of revelation where he was going to hide out from the mob, what he was going to go with his dead Philadelphians. He would go to Greece, to Crete, to some village where his family had lived maybe two generations ago. He could live like a king there, but quietly, maybe go into the big city now and then, but with a command of the language he could fit right in. They should never be able to find him. And if they did come after him, there in the mountains of Crete, he'd be the guy on home ground. And he started making his plans right away.

"Hey, take it easy, Thanassi!" Sam would say in Greek. "We been talking two hours now!" And Danny would laugh. Then he'd start talking in English again about his economics classes and the strategies of investment, at least the simplistic kind of theory that his junior college textbook thought kids could deal with.

Sam was mostly contemptuous. "It's good you should learn the basic theory, but you get into a brokerage, they're going to train you their way, and you're going to be just like the house in Vegas. You don't care what they buy or sell, just keep them buying and selling and collect the house percentage."

"But what they buy and sell makes a difference!" protested Danny. "My textbook has a problem: should you convince your client to buy, *A.* an Initial Public Offering, that might double in a week, or, *B.* a utility stock paying 9.8% yield, or, *C.* an energy stock paying 3.9%?"

"And what did you say?"

"I said, based on performance, you should recommend

66

the energy, even with a lower yield, because the growth figures over the last ten years show the stock actually doubling in value about every eight years or so."

"That's a good answer." said Sam. "But not the only one. Let me comment. All of them could be right. Let's take C.: the energy, let's say Chevron, or Mobil, is good because there ain't any more oil. Period. It's *always* going to go up. And the income is fair. Let's say, give it a B minus grade. But let's say you need some income over the next year, more than usual. Then buy the utility, but only after doing some research into the stability. It's riskier, but the income is right up there, about an A, A minus. But the IPO could be the big winner. Only trouble is you have to be an insider, know whether it's going to be a blockbuster, or just a bomb. I bought ten thousand shares of a restaurant chain once, all the Hollywood stars were partners in it, glitz up the kazoo, I figure it'll open, go up five points in a week, I'll sell and be ahead fifty grand. Instead, it opens at 26, bobs and weaves a bit, then sinks to 18, 19 forever. No dividend, no nothing. You get the same effect if you took two hundred sixty thousand dollars in cash, burn a quarter of it, then bury the rest of it in your backyard in coffee cans forever."

"So what did you do, just dump it?" asked Danny.

"Yeah, you gotta. Problem is, if in the meantime you convinced six hundred other people they ought to buy the stock too, you're going to have a lot of angry people at your trial. Doesn't help."

"And the up side of IPOs?"

"Well, like I say, if you're an insider, you make out like a bandit. It's happened to me a few times when you *know* it's going to go forth and multiply, like the Bible says, maybe six or eight times, even. But if ever they get you in court for whatever, parking in the handicap zone, I don't care, they'll go back over your record and say, 'Ahah! Insider trading!' and whether they can prove it or not, the jury is looking at you like you stuck people up with a gun, made them do it. That's the really risky thing, telling other people what to buy. So if you're a broker and playing it safe you just put them in the blue chips and then, someday, you gotta make a payment on your Porsche, you call around and get your clients to buy something you heard is moving, Texaco this week, Disney the next. If three out of ten phone calls get some action you get your commission, maybe four, five grand if they're heavy hitters. Then a few weeks later you call again, tell 'em, 'Texaco leveled off and announced the dividend. Probably time to sell.' So they collect a couple cents on the dollar on the stock going up, collect a dividend, maybe another four cents, you collect another couple payments on your Porsche. Everyone's happy!"

"That sounds too simple," said Danny.

"It is." said Sam. "You know what my father told me, a guy who made a million in the commodities market back then, when it was a lot of dough? He said, 'In the market, sometimes the bulls win, sometimes the bears win, but the pigs always lose.'"

"I think I get that," said Danny. "Greed always loses."

"You bet your ass it does! See. You've been trying to keep your client in what? a combination of blue chips, money market, maybe some bond funds for income, then you can't control these guys, they get out of the house once in a while and the guy comes to you and says, 'Hey I was playing golf with the vice president of a big biotech company and he tells me, completely confidential, you understand, that this Astrospasm, whatever, is going to take off'. And your client wants a hundred thousand shares at six dollars. Wants to buy it on margin too, which he's going to have to pay nine percent interest on.

"So first you gotta explain, if this guy, the golf player, is a veep and he tells you this secret, what he's doing is called insider trading, which is a felony, which is one of the reasons I'm sitting here telling you this. Second, what's probably happening is that this veep knows his own company is going in the toilet so he wants to sell its stock short, but he can't until it goes up at least a tick. That's an SEC regulation specifically created to keep insiders from selling short when they know they're going under. That's why he's calling all his friends, telling 'em 'buy Astrospasm!' Just enough so it'll go up —just one-sixteenth, say, so he's off the hook with the SEC when the stock goes into a black hole in space somewhere. You know what I'm saying?"

Danny nodded. The whole game sounded familiar even though he'd never been in it.

Another day Danny started asking about derivatives and Sam interrupted. "Enough about money, Danny. I got a feeling you'll never be short, you get out. Now let's talk about soul! What do you know about modern Greek poets? Let's keep on making you a better Greek." And Sam went off about the Greek poets of the twentieth century and how Danny should learn their poems, that make you forget about money and greed, that just get to the heart of the human condition. He told Danny to get some books from the library at the college, Cavafy, and Kazantzakis, and he'd show him some Greek soul. But when Danny passed on the request to Barbara Johnson and she brought the books one day, interlibrary loan from UCLA, the assistant warden wouldn't let them in.

"Prisoners can't have foreign language books. It's the rule."

Barbara protested, but the assistant warden, an older

woman, a spare, hard, angular authority figure, was adamant. "We can't check what it says. It could be pornography, or communist propaganda, and we wouldn't know."

Barbara was smart enough to realize it was useless to argue. Sam Papadakis just laughed. "People that dumb are the easiest to fool, Thanassi. Look, I'm going to write out some parts of poems, my father made me learn by heart. You learn these words, it's like learning to fly, you'll soar through the air with these poets, such ideas, such expression!"

So Danny started learning verses that Sam Papadakis wrote down, copying them himself, then memorizing them in his room at night. The third day they'd started, the assistant warden came around and said they couldn't be writing foreign languages to each other, things the staff couldn't read, wasn't even in the right alphabet. But Sam was ready for her, told her that the camp was one-quarter full of Spanish speakers who routinely wrote to their mothers and other relatives in Spanish, and if they couldn't read and write, they had friends writing and reading their mail for them.

"Is Greek different from Spanish?" asked Sam. The assistant warden furrowed her brow and finally said okay. Three weeks later five Mexican smugglers went over the wire and got away, undoubtedly in an arrangement that had been made by writing in Spanish to friends on the outside. Before she could think about it twice, Danny and Sam went to the warden's office and told her, look, we're studying Greek poetry. We're not going over the wire. We'll give you copies of everything we write down and you can get a Greek to read it. You find anything criminal in there you can throw us in solitary.

So they got to keep on studying Greek poetry.

*

After about fourteen months Goomba came by on a visit and told Danny his mother was not doing well. She'd been skipping some of the visits because of these headaches and now they were getting worse. The family was trying to get her to a doctor but she told them her husband had gone to the doctor, who sent him to the hospital for a test and he never came home again. So she was against this whole idea of tests.

Another six months and Goomba came by again. Johnny Z was not getting out of prison in Arizona. He'd gotten into a fight, somebody'd shoved a sharpened toothbrush handle into his stomach. It was a bullshit wound but they couldn't stop the bleeding and Johnny was dead on the operating table.

Danny used to lie awake at night thinking about his future. At first his big worry was Johnnie Z. The guy would get out of the joint and some big Chinese guy would be waiting to take him where Mr. Jolly could ask him about the bonds. None of the scenarios Danny thought about ended without Mr. Jolly finding out from Johnny where his dead Philadelphians were. That meant that Mr. Jolly's employees would pick him up too one step from the gate of the prison and inquire about their bearer bonds. Now Johnnie Z was dead and the connection might still exist but it wasn't clear, and if he hit the ground running when he got out, he might still get out of the country and out of mob jurisdiction.

More troublesome was the federal investigator who came to see him after he'd heard that Johnny Z had been killed. He was medium young, athletic looking, and friendly as if he really meant it.

"Danny, my name's George Kiosoglou. Hard to pronounce, I know." He chuckled.

Danny smiled. "You're Greek. You think I'm going to tell you all this stuff I'm supposed to know, just 'cause you're Greek like me, like a club or something?"

Kiosoglou just shook his head. "I dunno, Danny. You're going to need some help. We monitored enough from Mr. Jolly and his friends to know that they were interested in your pal Zafiropoulos and now they're interested in you. You can give us some help, you might get out of here next month, have complete protection from Jolly's people."

Danny sighed. "You guys been all over my bank accounts, my mother's business, everything. You gotta know I don't have anything belongs to Jolly. I never even heard of the guy until this came up!"

It was as if Kiosoglou didn't even hear him. "Just think about four thousand expensive homes in the Santa Monica mountains, Danny. That's what we figure this was all about. Four thousand, times half a mil, most of those properties? We know you been taking economics; can you do the math there?"

"Two billion, is what you're talking about?" said Danny with wonderment. "And you think this deal has something to do with me?"

"Four thousand homes," went on Kiosoglou, "You're not supposed to build this kind of house on park land, on unstable slopes, on land zoned for agriculture, or on land zoned for huge hundred-and-sixty acre lots. Four thousand homesites need convenient residential zoning at two acres at most, they need park boundaries erased, they need engineers to approve building on steep slopes. Bottom line, Danny! They need votes in city councils, on county boards of supervisors, and they need votes in the State Legislature and finally in Congress, to slide those park boundaries around a little. Then of course they need clearance from the State Coastal Commission. That's what Mr. Jolly is doing right now. He's getting big chunks of cash to people like Ottie Shamus, who know how to slip the money over the transom into the offices of city councilmen, county supervisors, state assemblymen, and Congressmen. Am I making my point?"

"Mr. Kiosoglou," said Danny. "It sounds interesting to me because I'm taking these economics courses, but I just vaguely heard of Jolly, that he's the mob man in L.A. So what does he care about real estate?"

"Way we figure, the last four or five really big real estate deals here in California, Nevada, Arizona, all had the mob as a silent partner. In fact not even completely silent. You take your H&D Enviro Development Partners? It's a big mover in a lot of development? It's got no offices, no phone number, but it files all its K-Ones, pays all its taxes religiously? H and D is Herschel and Dolly, who is Mr. Jolly's mother, and they basically make real estate loans. Like multi-million dollar loans."

"Dolly Jolly?"

"Right, you got it. Herschel's mother. She's a great character. You put her on the stand, like we did once a few years ago for the Grand Jury, trying to clarify some fraudulent deal Herschel is trying to pull off, and she starts doing a stand-up comedy routine, Jewish den mother to the mob, in five minutes she's got the whole courtroom laughing and the DA's having a fit. Just forget it. Worst fuckup of a serious investigation I ever seen."

Danny was laughing. But he asked anyway, "I wonder if she ever saw anyone hanging on a meat hook."

"The old meat hook story? It's bullshit. Also, stretching

guys on the lube rack? Jolly makes sure those stories go around and around so people are terrified of him. Listen, if you can help us nail Jolly on this whole bribery scheme he's going up for twenty or more, he's not going to bother anyone, and you can name where you want to go on the witness protection program. You could be out of here next week!"

But Danny had to shake his head and apologize. He couldn't be any help, he only knew Johnny Z to say hello to. The guy'd left this envelope in his car like he'd said a hundred times and he'd never been anywhere near the mail truck robbery in Phoenix. He'd been looking for Johnny to give the stuff back when he got busted. As to the bearer bond Johnny was carrying, Danny said he was completely ignorant. So the FBI guy sighed and got up to leave.

"*Adío, sto kaló,*" said Danny.

"*Yah....*" Kiosoglou started to say automatically, then looked back, his eyes narrowing. He pointed a finger at Danny, cocked his thumb, like a pistol. "Take it easy, kid. I'll be back."

*

Mr. Jolly's Korean muscle man, Moon, was sitting on a stool in a garage in Hawthorne in the middle of the night. The garage was mostly dark but they'd hung up a few work lights in the middle. Moon was watching a skinny man who had his ankles taped with duct tape to an engine block on the floor and his hands way over his head, tied to the ends of a lube rack. The man was naked because he'd crapped in his pants and everyone started cursing and carrying on about the smell so they cut his clothes off and hosed him off. Moon told him that if he couldn't control his bowels they'd stick the high pressure air hose up his ass and blow the shit out his ears. The skinny man was now a model of concentration.

"Tell me again about the mailtruck," said Moon.

"Juh...juh...just like I said," said the skinny man. "Me'n Shorty Bean, my partner, we done a few banks, Phoenix area, minor stuff, then Shorty buys into a plan for a mail-truck job, supposed to be carrying a payroll."

"A *payroll!*" Moon was indignant. "This supposed to be the fifties, golden oldies, or something? Maybe there's a cash payroll somewhere in Bolivia, Africa, some fucking place. But Phoenix? Manny, lift this shitfaced liar up a few inches." Manny, sitting on a stool by the wall, carefully turned the valve a bit and the lube rack jerked upwards, stretching the skinny man so he was on his tiptoes, strad-dling the engine block.

"Oh shit! Jesus Christ! You're going to kill me!" wailed the skinny man. "Listen, listen! I don't know nothing about payrolls!"

"These guys weren't rocket scientists," conceded Tony, who was running the tape recorder.

"Okay, go on, go on," ordered Moon.

"So, uh, we needed a third guy and Johnnie Z worked with us a few times before. We hit the mail truck and there's no payroll. We even cut off one of the driver's fin-gers and he swears, there's nothing but a big bag of stocks and shit like that, being transferred. So Shorty grabs it and says maybe the insurance'll pay to get it back."

"Okay, okay, so what about the bearer bond Johnny Z had?"

"I don't know nothing about that...ah—*eeeegh!*" said the skinny man as he rose another inch.

"You got three seconds to start talking about bearer

bonds and then you go up another three inches!"

"Wait! wait! wait! Had nothing to do with us! Shit! Johnny had some deal with his pals back in L.A. You talk to them, you'll find out! *Aaag! aaag!*" Skinny was having a hard time breathing.

Moon looked over at Manny, then at Tony. They both shrugged their shoulders.

"Okay, Tony, get the blow torch."

Skinny's eyes got wide, his mouth opened, then his eyes fluttered and rolled back up into his head. A second later they could smell the rich, fetid odor of the tan drool that was running down his legs. Manny and Tony started cursing.

Moon sighed. "Lower him, Manny. And hose him off again. Shit, he doesn't know anything. Stick him on a bus back to Arizona."

"It's going to be those kids up in Santa Monica," said Tony.

Manny had been sitting back in the shadows, smoking one cigarette after another. "You hear what he said? About cutting off the guy's finger? Man, that's sick!"

*

Goomba was visiting Danny. He looked funny, wearing this suit and tie, a guy who used to wear shorts all year round, and tank tops to show his muscles.

"Mom isn't good, Danny. Your cousins are running the restaurant full time now. She finally saw a doctor and he said she's gotta go in the hospital. But you know her. She keeps saying she's gonna wait...wait...wait...shit!" His voice broke and there were now tears coming down Goomba's big cheeks. He blew his nose, sat up straight.

"She says she's gonna wait till you get out, Danny. She

doesn't want to, uh, die in some hospital without her son around. You think you can get furloughed, just a few days?"

"I'll try," said Danny, choking up. He struggled for control. "They do it sometimes," he said. They talked a bit more about Danny's mother, about mothers from the old country, which Goomba knew about too. Then Danny had to ask.

"So, what else is going on? You see Costa? Anyone else? And what's with the suit and tie?" He was trying to lighten up, knowing that if they kept talking about his mom he was going to lose control the whole way.

"Oh. The suit. I forgot to tell you, man. I passed those courses at the college and qualified for my PI licence. Antonio Scarlatta, private detective!" He thumped himself on the chest, grinning through the tears.

"I still drive for Ottie, now and then. But with my PI ticket I can finally work legit, even pack if I want. I'm renting part of an office next week, share it with a couple of insurance guys. It's not much, but it's a start."

"That's great!" said Danny. Then he spoke quickly, hoping no one was going to listen in.

"You can help me out then, when I'm about to get out. I'll send someone to talk to you. But we can't talk now."

The next day Danny sat down with Sam Papadakis.

"First of all," said Sam, "Let me say I'm really worried, hearing about your mother."

"How the hell..." started Danny, about to get mad, thinking that he'd intended to keep his grief private.

"Thanassi *mou*, my boy! Remember you're in the joint, not the Secret Service. Everybody knows you're trying to get a compassionate furlough. Everybody here likes you, hopes you'll get it! Accept the love and the sympathy. Not much of it around a place like this!" He came over and put his arm around Danny.

"Now, tell me what I can do to help."

"I'm...I'm afraid I'm not getting the furlough. There's an automatic check on my file. Anytime I need a favor, I'm supposed to volunteer what I know about...about some other deal. But I don't really know anything."

Sam looked at him intently, finally spoke. "Whatever you say, Danny. But don't hesitate to come for help or advice. Remember, I'm getting out next year. It helps to have someone on the outside, like your friend the private eye."

Danny looked at him with amazement, wondering at the kind of grapevine that could identify everyone's visitor, make that kind of information public so quickly, and then they both had to laugh.

*

Goomba looked at the card the big Korean had given him. It said, very simply, *Mister Moon, Private Inquiries,* and had a phone number, a fax number, and an E-mail address.

"Just a courtesy call," said Mister Moon, trying to get comfortable on the tiny folding chair, bothered by the two insurance guys, who were both on their phones, laughing and chattering with fraudulent cheer. "I been asked to find out about some guys, maybe used to be acquaintances of yours." He looked Goomba directly in the eye. "So then I find out you're a PI too. Should make it easier. Keep it professional, and there's a good commission in it."

The two big men were being pleasant, but sitting there sizing each other up and wondering how long it would take to whip the other guy's ass. Moon didn't figure Goomba for a kung fu guy, just a big bruiser he could take out in a hurry with a *shat geng fau*, maybe followed by a *kwai jarn*. Goomba, on the other hand, was confident that this Asian guy was probably a lethal martial arts master. But he'd met one or two of them and none of them had played football, they hadn't experienced a two hundred-eighty pound lineman coming at them at over twenty feet per second, all knees and elbows. They started out yelling "EEEYAAAAH!" and all that shit until they had been smacked up against a couple of walls. Then they tended to lose their concentration.

"So. Mister Moon. You gotta first name?"

"Just call me Moon. That's what they do."

"Okay, Moon. So give me the names of guys I'm supposed to know."

"We'll take 'em one at a time. John Za...za...Zafir..." Moon was having a hard time with the name.

"John Zafiropoulos," said Goomba. "Everyone called him Johnny Z, made it easier. I knew Johnny, saw him in the clubs now and then. But I heard Johnny got busted there in Arizona, couple of years ago. Got killed in a prison riot, something like that?"

"That's the guy. You ever heard he was working the rackets, stealing, anything like that?"

"Hey, Moon!" Goomba was warming up now. "You're a little outta line, don't you think? My PI licence says I gotta observe certain regulations and one of them is I can't have a background of hanging out with criminals. I knew this Johnny Z guy to say hello to, but frankly, I always thought the guy was dumb, a loser. What can I say?" He held his hands out in a plea for understanding.

"I was sorry to hear Johnny got killed in that prison thing, but I had no real contact with the guy, just to see him on the street, you know what I mean?"

"Okay, thanks." said Moon. "Just one more question. Johnny Z got busted in the first place 'cause he was trying to pass something called a bearer bond. You ever hear about bearer bonds floating around here?"

"Man! A hundred thousand dollars! Yeah, I read about it during the trial. But that's the only bearer bond I ever heard of. I asked the lady at the bank who does my mortgage. She says they're hardly any left out there, try to cash one in, it would ring some bells for sure. So. Who else you got there?"

Moon went through Costa and Danny Castle and two other young guys who'd hung out with them during the last five years or so. Goomba kept shaking his head, nah, nah, guys were never into anything heavy. Costa had moved back east, he thought. Danny'd gotten double-crossed by Johnny Z and was doing time at San Luis FPC. Hadn't seen the other kids lately. Ask me something I can answer. Moon was thinking, *yeah I'd like to ask you some questions tied to the lube racks, maybe speed up this investigation.* But Jolly had told him the deal was going forward, don't fuck it up unless it's completely secure. So Moon got up, finally, shook hands, both men seriously restraining their impulse to show each other some real grip, and told Goomba he'd get back to him sometime.

"Oh, and yeah. This Danny guy? He's still up there at San Luis?"

*

Danny looked at the big Oriental guy sitting on the other side of the glass. They were talking to each other through the phones.

"Nah, I never heard of bonds like that," said Danny.

"And I hardly knew Johnnie Z except he asked me to hold some kind of securities for him and then he got busted and fingered me. All respect for the dead, you know what I mean, but this guy fucked up my life, put me in here."

All the time, Danny was wondering if the Oriental would recognize him. A few years ago, when he'd fallen into Ottie's lap, there on the shuttle bus, trying to screen him off from the baggage rack, he'd been wearing long baggy shorts, a cap on backwards, and the stupidest look he could put on. Now he knew he had a great tan, he was about ten pounds lighter and he had a full grown mustache, a good Greek mustache, like his father's. But he remembered the Oriental back there on the shuttle bus and he felt naked, sure that this guy already knew who he was looking at.

"Okay, Castle, I'll let you go. But do me a favor. I'm leaving my card with the guard over there. When you get out could you come and talk to me and my client for a bit? You might be able to clarify a few things. If you misplace the card I'm in the book. Just 'Moon PI.' In the white pages. Looks like a private phone unless you know what the PI means."

*

Danny and Barbara were a couple of years into his courses now. He had finished the first segment of his Greek History course and now she was assigning the literature part. He'd read Sappho, the woman poet and had been amazed, such open and explicit expression of love for other women. It had made him a little hot and he couldn't hide it from Barbara when they were discussing the verses. She was listening to him and crossing and uncrossing her legs, thinking the room was getting a little stuffy. It got a little more intense when he'd read the *Lysistrata*, where the women withheld sex from their men until they ended the war. He was reading a modern edition and the translator had kept in all the rowdy and raunchy dialogue, talking about dildos and erections and how both the men and the women were going crazy for want of sex.

Barbara thought she'd calm down the discussion a bit.

"You know, Danny, that until fifty years ago or so, no one even knew any Greek writer had ever had an impure thought, because most of the translators were classicists who were, uh, sort of, uh..."

"Up tight? Wimpy?"

"Well something like that, but maybe even trying to protect the ancient Greeks from their own literature. You can read an 1900 translation and wonder, what's going on here? In fact, there was an English artist named Aubrey Beardsley back in the twenties who illustrated an explicit translation of the *Lysistrata* with charming line drawings, showing the ladies naked and the men with, uh, uh, well, you know what I mean." Barbara had a copy at home and had been looking through it the night before, seeing the drawings of swollen penises, beginning to wonder if Danny's looked like...and then slamming the book shut.

"When a bookseller first tried to import the edition into the United States in the thirties they threw him into jail. They asked him who'd written the book and he said 'Aristophanes.' So for a while there was even a warrant out for a pornographer named Aristophanes!"

They both laughed heartily, probably more than the story was worth, but relieved to be out of sex and into comedy again.

*

A few months later Danny's mother died. Goomba came up with Katina the next day.

"She didn't tell any of us, Danny." Katina was trying to talk, but had to stop and sob now and then. "She actually did go in for a scan or something, her doctor told me. They could see a growth in her head and from her blood test the doctor knew she had cancer and it had probably spread. She...she...she...oh Danny!"

"What happened," said Goomba, clearing his throat a lot, "Was that the doctor said, we can do this, we can do that. But your mom, Danny, like all our moms, from the old country, you know what I'm saying? Those ladies never wanted to make a fuss, go in the hospital, be poked and shoved and humiliated. So, they just go home, lie in bed, and...." Now Goomba couldn't talk for a while.

"Anyway," said Katina. "Father Adoni came over the day before, she always liked him. And they spent a long time together. And when he came out *he* couldn't talk, he was trying to keep from crying. He was just trying to smile and, you know, nodding, nodding. Anyway she never woke up in the morning....ah...hooo...oh Danny, Danny!"

Danny just sat there for a while after they'd left, completely numb. He couldn't figure out why he couldn't cry, why nothing seemed wrong, nothing seemed to hurt. He was trying as hard as he could to bring back old memories, sometime comforted in his mother's arms, her kind words, good advice...but all he could come up with over and over was, "Not the good oil, Danny...not the good oil" over and over. He wandered out of the administration building aimlessly and was passing by the makeshift boxing ring when someone hailed him.

"Hey, Castle! Try your luck again, man?" It was Soose Mendosa, a former promising light-heavyweight from East

L.A., more recently a failed drug dealer. Danny had sparred with him once and been beaten on like a drum.

Danny walked over silently, took his shirt off and put on the other pair of gloves. Then he turned around and waded in, catching Soose by surprise, nailing him with a good jab on the nose and a short jolting right that caught him on the forehead as he started to duck. Soose stumbled backward but stayed on his feet. Danny kept coming after him, threw two hard rights which Soose caught on his left shoulder. Soose spat and glared at Danny.

"Tha's what you wan', fuckhead, here it is!" For the next minute Danny absorbed the beating of his life, trying vainly to ride the punches, trying to counterpunch, nothing working, seeing Soose vaguely through a red haze. Finally a looping left hook caught him below the right ear and he found himself on his hands and knees in the dust, sobbing and bawling now. Soose was yelling something at him but then he could sense a crowd growing, murmuring, hands under his arms lifting him up. He was looking at Soose standing in front of him, tears flowing down his face.

"Hey man, shit! I din' know your momma died, man! Shit! I'm sorry!" All around he could hear sympathy, friendly words, arms around his shoulders, someone giving him a wet towel to wipe his face. Now Danny had no trouble weeping as a terrible pain began in the middle of his chest. He stepped forward and embraced Soose.

"I'm sorry, Soose, I just went crazy. I didn't know what I was doing. It was like I couldn't feel anything, I needed to get whacked around or something."

Now Soose was laughing and crying at the same time. "Hey, you crazy fuck! I'll whack you anytime, man! But shit, you don' have to hit me first, man, like you almos' bust my head! But tha's okay. I'll say a prayer for your mom." Soose crossed himself and most of the surrounding crowd automatically did the same.

They finally let him have a furlough for the funeral. One of the assistant wardens, a younger guy, drove Danny down three hours to Santa Monica and to the big Greek Orthodox church. Danny endured the service and the hugs and tears of relatives and friends afterwards. It was so wrong, so corrupt, that he should be at his mother's funeral and not be able to just walk away afterwards. He was saying to himself, over and over. *twenty two more months, twenty two more months...*

The visible effects of his beating by Soose were a welcome distraction, enabling him to explain the recreational opportunities at San Luis FPC instead of dwelling on his mother's death. Unfortunately, an elderly aunt got it into her head that he'd been beaten by prison guards and started wailing. While Danny was hugging her and reassuring her about conditions at San Luis he had an opportunity to talk quickly to Goomba out of hearing of the alert assistant warden.

"I've got a friend getting out next month. I'm sending him to you and I want you two to do a few things, get ready for when I get out."

*

It was the evening before Sam Papadakis' release and he and Danny were walking around the perimeter of the baseball diamond.

"Sam, you practically saved my life," said Danny. "I was just sitting around feeling sorry for myself when I met you. Now I got plans and you're going to help me again, okay?"

"Now you tell me? You had three years to let me know!"

Danny laughed. "I'm just following your advice. Remember? 'Don't tell anyone what you're going to do until you do it?'"

Sam grumbled, but he listened to Danny.

"I got a few bank accounts. I'm giving you the account numbers of two of them and the names I opened them under, okay? Now, you'll be able to access the accounts?"

"No problem. I'm still a banker. I can transfer funds over the phone, or by computer, long as I have the numbers and your codes...mother's maiden name or whatever you gave the bank as your personal ID code."

"That's easy," said Danny. "When I opened the accounts I figured my buddy Goomba would be the only other person who might have to use them. So the code is his last name, Scarlatta. And the PIN is the same for both accounts: 5353. Now, write down the numbers."

Danny explained what he wanted. Most of the money was to go to Goomba to start some preparations for Danny's release. But twenty percent was for Sam, himself.

Sam protested. "You have to pay me nothing, kid! I got a few bucks squirreled away, you know!"

"No, no. This is legit payment for services rendered. Here's what I want you to render."

And Danny explained that he wanted Sam Papadakis, as a respected banker, to begin correspondence with some Swiss bank he trusted, to begin to arrange for the arrival of a colleague, a Mr. James, who wished to open a rather large account consisting of various securities.

Sam interrupted. "Okay, Danny. Now I finally find out what you been so close about all these years. What kind of securities we talking about here?"

So Danny told him about the dead Philadelphians. Sam stopped dead in his tracks and hooted with laughter.

"Bearer bonds! I shoulda guessed. Nobody's used bearer bonds for what, fifteen years, around there? Nobody but the mob and major white collar crooks. Like me!" And he laughed again. Then he got serious.

"Look, I ain't gonna ask you where you got bearer bonds because I'm afraid to know. But even the friendliest Swiss banker I know is going to charge you a humongous discount off the market value." Sam stopped and thought for a minute. "Okay, okay, leave it to me. I know a couple of those guys who would rob the dead. But if the paperwork is all squared away and they got their cut you can trust them. But the cut is going to be between ten and twenty percent, maybe! And your income is going to be piss poor. The Swiss think that paying two percent interest is shameful usury! Can you live on that?"

Danny calculated rapidly. Twelve million, let's say ten million after the Swiss banker took his cut. One third of that to Goomba, one third to Costa, if anyone could find him. A two percent yield on what was left would still bring him in over $65,000 a year, and a great deal more if he started investing it in more adventurous European funds. And, of course, he would have most of the cash he had put in the Reno banks.

"I think I can scrape along," he told Sam.

Soose looked him up a few days later and asked him to box with him again.

"No, no! Not real fighting, man!" Soose said. Danny had looked dubious. "No, man, I wanna show you some things. You know, you got a natural right hand, can do some damage. You ever get in a fight, don't even think about it, just throw the right first. I'll show you."

So the time went on, and on, and on.

*

A few months later Barbara Johnson told Danny that the college had recalculated his credits and that he was now eligible to get his degree with the June graduating class. Danny asked the warden if he could attend graduation ceremonies, not really expecting anything, and was surprised when the warden, looking through his file on the computer, nodded his head.

"You're due out relatively soon. I think we can take the chance. And, oh, the Feds didn't renew their check on you. Maybe they found out what they were looking for. Let's see, two weeks from Friday—I'll send Mason with you."

Two weeks later a high pressure ridge developed over the high desert and the hot air cascaded over the mountains and down on to the coast, sending the temperature twenty degrees higher than normal. Graduation day dawned bright and hot. When Mason picked up Danny to drive him into San Luis Obispo he told him he was glad *he* didn't have to stand around in a black robe that morning. Barbara Johnson met them at the parking lot at the college and told them they'd probably be through by noon and that she'd fixed a lunch for them at her house, if Mr. Mason thought it would be okay. Mason said sure, sure, and then all through the ceremonies he seemed distracted and kept looking at his watch. As the crowd let out, he stopped them at his car.

"You know, we all know you're not going anywhere, Castle. Listen, I got someone I'd like to look up in town. I hate to miss your lunch, Professor, but give me your address and I'll be by to pick up Castle around two thirty. Okay with you?"

Danny and Barbara drove silently, not daring to speak,

in her car to her house in a tract south of town with the midday heat beating down and reflecting off the black asphalt road surface. It was an airless day and almost no one was outdoors, escaping into the relative coolness of darkened houses.

Danny waited as Barbara unlocked the front door, then followed her in. They walked through the living room, past the dining room, with the table set and dishes ready to serve, and into her bedroom, where they fell on each other. Almost four years of sitting across a table and looking at each other had bred countless fantasies and they were ripe and overheated. With their clothes off Danny thought he should at least go for the minimum of foreplay but Barbara whispered, "No, no," found him with her hand and quickly guided him into her. She was already wet and eager to start before Danny was even all the way in. He started to slow down, thinking to prolong their lovemaking but Barbara clutched him and hissed in his ear, "No, no, Danny, come as fast as you can. Then we'll have more time for the next one!"

Willing and obedient, Danny came like a train whistle, a ragged groan bursting from his throat and then turning to helpless laughter as he plunged and plunged, finishing his climax for what seemed an eternity. Then they both slowly relaxed and just lay, slippery with sweat, panting. Barbara took his head in both hands and kissed him fiercely, her tongue driving deep into his mouth.

"Do you realize that's the first time we kissed?" she asked.

"Yeah, and we did it after, after..."

"After we fucked, I believe is the expression," laughed Barbara. "Now, let's get you ready for the next one. We have about two hours—that is, if we don't eat."

No one ate. The dishes remained neat and unviolated on the pristine table cloth, the German potato salad, the stuffed vine leaves Barbara had looked up in a Greek cookbook to surprise Danny, the rolls she had baked, while from the bedroom came soft noises, of conversation, then of pleasure, of wonder, of excitement, murmurs, laughing, continuing as the hands on the dining room clock slowly crept around the dial. Then a woman's voice began to exclaim, "Oh, oh, oh..." louder and faster until finally she called on the Lord with all her strength, and yet kept on calling, calling, as a man's voice was heard comforting, encouraging, and then rising sharply to join the chorus...

In the end they made love a third time before hurrying to the shower to wash away signs of combat and to cool off under the cold water before putting their clothes on and waiting for Mason to get back. Danny met him at the door, not wanting him to see the untouched table and dishes and after exchanging an unfathomable look with Barbara, he walked out to the government Plymouth.

They were on the outskirts of San Luis Obispo when Mason cleared his throat. "Uh, we got a little time, Castle. You mind if we stop so I can get a bite to eat? I ran out of time, never did get lunch."

Danny didn't mind. And if Mason was surprised to see his prisoner order two Whoppers, large fries, and a large milkshake he said nothing, perhaps taking it for granted that a lady professor's lunch might have been too dainty for a convict's lusty appetites.

Chapter Three
On the run

I<small>T WAS MORE THAN SEVEN MONTHS LATER.</small> Danny and Barbara had managed two more meetings at her house, each time Mason taking him in to the "Library" and then going his own way for three or four hours. Whatever Mason did made him hungry and they stopped for fast food each time but the two men never spoke about their activities in town, considering their bond too delicate to be stressed by confidences.

Now the warden had sent for Danny and he went into the administration building wondering what new complication the fates had dreamed up for him. When he finally entered the big office the warden, a meaty man with closely cropped gray hair, was reading a file. He gestured without looking for Danny to sit, then after a minute he sighed and leaned back.

"Damn DEA doesn't make it any easier for me."

Danny absorbed this observation silently. To him it was meaningless.

"Sometimes it's cheating on taxes, sometimes it's bank robbers, but you can count on it, every three months or so drugs heats up and every fucking politician, Sacramento, Washington, everywhere, they want the drug dealers in jail."

The warden just sat there, jiggling back in his armchair,

so Danny felt he had to say something. "I noticed a lot of dealers coming in lately, sir. Is that more than usual?"

"Is that more than usual, he asks!" exclaimed the warden. "How about thirty percent increase? You know what that means?"

Danny just sat there until he realized the question was directed at him, then responded, "No, uh, no sir."

Now the warden leaned forward and stared at Danny, as if holding him personally responsible for his situation. "It means your blacks, your Mexicans, all of the gang kids, that's who's running drugs in L.A. They kill each other there and they're going to kill each other here. You, Castle, you're a bank robber, right?"

Danny was going to protest, then realized his response was not necessary or wanted so he just waited.

"How many bank robbers up here you ever see slice each other up, gang rape each other in the shower, your bank robbers, tax cheats, mail fraud, white collar crime, huh? None! That's what. You guys got a certain class, even what's his name, Tolliver." The warden was referring to a black accountant who had managed to skim two-and-a-half million dollars from the huge bank where he worked by creating a computer program that directed all fractions of certain transactions less than one cent into dummy accounts that he controlled. The warden obviously didn't want to be taken as a bigot. Tolliver was definitely classy. He was the unchallenged chess champion of the prison and had completely reworked the camp computer system, enormously simplifying it, almost to the point where prison administrative employees could manage it.

"I guess you're right, sir," said Danny, who also knew computers and wasn't sure that all the time Tolliver spent on them was just to improve the camp's on-line standards.

"Fuckin' A, I'm right," said the warden. "And bottom line is, we gotta take in twenty-four new drug dealers next week, and no room for them. So..."

He hesitated for effect. "So...with my discretionary powers, I'm allowed to kick some of you lazy bastards out of here." He grinned at Danny. "And that includes you, Castle. You're out of here tomorrow. You do, of course, have the right of appeal..."

But Danny was out of his seat, jumping up and down. Then he had a quick sober moment. "You're not kidding me?" He stared at the warden, suddenly paralyzed.

But the warden got up, smiling, came around his desk and put his arm around Danny's shoulders. "You always been a good con, Danny. I think you got railroaded up here, but I'm not gonna say anything about that. Anyway, when you were up here you were straight arrow, took your college courses, which you was the first ever to graduate, last ten years. You stayed out of trouble and everybody liked you, even the trouble makers. When I heard your mother died, it choked me up a bit, you know what I mean? So. It's a real pleasure to release you tomorrow. Tell my secretary any arrangements you need to get picked up. Okay?"

*

Barbara picked up Danny the next morning and once again lunch waited on the table until mid-afternoon.

"I love you, you know?" he said, rising on one elbow and looking down at that sweet face, recently working in relentless passion, now in repose. Barbara just returned his gaze, no change of expression.

"Danny. Danny, Danny. My Thanassi. I love you too. So where do we go from here?" She smiled, knowing, having lived with the answer for three years and more.

"I...uh. Okay. I wasn't really starting a discussion. I was just making an observation, like." He smiled too.

She shook her head, still smiling. "Danny, 'I love you' is not just an observation. It changes dimensions. It alters orbits. It releases unimaginable energy into quiescent systems. Haven't you learned anything from the great works of literature you've been reading? When Helen caressed Paris there in Sparta, behind her husband's back and said, 'I love you,' did she say, 'Oh, that was just an observation. I didn't mean to launch a thousand ships and burn the topless towers of Ilium.'"

"Marlowe," he said.

"Close enough," she said, not wanting to give him full credit, and then throwing a leg over him. "But my love, you haven't taken *this* course, this *I-love-you* course. You just started it and you haven't even read the syllabus yet."

He started to speak but she shushed him. "No. You never studied the language of love, the way people really speak, especially when they're doing things like this." And her hand let him know what she was talking about. "When people say, 'I love you,' that's just the first line. And there's almost always a second line. With girl-type people the next line, whether they put it that way or not, can be translated, 'And let's get married.' With guy-type people the next line starts with the word, 'But...'"

"Isn't that a bit cynical?" asked Danny, trying to keep smiling.

"My love. Yes I'm cynical. But I love you, I do. And my next line is definitely not 'Let's get married.' There. I was honest. Now you be too. What is your next line?"

"It starts with 'But'" said Danny.

"Oh, thank you, thank you!" She grabbed him by the

hair and kissed him passionately. "You *are* honest!"

"Okay, I'll keep being honest," he said. "My next line is I gotta get out of here and get really well hidden because some people are going to try to kill me the second they know I'm out."

Now it was her turn to be taken by surprise. "But...but, what? You only had some worthless securities, stuff you couldn't even negotiate! What...Danny, what are you mixed up in?!"

And her tone of voice completely changed the atmosphere. They had been lovers, lazily musing after love, kidding about love words. Now suddenly she was the protective female, demanding to know what the foolish male, the husband-son-brother figure had done, so she could begin planning and working to get him out of it. Danny could hear, in the recesses of his mind, the phone ringing in his house, his mother answering, talking, her voice rising, then hanging up and coming after the twelve-year-old boy... "Thanassi! What did you do this time!"

They both knew what had happened. They both relaxed in sad resignation and at that moment they loved each other as never before, seeing the parting, the ending, and both of them had tears in their eyes.

"Barbara. My Barbara. All I can say is that I will be in touch. That you'll know I'm well...even if it's not safe for you to know where I am. I can't...I just can't tell you right now what it's all about. But give it a month, maybe two months, and you'll get a letter from me. I swear to God. And now..."

Barbara was rolling out of bed. "And now, my love, you better get moving. Because whatever you did, whatever you're involved in, I'm still your lover, in love with you, and I don't want you dead. I have priorities. So what now?

You need a ride? What can I do?"

An hour later she put him on the commuter plane to Los Angeles, a little puddle jumper with ten seats. She'd stopped at an ATM and drawn two hundred dollars for him although he'd protested bitterly, insisting he only needed enough to get to Santa Monica. A week later she would look uncomprehendingly at the package she had just opened, containing two thousand dollars in hundreds. Ben Franklins. Dead Philadelphians. And the note, "I can't repay one-hundredth what I owe you. This is at least a beginning. I love you forever!"

*

At five in the morning Moon snatched the ringing phone off the hook. "Yeah?"

"He left yesterday."

"The fuck! I told you to let me know the second..."

"Hey! Moon! This ain't the fuckin' Hyatt, man! Nobody knew until yesterday noon. Then I was on detail until now, and if they notice this call on the log my ass is in big trouble. I happen to be cleaning the warden's office right now. It's the only phone that's not locked down at night!"

"Okay, okay. But he wasn't due for what, a year?"

"Dope dealers, that's what. We're overloaded and they had to throw guys out. Anyway, I gotta get off the phone."

"Quick, then. Where's he headed, any idea?"

"The broad he's been banging picked him up. He could be there..."

"Johnson? That's the name?"

"Yeah. If he's still there..."

*

The phone roused Barbara from a blissful sleep full of amorous dreams. Like a dash of cold water.

"Hello?"

"Professor Johnson, this is agent Macready, FBI. We just found out that by an administrative mistake Daniel Castle was released from San Luis prison camp. There is a federal warrant still out for him and if you are aiding and abetting him you are liable to up to five years in federal prison. Now, where is Castle."

As sleepy as Barbara was, she was still alert enough to wonder at the slight accent in the FBI agent's voice, and to wonder why the FBI didn't know that Danny's real name was not Daniel, but Athanassios. She thought quickly.

"Ohmygod! That's terrible! I had no idea! Well, I put Mr. Castle on a plane for..." she hesitated, about to lie, then thought better of it..."For Los Angeles, yesterday afternoon. If you're trying to find him you should talk to his mother and father."

Moon was going to tell her that Danny Castle's mother and father were both dead, but then he realized he was talking to someone with intelligence, so he just hung up.

He spent the next hour trying to contact Herschel Jolly and finally gave up, realizing that sometimes people just got too important to be bothered before daylight for any reason. He left a message on three different answering machines, saying that the "bondholder" had left his previous location.

*

The phone woke George Kiosoglou. Outside his window he could see just the first streaks of dawn in the northeast over the San Gabriel mountains.

"Kiosoglou here. Better be important."

"I think it is, George. This is Jack downtown. I'm monitoring Jolly's taps. Pretty quiet usually this time of day but we just got three messages at three different phones, all the same, a guy saying, "Our bondholder has left, whereabouts unknown, will pursue a good lead."

"Jesus Christ!" was Kiosoglou's reaction.

"Yeah," said Jack, "I thought it might've been important. Anyway, George, I don't know the case, so I'll let you get moving on it, okay?"

Kiosoglou called Washington, which was at least awake, being three hours out of bed. His contact was bewildered.

"George, we had a hold on Castle. Lemme look here, yeah, a hold on anything Castle did or asked, let's see, oh shit! Two years ago we didn't renew. It wasn't automatic, had to renew officially every year!"

"How the hell does that happen? We had an automatic reminder in our software program!" Kiosoglou was indignant.

"George! I'm sixty-four years old! I remember up to a few years ago when all of us remembered our big ticket cases in our own heads, alright? So now, we all got computers, we file and forget."

Kiosoglou started to protest but his supervisor went on.

"So Castle got out early. It's not a big case, right? But whatever he was holding was mob payoff money, no doubt about it. More of those goddamn bonds been turning up and they're all connected with Pacific Estates."

"But I don't think Castle knew anything about Pacific Estates!"

"That's our reasoning. But Castle will know who owned those bearer bonds."

"But how the hell did Castle and that friend of his,

Zafiropoulos, luck into those bonds?"

"George, you're a detective, right? Our master, Mr. Sherlock Holmes, said something like, when you eliminate every other explanation, what's left has got to be the solution."

"But...."

"Shut up and listen, George. The only explanation left is that Castle and his friends stole a big payoff from the mob. They didn't know where it was going, they just found out somehow how it was being transferred and they hijacked it. It was fucking brilliant! A bunch of kids. Look, George, we have complete videos, ground level, helicopters, everything, of Herschel Jolly's mother going to the hotel that day and then to the airport. We spent maybe forty hours going over the tapes, over and over again. So we got one possibility, one only. A stewardess gets off the shuttle bus before it leaves, with a black suitcase. No one's watching her, so she just disappears. We've got more than a dozen high priced analysts watching all these tapes, they all agree. That's it. That's the window, the only one, where the payoff can disappear! Only thing we don't have is a logical connection to Castle and his buddies. But if we play Sherlock Holmes again, we gotta like *infer* the connection."

Kiosoglou had been trying to interrupt. "So why don't we get any kind of action from the Santa Monica kids? Scarlatta is still in Santa Monica, he doesn't spend money, he has to rent a cheap office, he drives a little shit car, a Ford Aspire, for Christ's sake! And this kid, Costa!"

"Right! Costa. Where is Costa, George?"

"Well, we don't know. He just up and disappeared."

"George, you're Greek. That's why we have you on this case. You know as well as I do that a Greek-American with a lot of relatives can disappear in what? ten minutes?"

"Well. Yeah, chief, you're right. But maybe I can find Castle today. I mean, he's gotta come back, see his family, whatever. Maybe I can pick him up."

"Yeah, George. But remember, you can talk to him. You can't hold him. 'Cause he's a free man, no parole, no nothing. That's the law. But listen, George, go find that son of a bitch so we can trace him. He's going to have mob all over him when he shows up. Number one priority, George, keep the mob out of this until we can nail them, okay?"

"Gottit, chief. Okay, I'm outta here. Phone you this afternoon."

*

Danny woke up in the alley behind Goomba's house as the first rays of the sun poked through the window of the camper top. He was sleeping in the back of Goomba's old Toyota pickup, still in his clothes from the day before. He'd been very cool about contacting Goomba yesterday, late in the afternoon, walking by the door of the office with the two insurance guys until the second time Goomba spotted him, went out back and around and met him at the corner.

"Jesus Christ, Danny! I didn't know you were out! You didn't go over the wire did you?"

Danny reassured him and explained. "Now, what I gotta do is collect the papers I hope you made for me, collect the money I stashed, and then disappear for a while."

"What d'ya mean, you hope I made! You jerk! Your pal Sam told me what you wanted, I got you exactly what you wanted! Three drivers' licences, two credit cards which I been buying stuff on and paying the bills, make them look legitimate. Two passports only, they're hard to do. But they're legitimate. You can even get back into the country with them."

As he was driving Danny back to his place he told him about the passports. "You gotta find some rummy, some homeless guy, not too burnt out, get him to clean up, go down to the courthouse and get a passport in his own name. Runs around a thousand to find the right guy and pay him off. But Mr. Sam paid all the bills already. He's some ballsy dude, Danno! Back up in San Francisco right now, but he said he wanted to see you, soon as you got out."

They were in Santa Monica now, approaching Goomba's house and Danny stopped Goomba in mid-sentence.

"I'm trying not to involve you, man, that's why I didn't call you or anything. Don't go to your house, just drop me in the alley and I'll meet you in the garage, okay?"

They'd stayed up late talking, laughing, plotting the next few steps Danny was going to take. It was hard for him to persuade Goomba that there was actually going to be a three million or so payoff for him from the dead Philadephians.

"Man, that is so weird! What the hell am I going to do with that kind of money? I been sitting on just the cash the last four years, not even spending much of that. It's in a money market account under a different name and it's way up over two hundred grand by now, the interest. I been doing things like paying my mom's mortgage payments, buying food, shit like that. But everywhere I go I get this feeling that someone's watching, just waiting for me to buy the Ferrari or the Rolex, start hanging with high class hookers."

"So it's a good thing you're just a simple Goomba, you big fuck!" laughed Danny, smacking him a good one on his massive shoulder. "So look. Here's what we'll do. I'll set up an interest bearing account there in Switzerland for you, you set up an account here to receive the interest, start buying some stocks, bonds, mutual funds, all in a different name. Some day they're going to forget about us and you can cash in, big time. In the meantime, you always got walking around money, right?" He paused. "The worst thing, really killing me, is that I can't go see Katina, the rest of the family. Anyone talked to them, they'd give it away in a second. You gotta promise me you'll wait a few days and then tell them I'm out, and I'm safe, and I'll write them. Okay?"

*

Danny looked carefully out all the windows of the camper top, then wiggled out the back, snaked around the alley and into the back door of Goomba's garage. He could smell coffee and the moment he entered the big man came in from the house with a pot of coffee and a bag of doughnuts. He was also carrying a small backpack.

"Got your coffee here, man. I'm going to give you the old Kawasaki in back of the garage. You get out of here on a bike, old clothes, old backpack, nobody's going to spot you. I got all your papers here in the pack. Here, have a quick coffee, I'll put up the garage door and you're out of here."

Danny gratefully took the coffee cup. He ate two bites of doughnut, couldn't swallow any more. He was too wired, wanting to get out of here, get on the road, away from old hangouts where he could be traced. He hadn't even wanted to stay last night but Goomba persuaded him that he'd be better off with a night's sleep.

Finally he walked over to the bike, set the choke, hit the starter. Nothing happened except the starter grinding over.

"Shit, man!" said Goomba. "No one's been on the machine for a couple months. Gas might take a minute getting to the cylinders. Hit her again.!"

The starter kept grinding, started to slow down with the battery getting low.

"Listen," said Danny. "I'm going to try it just one more time. It doesn't work I'm getting outta here down to the bus station. I don't want to hang you up, man! This is dangerous." He hit the starter one more time and there was a grind, then a wheeze and a whistling sound and then the Kawasaki was banging away on one cylinder, *bap, bap, bap, bap, bap, bap, bap,* and then finally began hitting on both cylinders, as the garage filled up with smoke. Danny turned down the choke, got off, came over and embraced Goomba one last time.

"Fuckin' ugly wop bastard!"

"Greasy Greek asshole!"

Danny got back on the bike and Goomba punched the garage door button. The door went up slowly, revealing a huge Korean man standing in the middle of the driveway.

"Danny! Get the fuck out of here! I'll hold him!" yelled Goomba, moving forward. But Danny was off the bike in a second and moved quickly to confront the Korean.

"I don't know what the hell you want, but you stay out of my life, you got that straight?"

Moon laughed, then just moved forward and into the garage. At the last moment his left hand flicked out and caught Danny on the throat with such force that he felt himself hurled into a corner of the garage where a bookcase full of paint cans toppled over on him.

"So. We meet again." said Moon to Goomba, without much imagination. "I'm taking your friend to see my client. You can make it easy or hard, doesn't matter to me one way or another."

Goomba had stepped quickly between him and Danny's prostrate form. "I don't know what you think you're doing, but I'm a licensed PI and I just witnessed an assault. I'm putting you under citizen's arrest." Goomba was stringing together bullshit, just looking for an opening.

Moon shut up and moved forward quickly, seeing Goomba start to throw a punch and then turning quickly away, then swinging back with a lethal kick and a follow up forearm. Goomba dodged the kick but took the forearm full on his temple and found himself sprawling in the front of the garage, winding up on his hands and knees. Moon was walking purposefully over towards Danny, who was just starting to wake up. Moon kicked him viciously in the ribs, going for pain rather than permanent damage. Danny felt a paralyzing shock go through him.

"Okay, get up, Castle. Let me break your arm, make it easier to take you in." He reached out.

Goomba almost came to his senses. He was under the impression that he was back in the only NFL game he'd ever played. He'd been trying to block Kevin Greene, concentrating too hard, and on a stunt the linebacker had nailed him from the blind side, speared him in the side of the head and knocked him out of his senses, so that he got up not knowing where he was, just seeing the big blond Kevin Greene going back to his position, laughing at him and flipping him the bird. He'd taken his stance on the next play by instinct, no idea of what play had been called in the huddle, then exploded out towards the blond man, who wasn't expecting him, play going in the other direction, and knocking him decisively on his ass.

Moon was reaching down for Danny's arm.

"Hey! Fuck you, Kevin!"

Moon looked over, startled but then Goomba was out of his stance and coming at twenty feet a second, every nerve and muscle in his body focused on blocking the defensive end. He was right. Moon had never played football, had no idea what to do with a two-hundred-eighty pound lineman coming full speed, head down, shoulders up. He swung a vicious chop at Goomba's neck but it just bounced off and then he was moving backward himself at twenty feet per second, Goomba's massive shoulder buried in his midsection. Across the garage they hurtled until they hit the area Goomba had set up as a weight room. Goomba finally tripped over a barbell on the floor and Moon went smashing backwards until he sprawled over the bench-press bench, with Goomba's 375 pound Olympic style barbell poised above it on the stands. Everything went crashing to the floor, Moon falling on top of the fallen bench The last thing Moon saw in his life was the barbell flailing down on top of his chest. The bar came down slantwise across his chest and crushed the life out of him in a fraction of a second.

Danny and Goomba stood in the middle of the garage, shaken.

"Jesus! You think he's dead?"

"I dunno. Slap him. Maybe he'll come around. Danny, you gotta get outta here, right now! Come on, get on the bike!"

Pure momentum and terror got Danny on the Kawasaki. Then he looked puzzled at Goomba.

"What was that 'Kevin' shit?"

Goomba was just shaking his head. "It's too complicated. I'll have to tell you some other time, man!"

And then with one last wave Danny was out the garage door and on the street leading down towards Pacific Coast Highway.

Goomba just stood watching him speed away for a moment. Then he turned back to the silent form in the back of the garage and began contemplating the various scenarios involving the transport of huge bodies into vehicles and then up the coast where they could be dumped and hopefully eaten by sharks before washing up on the shore again.

As he was standing there, hands on his hips, he heard a voice say, "Looks to me like you got a problem. Could you use a little help?"

He spun around, fists up, but the other man was only medium size, in a dark suit, not even pretending to fight.

"Agent Kiosoglou, FBI. Maybe we should talk."

*

It was a little after nine when Danny got to Santa Barbara and he had to wait for the bank to open. It gave him a chance to have another coffee across the street at a shopping center. His throat ached from the whack Moon had given him and when he tried to speak his voice was weird, real high and coarse, like the Godfather, but he kept clearing his throat and he thought the hot coffee helped a little.

At the bank they looked up his deposit box number and led him through the gate into the safe deposit vault. He'd worried they would be suspicious of his old clothes but they were all as friendly as could be.

A woman named Gloria used her key in the other lock and helped him release the box. "You take as long as you want, Mr. James. Just give me a nod at the gate when you want to come out."

Danny opened the box in the little room. There was the big, tattered manila envelope. He opened it just enough to confirm that his dead Philadelphians were all in there, all hundred and nineteen of them. Then he put them in his backpack and got ready to leave.

At that moment a horrible, high-pitched alarm went off and he saw a stainless steel barred gate zip closed in front of him. All he could think of was the dorms and playing fields of the prison camp, how he'd be going back to them now, probably for big time, and an absurd thought: what courses could he take from Barbara Johnson now? Then over the din he heard the voice screaming, "Get down, get the fuck down!" and other voices screaming, then a shot, several shots, a burst of shots and he just rolled into a corner of the vault hoping to avoid the stray bullets.

There was silence for a minute, then a babble of voices, and now sirens in the distance getting closer and finally the voices of big males in authority. Danny couldn't make out what was happening, but then he saw Gloria looking through the bars at him and then the bars rolled back.

"Oh, Mr. James! We're so sorry! That's the third time someone tried to rob us the last two months!"

Danny emerged into a crowded bank, cops all over, some of them with guns still out. There were two bodies on the floor. As Gloria escorted him to the door, urged on by one of the policemen, she told him briefly what had happened. They had an old retired policeman they'd hired after the last holdup. He hung around outside because he was a smoker and you couldn't smoke inside Santa Barbara businesses. Then this guy came in and stuck up her teller, there, Maria, the one talking to the cops. Maria hit the alarm button, but the wrong one, not the silent but the screamer, and the robber freaked out. The retired policeman came running in and tried to shoot him but the robber was faster, really wired, and got him first. In the meantime, Maria, who'd gotten fed up with holdups, pulled out of her purse the nine millimeter automatic her cousin had loaned her and put seven rounds through the robber.

"It's just terrible, Mr. James! I hope you won't change banks on us!" The police were now putting up yellow crime scene tape and they were standing on the lawn. Danny turned to go to the Kawasaki.

"Mrs.... uh, Gloria, I wouldn't worry. Looks like a safe bank to me! Just keep that Maria, okay?"

Going up the coast highway he really felt that now he was completely free, that he'd finally gotten away from cops, from mobsters. The scene at the bank seemed to be a sign. When he heard the alarm siren he'd thought that was the end of his life...and then afterwards, the cops hadn't paid any attention to him, just tried to get him out of the bank as quickly as possible. Now, going through the deserted coastal countryside west of Santa Barbara he felt like yelling with glee at the top of his lungs. So he did, startling an older couple in a Buick in the next lane. They immediately slowed down to avoid the obviously homicidal, drug-crazed biker rapist. An hour later he was going through San Luis Obispo on the freeway and he was tempted there, just for a second, to stop and see Barbara. But he realized the timing was all wrong, that he was pointed in a certain direction that had been planned almost three years ago and that it was time to get there.

He retained this prudent frame of mind. When it got dark up near Sacramento he left the freeway and got a room at a motel nestled among other motels in a long commercial strip in a nameless, faceless town where stores had names like "Mister Food," and Mister Gas," and he almost expected his motel to be "Mister Bed."

The bed was great, anyway, and he woke up late the next morning, already nine o'clock. But it was no big deal—he had a big breakfast and then got back on the Kawasaki, hit the I-80 and was in Reno by noon. Here he

was a little more careful to get a better class hotel and the
first thing he did was buy clothes, no suits or dress shirts,
or ties, but the kind of clothes he'd seen rich people of
leisure wear on the streets of Beverly Hills: good jeans,
some nice turtlenecks, a couple of silk shirts, a lamb suede
jacket that felt so good that he paid out the six-hundred-
fifty dollars, no problem! And then some real shoes, which
he hadn't worn for four years: a nice pair of boat shoes, and
he was going to go for something else practical when he
saw the Italian loafers, you picked them up and they were
so soft and warm they felt like live animals and he couldn't
resist them either, even at over four hundred dollars.

"Man, you are going to be in deep trouble, the ladies see
you in those loafers!" the salesman said. He was an older
guy, skinny, but with long hair and an earring, keeping up
with things.

"Chicks like *shoes*?" Danny asked, before he could think
about it.

"Hey! Where you been, in the joint or something! Listen,
real babes can tell within ten bucks how much your shoes
cost, which means to them, how much you can spend on
them? You know what I'm saying?"

Danny had had four years of training ignoring assholes
so he let that one go by. He paid for his loafers and headed
out for his banks.

In all, it took him four days to empty all the accounts
and he was thankful for having picked Reno, a gambling
town blasé about big wads of cash. The first bank showed
no surprise at a young gentleman showing up and wanting
to withdraw over ten thousand dollars in hundred dollar
bills; they just wanted a little time to get the money out of
the vault. In the meantime, could they call a security service in case he needed an escort? No thanks, he said, I'm

just headed for the club, and they nodded, okay, sure, not asking which club. The rest of the banks Danny called in advance, said he'd be by in a few hours and could they have the cash ready? No problem, Mr. James. There was a problem, however, one he hadn't foreseen. His carefully calculated deposits of under ten thousand dollars had been riding a boom economy and were now well over that amount and he had to leave money in every account to avoid having the transaction reported. He decided to empty the accounts by check later on. The last bank was in Carson City and as Danny walked down the block he saw the huge car lot across the street. *Merton's Mercury,* the sign blared, *Great Used Car Deals!* It only took about twenty minutes to buy the used Mercury. While they were doing the paperwork at the lot and putting Frederic James' name on the State of Nevada computer as a law-abiding legal owner of the car, Danny retrieved his Kawasaki, drove it down the street a few blocks and parked it outside a poolhall and bar, leaving the key in the ignition. He hoped that whoever stole it would stay out of trouble for a few months, at least. He'd pay Goomba for it, some day.

*

Danny woke up, disoriented, relaxed in the first class seat that was almost like a bed. The noise of the jet engines reminded him quickly where he was. Almost as quickly the tall brunette stewardess was kneeling by his side. Would Mr. James like his meal now? He considered, realized he was famished. She told him her name was Fiona, that she was a London girl all her life, going home now, and she'd be glad to give him anything else he needed.

At Heathrow he cleared customs without a hitch,

although he had worried about how the stacks of money would look in the X-ray machines as his bags went through. He just happened to run into Fiona on his way out. What a coincidence! And could she recommend a good hotel? Well, the one she stayed at sometimes was really super. They took a cab in together and on the way discussed the idea of having dinner at a really neat trattoria right around the block from the hotel. After he'd unpacked and showered for about a half hour—his first really indulgent and solitary shower for four years—Danny got dressed and called down for a bottle of champagne.

He showed up at her door with the bottle in a bucket of ice, carrying two champagne flutes in his other hand, feeling like Cary Grant in some old movie, and hoping that if he made the right moves he might get laid. Fiona, on the other hand, was absolutely sure that he was going to get laid. After putting the bottle down he kissed her and they went right on from there. They never did make it to the trattoria. Fiona was happy and playful and liked to do games. She gave the games all their own names, just to keep track. At first they did Undress me Slowly and then the Two Backed Beast, for tradition's sake. Then they did Tie Me Up and Make Me Crazy, taking turns. Then they did the Bad Little Girl and the Young Chauffeur and the Sweet Virgin at Confession with the Wicked Priest and that developed into the Riding Academy. Then she wanted to do Bad Boys at Winchester but he didn't think he could really get into that even though she told him Prince Charles had gone to Winchester so they did a variation and then it was natural for her to show him four different positions for *Pompier et Minou*, which was startling. They finished together with a reprise of the Riding Academy, enhanced with handfuls of body lotion. As the sky was turning light in the east and Danny was just dropping off to sleep next to a gently and sweetly snoring figure he had a quick remorseful thought. Oh Barbara! How could I have betrayed you so quickly? But it didn't keep him awake very long.

*

Herschel Jolly was watching the Korean man, an older man, not as big as Moon, wondering how old he was. He finally guessed, around sixty, or older, but the guy impressed him. Wearing a dark gray suit and a tie and moving like an athlete, sort of like Moon, but more...deceptively. The Korean was explaining the situation on the docks.

"Moon was running your operation down there, San Pedro. Every container ship comes in from Inchon, there's six, seven marked containers, all fixed in advance. Moon has his crew haul the containers down to an in-transit warehouse. Then, it works different ways. You got two custom guys on the pad, watchmen, whatever. Anyway, every week or so you got your half-million bucks of sport shoes, boom boxes, CD players. Anything we make in Korea. Good business, Moon was the best."

"So what happened to him, down there?" The Korean hesitated, expressionless.

"My guess, he was short on a payoff."

"They crush a guy to death 'cause he's short on the payoff?" Manny was indignant. "Here we gotta discuss a little..."

"Shush!" said Mr. Jolly. "Go on. So he was a little short...?"

"Maybe they discuss, maybe Moon said the wrong

thing. Korean people are very proud. You think you won the argument, they're smiling, but they're just thinking how to kill you, send a message, understand?"

"So, Mr...uh..."

"Sun. I am Sun. Just the one name. It's not my last name but it's how everybody knows me."

Manny was about to laugh about having Moon working for them, and now they got the Sun, but then he thought the guy might go away smiling and thinking about how to kill him. They had the police description about how Moon got killed. Here was a guy, about six feet, two-fifty easily, looked like he could throw around railroad ties, killed a lot of people, some with his hands, and they find him with his chest completely caved in down there on the docks in San Pedro, one broken rib sticking all the way through his heart. They'd been sitting around trying to figure out how someone killed Moon like that, and without a struggle, it seemed like. Then this guy Sun called up, wanted to talk to Jolly.

"Okay, Sun. So tell me, you got any idea who whacked our friend?"

"If it's a gang on the dock, we'll find out. If he cheated the contacts back in Korea, you maybe can find out, but there's nothing you can do. You run San Pedro. They run Inchon." Sun stood there calmly like a block of rock, waiting to see if there would be objections.

Sometimes Mr. Jolly didn't like plain talk but this time he nodded, understanding. "So. In the meantime. You understand the operation?"

"Yes. Moon and I were partners. I had the connections in Inchon. We sent faxes back and forth in Korean. I have all the shipments to date in our warehouse. All the stores are on the computer. Do we go ahead with the deliveries?"

Mr. Jolly had an interest in a chain of big-box discount stores, from San Diego all the way up to San Jose. With Moon hijacking Korean container ships for him he could get fifty thousand pairs of designer running shoes to fall off the back of a boat for the cost of a small payoff to a network of crooks both in Korea and San Pedro and then sell them for forty, fifty bucks a pair in his stores, twenty bucks under the competition.

"Yeah. We'll go ahead. Just as long as you know who runs the operation in this country. Know what I mean?"

Sun bowed his head. "It's a good business. Foolish to take chances. Now we got to shut down a little while, I think. Police are all over the docks, asking questions."

"You're a smart man, Sun. By the way, you know Moon did some other work for us."

"Yes. Moon was very hard man, very cruel. He did good work for you. He was working on something, I know."

"Uh. Would you consider doing some work, on a contract basis?"

Sun bowed his head.

"I would be happy to complete Moon's assignment."

Manny couldn't keep shut up. "Do you know that kung fu stuff like Moon did?"

Sun looked carefully at Manny. "I taught him myself. Everything."

"If you guys are all through with the bullshit," said Jolly. "I'll let Mr. Sun know what we're after.

"Here's what it is. Two weeks ago, just when Moon disappeared, this guy Danny Castle got out of San Luis. Like he went to another planet, no one saw him again. A week later, there's a police call all over the western states from South Dakota. Somebody with a hundred-fifty thousand in hundreds in a suitcase. They busted him for some bullshit thing, speeding, whatever, then they had to let him go 'cause he didn't do nothing and it was a dumb arrest. Then, again, he disappears. But he's heading east. Description matches Castle, a hundred percent. Mr. Sun. You got the facilities to follow up on this? Y'understand, I can't fucking move, I got the feds, the state cops, everyone looking up my yazoo! How about it"?

Sun nodded. "I already know what you are looking for. You want to pay percentage or per diem?"

PART 2

Chapter Four
Kali Vrisi

IN THE EVENINGS, while it was still light, Danny liked to walk eastward along the beach, past the three tavernas with their waiters out there in front trying to snag the early German for dinner. At the end of the beach the cliffs started and there was a path leading up. Two hundred feet up there was a saddle where you could look down on the coast further to the east for almost ten miles, to where the next craggy peninsula came down into the sea. There was a little spring up here and some trees and Danny liked to sit and look off to the south and just enjoy being where he was. He always reminded himself, he wasn't Danny any more, he was Thanassi, what his mother had called him. It was a common name. You could hear the mothers yelling to their kids, "Thanassi, where are you, come here, you'll fall down the well!" All the Thanassis seemed to be badly behaved here.

They said if you looked to the southeast you were looking right at Egypt but you couldn't see it, of course. It would take a small boat maybe six days to get there. But that's where the British submarines had come from in the big war, and sometimes even small boats from here had gone across the sea to Egypt with important people,

Englishmen. The old guys remembered and talked about the German occupation, mostly stories about how they fought the Germans, how cruel they were. The Germans had rules about everything. If one German got killed they would kill ten Cretans in revenge, sometimes burn the whole village. But the stupid Germans didn't understand Cretans and their old hatreds. They told the story of Limeni and Asteri, up in the mountains there, how the two villages had always hated each other, a hatred going back maybe three hundred years, the origins forgotten, but so much hatred still that when the Germans came in and announced their rules the young men of Limeni couldn't believe their ears, their good luck, and in the night they slipped over ten kilometers of mountain to Asteri and cut the throats of fourteen German privates, poor bastards, out on guard duty. The next day the German commandant dragged out all the men they could find in Asteri. There were only a hundred and twenty-one so after they shot them all they shot four cows, ten goats, and five donkeys, to make up the number; they weren't allowed to shoot women, or children under thirteen. So that took care of the men of Asteri. But then the next night some twelve-year-old kid from Asteri came over the mountain and nailed a German guard with a shotgun, trying to do the same thing to the people of Limeni.

This time the German sentries were more alert and they caught the kid trying to get back across the hills. But they still hadn't caught on to the feud between villages. They thought he was from Limeni. They strung the boy up with wire around his hands in the plateia in Limeni and told the people, we're going to set him on fire with gasoline unless you say who his parents are.

Well, at that point the villagers of Limeni knew perfectly well that the kid was from Asteri. But by now, they hated

the Germans so much that they wouldn't tell them anything, even to blame Asteri.

So the Germans told the kid, hanging there, the wire cutting his wrists and the blood running down, tell us who
your parents are, and he nods his head at just anyone and
says, those people there. So the Germans shot them, and
then he says, oh wait, I made a mistake, it was those people there, and the Germans got mad and shot twenty more
people and asked him, now tell us your parents, and he
said maybe those people over there and the Germans said,
you little shithead, we'll burn you to death with gasoline if
you don't tell the truth, and the little kid told them, burn
me then and I fuck your seven trumpets (a terrible Greek
curse, based on the *Apocalypse*) and may God kill your parents and your wives and children and may you die with
worms crawling out your assholes.

So they lit a gasoline fire under the twelve year old boy
and burned him to death. And later on someone told the
Germans about the hatred between the two villages and
they were so horrified at the willingness of these inferior
people to kill and be killed that they actually withdrew
from southern Crete. And after the war, the people of
Limeni and Asteri got together and pledged eternal friendship and there are memorials in the villages for the men
and cattle and goats and the little boy of Asteri and of all
the people of Limeni who got killed, and there were lots
more by then because the Germans were mad at them.

Thanassi had heard the stories and it was hard for him to
believe, looking over this placid landscape, knowing the
friendly people of the village, seeing their studied polite-
ness, especially to strangers. He couldn't imagine this idyl-
lic coastline erupting into violence. They were all poor here,
but they all had enough, and it seemed to him that they

shared, quite casually, when someone needed something.

And the Germans! Here where German troops had perpetrated some atrocity in nearly every village, fifty years later all they could talk about in May was when the Germans were coming and how many they would be, to fill the hotels and the restaurants, to hire the boats to take them to the beaches, to buy the local fruits and wine and cheese and fish for unbelievably inflated prices! It was still early in the season but there were already Germans in town, mostly older people, well to do, or retired, who could come to Greece when they wanted and beat the crowds later in the summer.

Manoli had explained it to Thanassi. Everything a Greek tells you, divide it by ten, he said. Maybe a hundred. Sometime go look at the memorials carved on big limestone slabs there in Asteri and Limeni. They will always carve the names of the people who were killed, no more and no less. The memorial in Asteri says that eighteen men were killed defending freedom. The one in Limeni says twelve. All the names are listed. That boy was caught but he never shot anyone. He was trying to steal sheep. The Germans beat him and sent him home. They did burn some people alive, but not him. He's there today, an old man, a communist, still steals sheep when he can, and he drinks too much.

Manoli was the first person Thanassi talked to when he drove down into Kali Vrisi in the old rental Fiat from Chania. Coming down from the north you were in the mountains with almost no sign of civilization until the road snaked down into a river valley, went around a long curve and there was the Libyan Sea shining in the distance. The road led through a long shaded colonnade of old eucalyptus trees, more and more houses now on each side, and ended at the beach, not a sandy beach, really, but smooth round stones. There was a little square at the end of the road where the beach began. To the west were some public buildings and then an L shaped breakwater forming the fishing harbor, completely deserted in the afternoon heat. To the east a group of restaurants marched off along the unpaved track along the beach, ringed with palms and tamarisk trees. He'd been hungry, it was two in the afternoon, and the first restaurant attracted him, a two story house built back in the shade of the bigger trees with a big courtyard on the pebbly beach under some smaller trees, with flowers growing in big boxes, oleanders and hibiscus, the smell of grilled meat and fish, and not too many people.

He'd ordered some *païdákia*—the baby lamb chops—and a salad, and a half-liter of the house retsina, ordering in Greek. When the food arrived it wasn't the waitress carrying it but a big rangy man, wearing an apron and a hibiscus blossom behind his ear. He was dark, black-haired, big black mustache, and a four day growth of black beard. He served the food, wiped his hands on his apron, then just pulled out the other chair, sat down and looked at Thanassi. When Danny had been at the prison camp Sam Papadakis had told him, when you get to Greece remember that they are prepared to hate Greek Americans. Greek Americans come back to the old county full of superiority, how much money they make, the factories they own in Brockton, Mass., Gary, Indiana, wherever. Remember, Greeks are prepared to love real Americans much more than Greek Americans, so be careful, always modest, always humble, always friendly in a modest way. Never suggest how anything could be done better, or how it's done in America.

So Thanassi just said hello to Manoli, picked up another glass and asked him to share some wine, talking in his stumbling Greek. Then waited.

Manoli narrowed his eyes, pursed his lips, did this exaggerated thing about how he was pondering serious decisions. Then he smiled and surprised Thanassi by speaking in English, bad English, but quite understandable.

"You see, I wonder who you are. Because you don't have a woman with you, you're not German, you're a Greek, anyone can see. So we Greeks here, we're always asking questions, how you say?"

"Curious?" suggested Thanassi.

"Curious. Yes. It's a good word. Curious because we want to know who the stranger is, to welcome him, if he comes to be here for some days."

Thanassi answered him in Greek, as imperfect as Manoli's English.

"I want to stay here for some days. Some bad things happened and now I am free, *eléftheros*," a word loaded with meaning in Greece. "I want to rest here, eat some good food, maybe swim a little, talk to the people where my father lived."

Thanassi was gnawing on one of the tiny lamb chops, only two scraps of meat on it, when he noticed that several other people had moved their chairs around his table. He wiped his hands and mouth, nodded at them all, asked how they were. They were all fine, and how was he? And who was his father?

He went on in Greek. "My father came from Kastelli, up north, a long time ago, he was just a boy. My mother was, was...born"—he struggled to remember the Greek passive verb—"In America, but her parents were from Sfakia.

"Ah! Sfakia. Several voices said the name. Trying to locate this stranger in time and space they had gotten a lot closer. Sfakia down the coast to the east. Maybe three hours by boat, a fast boat.

"Sfakia. *Pirátes*," said an old man, smiling. Others laughed. Manoli got mad and yelled something so fast Thanassi couldn't understand.

"I told him not to joke about pirates," said Manoli in English. "Everyone knows the Sfakiotes are pirates and smugglers. So are we all, this whole coast, but not so much now. I told him he's not polite, you might, how do you say, insult?"

"Be insulted?" asked Thanassi and Manoli nodded. "No. I'm not insulted." He held up his glass to the group around his table, which had grown by quite a few members, and said *"Yah sas!"* Your health!

"Yah sou, yah, yah, yah sas, kyrie!" the responses came rapidly.

Then came the rest of the questions: Where are you from in America? Are you married? Do you have children? What work do you do? and Thanassi remembered almost the same litany from the *Odyssey*, asking the stranger visiting some island, *where are you from, what city, and who are your parents and what ship brought you here, because I do not think you came by foot?*—this being what passed for good-old-boy humor in the works of Homer.

Then Thanassi had to remember his family's real name, before they got renamed at Ellis Island, Kateroudakis, and his mother's family name, Dimitrakis, and that set off the old men on a round of arguments as to whether that was the greengrocer down at Sfakia town or the fisherman and a woman said it's both, it's a big family, you go there and you'll never pay for a meal again, and Manoli yelled at her, are you trying to get him out of paying for this meal? And everyone laughed.

Thanassi had taken a room over the restaurant for a few days. That evening, after he'd had a little nap, he came down and sat in the restaurant and had an ouzo and watched the *volta*, the usual evening procession of townspeople taking a leisurely walk to look each other over, exchange gossip with their friends and neighbors, and check things out in the unlikely event that something new had happened since lunch. Today's news was the Greek American, Thanassi, who had suddenly appeared, seemed to have some money and, as the mothers had all decided, wasn't married, so that Thanassi had never seen so many pairs of girls, walking hand in hand, silently as they passed the restaurant with their eyes straight ahead and then dissolving into giggles and chatter once they were safely past.

Later that evening, after he'd eaten, the waiter came over to his table and put down a small glass of colorless liquid. "From those people," he indicated, pointing across the restaurant to where a priest and a policeman were sitting, holding their glasses in the air, toasting. Thanassi held his glass in the air in return, drained it, then instructed the waiter, "Give them each another glass," trying not to choke on the raw alcohol he had just swallowed, The two men interpreted the gift as an invitation to come over to his table and they were soon joined by two other idlers, as Thanassi found out later, the brother of the postmaster, and a prominent fisherman. They were too polite to ask immediate questions, but all the conversation was obliquely to that purpose: *this part of Crete is the loveliest, many people come here for many reasons.* In other words, who are you and what are you doing here?

Thanassi was enjoying speaking and understanding Greek so much that he realized only belatedly that his new friends were trying to get him drunk. At the end of a labored sentence in which he endeavored to praise the scenery, the ocean, and the simple, friendly people of Kali

Vrisi, he looked down to see that he was two little glasses behind.

"This is delicious!" he said, gaining time. "What do you call it?"

There was much laughter, and then a word he finally heard as *tsikoudiá*. "We make it from the grapes, what is left, when the wine is finished," said the priest, and Thanassi thought he understood that. It was just like brandy everywhere, so he could expect this to be anything up to a hundred and twenty proof. The thought occurred to him, *I bet I can drink these people under the table,* knowing that he had always had a hollow leg when it came to drinking. He didn't think of himself as a big drinker but when the booze was flowing he had always kept up and could never really remember having been drunk. But remembering Sam Papadakis' advice, he quit early. "I had too much," he told the reeling priest and policeman. "You people are too strong!" and he went to bed. The next day he was up early but the priest and policeman were said to have caught a vapor of some kind and weren't seen until the evening. But Thanassi had won a small victory: he hadn't shamed some important local people.

He had spent almost two weeks in Kali Vrisi, taking long walks up into the steep cliffs overhanging the southern coast, swimming in the ocean that the locals said was too cold, would make him sick, but which he found warmer than the Pacific at Santa Monica in August. It was also as clear as glass and he bought a mask and snorkel and spent too much time the first day exploring the reefs offshore; he came in with a bad sunburn on his back and the backs of his legs. And he walked around town a lot and talked to everyone, trying to improve his Greek. After the first few days he couldn't help getting into conversations.

The people of Kali Vrisi were shy at first, afraid of betraying ignorance in front of a stranger, as always, but when they found they could converse with him in a reasonable manner the thousands of questions in their minds found voice. These were people to whom the vast crowds of Germans and other tourists in the summer had no reality, no more than the shapes and voices that entertained them on television. But a stranger who spoke Greek, who had parents from nearby districts of Crete, this was a person of mystery and they wanted every detail of his past. It didn't help that he had blurted out some nameless bad things that had happened to him in the past. The gossips in town had now separated the possibilities into categories.

Sexual: the most popular, because Thanassi was obviously a good looking man, single, with hazel eyes, the mark of the satyr some said, undoubtedly capable of ravishing any number of young women in one night and he'd left some girl pregnant and her brothers out looking for him. This was popular with the older women in town.

Criminal: he was big and strong. He must have murdered a rival of some kind and was fleeing the law. Anyone could see he was a man of strong emotions.

Political: he was a communist who had been exiled from America for his convictions. There was a sizeable communist contingent in Kali Vrisi who had never given up their treasured images of the cold war and they argued bitterly whether it was the CIA or the FBI that was after Thanassi. The communists split quickly over the exact nature of his persecution. When he first heard that he was suspected of being an honorable communist fleeing political assassination by the American Secret Police, Manoli explained it to him.

"You know, Greece is the richest country in Europe in

some ways. We have two things of which most European countries lack even one."

"And what is that?" asked Thanassi.

"Communist parties," said Manoli, triumphantly. "Almost no other country in Europe still has a communist party, but we have two! There are the Eurocommunists, who are willing to negotiate, then there are the Stalinists, who look forward to the coming triumph of the hard-line Marxists and the revolution and will not compromise. The two local communist parties have, as usual, split over your circumstances. The Eurocommunists believe you to be fleeing prosecution for your views; the Stalinists are certain the CIA has tried to kill you. The postmaster and the woman who owns the Ariadne Hotel run the Stalinists. The postmaster as well owns the Mercedes taxi, the only one in town, the one that goes to Chania every day. I think there are four other members. The sixteen Eurocommunists have the butcher, Fotis, as their chairman. Do you know about the butcher?"

Thanassi had met old Fotis, a gentle looking old man, except when hacking up joints of meat with a huge cleaver. He would play a game with the town children every day— pretending to be furious and waving his cleaver at them as they ran screaming—then giving them all pieces of *loukoumi*, a chewy and sickly-sweet candy.

Manoli told the story. Fotis as a young man was a fiery leader of the local leftists. When he was just a teenager he had spent most of the big war up in the mountains, helping the British secret agents and taking part in raids against German troop concentrations and supplies. As soon as the war was over he emerged as a leader of the communists in a large area of southern Crete. They were in direct communication with the communist command during the Greek

Civil War of 1945-1949 and one of his duties was to eliminate those bourgeois elements that were impeding the success of the revolution. The communist command had set quotas and Fotis labored day and night to meet them. People suspected of supporting the royal family of Greece could expect to be hauled out of their houses in the middle of the night to face the *hasapis*—the butcher—a name doubly ironic because Fotis had worked even as a boy in his father's butcher shop. Now he was literally a butcher and during the year the communists held that part of southern Crete he rounded up all those elements suspected of royalist sentiments, or even prosperity, and put them before firing squads, making them first dig graves in the hard Cretan soil. When ammunition was in short supply he taught the executioners how to use the slaughterer's sledge, the hammer that was used to cave in the skulls of sheep and goats. The very name of the "Butcher of Crete" was used to frighten children.

"When the communists were beaten in the civil war, Fotis had to go to Makronisi, the prison island," said Manoli. "He was there fifteen years and then in 1963 he came back here again and took over his father's butcher shop."

"But didn't local people try to get revenge?" asked Thanassi. It didn't make sense to him and he was outraged.

"Well, maybe they felt that way. But they were all tired of war and killing and anyway, there were still lots of local communists to back up Fotis. Anyway, he hadn't been back four years before the Colonels made their revolution in 1967, you remember?"

Thanassi wouldn't have, four years ago, but he had read all the recent history of Greece and he nodded.

"What happened to Fotis, the police under the Colonels rounded up all the old communists and took them back to prison unless they would sign a statement that they gave up all political activity. Fotis refused at first but when his batch of prisoners arrived at Makronisi he realized he was in the same cell he'd been in for fifteen years that time before. There was his name carved into the wall with a spoon handle, and the beginning of the sentence, ΓΑΜΩ TON BAΣI..., 'Fuck the king,' you know, that they caught him carving and they broke both his hands with police clubs for writing it. So Fotis tells me, he's sitting there looking at his own name and at FUCK THE KI..., which no one ever bothered to scratch out, and his hands started hurting, and he realizes he can't stay here, he'll go crazy, maybe kill himself, so he yells for the guard and he signs the paper, he won't be political anymore."

"And he kept his promise?" asked Thanassi.

"Well, until the Colonels got kicked out. Then he joined the local communists again. But right away he thought they should be more moderate, mainly because the new government in Athens was giving money for socialist projects. So he organized the Eurocommunists and for a while we had a communist mayor and Athens rebuilt our harbor and paved the road north to Maleme and put in electricity and telephones. And the whole time the other communists, the Stalinists, called them whores and said their heads would roll when the revolution came. I'll tell you much more stories but I got to get dinner ready!"

*

There was a strange waiter at Manoli's. A week after Thanassi arrived the man was on duty for lunch, tall, very skinny, with a huge walrus mustache that accented his permanently tragic expression. Thanassi rattled off what he wanted in Greek, proud of his fluency, and the waiter just stood there. Then he tried him in English with no luck. Then the waiter took the menu and pointed with his finger.

"*Thixte*. You show," he said very simply in Greek. So Thanassi pointed slowly at the lamb and eggplant that was penciled in on the menu, then said "*krasí?*" and pantomimed drinking.

"*Nai, nai,*" said the waiter, "*krasí. wein,*" and he moved his hands apart to indicate big, or little.

"*Mikro*, small," said Thanassi, showing the height of the pitcher with his hands.

"Okay," said the waiter in English, disconcertingly and departed for the kitchen. Thanassi feared the worst but his lunch arrived exactly as ordered. About half way through Manoli arrived and sat down, as usual, wiping his hands on his apron.

"Sorry," he said. "I would have helped out but I wanted to see how this guy was going to be. He came last week and asked for work but he doesn't know Greek or English or German. He's Bulgarian."

"So what is a Bulgarian doing in southern Crete?" asked Thanassi, throwing up his hands.

"It's the same everywhere in Greece now. Albanians, Bulgarians, Serbs, they all sneak across the border because there's no work back home any more. This guy, Boris, I have a little talk with him, whatever we can understand with a few words, some signs. I think he's an engineer back in Bulgaria. He's much too smart for a waiter. You wait a week, he'll know the whole menu. He would have understood your order today except it's a special, *arní me melitzánes*, lamb with aubergines, how you say."

But a week later a Greek couple arrived, sat down for lunch, and after two words with Boris they got up, put him in their car and drove away. It turned out they were plain-clothes police from Chania and the government was cracking down on illegal immigrants because they were taking jobs from local people.

"Damn! I hate to lose him," said Manoli. "He was one good waiter, and he could cook too! Helped out in the kitchen when we were busy. Now we got a full restaurant today and only that dumb Pavlo who mixes up all the orders. What bastards they are in the government, having a woman policeman. Nobody expects a woman!"

"Hey, Manoli," said Thanassi, eagerly. "Let me help you out. My family had a restaurant. I worked there all my life!"

Manoli looked at him sternly, maybe waiting for the Greek American to explain how he could do things better, but Thanassi just shut up and finally Manoli said, "Okay, get an apron, learn the menu, and you better not make too many mistakes!"

Thanassi worked there that lunch and then dinner too. The next day Manoli needed help in the kitchen, so Thanassi went to work, cutting up the tomatoes, cucumbers, eggplants, peppers, keeping the charcoal fire built up under the grill, resisting every impulse to say that it would be better to do something differently—although he did turn up the heat under the deep fryer to get the fried potatoes crisper.

On Friday, after three days work, Manoli sat down with Thanassi in the kitchen, wiping his hands on his apron and sighing, the usual prelude to some kind of important decision.

"*Ela, paidí mou!* Come on! How do I pay you? You're worth two of any worthless bastards I hired before. No, no. Three, I hate to say, because it's me paying!"

133

Thanassi was ready. "Manoli, my friend. You just pay what you can. I need the money...I just came here because I heard I could live on little money."

Manoli gave him a look out of the side of his face, then laughed and rattled off, *ti malakía aftí pou les*! "What bullshit are you telling me!" But he pulled out a huge leather wallet and counted out fifteen thousand drachmas, slamming the notes down on the table in the eternal Greek gesture expressing both contempt for money and the agony of parting with it.

"Five thousand a day. And you pay me three thousand for the room. Tell me, kid, how you live on this?"

Thanassi just spread his hands, indicating, who knows, who can understand this crazy world.

This went on for another two weeks. The parade of eager young girls tapered off when it was learned that the Greek American was not wealthy but had to work for peasant wages at the restaurant. This suited Thanassi and he continued to present the profile of a modest and hardworking young man of slender means.

Manoli came up to him one day, wiping his hands on his apron.

"*Lipón, moré*. Okay, kid. I have a problem. Maybe you can help. Tell me, do you know how to farm, you know, grow plants?'

Thanassi thought. "A garden for the kitchen, yes, of course. We always grew tomatoes, corn, other vegetables, for the restaurant. Why do you ask?"

Manoli sighed with great sadness. "Ahhh. Thanassi. I have a problem with a little farm we own. We get our tomatoes now in the summer, our peppers, cucumbers, potatoes, we don't have to pay the thieves in the market for these things. But my tenant is an old man and he doesn't want to work, the Greek social security will support him in his sister's house and he doesn't want to break his back in the garden any more."

Thanassi waited, having learned the Greek manner, find out what the hell is going on. "Yeah, Manoli. That's a problem, alright."

Manoli looked at him sternly with his black eyes. "I was thinking, Thanassi *mou*, my Thanassi, that you could go live on my farm, raise the vegetables, bring them in every day. You don't pay rent, I pay you some little thing for the vegetables, you work at the restaurant and I pay you more what you're worth, maybe...six thousand a day. What you think?"

Thanassi had been in Crete long enough not to behave like some kid who just jumped off a donkey coming from the mountains. So he narrowed his eyes and pondered for a good minute.

"Manoli. I think ten thousand a day is what you meant to say."

Manoli smashed his forehead with a fist and cursed the sky, but they settled on nine thousand, Thanassi thinking, thirty-six dollars a day, for working a whole day in a restaurant, plus raising vegetables on a farm that's paid for, doesn't cost this guy a dime!

"Oh yeah," he asked Manoli. "And how far is the farm?"

"Just around the corner!" expostulated the restaurant owner.

Well. It turned out to be four kilometers and so Thanassi demanded an additional payment for the gas for his car. Manoli went off grumbling but Thanassi thought that he'd probably been screwed anyway. The important thing was that he'd preserved his image.

Chapter 5
Back in Biscuit County

SHERIFF MARIE BACON saw the Asian gentleman in the expensive looking suit come through the door, see her, then look around the squad room. She'd gone through that before.

"You looking for me, mister?"

"You are sheriff Bacon?"

"That's me, alright. Says M. Bacon out there, people don't always realize."

"Ah! You are like the sheriff in that movie, what was her name?"

Marie had been there, done that before too.

"Well, I'm not wearing my fur hat with earflaps today 'cause it's eighty outside and I think I got a few more pounds on than her, but yeah, I'm the sheriff. How can I help you?"

Sun stepped over to the counter, showed his private detective's license, which Marie observed with interest.

"I don't think we ever had a private detective come through here, Mr. Sun. According to all the detective novels I read, I'm supposed to get real hardnosed and tell you not to mess around in my jurisdiction."

Sun laughed. "I read all the same. Dashiell Hammett, Raymond Chandler. I was learning English in Korea and I always wanted to be a detective! But here no police are ever unfriendly. They only ask if I have lots of women chasing me!"

They laughed heartily, more than the comment was worth. Marie had never met a private detective, didn't even think there *was* one in South Dakota, but on the basis of this guy she figured they were all full of shit. "So here you are, Mr. Sun. What can I do for you."

Sun's face immediately became serious. "My client was defrauded of a great deal of money. We are certain that the thief came through Biscuit and was arrested for speeding. Mr. James. Frederick James. The sheriff's office here sent out a bulletin, let me see, four weeks ago, asking if there had been a robbery of over one hundred thousand dollars."

Now this is getting interesting, thought Marie. "Well, Mr. Sun, I'll get you a copy of the arrest report. That'll be fifty cents a page," she said apologetically, getting out of her chair. "But it doesn't say much. You can call the court reporter and get a transcript of the court hearing, that'll be five dollars a page—you gotta pay him, got nothing to do with the county. But the whole thing was, this James character had a valid driver's license, registration, it was a totally screwed up arrest, and there was no way to hold him."

Sun waited for the copy machine to spit out two pages...worthless, as she had said. He thought hard.

"Would it be possible for me to speak to the arresting officer, maybe get his description of the man?"

She laughed. "It won't be hard. He's not going anywhere soon!" And she told him where he could find a mobile home, double width, down by some trees near the river about ten miles away, and a highway patrolman with a broken leg.

*

"Damndest thing! We was checking out what sounded like a flat on the rear tire of our unit and the bastard slipped into reverse and ran both of us over! Artie's back on duty, but my leg was broke bad. So what'd you want to know about this guy, Mr. Sun?'

Sun had felt the bad vibrations of racism the second he got out of his car and confronted the man sitting in a lounger in the shade outside his mobile home, cooler full of beer at his side, listening to a baseball game on the radio. The man had a full leg cast on his left leg, halfway up his thigh, was slouched there in cutoff sweat pants, no shirt, and you could smell the last time he'd had a shower. Once Sun had shown his PI license and asked his questions the vibrations all turned into lies, lies, lies. He didn't know why this man would lie about how he got hurt but he suspected. Castle had got the jump on him, maybe ran him over. Then threatened him with death if he told? Sun couldn't figure out the details but he knew enough now for the right approach.

"Cecil? That's your name?"

Cecil turned hard. "It's 'officer' to you, pal. And why should I tell you anything anyway!"

Sun just shrugged his shoulders. "No reason. But my clients are some Italian gentlemen in Los Angeles. Let me put it this way. You tell me what I want to know, you'll get a consultant's fee. Let's say, two hundred dollars." Sun had been about to say five hundred, but looking at this miserable piece of shit he had immediately adjusted the bribe level drastically downwards.

"You don't cooperate with us, I'm sorry to say, someone is going to show up when your leg is almost well and break it again. And keep on doing it every six weeks. We just make a phone call, Cecil. It's like a service, we don't even have to check back. How about it?"

Sun could see the stupid man's face get ugly and he knew a gun was going to come out so when Cecil started dragging his magnum out of the bag by his side Sun was ready. He just bent it out of his hand, breaking the trigger finger, then stuck it in Cecil's crotch.

"Start talking, you idiot!"

*

Once Sun had the description of Frederick James, and other details that didn't show up on the arrest report, it should have been easier. He had the access codes to all the international airlines out of the major eastern cities because Herschel Jolly was a silent owner of six travel agencies. He sat in a hotel room in Omaha for two days, patiently going through every flight out of Boston, New York, Newark, Philadelphia, Baltimore, Washington, Charlotte, and he even went down and took a look at Atlanta and Miami. During that time the modem on his laptop broke contact fourteen times and the laptop—a top-of-the-line power model going for over four thousand dollars—stopped to whine over twenty times about too little memory or applications that could not be found. He never found a Frederic James and contented himself with the knowledge that the man named Danny Castle had left the U.S. on a passport with a different name. Nevertheless he took some satisfaction in smashing the laptop and modem to shapeless lumps with a heavy chair before he left. It also improved his temper when the cashier at the hotel told him his bill was $225 a day and that he had run up an e-mail phone bill of $384.67 and he was able to put it all on one of Moon's expired credit cards.

"Thank you, Mr. Moon, and you have a great one!" said the cashier. Sun was still going to bill Mr. Jolly for the laptop and modem.

When Mr. Jolly had sent him on this search his immediate reaction was not to trace this man across the U.S. but to look for him in the country of his ancestors. Sun knew that if he himself was in trouble in America and if he went back to Korea no one would ever find him, and if anyone even got close, all his relatives and friends would take great pleasure in killing whoever was looking for him. Now he knew he was right. He was sure than Danny Castle was back in Greece. From the final, true story he had extracted from the imbecile state trooper about his last meeting with Castle there on the deserted access road he had gained an appreciation of the fugitive. Castle had disabled both of the policemen, threatened them, and then made his getaway. If he himself had been in Castle's position he would have made both of the renegade policemen disappear, but he realized that Americans had different cultural patterns.

The next week a number of aspiring actors and actresses answered an ad in the *Los Angeles Times* and in a number of entertainment trade sheets. For hourly wages they visited Greek restaurants in the western part of Los Angeles and told the families they met that they were researchers for an author who was doing a major book on Greek-American families running restaurants. They taped all the conversations. Thanassi's cousin Katina, who was now married with two kids and running the family restaurant with her hard-working husband, was wary at first. She called two other restaurants she knew of, one in Venice, one in West Hollywood.

"Oh yeah, Katina," said her friend Ellie at the first place she called. "Somebody's doing a big story on Greek restaurants.

Who was your papa, your mama? What part of Greece did they come from? All that stuff. They came to you too? You think they'll make a movie? Maybe a TV special! This was the neatest guy who came over and interviewed us!"

Katina got the same reaction from other friends in Greek restaurants so she became less suspicious. She agreed to an interview.

Mr. Sun was listening to the tape his interviewer had given him. She was a nice blond American girl, trying to be an actress. He couldn't understand how anyone would believe her cover story, but it had worked. He listened to Katina, speaking on the tape.

"Oh, yeah. My grandfather came over from Crete. Don't ask me the name of the town! Lot of syllables, you know! Hee hee!...The name of the family back then? We're Castle now, you know? Actually since I'm married I'm Papalegakis. You know, I can't remember the name but we got a scrapbook here....you got a minute? Great. I'll be right back...Yeah, here it is, see the guy with the army uniform? The big mustache? I think that was great-grandpa. And here's the name—Kateroudakis. You can see why I didn't remember it! And the name of the town was Polyrhenia Kissamou, see right here? You know, I always promised my husband we'd go there some day, take the kids, you know...?"

Sun talked to a number of knowledgeable men in Los Angeles and Las Vegas, many of them with Italian names. He was directed to a man in San Diego named Papathanassopoulos, a hard guy. The name was funny, especially to Sun, since most of the people from his country had names with only one syllable. But Mr. Papathanassopoulos was not funny. He had a dark office in back of a pool hall in the southeast part of town, the part that didn't make the travel brochures. Papathanassopoulos was a tall, thin older man, with the kind of rangy look that always meant surprising strength. He looked as if he would kill people, even dogs, cats, just for fun. He listened to Sun seriously and then was lost in thought for a bit.

"What's the consultant fee?" he finally asked

"Ten K." said Sun. "We find who we're looking for. Otherwise it's five just for your trouble."

"Okay. For ten grand. You want to find a guy named Kateroudakis in western Crete? Greek Americans won't work, the Greeks there all hate them. They start asking questions, you know, everyone clams up, maybe they get hurt, you know what I'm saying? *You* can't go, obviously, stand out like a sore thumb. Same with any Americans, they never go to Crete, worry about the food, getting robbed." He chuckled mirthlessly. "You know there's almost nowhere you're less likely to get robbed than Crete! Dumb Americans!" He thought for a bit. "You know who can look around in Crete? You find some Germans. Not the old Germans from the west, but the new gangs from east Germany. In our operation we deal with them all the time. Drugs, weapons, smuggling, middlemen with the Russian gangsters, they know what they're doing. And you know what? Summertime there're more Germans in Greece than Greeks. You get some guys from the rackets there to go to Crete, pretend to be tourists, they'll fit right in. I'll give you some names, you got the right kind of money they'll do the job for you. Hard bastards, cruel. A lot of these guys used to be secret police. Shit! One out of five in east Germany worked for the secret police, the Stasis, they called them. When the system fell apart they went into crime. It figures, right?" Papathanassopoulos broke a rare smile, showing some very ugly teeth. "Very reliable. But not subtle, you know what I mean? You give 'em a job to do, they go do it. Anyone gets in the way, forget it! They're dead. But you have to go to Germany to meet the right people. They won't do business over the phone. And they want cash in advance."

"No problem," said Sun, putting a stack of bills on the table. "Give me some names."

Chapter Six
Kali Vrisi

THANASSI HAD MET THE OLD GERMAN in Kali Vrisi. His name was Hans, but when speaking of him most of the villagers just said *O Yérmanos*, the German, as if he had just arrived. Actually, Hans had come to Kali Vrisi thirty five years before. One morning he started talking to Thanassi at the restaurant and after many little cups of Greek coffee he had told his whole story. When he was fifteen the Nazis put a rifle in his hands and sent him to the Russian front. He and his entire unit were overwhelmed almost immediately, most of them killed, and he was sent to a POW camp just east of the Ural Mountains. He spent twelve years there building pipeline before he was repatriated to east Germany—to a country he'd completely forgotten, to distant relatives somewhere near Leipzig who were not happy to feed another mouth there in the dismal Soviet bloc. So they paid some money to the people who put you through the wire to the West and there was Hans, twenty-seven years old, with no skills, in capitalist west Germany. He took seventeen different jobs in a row, he told Thanassi, all of them paying just enough to stay alive, until he was hired to drive a rich family to Greece. The first time he felt the Greek sun on his body, frozen from so many years up in the

Siberian *taiga,* he decided to stay forever. In a few years, scrambling around, he had managed to persuade a rich Greek hotel owner to let him be the summer manager. Greek property owners tended to be raw-meat capitalists: they expected their properties to turn a profit without any further maintenance or expense. But Hans kept wheedling his owner into making improvements, toilets in every room long before everyone else did it, breakfast free, with coffee the way Germans liked it—thick and black. Maids who really cleaned the rooms, ads put in German travel magazines. And soon the Olympos Hotel was always full, always had a waiting list, and the owner moved away and let Hans run the place. Now he was seventy years old, but looked ten years younger, brown and lean, bright-eyed, funny, and in love with life. He joked with Thanassi about the Germans who were beginning to straggle into town in late spring. He spoke fluent Greek, English, and was waiting for the new Russian capitalists to show up so he could talk to them too."

"You see those fat behinds waddling down the street? My countrymen are beginning to arrive. Some are nice, but many are rude. They yell, they complain about food or wine that would cost them three times as much back home. They turn white like maggots for eight months of winter up there in Hamburg then they lie in the sun for four hours here and they can't even walk for the next three days. Sometimes I can fool them the whole time they are here that I am just another Greek. And I can listen to what they say in German about me, about the other Greeks here. How we are all lazy, stupid, dishonest. Dishonest! A big stupid porker of a woman accused the maid of stealing her sunglasses yesterday. Then a little girl came to the hotel with the glasses. That woman had left her glasses in a store and the store owner's little daughter went to every hotel in town to find out who owned them. I told the woman she should give the little girl something, a few drachmas, and she screamed things at me that would mean blood, blood, here in Crete if they were said in Greek! Fortunately I am seventy and have been in a concentration camp. It gives you perspective."

"I've been by the Olympos," said Thanassi. "It's a nice looking hotel, with the bougainvillea and other plants. You must spend a lot of time on the gardening."

"Yah, the gardening. But I wish I had some room to grow some real food. Tomatoes, cucumbers, peppers, melons! It would be a real money maker for the hotel for these people to see food coming right out of the ground. Now I have to go to the market every day and fight for a few vegetables."

"You know, I have a little farm, and I grow more than I can use," said Thanassi. "Maybe we can make a little deal, I can always use the extra money!"

*

Thanassi loved his little farm. It lay back from a curve in the road north to Chania, in the river valley that led up from the south coast and the sea. It was perched on a little plateau above the road in some kind of geological formation that had obviously trapped river runoff in past ages because the topsoil went straight down forever. When Thanassi first started working on it it was all weeds, but even under the weeds there were potatoes in the ground and squashes trying to grow and beans that had gone wild and some grape vines growing all over the house. It took him a week to restore some kind of order and then he had young tomatoes and cucumbers and peppers and egg-plants growing. And outside the back door in a little patch he had thyme, oregano, savory, rosemary, and other herbs, all growing wild in the neighborhood, but he transplanted them, and if you watered anything in this soil with the Cretan sun shining on it, it would grow.

The first day he was there, working near the fence, his neighbor, an old man, came over.

"Hey there, boy! Where's old Yanni?"

"He went to live with his sister. I'm working the farm now for the *aféndiko*, to raise the vegetables for his restaurant."

"*Bah!* That's work alright! I don't have a minute here with the chickens and the goats!" Thanassi had noticed chickens running around the ill-kept grounds and had heard goats complaining. It reminded him that he hadn't eaten chicken for many months.

"Maybe I could help you a bit, for an egg now and then, or some goat milk. I'm a hard worker, mister."

The old man gave him a stern look. "You don't seem a Greek to me," he said. "What are you doing here?"

"You got a good ear, mister," said Thanassi. "My people are from up around Kastelli, but I was brought up in America."

"America! What part?"

"Los Angeles. Santa Monica, really. Do you know it?"

Like so many Greeks, his neighbor did. His name was Yorgo and as a young man he had shipped out with the merchant marine. He'd been to San Diego, San Pedro, up the coast to San Francisco, then Seattle, over to Yokohama, then back. Sixteen trips over five years and then he made enough money to buy half of his cousin's farm here. His cousin let his half run to ruin—he was drinking, running after women in Iraklio—so Yorgo let his goats run on his property. He cackled at the advantage he was taking.

"Those goats get fat! Takes me two hours sometimes to milk them. And then I have to find some way to get into town to sell the cheese. I tell you, boy, I'm getting tired. And the hens! They get the run of the property. I could eat nothing but eggs, they lay so many, but who can find them all? Me, with my old eyes, can't see anything anymore! And those damn foxes eat one every other day!"

So Thanassi found himself taking care of two farms. First thing, he cleared some ground, brought some fencing from town, and made a chicken coop where the hens could roost off the ground during the night. Then he built some boxes he could fill with straw, also up off the ground. Being good hens they immediately started laying their eggs in the boxes, or at least most of them. Every day he would help Yorgo call the goats to be milked. He threw away all the filthy old cans and brought up clean, steamed plastic containers from the restaurant. He tasted the old cheeses Yorgo had hung up to dry over the last year. Some were good, others tasted like essence of goat odor, others were thrown out of range the second he unwrapped them a little. He tried for just a few minutes to explain the importance of cleanliness in cheesemaking to Yorgo, then just gave up and took over all the work himself, which Yorgo gladly conceded. In a couple of weeks he had made some tasty fresh cheese.

One day Manoli had to go up to Chania so he asked Thanassi to take over the restaurant until he got back that evening. Thanassi had just been waiting for the opportunity. He'd noticed in the hardware store that there were little folding grills that most people used for grilling fish. He bought three of them and that day he brought down ten freshly killed and plucked chickens from Yorgo's farm. He chopped them up in small pieces and marinated them in garlic, herbs, olive oil, and lemon juice, just like his father's recipe, then in the early evening put one of the grills over the charcoal fire. In a few minutes the odor of grilling chicken was going up and down the streets of Kali Vrisi and the tables were filling up. The last grill had been just sold when Manoli pulled up outside in his old diesel Mercedes.

"What the devil are you cooking here! Now, how much of my money are you spending for chickens? You know how much they cost these days? And give me some to eat, you bastard!"

Thanassi had a couple of wing pieces left, that was all, and while Manoli was gnawing the last shreds off them, his face getting greasy and his fingers blackened from the charred skin of the chickens, Thanassi explained to him.

"You know old Yorgo, next to my farm? He's got over a hundred chickens running around up there, and only the foxes are eating them. And they taste like something, not like the frozen chickens you have to get here in the store. And his goats! They're fat and happy! Here, taste a bit of this feta."

Manoli tasted, narrowed his eyes. "The chicken, the cheese. It's excellent! But what am I supposed to pay for it?"

"Well! Who knows? But Yorgo doesn't even know I brought chickens and cheese here. Tonight when I go back I'll give him some money, say, a hundred drachmas a chicken. He'll go out of his mind! Then when he finds out everybody likes chicken, he'll raise the prices, of course. So we go up to maybe four hundred a chicken, sell one half-chicken order grilled for twelve hundred, we're making a profit of two thousand drachmas on each chicken."

"But he doesn't have that many chickens!"

"Yes, but he says almost everyone up the whole valley runs a few chickens. And we don't have to offer chicken every day. Make people get hungry for it!"

Manoli looked daggers at Thanassi. "You got your mother's blood, those pirates from Sfakia, I don't care how much time you spent in America, getting soft."

"What soft!" exclaimed Thanassi. "I spent almost four years in college taking economics courses! What you can do with steel, oil, computer software, you can do with chickens!"

They were interrupted by a German couple, smiling, anxious.

"Please, is there more chicken?" the woman asked in English

"No, I'm sorry, it's a special tonight," answered Thanassi. "But we'll have it from time to time. Come back."

Chapter Seven
Los Angeles

THERE WERE THREE KOREANS loading the trucks at night in the big anonymous warehouse down in San Pedro on the docks. The new guy was retarded, giggled a lot and got things wrong but he was stronger than shit and was well worth any annoyance. When Kim, up on the catwalk, saw the headlights coming along the dock he yelled down that Sun was coming, that they should get ready with the invoices. Park was all ready to give him the checkout, all the goods that had fallen off the back of three different ships. It was a major load. But then Kim saw the new guy talking to the lapel of his denim jacket and suddenly he realized why the guy always acted so dumb. It was a setup, and he just barely made it to the panic button. The lights went on outside, super bright, and they could hear loud cursing outside, car engines revving, and then a big crash as a truck or something barreled into the main exit door, the one that rolled up. The truck couldn't get in, of course, but it pinned them inside and the law outside had obviously planned it that way.

Park had his niner out and was looking for the new guy, but he'd disappeared. He'd been a plant the whole time and he knew lots of details so Park went looking for him.

Sun saw the lights go on when he was still a hundred yards or so up the dock. Without a second's hesitation he spun the wheel, tromped on the gas and did a squealing one-eighty, going back the other way, fishtailing until he had the souped-up Hyundai Sonata almost up to seventy. Sun realized there must have been a setup and therefore all the exits were covered. So before anyone could get on his tail he made for his secret exit. Between warehouses 18 and 19 there was a narrow alley. At the end was the same fourteen foot chainlink fence with razor wire coils on top that surrounded the whole complex. But between the posts here the wire was fake. When they first started this operation Sun had cut the wire at the posts and then tied it back up with string. Outside of the fence was a big empty field strewn with trash. Just before Sun hit the fence he flipped his lights off. The Sonata took out the fake fence as if it wasn't there and then Sun was trying to control the big car as it surged across the field, skidding and swerving, and onto another access road. From here there was a maze of roads and warehouses and he was finally outside on a public street and he could slow down and be inconspicuous. Sun drove slowly three miles up into Long Beach, the sweat drying on his face, before he pulled off and inspected the front of the car. There was major scratching and paint damage. They'd be looking for the car. As far as he knew whoever planned the setup already had a good idea who he was. So he was hot, after all these years.

Sun was not the person to dwell on temporary misfortune, not here in the United States of America. When they had trained him so many years ago to operate against the North Koreans they let him know, if those guys catch you you'll be begging them for two weeks or more just to let you die. Here all that could happen was that you could go to prison. He wasn't ready to do that either.

The Hyundai Sonata disappeared into a brake and muffler shop in Koreatown. Sun made some calls that were relayed and then the answer came back. Dolly's, tomorrow at ten.

The next morning a panel truck with signs identifying it as belonging to Yueh Yung's Drycleaning and Tailoring emerged from the garage and drove to Dolly Jolly's apartment building where it was noted without much interest by the usual watchers. They saw a portly Korean with thick glasses wearing black pants and a white shirt with the sleeves rolled up get out and carry a bulky load of clothes on hangers into the building. They already knew that Herschel Jolly was in the building visiting his mother but they hadn't heard about the Korean connection down in San Pedro yet. Different operations.

Sun made his report. "They almost had me. Must a been a plant. But somebody got wise and hit the lights just before I got there."

Mr. Jolly sighed. "It's a fucking disaster, Sun. They got two of your guys and probably five others from connections they made. Are those guys going to talk?"

Sun shook his head. "I would be surprised. In our organization there is a severe stigma attached to giving information to outsiders."

Jolly figured he knew what that meant. "So they'll stand up?"

"They will stand up. First of all, they will claim not to know English. If they can get a good lawyer a jury can be convinced that they were just hired off the street to load trucks, that they didn't know the goods were stolen. I don't think they will do time. They needed to catch me too to make the whole case."

"Well that's the only good news I heard tonight," said Jolly. "Otherwise we're wiped out. Ten years of organizing that racket on the docks. Might be two, three years before we can start building it up from scratch again. You know what that load was worth last night?" Sun just listened. "Two-and-a-half fucking million dollars worth of stupid basketball shoes, TV sets, VCRs, computer parts, and radio-tape decks that go in Ford cars that people think were made in America!"

Jolly thought for a minute and Sun was silent, having been trained to find out what other people had on their minds before he said anything.

Now Jolly got up and went to the window. He was looking down at a phone company van double parked opposite the building, undoubtedly using some sophisticated equipment to hear what was being said in this room. Jolly went over and turned up the sound on the television, which was tuned to the Weather Channel.

"You know this is the worst possible time. There's a big payoff coming up for our real estate plans and I was counting on San Pedro. I'm actually a couple of million in hock to the Italians in New Orleans, my goddamned father-in-law, can you believe it?" He came to a decision. "Sun, we gotta act on that bundle the Greek kid got away with. I need that dough. And it's a good time for you to get out of the country. Lemme make a couple calls to my travel agent and we'll put you on a plane to Germany, date the tickets two days ago so you couldn't have been down in San Pedro last night. So. Tell me what you got lined up in Germany?"

Sun told him.

Chapter Eight
Kali Vrisi

WHEN THERE WAS A LOT OF WORK at the restaurant, Manoli brought in little Yanni. The "little" part was because Yanni wasn't little at all, he was bigger than most Greeks, about the size of a good NFL running back. He was also stronger than anyone Thanassi had ever met in his life, except for maybe Goomba. He didn't look strong, like weight-lifter strong, but he could toss a couple of fifty kilo sacks of rice up on his shoulders like they were sofa cushions or something and he could crush walnuts between his thumb and forefinger. The locals would challenge him to lift the front of a car. He couldn't do Manoli's old Mercedes, but the Fiats, the little Japanese cars, the Twingos—they were no challenge at all. He'd turn his back to the car, bend his legs, grab the front end, and up it would come, Yanni grinning like a little kid. And he was a little kid in his head, like he'd stopped in there at about twelve or thirteen and just grew muscles instead. He worked all over town at simple jobs that only required strenuous labor and he was infinitely cheerful and proud of his strength and endurance. The story was that when he was fifteen the family ox dropped dead just before planting time and his father made him pull the plow to get the wheat field ready for sowing. It was the hardest plowing of the year, the end of summer after the ground had been baking with no rain since May. He pulled the plow with his father and mother taking turns steering until they'd plowed almost a half hectare in one day—as much as the ox ever did. His parents died not long after, before he was twenty. They were old, maybe too old to have had children, people said, and maybe that's why Yanni was simple. He didn't even look like them, having light brown hair and different colored eyes, one grey and one green. Some old ladies still crossed themselves when they saw him coming.

But the village took over for the parents: Yanni lived in their old house and people gave him jobs so he'd have enough money to eat and buy clothes. Once an aunt went over to clean the house and came right back and told anyone who would listen that she hadn't touched a thing, that house was as spotless as hers or any woman's even on Clean Monday. He was also a superb shepherd and kept up his parents' small flock of goats, taking them far into the mountains to graze and then rounding them up effortlessly to be milked or shifted to another grazing ground.

Manoli made the mistake of letting Yanni take orders one weekend when they were really busy. Naturally the first table he waited on was a stuck up Athenian couple. He got the orders wrong and the Athenian woman was yelling at him, are you an idiot or something? Manoli got out there in a hurry and said, no he's not an idiot, he's just simple. But he has to have some kind of job. You think he should just sit around all day? We don't need you Athenians telling us what to do here in Crete! And the Athenians left.

Yanni only had one problem. Sometimes a fit of depression would come over him. He would sit in the plateia, his face like thunder and everyone staying away from him. He never hurt a soul, but when the anger had built up too much he'd go home and get his shotgun and a pocket full of shells and stand on the beach firing out to sea, throwing rocks high up into the air and blasting them into gravel. Nobody dared stop him. How could you stop a crazy person of superhuman strength armed with a shotgun, who could hit anything he aimed at? After he'd made everyone's ears ring for a few minutes the anger would pass, he'd go home and when he came out again he was the same old cheerful Little Yanni

One day Thanassi hired Yanni to come up and help him build a dry stone wall at his farm. They labored most of the day and when they were through Yanni looked around and told Thanassi that he had worked for the old man here before and taken his goats up the mountains by a secret way the bell goat had shown him.

"Come along, I'll show you." Thanassi had thought the cliffs behind his house were insurmountable, densely overgrown with the typical Cretan chaparral, all thorns and spines. But Yanni led the way, almost running, jumping just at the right places where ledges of rock wound their way almost invisibly between the thorn bushes until about half way up they came on a sloping rock face that wasn't as steep as it looked from below. The rough limestone was easy to walk along and cling to and when they had crossed it diagonally upwards they were on a well established goat path and reached the great shoulder of the mountain swiftly. From here Yanni ascended even more rapidly, from boulder to boulder. Finally they stood on top of a broad hill overlooking a shallow valley that led in turn ever northwards into the *Levka Ori*, the White Mountains, the high range of southwestern Crete. Thanassi was pouring with sweat and gasping for breath but Yanni wasn't even breathing hard.

"No one comes here but goats," said Yanni. "And the wild animals, of course. I saw an *agrimi* up the valley once, as big as a donkey. I had my gun but something told me not to kill it. And one day, far far away I saw a black bull standing on a cliff."

"Maybe the *Minotavros*," said Thanassi, joking.

"*Reh moré*!" said Yanni with a worried expression on his broad face. "You shouldn't talk of such things." Then suddenly he pointed.

"Look there, it's a goat, there on that rock!"

Thanassi could just make out in the distance a brown figure silhouetted against the sky.

"You know, that looks like Kanelli, old man Stavros' nanny," said Yanni. "He thought he'd lost her last month, hit by a truck or something. He cried like a baby!" And putting his hands to his mouth he began to call with a loud, clear voice, "KA-NEL-LI! KA-NEL-LI!"

Thanassi saw the goat drop off the cliff like a stone and thought she'd been scared away. But in a moment she appeared again leaping among the rocks and heading their way at full speed. Soon she joined them on the hill and went directly to Yanni, who began scratching her ears and scolding her.

"Kanelli! Aren't you ashamed? How could you run off and make Stavros cry! Come with me, baby, and I'll give you nice oats. You shouldn't run in the mountains! You need to be milked or your bag will hang down and you'll tear it on the thorns! Silly Kanelli!" And the goat nuzzled Yanni and smiled like a dog, wagging her tail like mad. The three of them descended the mountain in a line, Yanni and Kanelli surefooted, leading the way, Thanassi bringing up the rear by a long shot, thinking any moment he was going to pitch off down the slope and be skinned alive by the rocks and thornbushes.

Old Stavros was ecstatic, leading his nanny back home with a bit of cord around her neck, Kanelli strutting along as if she'd done something really clever. Manoli said Stavros had thought his beloved milk goat had become *agriokhátsiko*——wild goat.

"You mean, she'd gone wild in the mountains?" asked Thanassi.

"No. It's an old joke all over Crete. When a restaurant has "wild goat" on the menu as a special what it really means is that some driver at night, probably drunk, has hit a goat, so he sells it to the restaurant and they have the skin off it in two minutes, gutted and hanging up in the back room. You'll notice that "wild goat" is always a *stifado*——a stew. You have to cook an old goat three, maybe four hours before you can chew it, also to get the smell out, also so you won't notice the broken bones."

"You serve wild goat, Manoli?"

He smiled. "Sometimes. Also wild chicken sometimes, wild cat, wild dog. We have very skillful drivers here, especially at night. No, I'm joking about the cats and dogs," he said. "But you be careful crossing the road at night."

Chapter Nine
Los Angeles

GEORGE KIOSOGLOU was down at headquarters looking at the video coverage of Mr. Jolly's day. The crew of the phone company van was describing what they were viewing. Agent Bonnano was a heavy man wearing rumpled suit pants and a short sleeved white button-down shirt, open at the neck, that looked about three days—or six meals—from the last time it had been in the wash. He was not going to be the FBI poster boy. Agent Longway was a tall slim brown man in an elegant chalk stripe suit that had never experienced a wrinkle. His shirt was a delicate cream and he had a museum print tie, the kind that costs twice as much as your shirt. Bonnano was doing the commentary.

"See, here he comes out of his house, gets in the car, Manny is driving as usual. They pull out onto Rodeo, Manny throws his cigarette out the window. Littering, for sure. And isn't there something about being careless with a lit cigarette?"

"Probably attempted arson." said Longway. "It's high fire season."

"Woulda nailed him, except they're in Beverly Hills still. It's BHPD's call." They watched the Cadillac leave palm-lined streets and enter an area of tall apartment buildings.

"Here we are at mom's house. What a good son, visits his mom every day. Okay. We skip about an hour here, nothing's happening, he's gonna leave soon." The agent had his finger on the fast forward, watching the numbers on the counter. The picture stopped jiggling and came back into focus just as an Oriental came out of the building and got into a dry cleaning van.

"Wait a minute!" Kiosoglou was suddenly on his feet. "Play that part back! The Oriental guy..."

He watched carefully as they ran the sequence two, then three times. Longway was looking through the notes on his clipboard.

"Yeah. We got him when he pulled up, got his license number and called it in right away. It's a legit business. Driver doesn't fit any description we have since that guy Moon got whacked. You see something, George?"

"Moon! That's just it! The Korean connection! You heard about the docks last night?"

"Heard about it, that's just about all. Different operations," said Bonnano. "They're keeping us all compartmentalized and insulated so we can't give away secrets to Castro's secret police, or worse, the ACLU. We got a detail working with Customs down there as the lead agency. You think that guy's Korean?"

"What's the address of that cleaners?" They showed him the board. "There you are!" Kiosoglou burst out. "Right in the middle of Koreatown! I didn't make the name on the van right away, thought it was Chinese. But that guy could be Jolly's new Korean, the one that was running the docks. The Korean operation gets busted, next day a Korean comes to see Jolly at his mother's house..."

Longway was already on the phone, reciting the address of Yueh Yung's dry cleaning establishment. He hung up.

"What do you know. LAPD just got there. They were following up on the San Pedro bust, gave the Korean names to their Korean squad. K-squad had the cleaner's address on their computer as 'known associates.' They got the van there and they're printing it. No driver, of course, and nobody knows nothing, even in Korean."

"Goddamn!" said Bonnano with feeling. "Why don't we have a Korean squad!"

"So what's it all mean?" asked Longway.

"I dunno. I gotta talk to the boss," said Kiosoglou. "But my guess is Jolly is hurting. His Korean down there on the docks gets away, comes to report, maybe get a new assignment."

"Like what?" asked Bonnano.

Kiosoglou put his finger to his lips. "Need-to-know basis, my man. Fidel might be listening in, as we speak." He left to a chorus of profanity.

Chapter Ten
Toumba

Every day he could get off work at the restaurant Thanassi would go up into the mountains with Yanni. From down on the coast the great escarpment looked impenetrable. The dusty green of the chaparral shaded into steep grey limestone cliffs, tan slopes where the scree had fallen, patches of vegetation and stubborn, scraggly pine trees higher up. He knew the rocks were incredibly old, older than the first mammals, maybe even before dinosaurs. Their roots lay in the first earth, the oldest earth of all, cold and untouched by the heat of the modern Aegean, a second in time to them. The ancient Cretans had stood beneath the great range in reverence, crediting the heights with the birth of gods and monsters, as if crags hundreds of millions of years old had the slightest interest in religions with the lifespan of a gnat. The high mountain range of western Crete is not so apparent from the north, where the cities are, where the airports are and the tourists come, because the slope is gradual. But at the southern edge the mountains fall off precipitously into the sea. There, only the broader river valleys are populated and farmed and the few roads snake off to the north to wind around the shoulders of the heights rising on either side.

Elsewhere only goats and their solitary herders venture in search of isolated meadows, or springs that can keep hidden ravines green with grass through the long, hot, dry summers. Those who know how to look can spot the patch of color where oleanders have found a wet spot, or even wait by the great purple clumps of wild thyme for a bee to come and harvest and then follow it back to water. All these tricks and more, Yanni knew.

Thanassi remembered the thrill of his first trip through the mountains. He had flown into Chania, on the north coast, in May. It was already then in the low eighties—higher on the sunbaked asphalt outside the terminal where he rented his little Fiat—but to the south he was amazed to see the mountaintops still crusted with snow. He had driven westward along the north coast, all strip commercial, hotels and restaurants bedecked with gaudy signs in English and German, forests of postcards, stands clogged with suntan lotion and beach mats, and the first waves of tourists wandering the roads, pale white, or rosy red, or prudently working towards a tan that could be displayed in offices in Frankfurt or Manchester and other northern climes. He was wondering if this was really what Crete looked like. Then he turned south on the little road indicated on his map and was instantly in a different world. The din of traffic faded. He drove one block, there was a side road he had to cross, two more little houses, then he was in the countryside, lush and green after the last few rains of late spring. He passed fields and orchards, little whitewashed cottages with roses blooming in front along the road, goats and chickens wandering in the side yards. The road began to climb and he was now surrounded by olive orchards. He found himself behind a slow truck with nowhere to pass on the narrow road so after a while he just parked on a dirt track leading off the road and walked through the trees. He leaned down there in the heat of noon with the cicadas chirping and picked up a handful of light tan soil. This is my father's land, he thought, letting it spill out his hand slowly in wonder. Then he had to touch the trees, gnarled, ancient olives, pruned back year after year to keep the fruit within reach. The bark was rough and sent a shiver through him as he thought of the age of the tree, maybe already bearing fruit before the United States was born. And that reminded him of Ben Franklin, the dead Philadelphian, and he felt a wave of euphoria, thinking of all the dead Philadelphians, all put away in their safe places.

As the road began to enter the high mountains he realized he was hungry, he'd not eaten, only a roll for breakfast. And just then, coming around a curve, he saw the little taverna under the planc trees in the shade, hanging over the slope, with a big garden growing below. He stopped, parked the car under a tree, and walked over to one of the three wooden tables and sat down. In a moment a round woman emerged from the building and gave him a questioning look, waiting to see what language he was going to speak.

"Good morning, ma'm" he said, in his hesitant Greek. "It's early for lunch, I know, but I thought I could get a bite, maybe an omelette?"

"Rina!" cried the woman and a little girl came running out into the sunlight. The woman told her something so quickly that Thanassi couldn't make out anything but the word for eggs—*avgá*. But it was obvious what she had been told as she ran down the wooden steps into the garden, scattering hens in her path. She looked under a zucchini plant, then another and another and soon had four eggs cradled in her little hands. On her way back into the kitchen she gave Thanassi a triumphant smile.

It was the best omelette he'd ever had in his life, a meal interrupted only by the demands of the round woman to know where he had learned Greek, where he was from, and all the old familiar questions from the *Odyssey*.

The road reached a high plateau and for an hour he drove around the crests of the foothills. Then the mountains rose above him and the road led back and forth half way up a deep gorge until it finally snaked down and followed the dry river bed down to the sea, down to Kali Vrisi.

Here in the south there were no roads running east and west, only a few narrow tracks leading to the tiny villages perched up to the north and west, tracks that had been widened by the tractors of the villagers to allow them to bump along to market in their little Japanese pickup trucks. But to the east along the coast there was nothing but wilderness. From this valley to the great Samaria gorge ten miles to the east the mountains dropped into the sea in a series of precipitous steps. Thanassi could look up at the massive cliffs and doubt that anyone had ever lived there. A small party of Greek archaeologists was currently working at an ancient religious site up a valley to the north and once when they were in town for a meal he asked them about the mountains to the east.

"Some Canadians were doing a survey," a slight, middle-aged woman told him. "Two women, but they were tough. They walked almost everywhere, along the coast to Pikilassos, an ancient town, just a few stones on top of each other now. But they gave up on Toumba." Some of the idlers in the taverna echoed her. "Toumba. Yes. Toumba."

"Toumba. That's the name of that big peak there and everything below it." She gestured northeast where the last of the dying light struck a peach glow on a rounded summit. "They finally hired a little plane to fly over, from here to Samaria. They told me there couldn't have been any settlements among those cliffs Besides, the earthquakes move things around now and then."

"Too damn much," said Manoli, who was also helping Thanassi listen. "They knocked down half the church and a hotel one year."

"Yes, But the big one was in the year three hundred sixty five after Christ...a thousand seven hundred years ago almost."

"How do you know the date?" asked Thanassi.

"It was so big, the ancient writers mentioned it. One gave the year of the Roman emperor. It raised western Crete nine meters all at once. If you go over there to Phalasarna in the northwest you can see. The old harbor is just a big field, two hundred meters from the sea. Some big walls are still standing but everything else fell down. Maybe there were paths over Toumba once, but either they fell off the mountain, or the cliffs came down on them. It was something, that earthquake! The waves took ships inland a mile and left them on top of the houses, down there in Alexandria," she pointed to the southeast. "In Egypt. And up north there in Methoni, on the mainland too."

Thanassi didn't doubt it for a moment. *Toumba*, he knew, meant "somersault" in Greek. To the east on the coast was a rocky promontory dividing one beach from the next. It was as big as two or three of the huge buildings in downtown Los Angeles all put together. But it hadn't been there that long. He'd been told that just before the big war there was a little quake one night, nothing much. But then there was a rumble in the darkness and next thing anyone knew a big wave came through town and everyone was suddenly standing up to their knees in the sea. When it went back out it did some damage too, taking some weaker house walls with it as it poured out, some poor cats and chickens too. The next morning, there was part of the fallen mountain sitting in the fishing grounds below a new cliff, where it had split off and slid down into the water.

Yanni had been listening to the woman lecture. The next day he came up to Thanassi's house, having waved down a truck or car, as he always did.

"You heard what that woman said yesterday?" he asked.

"In truth! That was some story!"

Yanni smiled. "You come with me today." And he started towards the cliffs.

"But I have to help Manoli today..."

"No. I told him we were going to have a walk. He was angry."

"I bet he was!" Thanassi knew that people in the village tended to forgive Yanni everything and he hoped some of that good natured indulgence would rub off on him, although with Manoli that wasn't the way to bet.

They took the usual route up the face of the cliff.

"Are we going far?" asked Thanassi. "Should we take some water?"

"There is water there," was all Yanni would say.

Thanassi had gone with Yanni several times over a northern ridge and down into an interior valley, where goats grazed on vegetation greener than the parched stubble of the southern slope. But this time Yanni took off directly east, faster than Thanassi could follow, on a brutal route across the gorges of the Toumba massif. After a half hour Thanassi had to call a halt. Fit as he was he couldn't keep up with Yanni, barely sweating, who was now smiling at his weaker friend and waiting for him to recover. Down below more than a thousand feet they could see the electric blue sea and the daily boat, tiny in the distance, taking the hikers from the bottom of the Samaria gorge to the coastal town of Paleochora, where they would get their buses back to the north. Other than that, nothing moved in this landscape. They were on a ragged slope full of brush, thorn bushes and stunted junipers Many times they had had to clamber over massive limestone boulders and jump down onto ledges with nothing but air to hold onto on the southern side. Now, to the east, they were facing a sheer cliff and a drop-off and Thanassi started looking upward for a path around it. But Yanni was shaking his head. "No. We go straight across, Thanassi, you follow me."

Yanni stepped out along a tiny ledge until it ended. As far as Thanassi could see, there was nowhere to go—he couldn't even turn around to go back. But Yanni looked up at a crack in the rock above him. There was the usual brush, crowned by a low tangle of juniper that had found a grip deep within the crack. Yanni jumped forward, put his forward foot, the right one, onto an invisible foothold, caught a downreaching juniper branch, and suddenly swung completely out of sight. All Thanassi could hear was his voice. "Come on, kid! Do just like I did. Catch the tree and swing. Here there's plenty of room."

Thanassi had never seen Yanni make a false move yet on the treacherous slopes of the mountain but it took an act of sweaty-palmed faith for him to creep out across the rock face, locate the tiny foothold, up and forward, jump onto it, grab the juniper and then swing out into space.

As he swung around the corner he saw a broad ledge and a long gorge leading back north. He almost held onto the juniper branch too long, but Yanni caught his waist and just yanked him upright onto the ledge.

"Don't hold onto the tree, you just catch it and swing,"

said Yanni. "If you hold on, it might pull out. Then what would you do?"

So Thanassi had that thought to occupy him. Then he had another.

"Yanni, how do we get back?"

"Bah! Even easier. We go higher."

Now Yanni led along a recess leading deep into the gorge splitting the southern face of Toumba. Thanassi expected that they would reach the gorge and then come back out again, but this time Yanni looked up the gorge and began climbing it, although it seemed to get shallower and shallower. But at the top Yanni sat on a broad boulder and as Thanassi joined him, gestured down in triumph.

There below them was a hidden valley carved into the slopes of the mountain range. They were looking down onto the tops of real pine trees, not the scraggly cypresses and junipers they had been climbing among. Immediately Thanassi could hear running water and as Yanni led the way he finally could see the source. High above them a cliff split in two and a rivulet, gleaming in the sun, splashed down into shadow, to emerge below in a glade. They walked down the short slope onto the margin of the clearing. There Yanni stopped Thanassi with his hand and shushed him. Then he began to call softly.

"Madonna, Madonna, *pou eíse*? Where are you?"

In a second Thanassi could hear sounds in the forest and here came a black goat running, followed by two little black and tan kids. The nanny went right to Yanni to be scratched. The kids prudently stayed in the background, now and then prancing, throwing their heads up and their forefeet off the ground, timid, but showing their style.

"They won't come to me yet," said Yanni. "They want to stay wild. If they feel my hand it wouldn't be the same any more. I could make them come, but I won't. I like them wild. Like their father. You'll never see him but he's here. He's always watching. Many other wives too. Only Madonna would come one day. And now I give her oats." Yanni always had a pocket full of oats, or carrots, or dry corn. Madonna was now happily feasting out of his hand.

"Why Madonna?" asked Thanassi. "Is it after the *Panayía*? The Virgin?"

"No!" said Yanni, laughing. "How can you call a goat after the *Panayía*? No, it is after the actress, the one who is so pretty in Hollywood. Madonna. I want to marry her."

They walked down into the valley and into the trees, down to the little brook and drank deeply, with the goats standing watch around them. Then Yanni pointed to the cliff where the spring was splashing down, from boulder to boulder.

"Look on the ground there, Thanassi." And suddenly he could see the regular lines of stone blocks on the ground, almost hidden by the low undergrowth and the shadows of the surrounding trees. There was an obviously rectangular foundation, one end near their feet, the other end open and leading towards the cliff. There was a pool at that end and as they approached Thanassi could see a cleft in the rock behind the falling water. He looked at Yanni in wonder.

"It is all right. You can go in, Thanassi."

It was a shallow cave and almost immediately Thanassi felt broken pottery beneath his feet. He dropped to his knees and looked around and as his eyes began to pick things out in the gloom he saw masses of sherds and here and there a whole figurine. He picked one up...it was a small clay goat, painted in geometric patterns. Here was another, and another, and he realized he was in a cave shrine, obviously sacred to goats, where thousands of years ago worshipers had come to dedicate their little clay fig-urines. But to whom? All he could think of from his reading in mythology was Pan, the goat god. But now Yanni was next to him and pointing to the wall at the back of the cave.

Here there was a low step carved into the rock and what looked like a larger figurine, heavy, not moving when he touched it. Yanni scratched a match and the yellow light shone down on a crude bronze statuette of a goat, its head turned back and touching its flank. And then Thanassi real-ized it was not licking its flank, it was nuzzling two little bronze human babies who were suckling at its udder. The statuette was crusted with grime and verdigris but the bronze metal shone through. The shape was heavy yet graceful, a naive masterpiece of some inspired artist. The match went out and Yanni lit another. He fumbled on the floor and came up with a tiny clay bowl. It had a wick, which he lit, and then the cave was suffused with a warm yellow glow and Thanassi could smell the olive oil. It reminded him that he had almost stopped breathing from the excitement.and he was feeling a little light-headed. He took a few deep breaths, then turned to Yanni.

"When did you find this?" he asked in wonderment.

So Yanni told him about following a recalcitrant old nanny. He'd thought she was cornered back there at the cliff face but she'd just walked along it and disappeared. He realized there must be a path right around the corner.

"I was afraid, Thanassi. But I never saw a smart old goat like her fall, so I just followed. I grabbed the tree to help along the cliff. Then I saw her going up the rocks and over here."

He'd explored the whole glade, realized from the drop-pings that there was a big community of wild goats here. Taking a drink from the pool he saw the cave.

"Then I was really afraid, Thanassi! Because there are

bad things in places like this. But something told me to go in and not be afraid. I found the pots, and the goat there with the babies, and then I saw the little lamp, how it was an old oil lamp, black, you know, from burning. But it was dry for a long time."

I bet it was a long time, thought Thanassi. *Maybe fifteen centuries, or more?*

"So the next time I came back I brought some oil and lit the lamp. There are lots of them here. I was going to leave the bottle of oil but then I saw there was an old bottle." He pointed at a slim terra cotta jar in one corner.

"I thought it was better to put the oil in there, where it belonged. I lit two more lamps and looked at the bronze goat for a while. When I came out every goat in the valley was waiting on the other side of the pool. So I decided it must be a little shrine of some saint who lived with goats, maybe even Our Lady. I've seen pictures of her with sheep, why not goats?" Yanni gave a little laugh, as if theology was easy, once you'd thought about it.

"There's some writing on some of the jars," he added. "But I can't make it out." He lit another of the lamps.

Now in the brighter light Thanassi could make out the letters that he had thought were designs on some of the goat figurines. He could see NYM- on one, AI on another. Finally he found a whole figurine with the letters along its back: NYMΦAI. "Nymphs," he said to himself, and wondered what he should explain to Yanni, who evidently believed that any expression of faith could be folded into the habits of worship he had grown up with: God and Jesus, who were very remote figures in local churches; Our Lady, and the holy Saints, who figured prominently in any conversation with older people, particularly women, in Kali Vrisi.

"I think it says 'nymphs,'" said Thanassi, using the modern Greek word, *nymphes*. "So I don't think they were honoring the *Theotokos*, the Mother of God, here."

There was a moment of entire stillness in the world, there in the cave, outside, everywhere on that mountain range in Crete. Then there was a tiny earth movement, not even a rumble, just a momentary tremor of the roots of the earth under them, the sort of mild tremor that Thanassi had felt every day or so there on the edge of Crete, where it sat poised over the powerful African plate, plunging down into the molten core of the earth.

"Maybe I was wrong," said Thanassi, quickly. "The Mother of God is probably everywhere." He looked over at Yanni, who was smiling broadly. "Nymphs, Our Lady," he continued. "It's all part of the same thing, honoring the Gods."

He could almost feel the ground under him settle in relief and Yanni nodded vigorously, not even noticing the pluralization of the Gods.

Later they walked to the edge of the little forest and Yanni showed him where the cliff had sheared away unknown centuries before, leaving a broad shelf of the for-est floor poised above an abyss, maybe a thousand feet down to the next great pile of shattered rock. Thanassi looked over the edge, thinking of the tremendous earth movement that had terminated the life of this religious precinct. There were still ways in, but the ancient people might have taken it as a message, and never bothered to return, leaving the little valley to the goats.

"So now, Yanni," he said, "How do we get out of here?"

"That's the best part!" said Yanni, springing to his feet. "First, let's leave the food for the goats." and he turned his pockets inside out, spilling oats and dry corn onto the grass there by the pool.

"Now, we climb by the water," and he jumped up onto the cliff face, next to the thin stream of water spilling down from the unseen spring above.

Thanassi followed him, ledge after ledge, suddenly noticing that there were footholds carved into the cliff, and the first one obviously invited the right foot. But Yanni was looking down carefully and shouted. "No, Thanassi. It looks like the right foot, but put the left foot first."

And they clambered up the sheer face of the rock. At the top Thanassi saw Yanni pause, then leap upward out of the last foothold. In a moment he reappeared at the top, looking down, ready to offer Thanassi a hand. When he arrived at that point and had his foot firmly placed in the last foothold he pushed off easily and sprawled on the top, not needing Yanni's help.

"You see, Thanassi," said Yanni. "They were smart. They didn't want enemies coming. You can't climb down from here. And if you come up on the steps with the wrong foot you can't jump to the top.

And Yanni explained, haltingly, the first time he had come, realized that he couldn't swing back across the cliff on the juniper. He'd been stuck three days and that was when he made friends with Madonna, touched her, scratched her, and finally drank some milk from her bag, otherwise he'd have starved to death up there. Then he decided to try the cliff and he took the wrong step, right foot first. So when he got to the last foothold he was on the wrong foot and he realized he couldn't go back down—there was nothing to hold on to with your hands—so he just gave a great leap, caught the edge, and was able to scrabble over.

Thanassi looked at Yanni, at the great lump of sinew and muscle in front of him and thought that very few members of the human race could have had the strength to jump and then pull themselves over the edge of that precipice.

The rest of the day was an anticlimax as they walked easily downhill to the cliff over Thanassi's house and then took the well-known route down. They had some water there in the house, and Thanassi brought out bread and cheese. He knew he had to settle some questions with Yanni.

"Yanni. You've kept all this a secret, all these years?"

"Oh, yes, Thanassi!" His face was very serious. "Once when I was young I told people things I had seen somewhere else on the mountain. Very old things. Some people didn't believe me. And the priest wanted to send me to live in a home in Chania, I don't know where. He said..."

And Yanni fell silent, as he always did when the subject of his poor head came up.

"I don't know what the priest said," interrupted Thanassi, with heat. "But he was foolish! What we saw today was beautiful, very beautiful. But the people down here wouldn't understand it. So you and me, we'll keep it a secret, okay?"

Yanni broke into a big smile and Thanassi realized the big youth had been worrying whether he had revealed too many of his secrets, whether Thanassi would rush into the village telling everyone what he had seen.

*

A few days later the archaeologists came back down to Kali Vrisi for a swim and some civilized drinking after their hot and dusty days up at the temple site. Thanassi sat with them at Manoli's, having a polite ouzo, making idle conversation at first, wondering how to ask questions. Then they started talking about an inscribed vase they had found the day before, with ΠΟΣ- on it, probably a dedication to Poseidon, whose sanctuary it was.

"I saw a pot in a museum," he said. "It had the word *NYMΦAI* written on it. Would that mean something about the nymphs?"

"That would depend," said the older man, Stavros. "In ancient Greek it could mean..." But the woman Maria interrupted him, looking at Thanassi with one brow raised.

"Where did you see this pot?" Thanassi wondered if he had made a mistake.

"Was it Chania? Or maybe Athens? I don't remember." He smiled engagingly and shrugged his shoulders.

"I only heard of one or two vases like that," said Maria. "And they're not on display anywhere." She was still giving Thanassi a searching look.

Both Stavros and the other man, Vasili, started talking at once, evidently embarrassed at the close questioning of a drinking companion.

"Maybe he saw it in a book..."

"Who knows what they have there in Athens..."

Stavros' voice was louder and he won. "They keep changing the display there at the National Museum. Who knows? Anyway, Thanassi, it could mean 'nymphs.'"

"But more probably, it is singular. It means 'To the Nymph,' The nymph, singular," said Maria. "That's what the ones from the cave on Akrotiri say."

"What cave?" asked Vasili. But Stavros was nodding in agreement.

"Yes, I remember now. It was in the sixties sometime. They found a cave in the mountains there north of the airport, Chania airport."

"And there were dozens of little pots," went on Maria.

"Some of them had the same inscription: NYMΦAI, to the Nymph, meaning a particular nymph. The reason I questioned you is that the spelling NYMΦAI is Cretan."

"Well, it could be Boiotian too," said Stavros, quickly still trying to avoid the appearance of an inquisition.

"The ones in the cave," asked Vasili."I never heard of them. Come on! I was in grade school then! What nymph was it?"

"It was a Frenchman who found it, an archaeologist who used to walk around in the mountains by himself. He thought it was sacred to Akakallis," said Maria. "But he's a crazy man. It could have been any of the nymphs. Crete is full of them."

"Who was Akakallis?" asked Thanassi. "It doesn't even sound like a Greek name."

"Probably very old, even Minoan. She was the mother of the hero Kydon who founded Kydonia. That's the old name of Chania," explained Stavros. "There are old coins of Kydonia that show the infant Kydon being suckled by a dog."

"A dog?" Thanassi asked, trying to sound casual.

"She was a very bad mother, Akakallis," said Maria. She would make love with a god and then abandon the baby because she was afraid of her father, Minos. Down there at ancient Tarrha..." and she pointed off east towards the Samaria gorge, "There must have been a cult. The author Pafsanías said that he saw a bronze statue at Delphi that had been dedicated by the people from Tarrha. There was a goat suckling two baby boys and he said the mother was Akakallis."

Thanassi almost fell off his chair. Now he didn't dare say anything because he thought his voice would betray his excitement.

"That sounds like Romulus and Remus with the wolf," said Vasili.

"Hah!" "Romans!" said Stavros and Maria at the same time, scornfully. They looked at each other and laughed. "Much later," Maria continued patriotically, "All the Roman myths were stolen from the Greeks," Then she looked suspiciously at Thanassi again.

"If you remember where you saw this 'nymph' pot, you tell me, okay? We'll be around all month."

"Or until the funds run out," said Stavros, and they all laughed again.

Thanassi left the restaurant that night troubled. On the one hand he had been inspired by the very idea of the local archaeology. The idea that you could use ancient texts and actual excavation to learn new things about old Cretan civilization. Why couldn't he be a part of that? How difficult could it be for him to go on to graduate study in a university that had excavations in Greece? A university that would admit him to a program where he could learn archaeology? He knew modern Greek, after all, and Sam Papadakis had told him that ancient Greek would come easily, it wasn't that different. And he already knew of an amazing archaeological site completely unknown to these archaeologists. He wasn't sure that he would ever reveal the little grove of Akakallis to anyone but he thought that with Yanni's help he could find many other ancient sites along this coast. He'd seen a map in an Italian book that showed all the ancient sites here, some of them known from coins or inscriptions but never really discovered.

"Dr. Castle," he thought. Dr. Castle, famous Greek archaeologist. And he could picture himself digging along this coast where there were so many sites and so few excavations. He could even afford to fund the excavations.

And then he was reminded of the source of his funds. He was a hunted man. He could never go back to the normalcy of graduate study at a university. He could never risk the publicity of an archaeological excavation. He loved the town of Kali Vrisi. But how long could he live here, just growing vegetables, working at a restaurant, never reading a new book, never seeing a newspaper from home, or anywhere else... He thrust the thought from his mind, thinking it uncharitable, unkind to these fine, friendly people who'd been so good to him. But the corner of his mind where he filed the thought grumbled a bit, reminded him: *you're going to have to work this one out a little bit more!*

Chapter Eleven
Berlin Game

Sᴜɴ ᴄᴀᴍᴇ ɪɴ ᴏɴ ᴛʜᴇ Lᴜꜰᴛʜᴀɴꜱᴀ ꜰʟɪɢʜᴛ ʟᴀᴛᴇ, having missed the connection at Kennedy. The taxi driver took him to the Hilton and before he unpacked or even took off his raincoat he called the number he'd been given by Papathanassopoulos.

"I'm sorry, I don't speak German," he said when someone answered and barked rough phrases into the phone.

"So. No problem. Your name?"

"My name is Sun. The Greek in Los Angeles gave me your number." The man on the other end of the line did not bother to respond. Sun heard low conversation in the background. Then another voice came on, polite and cultured.

"Yes. Mr. Sun. We expected you earlier."

Sun never explained difficulties. After all, it was a hard world. "What time shall I come tomorrow?"

Once again there was a conference in the background.

"We think all the personnel will be here at fifteen... That is..."

"Yes, yes. Three o'clock. I have an address..." and Sun recited it.

"Of course. That is not the address, however. Call this number again tomorrow at two thirty, we will give you the address and you take a taxi immediately, understood?"

Sun understood. Having worked much of his life for two of the largest intelligence agencies in the world he found the security operations of criminal organizations laughably simple. He wondered why the German police couldn't just fold up all these gangster networks on some slow weekend when they had nothing else to do. But he didn't bother thinking about it.

He phoned down for a small meal, shook his head at the bill when it arrived, but paid a good tip. He ate his meal, showered and washed his underwear as he always did, then went immediately to sleep for ten hours with no difficulty.

The next day was gloomy and drizzling. Sun looked up the location of the hotel's fitness rooms, then went down and exercised for an hour and a half, sweating out all the bad chemicals that build up from sitting in an airport and on an airplane for twenty-two hours. Thirty years ago he could have stepped off the plane and started an operation immediately. But he was sixty-two now and needed some warmup. He swam ten laps in the small pool. Showered again and dressed, he went down and had the breakfast buffet. After four cups of strong German coffee he felt like himself again.

At two-thirty he phoned for the address and then hailed a taxi outside the hotel.

"Not so good place," said the driver, who Sun figured for a Turk. "This right address?"

"Yes. I'm sure. You have a problem? I can take another taxi."

"No, no! But you look like nice man, with money. Sometimes there are bad people..."

Sun insisted and they drove off with him wondering, *should he have worn such a good suit, shirt, and tie?* He realized as they drove through a depressing neighborhood that he might be a bit overdressed. But he didn't worry about it. Maybe a few 'bad people' would complete the morning's workout.

The taxi was going through an interesting neighborhood of little coffee shops and restaurants. There were several Turkish restaurants, Greek restaurants, signs in Chinese, Italian, and suddenly, to his amazement, Sun saw a placard with Korean letters. A very small Korean restaurant. A sign in English said, "Kimchi, Grills," and even as they drove by Sun believed he could smell roasting chilis and garlic. He almost salivated.

But now the taxi was in an industrial zone, passing empty lots full of construction equipment, big faceless buildings with complicated German words on their facades, grimy yards full of what looked like rejected machines and parts. The taxi finally stopped in front of a factory of some kind—a long three story building with almost no windows, fenced lots on either side with razor wire on top. On the street was one small metal door.

"Wait for me just a second until someone lets me in," ordered Sun, as he paid the driver. He got out of the taxi, looked around at the deserted street, then walked rapidly over to the door. He was still looking for a bell of some kind when the door clicked open. A large man silently beckoned him in, closed the door, then led him through a hallway to the open part of the factory. Here at some time some sort of machinery had been assembled. There were high rails with cranes that could lift things with chains. There were empty outlines on the concrete slab floor beneath where machines had once processed whatever it was the cranes carried along their rails. The side of the building away from the street was almost all windows and there were several loading ramps.

But the place was entirely deserted.

The large man pointed Sun at a cage elevator against the north wall, closed him in alone and pressed a button. Slowly the cage rose through the interior of the factory, maybe the only thing that still worked here. On the third floor landing there was an entrance to an enclosure that occupied the whole northwest corner of the building. Sun expected a little office of some kind. Instead, when he opened the door in front of him he found an open stairway descending into an opulent room, at least forty feet square. As he descended the stairs he could see the group of people waiting for him, inspecting him as he walked down. Four men and one woman. And three Rottweilers.

At the bottom of the stairs one of the men walked over and shook his hand, while the dogs romped about him and sniffed the visitor. His host was a man of medium build, stocky and of more than middle age, but obviously vigorous, from the feel of his handshake. He had a broad face, receding gray hair and was wearing all black, a black turtle neck sweater and black slacks. Out of all this blackness peered a pair of very pale blue eyes, and the face crinkled now in a smile.

"Mr. Sun. I'm so glad to meet you," he said in nearly perfect English. "I've heard a great deal about you. *Platz!*" he added in a sharp tone of voice, and the dogs retreated and sat down. "Friendly dogs," he said. "Much nicer than Shepherds or Dobermanns."

Sun just bowed his head, reserving judgment. He'd seen Rottweilers at work before. Also, he was wondering how his host had heard a lot about him..

"Yes, Mr. Sun. You are going to be modest, but you were known in certain data banks from the, um, Eastern bloc, ten or fifteen years ago?"

Sun faced his host squarely. "In that case you will know that I don't play any games at all. And forgive me for not speaking your language. You have the advantage of me."

"No, no. Not at all. German is a hard language to learn. And I know that you can speak not only Japanese and Chinese, but Russian as well, I believe? As well as your excellent English."

Sun bowed once again."You are well informed, sir. But in the present matter I am only an agent. I have been asked only to approve certain personnel, certain procedures, and then to guarantee payment."

The other members of the group had been silent and still, listening to the conversation so far. Now suddenly a young man spoke up, in very bad English.

"Payment. You say payment. But you have nothing with? Where is payment?"

There were swift and angry sentences in German from several people in the group, evidently trying to shush the young man. Sun turned slowly and inspected the speaker. He was taller than Sun by two or three inches, with very blond hair, and not as young as the first impression. Sun noted immediately that he had a weightlifter's body, with enormous biceps, and that he intended the world to notice because he was wearing a thin muscle shirt that showed all of his arms and the bulges of his chest. He was standing casually, bouncing up and down on his toes, with his arms crossed over his chest. But what made the lasting impression was the face with the crazy eyes. His face was broad, descending to a long pointed chin. His mouth seemed to be split in a permanent grin, from ear to ear. But his eyes were insane, light brown, wide open with excitement and totally mad, spinning, out of control. Sun believed that if he had encountered such a man in an alley alone he would have instantly tried to kill him or hurt him badly enough to escape. He did not scare easily but this sort of creature he had rarely encountered, and they always scared him.

Sun was about to address him politely but the man in black anticipated him.

"Jürgen. Please do not be stupid. Financial matters are settled these days in the offices of banks, with papers that are worth more than as much money as you could carry." Jürgen kept on grinning but he made no attempt to argue.

"And now, let me introduce myself and my colleagues," the older man said announced loudly. In a much lower voice and in Russian he said quickly, *"The boy has been in prison too long. A problem with a little girl. He gets excited. But his brother will not work without him now. He thinks it is good therapy."*

He turned to the excitable young man, who was now standing next to his brother, a man of similar build and coloring, but so calm and silent that he almost appeared to be invisible next to his brother.

"May I introduce the brothers, Jürgen and Werner Jaeger. Werner is the director of your operation."

Sun ignored Jürgen and nodded to the other Jaeger, an older man, dressed as a businessman, but any trained observer could see the brutal strength under the expensive suit. Sun turned back to the man in black.

"And you are Mr. Knoblauch?"

"Yes. And please, call me Walther. This is my company headquarters. Knoblauch International Security Systems. I am here only to organize and to finalize the financial arrangements. I have worked with your friend Mr. Papathanassopoulos before several times. He was kind enough to give me a good reference?"

Sun nodded. "He said you can supply reliable personnel."

Knoblauch laughed heartily. "Ja, ja! And I can! Werner Jaeger was an intelligence professional of great promise there in the East. Since the East is no longer he has moved here to the West, where his qualifications are in great demand and he is one of my most trusted executives."

What bullshit, thought Sun. To put it simply, Jaeger was a former east German secret policeman. A thug. When east Germany fell apart he just looked for the nearest place where gangsters like him could get top pay. *And his crazy brother is a child molester,* he thought. *A good start!* Sun stepped forward, shook hands with both men, expecting the younger one to give him some grip. But Jürgen Jaeger was behaving himself now, smiling broadly and chuckling to himself.

Seated on a sofa was the middle-aged woman and Sun wondered if she was the wife or girlfriend of one of the Jaegers.

"And may I introduce Frau Doktor Ilse Wilamowitz? She is most valuable in technical support."

Doctor Wilamowitz tended to fade into the background, like most former intelligence professionals. But Sun saw another face that frightened him. Under a severe short hair cut, graying around the sides, was the lean face of a predator, without expression now because none was expected or required. She had eyes of the darkest gray, eyes that caught Sun's gaze and gave him vertigo, thinking that if you lost your balance and fell into those eyes, you would find yourself in an unbearably bright place, shrieking in endless agony. She made an attempt at a smile now, actually just baring her teeth, giving Sun a momentary weakness in his knees. Although he had met such professionals before, he never got used to them.

"Ilse is also untiring in the field," said Knoblauch. "She runs the Berlin Marathon every year."

Sun could believe it, the stringy body, the impression of restless energy.

Jürgen Jaeger was now laughing. "Our Ilse. She is vurst doctor in de vorld! She has not one living patient!" And he convulsed at his marvelous joke.

Sun had expected a swift hostile response from the woman. But she smiled, even warmly this time, at Jaeger, then turned back to Sun.

"Herr Knoblauch is so kind to say. But I give always good results. Sometime I show even you, Jürgi!" grinning now back at Jürgen Jaeger.

Sun was beginning to wish he could have hired some less spectacular help. All he needed was a few strongarm guys, someone with brains directing. But Knoblauch was introducing the last man.

"And last, Mikali Stavrakis." Stavrakis was a slender dark man, who nodded silently.

"Mikali has worked here in Germany for twenty years. But he is from Crete, from the south near Sfakia, and he knows the terrain and the people well. He speaks some English too. Do you have any questions?"

"First of all," said Sun, bowing, "I am happy to meet all of you. I apologize again for not speaking your language. I have only one question and that is, what is the general outline of your plan?"

Knoblauch looked at Werner Jaeger, who waved back at him, saying "You explain, Walther. We have all discussed this but you know the English better."

Knoblauch nodded. It was obvious that he had been designated to sell the operation, probably had planned it himself.

"Yes. Mr. Sun, we studied your problem thoroughly and consulted with some of our experts on Swiss banking. It is almost certain that Castle will have remote access to his account or accounts through codes. In his situation he would not want to risk frequent visits to Zurich. At the same time, his banker would not be surprised if he made large investments very soon to capture a higher return. There would be nothing unusual if he designated large transfers to certain holding companies with all the correct codes fairly soon. In fact it would be unusual if he did not, given the tiny interest rates offered by our friendly Swiss neighbors.

"This is the problem," said Sun. "One can always extract codes, names, anything, under interrogation. But if the codes are wrong, or they give an alarm? Then what?'

Knoblauch looked at Jaeger, back to Sun. "We have been in touch with a security service in Chania. They have rented a large villa outside the city for us and will have a rental car ready. Otherwise they know nothing. Our only problem is to get Castle there. Once there, I promise you, several treatments from Doctor Wilamowitz will not only supply the codes but instill such terror of repeated treatments that it is unthinkable that he would try to trick us. Can you imagine him chained to a wall in a cellar after many hours of strenuous interrogation with any desire other than to give up his money and then his life without any more pain. I believe you have observed North Korean intensive interrogations?

Sun nodded, forcing himself not to betray the slightest emotion. He had been an unwilling observer, in deep cover, in the blood splattered gymnasium there in Pyongyang and was still sickened by the memory.

"Well then. While many experts at torture, and the North Koreans not the least, have been able to extract every last twitch of agony from helpless nerves long after the subject is brain dead, Doctor Wilamowitz is a trained psychiatrist, who can force the subject's mind to accompany the various parts of his body on the long journey of pain. Castle will be waiting anxiously, hoping against hope that his instructions will be followed. Am I right, Ilse?"

"Ja, Walther. We like to remind the subject exactly why zeze horrible tings are happening, every second. We want cooperation, not punishment. Punishment can always come after." And she grinned a toothy grin again.

Sun had killed many people. He had had others killed. He had hurt people severely to make a point. He had been forced, from time to time, to apply pain to get some quick answers but he had never liked it. Now he felt himself in the presence of a deeper evil and if it had been up to him he would have looked for another solution. But he had given his loyalty to certain principles and his bond to his present employer was a matter of principle. So he shrugged.

"That is up to you as long as it is effective. My part of the operation is to stand by in Zurich ready to assist in any transfer of funds. Now some of you may have questions and I want to know some of the other details."

"Of course, of course," said Knoblauch. "Sit, sit. And we can have something to drink. Would you like coffee? Or maybe something stronger?"

*

Sun's taxi had not waited and they called for another. This driver was a German and looked like a tough guy. Sun thought the Knoblauch people probably had their own favorite drivers who were willing to drive deep down into the Kreuzberg to pick up clients.

But after a few blocks he had another idea. After being closeted with people who made him feel clammy he wanted to get out and walk, even though a light drizzle was falling. He thought he could find his way back to the Korean restaurant he had seen and he could almost taste the peppers and the garlic. So he told the driver to let him out, he'd walk back himself.

But after only a few blocks on the same street he had to admit that it wasn't the same route; this second taxi had taken a different street north. He thought that if he turned left and walked a few blocks he could find the parallel main road up to the north. But the cross street he took kept winding back away from his route. When he tried a right turn and encountered an endless street with no businesses, no signs, no phone booths, he realized he was lost and that under the heavy clouds above he could no longer tell which direction was north. Ahead was a small square and Sun felt relief. There must be a bar or cafe where he could call for a cab. But when he stepped out into the square he could only see one bar and that one had an entrance crowded with young men in tank tops and black pants, all of them wearing heavy boots. And in a second he noticed they all had shaven heads. He would have retreated but he had already been noticed.

"Rudi! *Pass auf!*" And faces turned to him. A chorus of cheers erupted from the crowd around the door and many of them came loping towards him.

Now a tall man emerged from the door of the bar and parted the crowd, walking deliberately towards Sun. He had a solid round head, brutish brow, and a stupid grin on his face and Sun knew, this was the kind you could break your hands on, you would have to fracture bones to stop this kind of Neanderthal. Now the man was surrounded by his followers and Sun, not understanding the language could at least interpret the hostile shouting of the mob forming up in front of him.

Some were yelling "Jap," or "*Schlitauge*," which were terms that never improved his humor. So he bowed to the tall man, as he did to persons he would probably have to kill.

"I apologize for not knowing your language," he said. "I am a visitor in your country." All the time he was looking right to left, every member of the mob in front of him.

Rudi knew some English. "Ja! A visitor! Ve don't vant your kind here, dirty Jap! You come viss much money, buy business, ve lose jobs!

Ahah! thought Sun. *A gangster with a social conscience.*

"So it is a job you want?" he asked. "Fine. Get your car and drive me to the Kudamm and I will pay you one hundred."

There was a peal of laughter from those who could follow his English, and Sun was able to continue his examination of the crowd in front of him. Most of them were carrying sticks, or pipes, which was bad. The tall man facing him had a four foot length of steel pipe in his hand and Sun did not consider this a fair match. So while the crowd enjoyed their jokes he picked out his target. *If your opponent has a weapon, get a weapon yourself,* he told himself. Then in the background his searching eyes found a pudgy, fat-faced youth, yelling obscenities, but keeping himself well back behind his leader, a natural coward. He also held a long length of steel pipe. *There is my weapon,* thought Sun.

The tall man advanced. "Take all your clothes off, Jap! Denn ve let you go vit a beating!" And the chorus rose, "Ja! Take off, take off, take off!"

Sun started to shrug off his jacket, then pretended to unfasten his belt. At the last second he dashed forward, made a feint at the leader, Rudi, who was raising his steel pipe, then he cut hard to his right and threw himself at the fat youth. In a second he had broken his wrist and seized his length of pipe. Two hard kicks took down the nearest louts threatening him and without hesitation he reversed, blocked the blow that Rudi was swinging at him, then thrust the end of the pipe like a spear into the center of his forehead. Rudi went down like a ton of bricks and Sun took out the next man with a back swipe of the pipe. An attacker trying to cut inside the radius of his pipe received three fingers right in his eye and went down howling. Turning this way and that, dodging blows, or parrying with his pipe, Sun could see that there was a narrow alley in front of him now and he thought if he could run into it and force them to chase him one man at a time, the natural cowardice of bullies would prevail and he could get out of there. But unfortunately there were some real fighters in the mob. As he sprinted for the opening, a charging figure caught him from the side and knocked him off his feet, he twisted this way and that, avoiding blows, but some of them landed, and as he tried to regain his feet, a glancing blow from a club swiped him across the top of his head and he went down again. Now he could feel the crushing blows of kicks and a rain of clubs and pipes down on his arms and shoulders as he tried to duck. Finally a glancing blow on the top of his head dimmed his consciousness. His last thought was sadness at giving his long life up at last to such vermin.

*

Knoblauch heard the banging on the door and rushed down the back stairs. He threw the door open and saw the taxi driver upset, waving his arms.

"Herr Knoblauch! Your guest asked to get out and walk. I knew you were concerned so I followed him, a long way back. But he turned and went left into the Platz Ernst Sturm! You know what..."

"My God!" yelled Knoblauch. "Werner, bring the dogs!" There was a great scramble as Knoblauch, Werner Jaeger, and three Rottweilers piled into the taxi and it screeched off. They roared down the main street for several blocks and then as they squealed around a corner to the left they could hear the roaring of a crowd and pick out a sentence or two: "Kill him! Hit him in the balls! Break his fucking head! Fucking gook!..." At the entrance to the square Knoblauch barked orders. "Stop! Let the dogs out! Werner! Shoot into the crowd low, their legs!"

The Rottweilers made their point immediately. A few vicious snarls, a few crushed wrists and ankles started a quick migration out of the Platz. The few stalwarts who stood their ground and faced down the dogs with their sticks and pipes were shot down. Suddenly the square was empty again except for five writhing skinheads on the ground holding their legs and the big Rudi, who seemed dead. Knoblauch looked down at another motionless figure crumpled in the middle of the square. He advanced and knelt by his head. Sun was still breathing but the right side of his face was a sheet of blood. As Knoblauch examined him his eyes opened, startled at first, then relieved when he saw the worried face in front of him.

"What do you think? They broke some bones?" asked Knoblauch. The dogs had come back from the pursuit now, happily panting and wagging their tiny stub tails.

Sun took his time, wiggling one limb at a time, grimacing and wincing as shafts of pain cut through his consciousness. He made a major effort and turned over onto his back. He gave a deep sigh. "Let me just lie here a minute unless the police are coming or something."

"Nobody calls the police here," said Knoblauch. "Did you put that big Rudi on the ground? Man, that's some fighting!" Then he walked over to one of the skinheads with a bullet in his leg He barked in German.

"I have a message for your friends. You don't hang around in this square any more. If I see a skinhead one kilometer from my place he's a dead shithead! Understand?"

The youth looked up. He obviously knew who Knoblauch was and he cringed, expecting a blow.

"You garbage go somewhere else now. You see what a sixty-two year old man did to big Rudi? You better find some real weaklings to beat up from now on. You hear me?"

"Yes sir," said the wounded youth meekly.

"Werner, put Mr. Sun in the taxi and I'll take him back. You'll have to walk with the dogs." And Sun was gently helped into the taxi.

*

"You are lucky, you haff no broken bones," said Dr. Wilamowitz. "But you vill hurt like hell tomorrow!"

"I hurt like hell now," said Sun, with a grin. "But I enjoyed the exercise."

The doctor was smoothing a bandage over a cut on his forehead. She had had to put in a few stitches which Sun thought she had done remarkably painlessly, for a professional torturer. He had massive bruises on his thighs and shoulders and she had made her associates hold bags of ice on the larger ones for a few minutes to stop the swelling.

"We checked Rudi, Mr. Sun," said Knoblauch. "You killed the imbecile. Now the police will have to investigate but I don't think too much. If they ask us we will all say we heard they had a fight with another gang. No one will shed tears for Rudi, and his gang goes somewhere else now."

Sun was impressed with Knoblauch's organization.

Werner had shown him the small caliber handgun he had used to maim the skinheads and he had to admire his marksmanship.

"Ve put in the bullets small...small.."

"Light loads?" Sun prompted.

"Yah, not so much powder," Werner Jaeger said. "Is good for shooting legs. But if you vant to kill too, no problem." Sun thought the search for Castle was probably in competent hands. He was glad at least to have seen a demonstration.

They had managed to sponge the worst stains off his suit but he had a tear in one knee and a split seam under his left arm. There would be comment at his hotel.

Knoblauch was looking through his desk drawer for a card. "Here is a good men's couturier, and near your hotel. Give them my name and they will have a suit ready in two hours. And they charge it to me."

Sun started to protest but Knoblauch waved it off. "I am ashamed you come into my neighborhood and get beat up. It's the least I can do."

Sun was leaving for the second time, with stern instructions not to get out of the taxi until they hit the Kudamm and Jürgen Jaeger started cackling.

"Ilse! Your record is broken! Now you haff one live patient!"

"Ach, little Jürgi," she smiled. "Someday I'll tie you to your bed when you're sleeping and then we'll have some fun, I tell you!" Her voice was soft and inviting, as if she were talking to a lover, but it gave Sun the chills.

Chapter Twelve
Kali Vrisi

Now and then Thanassi found himself bullied into driving Manoli's sister Anna to Chania on shopping expeditions, her and her two teenage daughters. Anna was a big woman, tall like Manoli, with long arms and legs and abrupt movements. Her black hair was parted in the middle over her severe face. Anna's husband, another Manoli, was a fat little fisherman who faded into the background whenever Anna was around. On these drives she had given herself the mission of finding out Thanassi's mysterious life history and background and when he laughingly put off direct questions she would bring up stories she had heard about life in various American cities, New York, Chicago, Los Angeles, hoping that he would be tempted to supplement her information and give away his origins. Instead he would invent stories in response about events in Cheyenne, or Des Moines (she wanted to see how that was spelled and then accused him of lying), or Pawtuckett or Alamogordo. Whenever he pronounced the absurd name of a city the two daughters would giggle and carry on. Roula was the older at eighteen and the most brazen, making goo-goo eyes at Thanassi at every chance, or stretching exaggeratedly to allow him a view of her maidenly young breasts. Like her mother she was a nonstop talker and at those moments when Anna had finally given up her questioning mother and daughter would comment on the scenery, on towns they passed through, on the failings of most of Kali Vrisi's inhabitants, their voices rising dramatically in pitch as they made a telling point or two. Sometimes they would take turns talking but most of the time they spoke at the same time, a seemingly efficient way to increase the speed of communication with no discernible loss of comprehension.

Elli was seventeen and the quiet one, an almost identical younger version of Roula. Although she could giggle and chatter her share in a three-way conversation she rarely initiated one and she was shy with Thanassi, lowering her eyes and blushing when he addressed a remark directly to her.

Thanassi suspected that Anna might have picked him out as a prospective mate for Roula. Once on the way back to Kali Vrisi in the heat of the afternoon Anna pointedly made Elli sit in back with her and Roula lounged in the front seat, squirming and posturing in her shorts and inadequate halter all the way home until Thanassi felt as if the whole seat next to him was full of thighs, tits, and belly buttons. Her mother didn't say a word although Thanassi knew very well that Cretan mothers usually demanded excessive modesty of their daughters.

*

Now the tourists were in Kali Vrisi in full force, the end of July, and just waiting for the flood when most of Europe stopped working the last day of July and went on holiday. Thanassi had already seen his share of Germans and Scandinavians, the ones who had the good jobs and could take off earlier in the summer. Now the English were arriving, and the Irish and unfortunately the Australians. He had begun to believe that no Americans ever came to this part of Crete until one day when he had parked his Fiat at the end of town, seeing the endless rows of rental cars already crammed into all the available spaces in the long lane of eucalyptus trees. He started walking towards Manoli's taverna down the main street and halfway there he saw two men come out of a hotel down the block and walk in the same direction.

"Goddamn!" he thought, "Those are Americans!" And indeed they were unmistakable from the top down, the too small T shirts, the too long shorts, the long white gym socks, and the brand new Nike running shoes. And nerdy floppy white hats to keep them from skin cancer. One of the Americans was huge, lumbering along, the other was smaller, well built, but walking along like a penguin, his toes out. And both of them pale, pale white, ready for the sun to redden them, crisp them, send them indoors for days of agony, twisting on Kali Vrisi's hard mattresses.

So it was a profound shock when Thanassi drew abreast of them in the plateia and saw that they were Goomba and the FBI man, George Kiosoglou.

"Don't make a big deal out of this," he said out of the side of his mouth. "Follow me to a taverna and we'll sit at different tables."

He walked to the end of the beach, as far as he could get from Manoli's and sat down for a coffee at Yorgo's. Yorgo himself came out and asked, *"What's happening, Thanassi? You mad at Manoli or something?"* And Thanassi took his time and smiled and made small talk and then said, *"Hey Yorgo, go wait on those two Americans. They're helpless, fish out of water."*

After a few fruitless minutes Yorgo waved over to Thanassi. *"Hey, man, come talk to these dummies! They don't speak a word!"*

Thanassi ensconced himself at their table, arms folded, looking grim. "Okay, you guys, what the fuck is going on? WAIT!" He held up his hand. "Don't be giving me these dumb grins. I don't want everyone here to know you know me!"

So big Goomba, who'd been wanting to throw his arms around him had to settle down and pretend to be just another tourist needing menus to be translated.

"Danny! This is going to be hard to explain!"

"Okay, so you guys explain first. What the hell are you doing together? And how the hell did you get here?"

They looked at each other. Then Goomba spread his hands.

"Danny. Things are moving fast back home. We need your help. And believe me, you can get out of this with no sweat!"

Kiosoglou started to speak but Thanassi interrupted.

"In order, in order. I want to know, first, how you found me, second what you and this FBI guy are doing together, how you two became 'we,' and then, what exactly is moving fast back home? Alright?"

Yorgo was standing and watching from the door of his kitchen with his wife. "See," he said. "They say only Greeks wave their hands around and talk loud. Now look at them. And they are only discussing what they'll order!"

"Danny," said Goomba. "George and I been cooperating a long time. I'll get to that. But when he said we *had* to find you, I went and asked Katina where your grandparents came from. So we went to Chania and hired a private detective who checked car rentals the last two months even with your new name and nailed you in fifteen minutes. Where you think you are, New Guinea or something?"

Thanassi started to protest, but Goomba put up a huge hand. "Now here's the scary part. Katina said some pretty woman came by just a few weeks before and asked the same questions. Supposedly she was doing a survey for someone writing about Greek restaurant owners. But Kati never heard from these people again although they said they'd send copies of what they wrote."

"And we checked the ad that hired that lady," said Kiosoglou. "It showed up in entertainment trade papers, where out-of-work actors get part-time work. Totally untraceable, with a one-time phone number that doesn't work any more. You actually think there's somebody out there who doesn't know where you are?"

"But this is such a little village..." Thanassi was starting to say. Goomba broke in. "I looked in the post office. You got two fax machines in there. The postmaster's got a computer, you can send an e-mail if you know the address. For five hundred drachmas. I asked. Less than two bucks. In the square they got a phone booth, you buy a card next door, got a chip in it, put it in the phone and talk up to twenty minutes, to Athens, New York, Hong Kong! They don't even have that technology in the States yet! A block away they got an ATM, you can put in your bank card from back home, get fifty thousand drachmas." He pointed out to the street, where a little girl was leading a goat on a rope.

"Maybe this is a village where there are little girls leading goats around, but believe me, Danny, they are wired into the world. Some guy out there who was smart enough and with enough time could probably find you on the Internet."

Thanassi was quiet and Yorgo interpreted this as meaning

that the drink orders were all settled. He came up to the table, slammed his tray down in a friendly way, making Kiosoglou jump

"*So. They decide?*" he asked. "*Three cokes,*" ordered Thanassi.

"*For three cokes you discuss for five minutes?*" Yorgo showed no signs of moving.

"*The great big guy is in a bad temper,*" said Thanassi. "*I had to calm him down. He wanted to break the table because he was cheated last night in Chania.*"

Yorgo consulted Goomba's face, found it grim and foreboding. He looked at the weight of the forearms resting on his weak table and gave Goomba a sympathetic smile.

"*Oh, those masturbators in Chania! They give Crete a bad reputation!*" he said, and decided to leave before the big man felt any worse.

"What did you say?" asked Kiosoglou. Just then Roula and Elli walked slowly past the taverna, hand in hand, and when they caught Thanassi's eye, giggled and walked on more slowly, twitching their behinds under their flimsy cotton dresses.

"You see that, George?" Goomba smacked Kiosoglou on the arm, almost knocking him off his chair. "Now we know why this fuck is hanging out here. He's sitting here in paradise spending all his dough and bonking the local beauties!"

"Spending!" cried Thanassi. "I actually have a job here that pays me more than I can spend. And those girls are just kids! Their mother wants me to marry the oldest one. That's why she's always shaking her ass at me like that!"

"Well, now that you mentioned it, it's the money aspect we need to talk to you about," said Kiosoglou. And Goomba nodded, serious now. Thanassi saw that a longer discussion would be required so he sighed and told them both.

"Look. Pretend you're going for a walk on the road north out of town. Give me about fifteen minutes and I'll pick you up in my car. We can go to my house and talk this over."

*

"First of all, what are you two guys doing together?" demanded Thanassi. "Are we all on the same side now or what?"

They were sitting in the shade of the olive trees behind Thanassi's house, drinking lemonade, Goomba wolfing down a big piece of bread covered with olive oil and fresh goat cheese. Goomba started to talk but his mouth was too full so George Kiosoglou spoke first.

"Okay, picture this. Last May you had just left this guy's house on your motorcycle. I come in the back way, walk into the garage and find Goomba here looking at one big dead Korean, guy I know right away as Moon, runs all the major hijacking on the docks for Herschel Jolly. So I go, 'Looks like you could use some help,' some dumb shit like that, and first he wants to fight me."

"Yeah, so he pulls out his niner," said Goomba, wiping his mouth, "And I'm like, 'Oh boy, now what?'"

"Anyway," went on Kiosoglou, "I explained that the feds were really interested in the connection between Jolly and Ottie Shamus and that killing mobsters was a matter between him and the Santa Monica P.D."

"And so I go, 'Killing? What killing? Looks to me like he slipped, tried too much weight on the bar, something like that.' And George here..."

"I told him we had to talk but we had to dispose of Moon first, which feds aren't supposed to get involved in—it's in all the FBI manuals—but there were what they call overarching concerns and I asked Goomba what he was thinking of and he said feeding the sharks up around Point Mugu..."

"Bad idea," said Thanassi, interrupting. "I used to surf south of there, just where the body would drift. Major curl. Everybody goes there on a good day. Either the surfers would find the body or you'd be bringing a whole bunch of sharks right into the middle of a good surfing ground."

Goomba laughed. "Yeah? George gave me about six other reasons it was a bad idea. That makes eight. Anyway..."

"Anyway," went on Kiosoglou, "I told Goomba, why don't we wait until tonight, then we'll dump Moon down on the docks in San Pedro. It'll look like he had an argument with his pals or something."

"Amazing!" said Thanassi. "So what happened?"

"We're not exactly sure," said Goomba, "Except that they seem to've bought it. Them and the cops, both."

"Well! That's the end of the connection to me, right?" asked Thanassi, hopefully."

"Wrong!" pronounced Kiosoglou, pointing a finger directly at Thanassi's chest. "What happened was that this other Korean, Sun, took over on the docks. He's older and smarter than Moon, way I figure. They had a great racket with their own mob in Inchon, knew what was going to be in every container docking in San Pedro, stole millions of bucks worth of running shoes."

"Running shoes? There's money in that?" Thanassi was incredulous.

"Yeah, running shoes," said George. "Would you

believe that this designer brand running shoe, made in some sweatshop in Korea, if you put a pair on the scale, costs three times as much per pound as filet mignon at a fancy butcher shop? In the mall in America, anyway. The point is, that Sun took over on the docks, we had a major operation to nab everyone and we got everyone but Sun. He disappeared and my hunch is that Jolly used the opportunity to send him after you! So. What do you think about that?"

Thanassi grew serious. "George, I appreciate the work you're putting in on this. But how is a Korean going to show up on southern Crete?"

"That's what we don't know. But here's what we do know. Jolly's real estate deal is about to fall through. It started out as Pacific Estates, then it became Mountain Meadows, and it's now Malibu Horizons. Originally there was a little bit of National Forest land in there and the developers offered a trade of some land they somehow owned on the northwest for some National Forest land on the southeast. A congressman from Ohio, of all places, very quietly attached a rider to an appropriation bill, rider's titled, 'National Forest enhancement adjustment,' supposed to look like he's improving our National Forest. Nobody woulda said anything except this freshman congressperson from Santa Monica just happened to look into it and she's thinking, 'What the hell is some guy from Ohio doing messing around with a National Park in my district?'"

"Mandy Clark," said Goomba. "Good woman. I sure voted for her."

"Right. So Ms Clark, instead of doing the traditional thing, like going up to Mr. Ohio congressman and asking, you know, like 'What the fuck're you doing in my district?'—she comes straight to the FBI and says this guy is a crook, he doesn't know the Santa Monica Mountains from the Alps. And she threatens to bring it up on the floor of the House."

"Right on, Mandy!" said Goomba. "Did you vote for her, Danny?"

"Hey, man, I'm a convicted felon, you forget? But I will vote for her if I can get this thing quashed, couple of years from now, or whatever."

"That's what I'm trying to say," said George, patiently. "Mr. Ohio congressman, when we started asking him questions, just completely folded. He thought we had more evidence than we did so when we promised him immunity he mentioned some bonds a true supporter had contributed to his campaign fund. And where in his legal campaign accounts can we find the record of these bonds? we ask. He gets very embarrassed and says there was a mistake he just found out about and was going to rectify and he's eternally grateful to us for reminding him 'cause he didn't want to besmirch his honorable record, blah, blah, blah. But, bottom line, what happened, he says, is that a loyal aide accidently transferred the bonds to Mr. congressman's personal overseas account."

"Oh yeah?" said Thanassi. "And what kind of bonds were these?"

"Dead Philadelphians," said Goomba.

"Matthias Wingerden?"

"You got it! Lower Schuylkill sanitation district, or whatever. The same bonds we stole from Jolly," said Goomba.

"Hey, wait! What do you mean, 'We,'?" burst out Thanassi.

George started to speak but Goomba cut him off.

"I told them everything, man. And listen, you gotta

believe, no one is going to prosecute us for stealing from Herschel Jolly. It's almost like a public service. The thing is, they need to know about the rest of the bonds. If they can get consecutive serial numbers, our bonds, other bonds, Ohio congressman bonds, they can nail Ottie Shamus and Jolly and the developers and the lawyers who are fronting for them."

"But..." Thanassi was thinking quickly. "But, how can the feds get Swiss banks to give them serial numbers on bonds? All that stuff is completely secret, isn't it?"

"Well, yes and no," said Kiosoglou. "Thing is, a few years back, we managed to embarrass some Swiss banks about Jewish deposits they'd been sitting on for the last fifty years, when they knew for sure that the owners had been gassed at Auschwitz or wherever. Along the line we managed to broker a little arrangement about revealing mob money, when we had good evidence. And that's what we need right now. You give us the serial numbers of those bonds and we can find out who has banked bonds with consecutive serial numbers."

Kiosoglou just looked at Thanassi, waiting. Thanassi was thinking of lying, telling him that he didn't know the numbers, but he did. So he thought about it for a minute.

"And what happens to me, and Goomba here, and Costa? What happens to our bonds, if we give you the numbers?"

"Well, first. You can't just give us the numbers. You have to testify before a federal Grand Jury. Grand Jury has the right to file charges for almost anything. But I don't see them filing charges against you."

"Yeah. But can we keep the money?"

Goomba and Kiosoglou looked at each other and laughed.

"That's the gray area," said Goomba. "We talked this over time and again. 'Cause we don't know how the bonds got into Herschel Jolly's hands. We have no record of a big theft. There is no record that Jolly ever bought the bonds. That's the whole thing with bearer bonds. No records."

"The deal is," Kiosoglou explained. "If we go to court and everything, with all the publicity, and someone comes out of nowhere and says, 'Hey those are my bonds,' and has some kind of evidence, then you guys are going to wind up in court."

"But the thing that worries me more," said Thanassi. "Is when we're back in the States testifying, what's Jolly going to be doing the whole time. Getting the meat hooks ready?"

"Ah, yes," said Kiosoglou. "Maybe you don't have to worry so much any more. Let me tell you a story."

*

George Kiosoglou had been on duty and got the call. It was mid-morning in Los Angeles. "George, we think Herschel is moving."

"What do you mean, 'You think'? Can't you see him?"

"It's the Merc with the dark windows. Came out of his underground basement. It's moving...uh...right now, east on Sunset, taking its time. Where are you, can you join the chase?"

"I'm downtown. I'm outta here. Keep up with me on my car phone and I'll try to hit Sunset at the 101. He turns before then, let me know."

Jolly's Mercedes stayed east on Sunset, heading downtown, and Kiosoglou was able to catch up to the chase east of the 101 freeway. They were moving through the Silverlake district of Los Angeles when the Mercedes signalled a left and turned at a stoplight. George was well behind the drab FBI car, a ten year old Plymouth van, and because of that was stuck at the light. He would have turned against the light anyway except the traffic was heavy in the other direction and when he finally got the green the oncoming traffic was even heavier. At last he just took a chance and cut in front of a slow moving customized low-rider Chevy and accelerated north along the cross street, hoping he'd catch the chase before it turned a corner.

He didn't have to worry. Eight blocks up there was congestion and the FBI van now had a portable flasher on its roof. As he parked behind it there was a scream of sirens and two LAPD black-and-whites moved in to block the street in both directions, roof racks flashing.

George got out and ran around the black and-white in front of him and the van, holding his FBI buzzer high up in the air. The Merc looked a mess. A big weapon, a shotgun by the looks of it, had taken out the driver's side window and gone through to wipe out the passenger's window as well. More than one shot had been fired and the driver's side door was pockmarked with holes, big holes, meaning the kind of shotgun loads meant for bear, or more frequently, for humans.

He joined an FBI colleague and two uniformed cops at the side of the Mercedes. They were all looking front seat, back seat, searching in vain for whomever had caught the blasts.

"No blood." said one of the cops, obviously disappointed.

"Where the fuck's the driver then?" asked the other.

As if in response, a head emerged slowly from the space below the steering wheel. It was a round head, closely cut black hair, the forehead was running with sweat, and the police would remember the rest of their days the eyes, brown eyes, open as wide as they would ever get, almost spinning, asking the question, am I alive, could I possibly be...?

They finally helped Manny out of the car and sat him down on the curb, where he sat, his head in his hands, just breathing in and out deeply. Finally he was able to talk.

"You guys...? Can you do me a favor? I give you some bills, fifty bucks, whatever, I don't care...before we go talk this over, I gotta say, I shit my pants. Can we stop, like a men's store, buy some clothes, let me wash up in the bathroom, put on the shorts and the new pants? Christ! Is that too much to ask?" And he started to cry.

"I dunno, man," said one of the cops. "I ain't takin' you in in my unit, smell it all up."

The other policeman looked over at the FBI van driver, then at George Kiosoglou.

"Hey, me neither, man. We got the FBI here. You know I hate to give up jurisdiction but hell, they're the feds, man. And this is their case!" The two cops laughed hilariously.

"Course, what we gotta do is follow the feds downtown, get a copy of their report. Have to do that, guys. But, what the hell, we get the glory all the time. Now it's your turn."

"Uh...there's a Ross Dress-for-Less four blocks down on Sunset," added the other cop. They both started laughing uncontrollably again.

The FBI van driver was furious. "I'm not getting the joke here! The guy I'm tailing is shotgunned in a major killing attempt and you jerkoffs are sitting around here laughing your asses off! Did anyone get the license, make of car, anything remotely professional like that?"

The first cop stopped laughing, but he couldn't get rid of the smile.

"Sorry, agent. We wouldn't of been hanging around here except that the perp's car hit a truck, high speed, trying to get back on the freeway. We got him back there, just go up to the corner, turn right, turn right again and you'll see the gumballs down a few blocks. He hit the truck right in front of a CHP unit. They been on our radio last few minutes."

Down near the freeway everyone was standing around the old Volvo sedan, battered, facing the wrong way just at the freeway onramp. The driver was outside, bloody face, being cuffed. He looked Latino. Police were going through his pockets and carefully wrapping a shotgun in a couple of big garbage bags.

Downtown LAPD and FBI had talked about jurisdiction and because attempted murder was a State offense the feds handed off to the Los Angeles DA's office. But the police had agreed that federal officers could debrief Manny privately first, which they did after he had freshened up and changed clothes.

∗

"We thought Manny would clam up as usual," said George "We couldn't hold him on anything and I'm fully expecting him to say it was just 'road rage,' or something.and walk out on us. But instead he tells all. Jolly'd been getting threats from his father-in-law in New Orleans, Edward Charbon, the major menace down there. Manny says Jolly had to borrow money on the street for his real estate deal and nothing was happening and he wasn't paying back."

"So they send a guy to shoot Jolly? That's a dumb way to collect a debt!" said Thanassi.

"We figure the hit man *knew* Jolly wasn't in the car. He was just sending a message."

"Nice for Manny!"

"Yeah. That was his take on it too. Manny is really Aristide Manfredoni—that's his real name. His father owns a garage in Hawthorne and he claims he's just a driver but he seemed to know a lot more than a driver. Anyway, by now he's long gone, headed back east he told us, take it easy for a while."

"Tell him about the hit man," said Goomba, who'd been sitting there enjoying the story and Thanassi's reactions.

"Oh yeah, the hit man. He had no ID on him, naturally, stole the car, just walked in and bought the shotgun at a sporting goods store. And a box of 10 gauge shells although that's supposed to be illegal, guns and ammo at the same time. He puts five loads through the windows of Jolly's car, we're wondering how Manny can still hear. Then the genius blows the getaway and in his pocket he's got a keycard to his room at the New Otani Hotel downtown. We go there and find all his ID, Jacques Piccomini, from Plaquemines, Louisiana. Got a return ticket to New Orleans. We called the law there. Sheriff at Plaquemines Parish says he's a shooter, how'd we ever catch him?"

"He stole a *Volvo?*"asked Thanassi incredulously.

"Bottom line," said Goomba, "Is that Herschel Jolly is in big trouble. He has to make payoffs to politicians to get his development approved but now he's short of money and he thinks his father-in-law wants to kill him. I been talking this over with George a long time."

"But the Dead Philadelphians?" asked Thanassi. "The bonds. He must have some of those left. How much are they worth, face value? Don't tell me they're worthless!"

Yanni came walking up to Thanassi's house. He grinned at the two other men and sat down as if he was willing and eager to join in the discussion.

"*Yanni, these are some other Americans,*" said Thanassi in

Greek. *"They want me to tell them places to visit, good swimming, good fishing, things like that."*

"Sure. You know all those places," answered Yanni. *"Yorgo down in town said he thought you knew them from before. Back in America?"*

"You see!" Thanassi spread his hands in wonder. "You guys're in town for what, ten minutes, and everybody knows you're old friends of mine!" Then he turned to Yanni. *"I just wanted to know the football scores from home, that's all!"*

"So now, quick, tell me scores and stuff, how are the Dodgers doing? Tell me numbers and stuff. This guy is a real good friend. He's supposed to be simple but I dunno. In some ways he's the sharpest guy I ever met."

"I can understand most of what you're saying," said George. "Should I let on I know Greek?"

"No, no, no! Bad move! *They lost again, my team!"* said Thanassi, trying now to talk to both Yanni and the Americans.

"Well, we're still trying to find out how your team the Dead Philadelphians did," said Goomba. "But that's another whole deal that needs a lot of explaining. I can't figure it out, George here is having trouble, maybe we could get the Secretary of the Treasury, or what's his name, Greenspan, or like that to make sense of it. Have you talked to a banker anywhere, where you put your Philadelphians?"

Yanni sat listening smiling peacefully. He'd gotten a piece of bread and cheese and was nibbling at it.

"You gotta realize, I came here in a hurry from...from where I left my bonds. Well. Shit. Zurich, all right? I opened an account at a private bank I had an introduction to, guy I met in the joint gave me the name. This Doctor...they all seem to be doctors there, he was really impressed at this stack of bonds and he asked first thing, 'Where are the coupons?' So I told him we got the bonds, they were mature already."

"Hey! What's that mean?" asked Goomba.

"*You have long games in America? Here not much happens—one goal, two goals—then they all jump on the man who kicked the goal,*" said Yanni.

"*Yes, but we have lots of games, basketball, baseball, volleyball,*" said Thanassi. "*I want to know all the scores.*"

Now he saw his neighbor, the other Yorgo, come wandering into his yard. Old Yorgo looked around, asked everyone's health and sat down, sighing, giving the impression that the conversation could start now, now that he was here.

"*The Americans are telling Thanassi the volleyball scores,*" said Yanni to Yorgo.

"*That's a wonderful thing,*" said Yorgo, "*I didn't know you cared about volleyball! And don't they play in the winter there in America?*"

"*Sometimes the summer too,*" said Thanassi. "Listen, I'll explain later. My neighbor, Yorgo..." Yorgo smiled at Goomba and George. "Yorgo can understand a little English."

"Yes, English...I speak...San Francisco...many years...I was sailor, you know, sailor? On ship?" Yorgo gave them a toothless grin.

"Okay, you guys, what I gotta do now is get up, make some more lemonade, maybe bring out the ouzo, bring some olives, nuts, some more bread and cheese. Come on, give me a hand." And Thanassi got up, gesturing to Yanni and Yorgo, *no, no, don't get up, I'll bring something to drink, some mezé, it's a hot day.*

Chapter Thirteen
Zurich

Sun was sitting in Dr. Liebling's office at the Liebling Bank, GmbH., in Zurich. It didn't feel like a bank. There was no big glass door, no lobby, no ATMs outside. He'd come up a residential street looking for the address, thinking he was on the wrong street, but there it was, a solid door, no sign of any kind, with a speaker phone. You couldn't even speak into the phone unless you knew the numbers to punch onto the keypad under the phone. Sun had been told the numbers over the phone from his hotel when he made the appointment.

Two flights up in the elevator and then he was in a small anteroom facing a stern middle-aged woman behind a desk. She was not expecting an Asian and her face tightened.

"I am Mr. Sun," said Sun in the friendliest tone he could manage. Sometimes racism even amused him. "Dr. Liebling is expecting me."

Dr. Liebling was not expecting an Asian either, but it didn't bother him. Sun's new suit got a second look and almost a nod of approval. Liebling was a stocky man of about sixty, receding gray hair, cold blue eyes behind rimless glasses, and doing his best to pretend that he was relaxed and good natured. He spoke excellent English, virtually without an accent.

"Your principal wishes to deposit a considerable sum, you say? What would you regard as considerable?"

Sun resisted the urge to sit forward in his chair and be earnest. It was always better to be relaxed yourself, as if you were just passing the time of day. He waved his hand.

"That depends. The securities are unusual. I cannot estimate their worth. Would it help if I said that the face value is approximately twelve million US dollars?"

Dr. Liebling now relaxed even more and smiled a thin smile. *Now,* his body language seemed to say, *we are talking about real matters and I am not just wasting my time.*

"Mr. Sun. If you could be more precise about the nature of these financial instruments, perhaps I could consult local experts. Zurich is not without its resources." They both laughed politely. Sun was thinking how invigorating it would be to throw Dr. Liebling together with his armchair out the window in back of him.

"I have a facsimile of one, and they are all the same," said Sun. "But before I reveal its identity we should have some sort of agreement. Confidentiality, of course, and a contractual arrangement—nothing complicated, just an understanding that you and my principal have agreed to do business."

"It is not necessary to explain more, Mr. Sun." Dr. Liebling was almost jovial now. "Swiss banking laws define precisely the various sorts of arrangement you are talking about. Elise outside no doubt has blank forms in her files. If not, she can access a form on her computer and we can edit it at will to suit your concerns, ja?" Then his face became more serious.

"As to confidentiality, I must confess that certain interests have pressured certain governments into forcing the Swiss government to relax our previously impervious laws of confidentiality." He looked around, as if afraid of being overheard, then inspected Sun thoroughly once again, as if reassuring himself that his visitor was not Jewish.

"The Jews." He said, almost in a whisper. Then he became affable again. "And of course you may have heard that Swiss banks have revealed deposits made by what the media calls the 'Mafia.' Any reports you may have heard are of course wildly exaggerated." He chuckled and Sun allowed himself to be amused as well, with a brief rumble of mirth at the very notion. He was actually wondering what Liebling's reaction would be if he explained that his client was not only Jewish but a mobster.

"No, no, Doctor. We are not talking about Jewish deposits or so-called mob money. This is just a substantial sum that has been in a certain family for a long time and may or may not be worth its face value. In fact, one of the reasons I came to you was that I was informed that you are one of the world's experts at analyzing financial documents that are...shall we say, out of the ordinary."

"Quite so, quite so. And therefore, our arrangement should specify that if you do not, in fact, choose to deposit these securities in our bank, that you promise to pay our hourly consulting fee for establishing the exact market value of whatever it is you wish us to investigate."

This was proceeding the way Sun intended. "That is completely satisfactory, Doctor." He found himself leaning forward in his chair and forced himself to relax again. He could imagine the size of the consulting fee and determined not to ask. He was sure Jolly wouldn't pay it anyway.

"Shall we have a look at the printed agreements."

The banker looked almost shocked. "Oh, certainly not! I shall leave you with Elise...Frau Stockner. I have no expertise in these matters. That is her kingdom. She would be offended if I interfered!"

Sun spent a miserable hour with Frau Stockner, having every motive questioned, every doubt raised about his securities, his trustworthiness, his credentials as a financial representative. She finally expressed surprise when he revealed that he was not, in fact, a lawyer. Her face turned to stone and she said, "But Doctor Liebling cannot sign an agreement except with a lawyer."

Sun stood up. "Very well. I believe I have heard that there are other bankers available in Zurich. Some of them have been perfectly happy to sign agreements with thieves and mass murderers in the past and may not be so particular."

Frau Stockner immediately realized she had gone too far. She swiftly found an appropriate form on her computer that could be adjusted to the circumstances.

"If you believe you could sign this for your principal, Dr. Liebling will see you at the same time tomorrow."

Sun simply nodded his agreement and left, with a sudden random fantasy of Frau Stockner actually meeting Herschel Jolly under adverse circumstances. A mental image of Frau Stockner suspended from the lube racks brightened his day.

Liebling took one look at the facsimile of the bearer bond the next day, looked quickly up at Sun, then back again at the visage of Matthias Wingerden and the face value of the bond, $100,000. Once again Sun was told he should return the next day at the same hour.

"If I think it will take longer to trace this bond, I shall phone your hotel. You will have your evening free? Have you perhaps never eaten at Petermann's? It is the best restaurant, just outside of Zurich. Reservations are impossible but we have a special arrangement with the management and Elise will call for you."

Sun had Frau Stockner phone for a reservation just to give her trouble. Later on, he called the Korean consulate in Zurich and a friendly receptionist gave him the name of a little Korean restaurant downtown near the consulate. There he spent one of the few enjoyable evenings in the last few months eating searing, garlicky foods and talking and laughing away the hours with his countrymen, the few people in the world who understood honor and courtesy and humor and friendship and the pleasures of companionship.

*

"I was fortunate to identify your securities almost immediately," said Dr. Liebling. "It took only about four hours of research." Dr. Liebling had actually found out everything he needed to know within fifteen minutes because he had heard of the deposit of the Dead Philadelphians a month before from a friend at another bank. A swift call to his friend and the promise of a fee of five hundred Swiss francs, to be charged to his client, had elicited the required information.

"These bonds were issued in 1973 to redesign and construct a major sewage system for the city of Philadelphia. They were revenue bonds, to be repaid from taxes and utility fees. You understand, ja?" Sun nodded.

"The term was ten years. Investors buying these bonds could clip off one of the attached twenty coupons every six months and cash them to any bank as accrued interest. From what I know, the bonds still on the open market are mature, and their coupons have all been cashed in."

"Mature," said Sun. "This means that they are worth their face value?"

"Well, there is a problem. You see, the First National

Bank of Upper Darby served at first as the brokerage bank."

"So. It's a bank. What's the problem?" asked Sun. He was beginning to be glad it wasn't his money.

"You understand, as the sanitation district collected its taxes and utility fees—many of them substantial because there are state and federal facilities using the system and quite a few industries—they were deposited in the bank of Upper Darby to pay off the coupons and eventually the whole loan. Do you see what I mean?"

"I think so," said Sun. "At some time within those ten years the sanitation district deposited the whole repayment of the loan into the bank to pay off the bond holders."

"Exactly. And all the bonds were redeemed in the normal manner. Except for twenty million worth that never appeared again."

"But now some of those bonds have reappeared," said Sun.

"Is there any reason the Bank of Upper Darby would not pay off the debt, considering that they have already collected the required sums."

"Ah. Now it is necessary to discuss the laws regulating banking in the United States. And specifically the laws during the regime of your most admired President Reagan which *deregulated* banking."

If Sun had been among friends he would have said, "Uh oh!" But he just smiled, leaning back in his chair. "These are the details we particularly wanted to learn, Dr. Liebling. Please go on."

"You see, the First National Bank of Upper Darby, like many other banks in the eighties, made numerous loans on commercial real estate which, shall we say, turned out to be overly optimistic."

Sun thought that Dr. Liebling was having entirely too

much fun with this topic.

"So they went in the toilet?"

"In the toilet. Yes, I see. Ha ha. No, not completely, Mr. Sun. The bank no longer exists, but before it closed its doors it sold its assets at a discount to the Longhorn Savings and Loan Bank of Bryan, Texas. You may wonder how a debt can be considered an asset, but we bankers do this all the time."

Sun smiled. "And now you're going to tell me what happened to the Longhorn Savings and Loan, aren't you?"

"Well. Yes. Longhorn went bankrupt in 1990 and its creditors were guaranteed part of their money by the federal government, through the Federal Deposit Insurance. This is evidently a uniquely American institution which allows bankers to engage in foolish and irresponsible practices and then have the American taxpayer pay off the money they have lost their depositors."

Sun realized that Liebling would not be talking in this plummy, self-satisfied fashion if he had bought some Upper Schuylkill bonds himself at face value. He decided to bring the meeting to a head.

"Then I must tell you, Dr. Liebling, that within a few days I expect a large consignment of these Schuylkill bearer bonds. Can you give me an estimate of their value."

Liebling was through fooling around. He looked Sun directly in the eye and said, "Fifteen cents on the dollar. You spoke of twelve million? This would be now one million, eight hundred thousand dollars, minus banking fees. By our agreement you are to pay our consulting fee for four hours time of, let me see the rate today for Swiss francs...yes rounded off, about two thousand dollars. Naturally, should you deposit your funds in this bank in the near future your fee will be returned. I am sorry if there was a disappointment?"

Sun spread his hands. "My client will not be pleased. For myself, I am on straight salary. At any rate, it's only money." Sun smiled and the smile became even broader when he saw the shock on Liebling's face at this heresy.

*

Sun was at a private phone in the extensive business facility that his hotel made available to guests. After almost a day he had made arrangements to receive a conference call from Herschel Jolly and someone else, he wasn't sure, from what he'd been told by the woman at Jolly's office. It was eight in the morning, meaning that Jolly would be calling from California at eleven in the evening the day before.

The call came through and the international operator asked him to identify himself. "All parties are on the line, sir," she said. "Go ahead with your call."

"Sun!" said a familiar voice. "I'm talking here with Eddie Charbon, from New Orleans. He's sort of like family. Eddie, say hello to Sun."

A low rumble acknowledged the introduction.

"Anyways, what's the deal with our friends in Berlin?"

"The plan seemed appropriate and well thought out. I approved it and expect to hear from them as soon as they get the information so I can make the transfer."

"So. What about the bonds?"

"The banker recommended to me did some research and says the market value is fifteen cents on the dollar."

"Jesus Christ!" expostulated Charbon. "That's only one point eight mil!"

"Unfortunately, I believe his figures are correct. He knew the history of the various banks that had difficulties about seven...."

"Christ, Herschel!" Charbon burst out. "How many of these you handed out already? Some politician finds out you gave him fifteen cents you're going to be dead meat!"

Jolly sounded strangely calm and resigned. "That was my first, uh, consignment. And I only got a few more, about three mil, face value. But when I got the bonds I traded a few offshore, a discount, you know what I mean, but they traded at face value."

"And when did you pick up these great bonds?"

"Let's see, I remember thinking Dukakis is going to win, so I sold this option I had in Florida..."

"Come on, come on! Eighty-eight. So they were still good then. Why didn't you cash them then?"

"Well, selling the option was something that couldn't show up on the books and I didn't want fifteen mil showing up anywhere either, so..."

"Okay, okay! No reason your guy Sun has to listen to all this shit. Let's make it fast. Here's the deal, Sun. Your boss here and me are partners now. Right, Herschel?"

"Yeah, like he says."

"He explained what's going on there in Greece. So when you get the transfer information, put it in that Swiss guy's bank. Jolly's going to send you the rest he's got, the three mil, and you put that in too. And tell your banker to liquidate!"

"Shit! We'll have to take a discount on that too," moaned Jolly.

"Yeah? We already got discounted eighty-five percent. Now let's get rid of the fucking things. Next year we might get a Democrat again as chair of the Senate Banking Committee and who knows what the hell'll happen."

"You're right. Sun, do what Eddie here says..."

"And listen! You in touch with those guys went to Greece?"

"I expect them to check in when they move into their villa in Chania."

"Good. Listen. Have them go ahead as they planned. But if it isn't working out, tell them not to make a fuss, get any attention. Just tell 'em to whack him. Got that?"

Sun spoke carefully. "Mr. Jolly, I'd like to clarify our relationship. When I work for you I guarantee complete loyalty. Do I understand that I am now working for Mr. Charbon too?"

Charbon interrupted. "Listen, pal, just do what I tell you or you're in big trouble."

There was silence on the line for a minute. Then Jolly spoke.

"Uh, Eddie, when Sun agrees he's working for you, you got a great deal. It's a Korean thing, they never back away."

Sun could just picture the New Orleans mobster mulling over this unpleasant message, someone he couldn't order around. Sun didn't mind. If he got insulted in this deal he'd take a trip to New Orleans, straighten things out, then try out some of that great food they were supposed to have down there. Eddie Charbon sounded to him like soft goods, someone who'd been on top too long without paying the dues.

Maybe Charbon had shared the thought. "Okay, Mr. Sun," he said. "This is the deal. Your boss has agreed to be my partner. And if I ast you to do something, it's like he ast you, you got that straight?"

"That's what we agreed," said Jolly.

"Then that's the deal," said Sun. "Your orders, Mr. Charbon's orders, that's what I'll do. And also, if you are not available to pay my salary and expenses then I assume that Mr. Charbon will do so." He made it a statement, rather than a question.

"That's the deal, then," said Jolly. Sun noticed that Charbon had said nothing.

"Until the transfer, then," he said, and hung up.

Later that night Sun was at the Korean restaurant again enjoying himself. When he went to the men's room another Korean came in behind him and checked to see if the booth was empty. Sun relaxed, waiting for trouble but the other man smiled and spoke rapidly in Korean.

"Sun. I'm Kim, from the consulate. You can probably guess the department. Listen, I saw you here last night and told my boss. We wanted to know, are you free at the moment?"

"Kim. Yes I think I know of you. I'm not really available right now, just finishing something up. But I will be next month. What's up?"

"We could use an independent contractor in Hong Kong, straighten out a little situation there. An easy job, good pay and you'll love the food and night life. Give me a call when you're ready."

Sun went to bed that night happier than he'd been for months. He figured he'd never have to work for Americans again.

PART THREE

Chapter Fourteen
The Great Adventure

A FEW DAYS LATER Goomba and George Kiosoglou were at the airport at Chania, standing in a long line for check-in. They had an hour flight back to Athens before them, a five hour wait there at a different airport, then a United flight to Heathrow and finally a three hour wait for United back to LAX. They weren't looking forward to it.

"Fucking FBI, couldn't you at least get business class?" asked Goomba. "I don't really fit into those little seats."

"Are you kidding! Remember President Bush, that fat chief of staff he had, took first-class once and got nailed! Had to resign. And you think *we* can go business class?"

They were closer to the check-in counter by now and had successfully headed off three large Greek families trying to cut in front of them, all of them smiling blandly and pretending not to understand the system.

"You think he'll go for it?" asked George.

"I dunno. It's hard to say. You know that's a great life there Danny's having, the sun, the sea, good food, great looking young broads..."

"Yeah but don't forget, there's no cable, no American shows, no..."

"Sure! How often do you watch some bullshit all the

way through on TV? Nine commercials a half hour? And Danny can watch the Greek shows if he wants. Hell, he never watched TV at home much. We used to catch the Dodgers now and then, or the Rams, then the losers went to St. Louis..."

"No, what I'm saying. Some day he's going to want to come home, see his family, sit in his restaurant—it's his, after all, it was in the will—and, you know, be an American. Shit, Goomba, I'm Greek too. I love this place. But I could never come back here and live forever, you know what I mean?"

"Yeah, I do. And I think what Danny would like, is have both, a place here, and a good life back in the States too, he could go back and forth, if he could afford it and if the mob doesn't have a contract out on him. But we have no idea what kind of income we're going to get from those Dead Philadelphians. How come the damn FBI doesn't know?"

George knew but he wasn't telling yet. Now he pointed.

"Look, our plane is in. Look at the Germans coming off it!" And there was a parade of Teutons on holiday coming into the terminal, mixed with the Greek commuters from the Olympic Airlines Airbus. Their attention was caught by a party of four marching their way on the other side of the barrier: two big blond muscular men, looking like brothers, both wearing shorts, Hawaiian shirts tucked in, and sandals with white socks; then an older couple, a darker man who looked Greek, wearing jeans, and a thin wiry woman, dark grey eyes, with her colorless hair pulled back severely. She was wearing a warmup suit and running shoes and looked fit enough to go out and run ten miles or so. One of the blond men had crazy eyes and was turned around trying to say something to the woman over the din in the terminal. He guffawed and she gave him a thin smile.

"That's a weird group," said Kiosoglou. "You know in our training we would have a notation on a group like that coming through an airline terminal, a bus station, whatever. It would say, 'Unusual profile, have another look.' You know? Three guys and an older woman? Not your usual holiday grouping."

"I would bust the two guys right off for the socks with sandals," said Goomba. "Here we go, the line's moving, maybe we can get on at last."

*

The news flew through Kali Vrisi like a hot evening wind off the mountain. Elias and Katerini were finally going to get married and Manoli told Thanassi not to go wandering away for the next few days; there'd be a lot of work, and extra pay. The young couple had been formally engaged for three years, and everywhere in the Greek countryside that was considered sufficient for them to move in together and start housekeeping. The financial arrangements had long ago been settled between the families and that was the important part. But now Katerini was visibly pregnant and all parties had agreed that a big wedding and an even bigger celebration was in order. The last really memorable gathering had taken place almost a year ago when Kostas Hadjimikalakis had his eightieth nameday and his seventy-three descendants gave him a party.

The church was decorated by the priest and a number of local matrons, under the demanding supervision of Manoli's sister Anna. The celebration, as usual, would take over the entire plateia down at the bottom of town, the beach to the south, Manoli's taverna to the east, the post office and city hall to the west. The plateia preparations were thought to be men's work and most of the males of Kali Vrisi who weren't actually working spent a whole day collecting tables from all over town, as well as the sawhorses and boards that would be covered with butcher paper to support the masses of food and drink. A mournful parade of lambs was collected and led up the road to Fotis' long green butcher shed where they disappeared in one door and came out another butchered and skinned and ready to be hung on trees by willing volunteers. Boys stood around with palm fronds and kept most of the flies off the carcasses.

Stores of the fiery *tsikoudiá* and the locally homemade brown wine were collected. The wine was of various grades. Everyone in the valley who had space for vines tried to grow at least some grapes and after the long established Cretan custom the grapes were all pressed together, red and white, up the valley at the tiny village of Agia Eleni where the wine cooperative was. After the barrels were stored in the sun for a month or two to "cook" and raise the alcohol content, the various producers collected their shares, according to how many kilos they'd brought in. Small growers generally drank all their wine in one year but the big producers kept huge barrels where they'd stored the wine over the years, decanting enough each year into smaller barrels to make room for the current vintage, which then got mixed with all the previous years' vintages. The family of Hadjimikalakis swore that a few drops of their stored wine went back more than a hundred years, when the Turks still ruled Crete and they had to hide their *vareli* in a cave. Good, old local wine was delicious, went down smoothly and warmly. Manoli had told Thanassi that well-aged wine would never give you a hangover, which was a sordid piece of misinformation he had himself disproved many times.

In addition to food and drink Katerini's father (yet another Manoli) had engaged a famous bouzouki band from Rethymno to play for the dancing. The father owned forty *strémata* of olive trees and two fishing boats so everyone knew he could afford it. Besides, he was so relieved to have paid his last dowry and to have his youngest daughter finally honorably married to a promising young man that he was ready to dispense legendary sums to give a party everyone would remember.

The wedding day dawned bright and hot. The women of the town spent the early hours preparing dishes they would bring to the plateia and then cleaning themselves and choosing the dresses they would wear to church. The men felt that their mission was more important. At the bottom end of the plateia, where the paving gave out, and before the pebbles of the beach began, they assembled with picks and shovels in mid-morning. Taking turns on pick and shovel they dug six long trenches two feet deep. Into these they piled dried bramble bushes, old cuttings from vines, small branches from the copious chaparral from the hills around town. Once the fires were alight they started piling on logs of olive, chestnut, carob, and other hardwoods. In a couple of hours you couldn't get near the pits, it was so hot. In the meantime the experts had gone up to Fotis' butcher shed with the spits, long iron rods with insertable cross pieces. Fotis had taken in the carcasses to cool during the night and now they brought them out, laid them on a canvas, and ran the spits through them, The points emerged through the top of the skulls, which were skinned and left on the animals in the Mediterranean fashion. The numerous children in attendance had great sport, the older ones having informed the youngsters how gross it would look when the bloody points burst through the center of the forehead, smeared with brain, and the staring eyes on either side. Forewarned, they all ran around screaming at the sight and then stood eagerly awaiting the next one. The men bound the spines to the spit with twine, then tied the ends of the legs to the spit with wire. Twelve men went down to the beach with six lambs carried on a spit between each pair of men. And there they waited for the fires to burn down. Fotis looked over his shed. There were still eight more lambs and he figured they'd all go before next day dawned.

Now a covey of women showed up at the butcher's shed with smaller spits and Fotis brought out big plastic lugs full of the lamb hearts, livers, kidneys, spleens, and lungs. The women started working at makeshift tables cutting up the organs and threading them on the spits, adding many gob-bets of lamb fat that had come with the organs, sprinkling the spits with freshly picked thyme, rosemary, and oregano, salt and pepper. Finally they took the long strings of intestines that Fotis swore he had cleaned thoroughly. They scorned his protests and ran copious bursts of water from a hose through the intestines again until even they were sat-isfied. Then they wound the intestines around and around the spits full of organ meats until they were completely cov-ered. One of the women shook a spit at Fotis.

"*Aftó eínai kokorétsi!*" she exclaimed. THAT'S *kokoretsi.* The same ritual went on every time there was a feast, the women claiming that only they could clean the innards properly. All through the afternoon, as the lambs slowly turned over the coals in the fire pits, the *kokoretsi* would cook over braziers in many different homes.

At five o'clock all sounds in the village were over-whelmed by the clangor of church bells and everyone except the most essential food preparers filed into the church. Thanassi was helping Manoli finish up the last minute dishes the taverna would contribute: six huge lugs full of tomatoes, cucumbers, green peppers, olives, and feta cheese, with a liter of olive oil poured over each one; two lugs full of fried potatoes, which would be replenished with fresh ones as they emptied; twenty platters of cut up melons, if anyone got around to them.

Most of the hotels in town were now full of relatives from other parts of Crete and Greece and only a few rooms had been left to be reserved ahead of time by tourists.

"Vat is de big party?" asked a big blond man at his hotel. "Vill de restaurants be closed tonight?

"Oh, no, no, sir," said Hans, the hotel manager in English, trying to sound Greek. He'd been watching this group of four Germans with growing suspicion and was not going to reveal that he was German too.

"It is a wedding," he said. "And if you are in town, they give you food, wine, what you want. You are guest!"

The Greek archaeologists had heard about the party and, being Greek, knew they didn't need an invitation. They strolled down the hill far too late to attend the church wedding.

Yanni was being superhuman, being asked from all directions to bring huge loads...of wood, of cases of drinks, of sacks of potatoes, to move this table here, that one there. He was sweating and happy.

After what everyone agreed was much too long a church service the doors burst open, the bells rang, and most of the population of Kali Vrisi flowed out onto the street and headed for the plateia, most of the men stripping off their jackets as they went. An unspoken convention held that nothing could be consumed until bride, groom, and entire families were present and the mother of the bride gave her blessing. Unfortunately, the mother of the bride believed she was having a heart attack and went home with fifteen other women to lie down for a moment and fan herself. Once out of her best clothes she decided that it was only the tight clothes that had deranged her, so she put on something looser, had a quick glass of a sticky sweet aperitif for her circulation's sake, and feeling better immediately, came back to the plateia.

The villagers had been trying to content themselves strolling around just looking at the first batch of lambs, which were now being taken off the spits, dismembered and boned out, smoking and steaming, into piles of meat on great platters; or inspecting the next bunch, being turned on their spits over the coals by the young boys who always volunteered for the task. On every table was a long array of liter-and-a-half plastic orangina or coca-cola bottles which had been refilled with brown wine. For those requiring stronger medicine there were glass bottles of *tsikoudiá* and just plain ouzo. A whole table was covered with cans of cola, lemonada, and real orangina for the children. The father of the bride had asked Manoli if he would donate some beer as well but Manoli had refused.

"Nobody drinks beer at weddings except Germans, I don't know, maybe Australians. If there're any here and they want a beer they can come here and buy it!"

For two hours Thanassi barely stopped moving. It was his job to see that every empty platter was refilled, so his impression of the feast at first was limited to carving meat off lamb bones, pulling the *kokoretsi* off the spits, rushing back to get lemons to squeeze on everything, rushing back to the kitchen to slice up a dozen more tomatoes, cucumbers, cutting loaves of bread. Now and then a reveler would come by and hand him a plastic glass of wine, slopping it over his arm and demanding that he drain it.

"*Ela! Thanassi, ya sta héria sou!*"

Finally there was a lull in the action and he was able to go in back of the kitchen, strip off his sweat-soaked T-shirt, hose off in back, dry himself rapidly and change into a loose, short-sleeved white shirt. But he kept his apron on for a while. The work was not over.

By seven the sun was low in the sky and the first feeding frenzy was over. Most of the town's inhabitants were now leaning back in their chairs, amiably toasting each other, and now and then returning in a more leisurely fashion to the serving tables. A party of four German tourists turned up and stood around aimlessly until Manoli yelled at them in English.

"Hey! *Mach schnell!* You better get some food or there won't be any left!"

Thanassi at the moment was manning the service table. As a large blond man came up to him he held up his hands. "I'm sorry, just a minute, you don't want cold lamb, it gets very greasy. I'll put some back on the grill, it won't take a minute." He was doing his best to speak English with a Greek accent.

"You are from here?" asked a thin woman standing next to the first German.

"Yes. I help run this restaurant," said Thanassi, smiling. "Let me give you some salad, some bread. The meat, one minute, it will be ready. You had some wine yet?"

The woman's husband, a dark man, looked questioningly at Thanassi. Then he asked rapidly, in Greek. "You are from here? Or maybe from America, originally?"

Thanassi just stared at him. He couldn't think of anything to say. The woman hit her companion in the side with an elbow. "What are you asking, you imbecile? Be polite.

I'm sorry," she explained to Thanassi in English. "My husband is a German Greek. He is from the modern, how you say, *diaspora*, when so many Greeks went to Europe. Now he thinks every Greek is somewhere else!" She crinkled her lips at her husband but it didn't look like a smile to Thanassi. He relaxed and answered the German Greek man in a mixture of Greek and English.

"*Then birázei.* It doesn't matter. I lived in Athens a long time, *katálaves*? I spoke much English there. Come on, now! Take some more lamb! There's more. And have some more wine, the table over there!"

Then the large blond man was joined by another, who could have been his brother, a muscular man who seemed always to be laughing, his eyes darting this way and that. They had no trouble taking large helpings of lamb and salad and bread, and filling their glasses with wine. They were now being surrounded by a few of the villagers who had at one time worked in Germany building cars and Thanassi was relieved when they began to be bombarded by questions in atrocious German from the former *Gastarbeiter. What town are you from? You know I worked in Wiesbaden ten years? What are they paying for factory work now, you know, the union wage?* It took the attention off him. He turned to Manoli.

"I just have to take a break, go sit down, rest a bit."

"Sure, go ahead, Thanassi. You worked like a mule today. And take Yanni with you. Make him sit down, have some food and wine. He hasn't sat down since noon!"

*

The band arrived at sundown, stuffed themselves with food and wine and then began to play some dances, the easy ones first.

The crowd was timid, as usual, no one wanting to be the first dancer out in the middle of the plateia. Then Manoli's brother-in-law, short fat Manoli, got up, wandered casually across the plateia and then grabbed Manoli, the father of the bride, by the hand and dragged him out into the circle of light from the overhead bulbs. Everyone cheered. Hand in hand, they danced an older, traditional dance, and soon other men ventured onto the plateia, dancing in male couples, in the Greek fashion.

The next tune, the band speeded up and played a livelier, more rhythmic bouzouki number, and now the men rushed to get on the pavement of the plateia. As the tempo of the dancing picked up the children noticed the infectious beat and began to jump and pirouette at the edge of the pavement, not quite daring yet to join the grown men. For several hours no one had paid any attention to the children of Kali Vrisi. In fact, they had been playing a game taught them by an older delinquent, who had been through this before. The game was, *Oh look at all the orangina bottles, let's drink some orangina!* So the children had been picking up all the half empty plastic cups of wine put down aimlessly by grownups on any flat surface, and draining them. *Oh boy! This is really good orangina! Giggle! Oh, but you should taste this Coke! Ha haha!* By now the children of Kali Vrisi were all shamelessly tipsy and finally they could not resist the dance floor; they ran, swooping and swirling like flocks of swallows amidst the feet of the older dancers, shrieking with joy and laughter.

The advent of the children into the mass of dancers coincided with the beginning of another old Cretan wedding tradition. Some of the older men had brought their pistols concealed in their clothes and now they began to pull them out and fire them into the ground to celebrate the wedding in the noisiest way possible. Thanassi was watching in horror as drunken children ran around and between the legs of drunken men who were firing pistols of every vintage into the ground, modern automatics, revolvers, antiquated Lugers and Walthers that had been liberated more than fifty years ago from unlucky occupying forces.

"They never kill anyone," shouted Manoli into his ear. "Although God knows why not! There's no use trying to stop it. In a bit they'll run out of bullets. You can't buy those anywhere, here in Crete, you know. and they don't want to use them all up!"

Now the band began a classic *syrtáki*. The clumsier men were jeered off the floor and a line of five dancers known for their grace began the steps, arms over each other's shoulders. As they turned the second time, one of the men saw Thanassi watching.

"*Ela, Thanassi!*" he cried. "Come join us, we saw you dance before. You know the way!"

A roar from the crowd forced Thanassi to join them. He found it effortless, doing the old steps he had learned so long ago in Santa Monica, and he knew the tune they were playing. The line of dancers moved in unison, in fluid perfection, making the turns together, stooping together, pausing to slap their shoes, ending precisely and proudly under the swaying light bulbs that had begun to move before a warm night wind now flowing off the land and out to sea. The band quickly picked up another dance, this one faster, and two of the dancers dropped out to let Thanassi and two young bravos of the village become more energetic. Thanassi let himself go, did the extra turns, squatted and kicked with extra energy, and the three ended in a line, arms linked, to feverish applause.

Now there were calls, "Zorba, Zorba..." Thanassi was walking back to his table, when Manoli caught his arm.

"*Moré!* They're calling for you!"

"Manoli! I hate that Zorba shit! That's for tourists!"

"No! You're wrong! We love that Zorba shit! Why you think they made that Mexican guy, that actor, a Greek citizen? Get your ass out there and do some Zorba!"

So Thanassi did the dance he'd always hated back home, the Theodorakis song that started slowly, then built gradually, gradually.

He paced off the first steps precisely, looking down modestly, as the mandolin picked out the melody sweetly. A few of the audience were still calling to each other raucously, but as the dance went on others shushed them and now it was almost silent except for the music. The swaying lights cast dappled shadows across the faces of the audience and Thanassi saw, once, as he turned, the faces of the two sisters, Roula and Elli, entranced, staring at him as if they'd never seen him before. They were wearing identical light blue dresses. Roula had a red ribbon in her hair and the younger Elli a yellow one. He gave them a big smile and spun away. Most of the smaller children had collapsed and were lying in lumps, asleep, under chairs and tables. And now the music began to pick up, the beat intensifying, and he had to concentrate on the footwork, this foot crossing the other, then back again behind the other foot, three steps this way, two that, turn, sink to one knee, slap the shoe, up and do it all in reverse...now it was speeding up, speeding up and he went into the floor dance, squatting, twirling, one hand on the ground, squatting, kicking out like a Cossack, on his feet, squatting again, twirling, as the noise grew in the audience, clapping, and yelling, and then just a roar as he finished the most strenuous part and then ending standing, his arms over his head, face split in a beatific grin, sweat streaming down his face, his body, and he realized he'd stopped directly in front of the two sisters again and Roula was clapping as hard as she could and yelling something and Elli was just sitting there petrified, her mouth open as if he had danced her into a trance, and he thought, *why do I keep doing this phony thing?* But he admitted to himself for the first time, *I do enjoy it, when my people are watching. For the first time I felt Greek when I danced!*

"Shit! I'm ruined," he complained to Manoli, who greeted him at the edge of the plateia with a large glass of wine. "I'll never make it up the road, and I'm ready to collapse right now!" He drained the plastic cup.

"Don't worry, kiddo! You were great! And don't worry about the cleanup here. We'll take care of everything. Don't you dare go to your car, the way you've been knocking them back. You take your old room, the one you used to rent. Sleep here tonight!"

Thanassi went gratefully off into the kitchen, hosed himself off once more, climbed the back stairs and collapsed onto the bed in the little back room. He could see the half moon out of the one window and he was beginning to wonder what part of the month it was, was the moon getting bigger or smaller, when he dropped off completely. He was unaware that several pairs of eyes had watched him disappear.

An hour later the crowd that remained in the plateia was, for the most part, disgracefully drunk. The band had taken a break, a young man had brought out his boom box and put on some rock and roll, and some daring teenage boys and girls had actually started to dance with each other, as the elders tsk-tsked helplessly

In one corner of the plateia the locals had gathered around a table where they were making Little Yanni arm wrestle with strongmen from other towns who didn't know his reputation. Yanni put on his usual act, smiling, modest, saying, oh you look too strong for me, then when they started, getting a worried look on his face, letting his fist fall backwards, grimacing now, holding, holding, holding, and then slowly coming up the other way relentlessly and putting his opponent's wrist on the table, never slamming it, or playing the big shot, just being Yanni, always apologizing afterwards.

The big men from the other villages either went away shaking their heads or stayed to watch others get beaten. Yanni always changed hands, right and left, not to get worn out, and he was on his left hand when a big blond man sat down, a German with a crazy grin on his face, and put his massive bulging arm on the table.

"How much you bet?" he asked in English.

Yanni looked puzzled but a few of the crowd knew enough English to answer. "Yanni doesn't bet" "His mother said it was wrong!" "But I'll bet you!" "Yes! Me too! I bet a thousand!"

There was a chorus of voices and the notes fell on the table, five, ten thousand, getting close to twenty—about fifty thousand drachmas—when another big blond man stepped up and caught the money. He handed it to the nearest villager.

"Ve don't bet for money. Only friendly, Okay?"

Everyone murmured assent, disappointed, seeing a sure thing get away.

Yanni put his left elbow on the table, held his right hand in the air to signal the rules—you couldn't touch anything with the other hand. Then the German reached out and grabbed his hand, squeezing to test the strength of his hand and maybe to inflict a little pain. But Yanni just grinned.

"Ena, dyo, tria!" chanted an older man and the contest started. The German went for the fast put down and bulges stood out on his shoulder and back as he tried to use his whole body strength. Yanni gave way, more quickly than anyone had seen, his forearm making a forty-five degree angle with the table before he finally held, and now he wasn't pretending, no grimacing, no worried looks. He just seemed to get calm, like a statue, his arm bent over, no expression on his face, as if he was out there somewhere else watching what was going on, leaving his body to its own devices.

"Ungh! ungh! ungh!" The German was pulsing, giving a bit, then surging back with all his might, trying to wear Yanni down. And then everyone noticed that each time the German gave a little Yanni took up the slack and his arm slowly but certainly began to move upright again. Now they were straight up and down again, both sweating heavily. Yanni was content for the moment just to hold where he was. He signaled to an onlooker who rapidly passed to his free hand a glass of cola, which he drained.

Then he said something to the German, who looked around in amazement, not understanding.

"He says, take a drink, he won't push," said one of the English speakers and handed the German a plastic cup of wine. The big German laughed, casually took the cup, drained it, and then tried to take Yanni by surprise, putting everything into a crushing attack while the cup was still to his lips.

Yanni was a simple child, but he had arm wrestled countless times and had seen every trick, including this one. He was ready and the attack went nowhere, their arms remained upright and now, inch by inch, Yanni started to put the German down. He was halfway there when suddenly the German's slippery hand suddenly escaped his grasp.

"Too vett, too vett!" yelled the German leaping up and waving his hand.

"Dere vas too much sweat, you understand?" said the other blond German. Everyone understood. The guy'd been beaten and was pretending his hand slipped out of the sweaty grasp. But they were polite and waited to see what other breaches of fair play these visitors could come up with.

Yanni shrugged and made as if to leave. But the German grabbed his shirt. "You come, ve do right hand, maybe you not so good, okay?"

Yanni looked around the crowd as if hoping someone would tell him to go home but instead they all shouted at once.

"Akóma, akóma, me ti dexá!" Again, again, the right hand.

Yanni was tired, he knew his opponent had cheated, he wanted the evening to be over. So when the contest started he didn't go through the usual ritual, he just gritted his teeth and started pushing. The German had obviously never felt strength like this. A startled look came over his face, to be replaced by determination: aha! so that's the way you want it? And he pushed back with all his force. But slowly, inexorably, his forearm went backward, even when he grabbed the edge of the table with his free hand in complete disregard of the rules and used the extra leverage, with all the Greeks shouting, no fair, no fair, still he was going down, down, down...

And then suddenly he was on his feet, tore his hand away and hit Yanni in the face with his left hand. There was immediate silence, an intake of breath all over the plateia. Yanni sat stunned, looking around, as if somehow it was his fault. Then suddenly the German realized he was looking at pistols, one, two, four, many now...

Suddenly Manoli was in the middle yelling in Greek and English.

"*As ti malakía!* Alright! enough of this bullshit! All you masturbators go home! *Drópi sou! Drópi sou!* What shame you should fight on Katerina's wedding day! No more drinks now. Everyone should go home."

The villagers gave way before his outburst, although many of them were thinking, I'll find this German bastard tomorrow and kill him. Manoli was now facing the German, speaking softly in English although he was so mad he was spitting.

"You come here and push around, hitting, like you do at home? Don't you know? You hit a Greek in the face you could be a dead man? And no police will arrest the man you hit! But there are no police here. Just many Greeks with guns! And some with knives, maybe better! This boy was beating you. Now you say to him, apology, then go to your hotel. You not welcome here any more!"

The other blond German put his hand on his friend's shoulder, looking at Manoli.

"Ve apologize. My brother made a big mistake. Too much vine. Now let me buy everyone drink!"

It was just the wrong thing to say and all the villagers turned away in disgust. These weren't even worthy enemies, they were just clowns. Some of the oldest men, walking away were telling anyone who would listen, these are not like the Germans who were here long ago, the ones we beat. Those were real men, cruel bastards, brave. They wouldn't cheat wrestling, they'd just shoot your arm off. By God, these assholes are not worth shooting.

The two blond Germans walked away from the plateia toward their hotel. The crowd that was left noted that the crazy one had never apologized himself, just let his brother do it. A few looked around for the older couple that had come with the two blonds but they had disappeared.

Jürgen Jaeger found Ilse sitting in front of their hotel in the dark, tapping her foot. She spoke softly, viciously in German. *"How brilliant! Such a low profile! Certainly no one will remember us tomorrow or the next day! Maybe you could have put off a bomb instead, you stinking, crazy bedbug!"*

Jürgen lunged for her, snarling with hate, but she was on her feet, holding a long needle in a wooden handle in front of her.

"Go ahead, you stupid maggot! I'll make you scream with agony in places you didn't know existed! Werner! If you can't control your brother I may have to drop him from this job!"

"You bitch!" said Werner Jaeger. *"You are not in charge here. And there's work to be done. Maybe tonight!"*

Mikali appeared out of the darkness. *"He's the one. The dancer. Everyone calls him the American. They don't know him as Castle...it's Kateroudakis, his father's real name. He came two months ago, maybe more. He lives up the road four kilometers. But he didn't go home tonight and I don't think we can grab him now. He may be in the taverna, upstairs, there are four, five people there tonight."*

"Well, well," said Ilse Wilamowitz. *"Don't tell me someone actually is doing his job, finding out things, instead of stupid wrestling in the middle of the square. Mikali. Did you find out where he lives?"*

"Sure. He's up the road, right side, a little driveway goes up above the road a bit. You don't even have to ask questions in this town, they tell you everything sooner or later."

"Okay, then." said Werner Jaeger. *"That was good work. Let's all calm down now, get some sleep. When Castle goes home tomorrow morning we'll go pick him up and get out of this goddamned place!"*

No one noticed the old man sitting silently behind the hibiscus hedge in front of the hotel.

*

Thanassi woke suddenly in the darkness. The moon had set and the night was impenetrably black. He realized he couldn't have been asleep more than a few hours. It took him a moment to remember where he was. Upstairs in Manoli's taverna. What had he heard? he wondered. Then he heard another sound, unmistakable, the sound of clothing slithering off a body and falling to the ground. And then a giggle. Roula! he thought, automatically, and was trying to decide if he should turn on the light and sternly order her out of his room. But it was too late. A hot naked body was suddenly on top of him and hot, wet lips were clamped to his, and a soft thrusting tongue seemed to be half-way down his throat. Thanassi was wondering what was the right thing to do and then he was half worried whether he could even function, with all he'd drunk, but then the girl on top of him started playing with his nipples and it became academic. In a minute she started feeling behind her, caught hold of the object she was looking for, and guided it into herself. She was hot, hot, wet, wet, and her hips were going like a well oiled machine before he was even all the way in. *She's either done this before or she's thought about it a lot*, thought Thanassi, and joined the action. He put both of his hands on the fine, round bottom that was going up and down and added to the motion, making her go round and round and rocking her from side to side. They were slippery with sweat and now she had both arms wrapped around his neck, her head buried next to his and her breathing picked up and now she was hurling her body up and down and beginning to groan, oh, oh, oh, and then her voice rose and Thanassi just managed to get his hand over her mouth before she screamed and he felt as if his head was being torn off by her arms around his neck and he wondered if everyone in the building couldn't hear the old bed going creak, creak, creak, creak and now and then the headboard hitting the wall, bung, bung, bung and then there was no doubt about it, she came, and clamped him to her, and shuddered once, twice, three, times, and he had the idle thought, Jesus! these girls are strong! And then she was relaxed, panting, on top of him, crooning into his ear, and they both rested for a few minutes, neither wanting to say anything. A minute, maybe several minutes went by. Time passed.

A star, or maybe a planet, had now swum into view of the room's window and by just its distant faintest light Thanassi could see past the tangle of dark hair the gleam of sweat on beautiful round arms, on a long, supple back, on two gloriously curved buttocks, still cocked up in the air a bit, stilled in mid-thrust. And as they lay there they both became aware at the same time that Thanassi still had a huge, rigid member buried deeply within her and that one of the partners in this dance had saved his energy for another bout atop the sodden sheets.

She murmured, hmmm, at the recognition, at the anticipation of unfinished business, and began to move again, slowly, slowly, just trying it out, then seeing how far she could let it slip out, and how far she could press it in again, being slow, slow, and careful, solicitous of every tiny motion, every bit of friction. The time went by. And then, playful, she sat up, perched over him, bouncing very slowly, touching his face, his lips, running her hands down his body and then up to brush her hair back and tuck it behind her ears.

Thanassi still couldn't see her face in the darkness. But the starlight fell on her breasts and the little erect nipples and Thanassi had to reach up and run his fingers over them until they hardened and her breath quickened again and she eased herself down on top of him again. But now Thanassi clutched her to him and turned them both over so he was on top and her legs met across his back instinctively and the sap rose within him and his loins turned to fire and he began to plunge, deeper and deeper until it seemed that their flesh had joined and he could feel the spurting, spurting, spurting as if it would never stop and he was laughing uncontrollably and the bed was smashing against the wall, and once again her arms were around his neck as if she was trying to break it and then they were still and she was just barely murmuring in his ear, *s'agapó, s'agapó, agápi mou!* I love you, I love you, my love.

Thanassi thought later that they must have slept awhile like that. And then they lay side by side for a bit, and then he slept and she must have taken her clothes and left and in the morning, there was the ribbon on the floor, the ribbon from her hair, and it was the yellow ribbon, and it had been Elli all the time, the quiet one, not Roula.

*

Sun called the villa in Chania a couple of times and never got an answer so he assumed the Germans were off hunting down Danny Castle. He expected the needed information any time now to transfer the bonds to Liebling's bank. Then one evening he got a call from Charbon.

"Mr Sun. Sorry if I was a little rough the last time we talked on the phone. I was nervous, you know, having a little problem with your boss, you know what I'm saying?"

"No problem, Mr. Charbon. What can I do for you?"

"Well, Herschel and me decided to change things around a bit, you know? The deal now is, when you get the bonds, don't deposit them there, bring 'em here and Hersch and me are going to split 'em up, both sets, the ones you're getting and the ones he's still got. You with me?"

"I understand. I get the bonds and we meet in...where, there in Los Angeles?"

"No. No, we decided a neutral place. The Times Square Marriot in New York. Call the hotel a week from today, ask for my room, give me the news, and if you got the bonds be ready to get the next plane to Kennedy. If you get the bonds quicker than that call me at this number." And he read it off slowly. "That's the New Orleans area code. But we're all ready to move at a second's notice. Okay?"

Sun wondered how Jolly had been pressured into putting his bonds into a gangster's hands in a city far from home. But he was aware that Herschel Jolly's power was out of balance, as a Korean would put it, was now sinking, and another's was on the rise and nothing he or Jolly could do about it.

The next day he got a fax. The letterhead read "Yueh Yung's Drycleaning and Tailoring" but the body of the fax was hand-written in Korean. Herschel Jolly had sent along some instructions, translated into Korean, that were significantly different from the ones he had received from Eddie Charbon.

*

The sun came up over the mountain called Toumba, reaching out to sea with long golden arms over the deep blue, flat in the dead calm of dawn, turning it bright and sending up a few tendrils of mist over the broad waters before the relentless heat of August settled down to make the surface shimmer gently until the afternoon wind came up. In the village of Kali Vrisi the only living thing to be seen was a nondescript brown dog lying sprawled in the middle of the plateia. As the sun hit him he stretched without waking, then turned onto his back, legs splayed, to present his genitals to the new day.

The sun streaming through the window at the back of Manoli's taverna found Thanassi in much the same position. It took him a minute to wake up, to remember where he was, and to remember what he had been doing in the darkness only a few hours ago. It was then he sat up and discovered the ribbon.

Oh my God! was his reaction, sitting on the edge of the bed, holding his head in his hands, with the destroyed bedding in heaps behind him. He had been tempted, he had to admit, during the past few weeks, to see what Roula really had in mind, wondering if all young Greek girls were put on the pill by their mothers, as the loungers in the taverna said, and whether a moment's temptation might lead to a fatal entrapment. But Elli! Probably not on the pill! And so impulsive, wouldn't she just blurt out to her mother what she'd done, probably blaming him for it. In his mind's eye he could see, almost hear, the tromp, tromp, tromp of indignant villagers coming through the plateia, many of them armed, the mothers tight lipped and grim, the priest bringing up the rear, ready for his office...

Thanassi decided to stop thinking about it until later. He gathered his clothes and put them on, from time to time having to lean against a wall until his head cleared and the pain went away. He looked around the room. No sense leaving the bed in that state, they'd change the sheets anyway. So he gathered up all the sodden bedding and stuffed it into the pillowcase, the way he'd been taught so long ago at the federal prison camp in San Luis Obispo. And that made him think of Barbara. Barbara, Barbara! Would you forgive me for this? And then he remembered again, he wasn't going to think about last night for a bit.

Thanassi crept down the stairs. In back of the taverna his Fiat was wedged behind Manoli's old Mercedes and a *trikyklo*, one of the local three wheeled mini-trucks powered by a motorcycle engine. The owner of the *trikyklo* had obviously pulled in last night in a hurry to join the merriment with not the slightest concern that the little Fiat might want to get out sometime. There was no way he could get it out. He'd have to wait until someone woke up and that didn't seem imminent. So, he thought, *I'll walk. It's better. I'll get some exercise and clear my head. Half an hour at most if I walk quickly.* So he started off up the lane of eucalyptus trees northward out of Kali Vrisi.

An hour later four figures wandered out of the Olympia Hotel, carrying light luggage. They went to a light green Volkswagen van with the decal of a Chania car rental firm on the rear window and started to get in. Then the woman paused as if thinking of something.

"*Just a moment,*" she said in German. "*Maybe we forgot something.*" And she went back into the hotel.

She came back in a minute shaking her head. "*I can't find that guy.*"

"*What guy?*" asked the driver, a big blond man.

She laughed, but it wasn't funny. "*Am I the only one here who figured out that the hotel clerk was German?*"

"*I knew he wasn't Greek,*" said the slender dark man, who was Greek. "*But I thought he was Italian, Albanian, or something. He spoke Greek almost perfectly. So what did you do to this German?*"

"I thought he was sneaking around us last night. I was going to give him an inoculation, an anti-sneaking kind of inoculation. But he wasn't there. Hasn't been there all morning. Let's go finish this business."

They drove off towards the plateia and the road to the north just as Yanni came walking down the road from his house. Hans came running from behind the hotel where he'd been hiding and grabbed Yanni's arm, startling him.

"Yanni, Yanni! We have to do something! I can't wake the policeman!"

Yanni laughed. "The policeman? Stavro? I saw him drinking last night. You're not going to wake him up, Hans. Maybe later."

"Yanni, you must understand! Those people in that van! I heard them talking last night! They're looking for Thanassi! One of them has a gun in his pocket! I was peeking out the kitchen window! Now we must do something quick!"

Yanni immediately turned serious. "Come, we'll go to the plateia, get some help." The two men ran down the street. But the plateia was still empty. Yanni started to beat on the door of Manoli's taverna but just then there was a hellish racket from in back of the restaurant. They ran around the building and found a *trikyklo* slowly backing out, its motor sputtering and backfiring. The driver was plump and bald with a three day growth of beard and was staring at the two men who seemed to be so agitated. Yanni started to ask the driver for a ride when Hans spotted Thanassi's Fiat behind the spot the *trikyklo* had just vacated.

"Oh, look! Thanassi's not at home. His car's here!"

"Just the same," said Yanni. "I'm going to go up to his house. Those Germans might do something bad there. Spiro!" This was addressed to the driver of the little scooter truck who was still sitting there idling, his motor clattering away.

"Spiro, will you take me up to Thanassi's house? Maybe he's in danger!"

"What danger, Yanni? And what can you do?"

"What can I do?" Yanni thought for a second. "Wait a minute. First drive by my house, I'll get my shotgun!" And off they went at the *trikyklo's* top speed of twenty kilometers per hour, Spiro now an eager participant. Anything involving shotguns and Germans seemed promising to him.

*

Thanassi was sweating and thirsty when he reached his house. The first thing he did was drink half a jug of well water. Then he poured the rest over his head. He gave his bed a long look, wondering if he could indulge in a daytime nap, but there were animals to be fed and plants to be watered so he compromised by sitting at his kitchen table and drinking another glass of water. He was leaning back, rethinking the daytime nap situation when he heard a horn honking in his driveway. He went out into the bright sunlight squinting and saw a green van, all the doors open, and three men standing by it. One of them came running forward now and he was surprised to see that it was the big blond German, one of the group of four he had served at the party the night before.

"Is something wrong?" he asked in English, once again trying for a Greek accent.

"My friend's wife, I think she is sick! She suddenly started groaning! Maybe she could lie down a bit, in your house, in the shade?"

"Of course, of course, let me help!" Thanassi rushed to

the sliding door of the van and saw the thin woman, dressed in warmups, slumped on the back seat. The other blond man and the darker one, her husband, Thanassi guessed, were trying to get her to sit up and get out of the van. She struggled, her eyes wandering and unfocused, and managed to get both feet on the ground. But she immediately sat down on the floor of the van and began to whimper.

"I can't...too weak. Maybe my heart...please..."

"If you can help carry her...?" offered the darker man.

"Of course!" And Thanassi picked her up, an arm under her legs, an arm around her back. She was light, but he could feel the wiry muscles and he thought, disconcertingly, "She doesn't *feel* very sick." The first blond man went on into the house and the darker man held the door open. The second blond brought up the rear.

As Thanassi reached the door of his house with his burden he turned sideways to slip through the opening and, as he did so often, hit his head on the low lintel of the door frame. As usual he cursed and then quickly shifted his grip on the women, thinking he might drop her. And that was how he felt the slight tug on the fabric of his pants and looked down. Just when he'd shifted his grip she'd been about to plunge a hypodermic needle into his thigh but his movement had made the needle catch in the tough fabric of his jeans. Now she stabbed again for his thigh and the needle pricked him but he'd thrown her away from himself now and the needle went flying before she could depress the plunger. Thanassi looked in disbelief at the three assailants in front of him and then turned to flee out the door.

"Jürgi! Stop him! Knock him down!" And Thanassi saw the big man grinning in the doorway and his crazy eyes light up and his massive arms spreading wide to stop the fugitive.

What happened was pure instinct, remembering Soose's words back at San Luis. *"You got a great right hand. And fast. Never think, just punch!"* Thanassi punched Jürgen Jaeger with every ounce of power, his hard fist hitting him about an inch under his left eye. Jaeger went down like a rag doll and Thanassi ran right over him, starting at first for the road, but then realizing they'd catch him there, then sprinting for the base of the cliff in back of his house. He went up the goat path faster than he'd ever believed possible, putting on an extra burst of speed as a projectile whistled past his ear. "A silenced pistol," he thought, and did his best to outrun it. At the top he turned immediately for the swiftest path, the one that led towards the gorges of Toumba, thinking that there he could hide himself indefinitely.

Back at the house Werner Jaeger barked orders.

"Ilse! Fast, after him! Keep him in sight. You're the fastest of all of us! Mikali! Come with me, we can catch him!" And to his brother, who was trying to sit up, blood streaming down his face, *"Jürgi! You can't run with us. You stay here, hide, he may try to double back! And this time, hammer him one, a good one, ja?"* Then he was off.

Thanassi hit the first gorge and considered sneaking down it instead of crossing it, but then he heard a high voice yelling in German and realized the woman had taken a higher goat path where she could keep him in sight and direct the other pursuers. So he labored out of the gorge and on eastward, settling down to a jog now, thinking that they couldn't keep up in this terrain, not unless they were in terrific shape.

At the driveway to Thanassi's house the *trikyklo* squealed to a stop behind the van and Yanni vaulted out of the back with his shotgun. He started for the house but saw a blond man, all bloody, sitting in the doorway. He realized that it was the bad man from the night before, the one who'd hit him. Thanassi must have knocked him down. It seemed obvious to him. Thanassi would be running up on the mountain with the others after him. He started running towards the cliff face himself. Jürgen Jaeger thought for a moment that he should try to stop him but Yanni gave him a grim look and kept going without breaking stride. Spiro was getting out of his truck but when he saw the big German with blood on his face he decided that this was all getting too exciting. He backed down the driveway and took off at his full speed for Ayia Eleni up the road to the north. Later today when he got back, he told himself, he'd stop again and see what had happened.

*

Down in the village Hans had made another visit to the policeman's house. He finally managed to raise a blowsy, irritated policeman's wife.

"He's sick. I think food poisoning from that tzatziki that rotten bitch Maria brought to the party. She thinks she's sexy. They should tell her..."

Hans quickly recognized that they had conflicting agendas. "Okay, okay! I just want him to know that those Germans last night might be going up there to hurt Thanassi. One of them had a pistol!"

"Thanassi? Germans? That boy, the way he danced last night, he could take his fist and, pom, pom! That boy's a superman. Don't you worry about Thanassi and Germans, my uncle—THA-NAS-SI!!" she suddenly yelled.

"What are you saying?" quailed Hans, "Why do you cry out?"

"No, no, not that Thanassi, my Thanassi, five years old and he won't live to six, you wait and see!" And in the dim light of the kitchen Hans could see a little boy running around chasing his sister with a butcher knife.

"THA-NAS-SI!! *As ta*!! She turned and lumbered back into the kitchen and Hans could hear the meaty smack of a small boy being disciplined, followed by a rising wail.

"*Lipon, Katina!* Okay, don't bother, I gotta go talk to Manoli, bye bye!"

At Manoli's taverna Hans found Manoli out glumly looking at his tables, covered with spilled liquids, empty bottles and glasses, and his chairs, some turned over, one or two broken. He gave Hans a black glance.

"Your goddamn Germans last night, they fucked it up alright!" Now a couple of housewives were coming up the road and stopped to listen to the heated conversation.

Hans hadn't heard about the great arm wrestling debacle but at least Manoli was talking about the right subject.

"Manoli! Those other Germans were looking for Thanassi for some reason. I heard them talking about him. And today, when they left, one of them had a pistol! I saw him take it out of a bag and put it in his pocket!"

The two housewives looked at each other, *a pistol!* and beckoned to a third, who was coming across the plateia.

"And that's another one, that goddamn Thanassi!" said Manoli, oblivious to Germans for the moment, and not noticing the three women behind him, listening to every word.

"That bastard Thanassi kept me awake half the night. He was fucking some woman in my room up there, banging the bed against the wall, what a stallion! I tried to stay awake, see who it was who left but I fell asleep, the goddamn *raki* I drank last night!"

"Thanassi! With a woman?" Manoli turned to see the three housewives staring at him with amazement, then looking at each other wide eyed, mouths open.

"It could have been me!" said one of them laughing. "He's always been hot for me!"

"No, no, you slut!" said the second. "It was me the whole time!" And they bent over laughing.

The third woman just stood there with a bewildered expression. "Thanassi? With a woman? If I'd known...What a man! He must have a thing as big..."

"*Dropi sou! Dropi sou!*" exclaimed the other women. "Voula! Shame on you for even thinking...!"

"Well! And who started the whole thing...!"

"Yes, but we were joking!"

"Sure you were joking, as if you wouldn't..."

"*Kyries, kyries!*" interrupted Manoli "Ladies! Please! Hans here claims that those Germans from last night are going after Thanassi with a gun!"

"Bah!" the first woman said. "I don't believe it! And if they did, what a beating they'd get from him! And if I don't get my melons down at the market now they'll all be gone!"

She walked off with the others, one of the women saying, "We'll have to see who's got a loaf in the oven a few months from now..."

And the third said, "But four months after a wedding party like this every woman in town has a loaf in the oven..."

"Cover your ears, old man," said Manoli to Hans. "These women in town are a threat to the chastity and purity that we Christian men cherish in our hearts. Don't listen. Now tell me again about Germans and guns."

*

Thanassi paused on the path, leaning against the cliff face. Could he slip down the escarpment here? He knew there was a gully below, choked with oleander, where a tiny spring trickled all year. But there was no way out of there, and above he could still see the figure of the woman, really high now, but always keeping him in sight. She'd point him out to the men and they'd have him caught.

What a bitch of a woman, he thought. *To run like that in the mountains where she doesn't even know the paths!* And he thought that even Yanni would be impressed. He continued his run along the path, not even a path, just an absence of vegetation where generations of goats had found their way. He ducked around outcrops, dropped swiftly down into overgrown gullies and clambered up the other side. He thought about descending a narrow difficult gorge that was supposed to lead to the Forestry path to Agia Roumeli. But he'd never taken it before and was afraid they'd catch him there in that snarl of brush and clinging branches. He ran on. And above him the apparition of the scrawny woman ran on, screeching down to her unseen companions from time to time. Now there was no other solution. He'd have to go for the secret valley, swing around the cliff and hope they couldn't follow him. So he started off, jumping to a boulder in front of him...and it turned as he landed, flinging him to the ground with a terrible pain in his ankle. At the same moment he could hear a cry of triumph from the woman above. She was obviously screaming to her companions that he was down, hurry, get him before he can get up!

Thanassi struggled to his feet and tried to run. His right ankle immediately crumbled on him again and he cried out with the pain. Twisting around he could see the two men now, only a few hundred meters behind, loping along, in good condition, nothing to hope for there. So he got to his feet and just tried walking for a bit, one foot in front of the other, slowly, slowly, gently, and the right foot was actually able to bear a bit of weight so he hobbled on as fast as he could, trying to go as fast hopping on his left foot as he could. Then he heard the woman yelling again and although he didn't understand German he knew what she was saying because he knew where they were now. There were sheer cliffs where she was and if she wanted to continue she'd have to go higher, higher up the mountain, to find a way around. She must be telling them that's what she'd do. Now there was just a long straight stretch in front of him, an easy level path that widened almost twenty feet or so and ended at the cliff where he would have to swing across.

He looked back...and immediately turned and hopped off as quickly as he could. Werner Jaeger and the Greek, Mikali, were only forty meters behind him and coming fast, and Jaeger had a gun in his hand, a big, odd looking gun, maybe with a silencer, the one he'd shot at him before...

All these thoughts were going through his mind as he reached the end of the path, the cliff in front of him now, and he took the first tentative step off onto the tiny ledge in the rock, feeling his whole back vulnerable, now putting his right foot down...could it take the weight?...and then the shooting pain and he quickly took up the slack with his left foot, his right foot for an instant again...pain! and then his left foot and now, thank God, he could see the juniper branch within reach and he set his left foot firmly in the last foothold, leaped and caught the branch.

Werner Jaeger, coming to the end of the path, saw Thanassi working his way out along the ledge, looked down and saw the sheer drop of a hundred meters at least, and wondered, is he committing suicide? Then he saw the juniper branch and saw Thanassi start to jump and understood the strategy. In one swift movement he brought up the tranquilizer gun and from short range fired a dart that hit Thanassi right in the buttock just as he was swinging out of view behind the cliff.

Mikali joined him there at the edge.

"Where'd he go?"

"He caught the branch there, you see? Then he swung around. There must be a space there he knows. But I got him with the dart. He'll be unconscious now wherever he is, even if he was a fucking bear, with that load!"

"How will we get him down from back there?"

"You've got the rope there..." Werner Jaeger pointed at the coil of mountaineering line over Mikali's shoulder. "We'll get him down somehow, collect Ilse, and get the bastard up to Chania, he'll be sorry he..."

There was suddenly an inarticulate cry behind them. Mikali and Jaeger turned to see Yanni standing there, shotgun leveled at them.

"It's the idiot!" Mikali hissed. "He'll never shoot you, they never do, they can't, those dumb ones! Give him one of those darts!"

"I'm out, goddamn it! I tried to hit Castle when he was going up the cliff back there and I only had the two darts! Anyway, if he can't shoot, he can't shoot! I'm going across. Tell him something to calm him down. Tell him we're only trying to help." And Jaeger started to work his way out along the ledge.

Yanni watched helplessly. Just as he'd reached the little plateau he'd seen Thanassi swing on the juniper branch and he'd seen the big man shoot the strange pistol and hit Thanassi. He knew Thanassi must be dead or dying on the other side of the sheer cliff. He raised the shotgun.

"Hey, boy!" shouted Mikali in a friendly tone. "We're only trying to help!" And then he got out of the line of fire.

Werner Jaeger got to the end of the ledge and looked

back. He looked up at the juniper branch, within easy reach. He looked back at Yanni, saw the furrowed brow, recognized the true paralysis of the retarded youth, told since infancy that he mustn't hurt anyone. So he turned, grasped the juniper branch and swung outward.

Yanni had been told all his life. Never point a gun at *anyone!* So he was frozen in place until the bad German reached up and grabbed the tree and started to swing, swing across to hurt Thanassi. And then it became simple. He brought up the shotgun in one smooth, swift motion and shot at the juniper branch. It disintegrated. Chips of wood, brown earth, bits of cliff flew in all directions.

Mikali ducked away at the shattering sound of the shotgun. When he looked back there was no juniper branch, no Werner Jaeger, only Yanni looking at him, shotgun braced over one forearm. He tried to listen for something hitting the rocks down there but it must have been too far, not even Yanni was listening. So he straightened up and faced the young man.

"You know," he said in Greek, in a conversational tone, trying to keep the tremor out of his voice. "I've got people down there in Sfakia, near there, anyway. I thought maybe I'd go spend some time there, take it easy for a while. Do you know if there's a path I could get to from here?" He felt himself about to whimper, his knees began to loosen, but with a heroic effort he composed himself again.

Yanni now relaxed, let the shotgun down. "Yes. There is." He too spoke in a normal tone, as if someone had casually asked him for directions back on the main street of Kali Vrisi. "You go back to the last big gorge? Full of flowers? You turn left, work your way down? It's a bit of trouble at first, but then you'll see the gorge flatten out, you can walk easy and, I don't know, maybe halfway down to the sea?

You'll see the path. The Forestry Department marked it a long time ago with red dots. Sometimes it's hard to see, but follow the little goat pellets. The goats always use the path. Turn left again and you can go all the way to Ay Roumeli. There you'll get the boat for Sfakia. Twice a day it is, until September anyway."

Mikali said thanks and started to turn away but Yanni added, "Leave the rope." Mikali looked down, realized he still had the rope over his shoulder and then dropped it on the ground.

"Okay, no problem. You're welcome to it!" And he walked back the way he'd come, expecting any moment the thunder of the shotgun. But it never came.

Yanni sat down on the ground, his head full of terrible pain. He should do something, but every thought he tried to think just came to a stop, boom. And he had to go back again, start thinking and then the thought stopped, boom. He squinched his eyes closed and began to cry. Think, boom, think, boom. And he thought about something else, like what would happen if he just jumped over the cliff like the big German. But that was against God's law. And then he lay over on his side and curled up and wept.

*

Jürgen Jaeger woke up lying on Thanassi's bed. That bastard had hit him so hard he thought his cheek was broken. He'd lain on the bed just to organize his thoughts and must have dropped off. Thinking that Castle might have returned he sat up quickly, then screamed at the pain in his cheek. Oh, oh, oh! He leaned over, willing the pain to go away. There must be something to drink here, he thought, and found finally the cupboard with a bottle of ouzo, almost full. He gratefully choked down two, three big swallows and they seemed to clear his head, dull the pain for a moment.

They were all up on the mountain, he thought, chasing the bastard. And he might come back here. He looked around for a weapon. There was a lethal looking kitchen knife out on a cutting board. No. He was supposed to knock him out and hold him, not kill him. Good luck! Jaeger giggled. Christ, that bastard had hammered him one. How was he going to hold the fucker? He'd just knife him, let Werner figure it out. He took another big gulp of ouzo, leaned back on the comfortable chair.

It was an hour later when he woke again and finally realized once again where he was. Well. Shit! The cocksucker obviously wasn't coming back here after all that time. Jaeger realized he still had hold of the ouzo bottle and he took another sip, just to clear his head, he told himself. And what he'd really like was a cold beer. He was thirstier than hell! Nothing like that here. Just water, gave him a headache just to think of cold water. He'd go to town. Castle wasn't coming back anyway. He knew Werner would yell at him for taking the van but he didn't care. When he got to the van he saw the keys were gone. The bastards! He had another ouzo out of the bottle and determinedly started out for town. He didn't think it was that far.

About a kilometer from town, from higher ground, Jaeger could see that the main road made a big sweeping curve, following the river bed, but that there was an old dirt road that cut straight across, narrow between low stone walls that divided the fields. A shortcut. He took the shortcut and in ten minutes or so came to a long building of some sort. He'd been hoping it was a café but it was windowless, deserted. Now he was hot and tired and across the track to the east was a little grove of cypress trees. He went over and sat in the shade and had a few more ouzos. He lay back, just to rest for a minute and fell asleep again in that hot sun-blasted, deserted countryside, silent except for the cicadas droning their song in the heat of the after-noon.

He must have had erotic dreams because he woke with an erection and that difficulty swallowing he often experi-enced when he just had to have a woman. His whole body felt electric. The suddenly tender skin all over his body crawled as if there were ants on it. He felt the bottle under his hand and finished off the ouzo. By God, he needed a woman now! He wondered if there were naughty women in town, maybe someone he could catch alone and per-suade to be naughty. Jürgen Jaeger's brain had now given up thinking and was heating up to furnace temperature, out of control, giving way to pure impulse, fanning the flames of memory, of creepy pleasures he'd had and even creepier pleasures he'd imagined in the darker, stickier cor-ners of his sodden mind.

And now who was this coming along the track? A little girl, maybe eight or nine, leading a goat with a bit of cord around its neck. Just the perfect thing! Those little limbs, long legs beneath her too short dress. A sweet face of inno-cence beneath long black hair, parted in the middle, her cheeks just a bit sweaty in the sun. And in a perfect place! He could get her back deeper in the grove of trees and real-ly take his time.

As the little girl saw him sitting there he waved and got up. She said something that he interpreted as "hello" and didn't seem at all afraid of a strange man. All the better. Jaeger pointed to the goat and said to her in German, "*Your goat there? There's another one back in the woods there, a little one.*" And he spread his hands to show how little. A really little goat. A variation on the old "help me find my lost kitten" theme.

She looked at the trees and asked a question in Greek, obviously, she was asking, was there really a little goat in the wood?

"Ja, ja!" said Jaeger. "*Kom!*" And he took her arm and started to guide her into the trees. But something about him, his strangeness, his loony smile, the hot waves of insanity reflecting off him made her hesitate and she tried to pull out of his grasp. Too late! He had her off her feet now, holding her by her upper arms, and ran into the trees. The feel of her in his hands pushed him over the edge and then he had her down on the ground, face down, one hand over her mouth, pulling up her dress, then fumbling with his zipper, to let out the surging thing in there. He was trying to force her legs apart with his body when a sudden, shocking, painful blow on his hip knocked him to the ground on his side. He looked wildly up and it was the goat!...the goddamned goat the little girl had been leading and he'd forgotten all about. Its horns were down low and it was pawing the ground, getting ready to butt him again. At that moment the little girl slipped out of his grip and in a second was running across the track, headed for the deserted building. Jaeger leaped to his feet, aimed a kick at the goat and was after her, thinking, it would be even better in that building. No one to see, easier to catch her. He saw her dart through a narrow door and the door slammed. A second later he was there yanking the door open and looking into a cool, very dark interior. He couldn't see where she'd gone but he'd find her for sure now and he started to wander in the dark, his hands in front of him, crooning, *come here, little girl, come to Jürgi!* And then suddenly his hands felt flesh, but it was cold, hard flesh and he couldn't think what it could be and he never saw the dark shape of Fotis the butcher, the Butcher of Crete, come silently around the corner in back of him, the slaughterer's sledge hammer high over his head.

*

Yanni sat up suddenly. Of course! What an idiot he was! He'd had the thought in his head when the stranger, the other Greek had started to leave. "The rope, drop the rope." It was normal for him to have a rope if he was hunting a lost kid. To be able to get it from some corner of the cliffs it couldn't get out of. And he realized that when he'd shot the tree branch that somewhere in his mind was the thought: get a rope so you can swing around the cliff. Then he'd forgotten, the dummy that he was, and only now remembered. The rope.

He ran to the coiled mountaineer's rope, then back to the cliff. He knew there was no way up and over. He'd tried it. There was a broad vertical crack in which brush was growing, in fact, the juniper was growing, but beyond, a big sliver of cliff had dropped, who knows how long ago, leaving only empty space.

With difficulty, he clambered up to the crack where the brush was growing. He would have to tie an end of the rope here. What could he tie it too—what would be strong enough? Then he saw the remaining trunk of the juniper, its former branch hanging down in shreds. The main trunk of the juniper was only a few inches high, but the roots went off in all directions, burrowing into the rock. He grabbed the trunk in both hands and pulled as hard as he could. It felt like part of the mountain, so little did it move. So it must be strongly rooted, he thought. Yanni wrapped the end of the rope around the trunk three times, then knotted it securely. Now he retreated back the way he came, carrying the rest of the rope with him. On the level again he wrapped the rope in his hands, gauged the possibility of swinging on it. Too thin. It would cut his hands, maybe stretch and leave him hanging below the lip of the cliff. Leaning up, he tied a big double loop in the rope, like the loop he would make to rescue a kid. Now it felt better, as high as he could reach, and not stretching when he pulled down on it.

Without thinking any more Yanni grabbed the loop in both hands, stepped out along the ledge until it ended, then jumped out into space.

*

Fotis was sitting with little Mairy on the back porch of his butcher shop. Her goat was happily grazing in the stubble of the yard in front of them.

"He was a bad man wasn't he, uncle?"

"Yes, very bad. But you mustn't think about him. I chased him away, far, far, away, and he'll never come back. Don't worry. And you shouldn't tell your mother."

"But why not, uncle?" She was already wondering whether her mother would even believe what had happened.

"Maybe the bad man wasn't really trying to hurt you, maybe he tripped and fell on you."

"But Eleni hit him, she hit him hard! She thought he was hurting me!"

"Yes. She's a good goat." He thought rapidly, "You shouldn't tell your mother because she might not let you walk around by yourself anymore. She'll keep you locked in the house!"

"Oh." Little Mairy considered this, found it convincing. "Are you sure the bad man is far, far away, uncle?"

"Oh yes! He's far, far, far away. *Poly makryá!* He'll never come back here. And Mairy?"

"Yes, uncle?"

"You mustn't ever speak to men alone, when no one's around and you're out in the country like this. Not even men from the village, men you know. It's not...it's not what good little girls should do. Do you understand?" She did.

*

Thanassi was staring into circles in the water where a stone had landed. The stone had gone through the water, plunk, and the rippling circles had started to spread out and he was going through the circles as they spread around him, hurtling now through space and then a hole appeared in the water ahead of him and he had to go through the rippling circles expanding around him again and it was unpleasant, so unpleasant he wanted to scream, being there in the black water not able to breathe, and with more water ahead, and the circles kept coming and the water was ice cold on his face and he felt as if he was sliding much too fast on a glass sheet, too fast, sliding to a point on the horizon and then he opened his eyes and Yanni was shaking him and there was cold water on his face.

"Thanassi! Come on! Wake up!" Yanni had tears in his eyes. "You were screaming! Wake up, *moré!*"

For a moment Thanassi didn't have the slightest idea where he was, didn't know who Yanni was, and the circles were still going by his head until he shook it hard and tried to sit up. Then he was seized by massive nausea and he just managed to turn his head before he retched over and over again, helpless retching, with nothing coming up. But he could feel the blood returning to his brain and like a curtain going up somewhere in there consciousness returned.

He remained on all fours, his head hanging down, a great feeling of relief coming over him. What should he be relieved at? And now he remembered. The Germans chasing him. And the last thing he could remember was the pain of turning his ankle. He looked around now and saw immediately that they were in the grove of the goats. Yanni had been dribbling cold water from the pool onto his face.

"Yanni! What happened? The Germans, where...?"

"Thanassi! Oh thank you, Jesus and Mary and all the angels! Thank you God! Thanassi-the-bad-German-shot-you-with-a-gun-and-I-thought-you-were-dead-the-other-one-the-Greek-man-he-went-away-he-has-family-in-Sfakia-the-German-fell-but-I-got-around-the-cliff-and-found-you-and-look-what-he-shot-you-with!"

All this came in a great burst and Yanni was now holding up a metal dart. Everything was suddenly clear to Thanassi: the strange attack in his house, the hypodermic needle, the dart—obviously a tranquilizer dart—meant to immobilize him so they could get him somewhere alone and...what? That was obvious. Find out where the Dead Philadelphians were and how to get them. How would they find out? Long, slow torture, no doubt, and he wouldn't be able to give them the right answers, the way he'd fixed it. Oh, my God! he thought. What have I done?

Yanni told him about the chase, how Hans had heard the Germans talking, how he'd come up on the *trikyklo*, saw the crazy German, how he'd run up on the cliff...

"Yanni! The crazy German? Who was he?"

And Yanni told him for the first time about the arm wrestling and how the crazy man had hit him, and how he'd been there, sitting in Thanassi's doorway with blood on his face when he went by.

"So he never came up on the mountain? Good! I hit that *maláka* as hard as I could. But he's still down there. Maybe he's waiting for me!"

"Thanassi! Don't you worry! He's just one man, how can he hurt us? We'll tell the policeman to arrest him."

Thanassi had a sudden relapse of dizziness. The circles returned and he put both hands on the ground and shook his head. Yanni was reaching out, worried. Thanassi felt the pulse pounding again in his head and he recovered.

"It's the drug, Yanni. They shot me with a drug to make me sleep. They were going to...uh, take me back to Germany."

"But why would they do that, Thanassi?"

"Because...because they thought I owed them some money. But it was a mistake. They were cruel people. Don't worry about them, Yanni."

And then he finally asked Yanni, how did the bad German fall, and Yanni didn't want to tell him but didn't see how he could not answer the question so he told him, I shot the tree. I shot the tree and the tree fell down the cliff.

The two men sat there on the grass. Yanni looking worried, Thanassi with his head in his hands, trying to make it work again, slapping his own face now and then. Shot the tree, he thought. Yanni shot the tree, with the bad man hanging on it. Of course. And he had a crazy thought, I wish I had that on a video. He could see it in slow motion: the German cocksure, knowing that the youth would never shoot him, swinging out on the branch, the branch suddenly shattering and nothing but space under him, plenty of time to think it over before he landed. And then he remembered something else.

"Yanni! The woman! Where did the woman go?"

"Oh, the woman? I only saw her at the end. She was climbing high on the mountain, yelling down at the men. Bah! You don't have to worry about a woman, Thanassi!" And he laughed. Thanassi was thinking about a woman who could pretend to be sick and then stick a hypodermic in someone. What would her role have been in the torture? And he didn't even want to think about it. He had to chuckle at the innocence of Yanni who had lived in a Cretan village all his life and couldn't imagine a woman who was really dangerous. Just noisy, maybe, might bounce a pot off your head if she was really angry, but dangerous? Unh unh!.

After a while they tried Thanassi's ankle and he couldn't walk on it at all; it was swollen like a melon, and Yanni helped Thanassi slide down to the pool where he could put his whole lower leg in the water to cool it off. Lying there in the shade, listening to the cicadas' endless chirping and the spring dribbling down Thanassi went back to sleep and this time it was a good sleep, no dreams, no panic, and when he woke again it was dark.

"Thanassi, drink some milk."

Yanni was holding a clay cup full of goat's milk, still warm. It tasted delicious and Thanassi lay back down, but after a moment the nausea returned and it all came back up.

"I'm sorry," he told Yanni. "I think I still have the drug in me. Maybe I should just sleep."

So Yanni pulled up a big pile of brush and soft pine boughs and made him a softer place to lie and Thanassi thought that he'd never been so comfortable and he could almost feel his brain trying to sort out the right connections, get rid of all that weird shit left over from the drug, and for some reason now his sense of smell seemed to be unnaturally keen and he could smell the pines, first, and then in the background a layer of goatiness, their droppings, of course, but also he could smell goat milk, and their skin, their goaty hair, and there was a little of Yanni too, who was not always washed to perfection, and he could smell the spring water flowing down the cliff and it seemed that he could smell the cave too, the cave on the other side of the pond, with the little altar and the ancient oil lamps with their oil, and the roof of the cave, it seemed, blackened with soot from centuries ago, and from the roof of the cave his sense of smell penetrated inward and he could smell the rock itself, the great massive rock of Toumba, the mountain itself, the limestone hundreds of millions of years old and he could see the stars overhead through the pine boughs and it seemed to him that he could smell the air itself and all the way through the atmosphere out into space and that he could smell the stars...

*

In the end, in the light of day, they agreed that he couldn't walk for a while. He could have walked down a road, but to climb up the cliff in the little footholds his ankle had to get better. Yanni wanted to go back down the mountain and call the Forestry Department, have them bring their helicopter, which was used sometimes to rescue unwise hikers from the slopes of the White Mountains, the *Lefka Ori*, beautiful mountains, mild and forgiving, they looked, but they could kill soft, stupid creatures like humans in an instant and the helicopters had plucked corpses frozen stiff out of snowbanks in the middle of April. Yanni told Thanassi that there were caves high on the mountain. His parents had told him that in the war the partisans had hidden in the caves but they didn't explore the back parts.

Only silly foreigners went exploring in the caves and once high above Toumba some French people went in a cave and never came out and the Forestry people found where they'd left some gear outside the cave so they went in looking for them and the Forestry people never came out either so from now on, if you went in a cave in the *Lefka Ori* it was up to you to get out, no one was coming in to save you.

But Thanassi said no. He didn't want anyone to find this place. It belonged to Yanni and him and no one else, he said. Yanni seemed relieved to hear this. But they both got hungry over the course of two and a half days. They had goat milk from time to time but that wasn't enough to live on for two big men so finally on the third day Thanassi was tired of lying around and he told Yanni how to climb the cliff with the footholds and then lower the rope so that he could come up, step after step, with some support. It hurt, and he lay for a long time on top of the cliff panting because the drug had sapped his strength and he knew he would have to eat and drink well to get it back again.

It took them half a day to walk back down to Thanassi's house, a hike that normally was less than two hours, taking it easy. They found the Volkswagen van gone from the driveway and Thanassi was looking around for his Fiat and finally remembered that he'd left it in town so long ago, it felt like a month. So they went down to the road and Yanni flagged down the first local going by in a pickup truck. They rode into town and everyone came out to find out what had happened.

*

The people of Kali Vrisi had always just thrown their garbage away, down a cliff somewhere, in a ditch, out to sea, but as the benefits of technology increased so did the kinds of trash that wouldn't go away, the plastic bottles that just washed back up on the beach, the soiled food containers that brought flies, and of course the ordure from the fish market and from Fotis' butcher shop. The mayor and town council had eventually decided to bulldoze a solid waste dump in the hills north of town and they were using that until engineers came from the government in Chania and told them the germs and bad chemicals were draining right back into the stream bed that led directly to town and the engineers did tests on the town's well water, of which Kali Vrisi was so proud—that's what the name of the town meant, after all—and they let the townspeople look at the water under a microscope and there were germs swimming in it and there were chemicals that they said could kill a baby if there was too much.

Then they found out that the government of Europe, way up in Belgium of all places, that strange new government farmers and fishermen had so often cursed for interfering with their private business, these bureaucrats had actually arranged to give money to little towns like Kali Vrisi so they could dispose of their garbage in a sanitary manner. The money helped buy a truck that would take some kinds of trash further north to a properly engineered solid waste landfill. It was also used to rent a fishing boat certain days of the week to take big plastic garbage bags weighted with stones out into the really deep water offshore and dump them. For some reason the money was designated to rent the boat of the mayor's brother, a fisherman, another of the many Manolis.

Manoli, Spiro, and an Albanian illegal immigrant were working on the second day after the wedding, loading big black plastic bags on Manoli's *kaïki*. Most of the rubbish was the trash from the big wedding. Spiro was struggling with a trio of bags that had been brought down by Fotis the butcher in his pickup.

"*Panayía mou*! These fucking bags are heavy!" said Spiro. "I think Fotis has been butchering mules or something."

"Remember all the lambs we ate, man!" counseled Manoli. "That butcher slaughtered a lot of animals that day, after all."

"Well, maybe," said Yorgo. "But I'm going to watch what I eat in town the next few days."

"I wouldn't say that around Fotis. You want him to get mad at you?"

"That guy? He killed more people than cancer in his day! No way I'll get him heated up!"

"Well alright then. Don't forget to stick some little holes in the bags so they won't float. Not now, idiot!" This was to the Albanian. "You want to smell what's in there all the way out to sea? Just before we dump them!"

And later that day the three heavy black plastic bags went over the stern into five hundred meters of wine-dark sea off the southern coast of Crete and what was in there only Fotis knew.

*

Thanassi thought maybe the whole village had turned up, standing around the chair where he was resting his ankle in Manoli's restaurant. It seemed that everyone wanted to talk but that no one knew anything so they finally shut up and listened to him and Yanni.

"The Germans came to my house and wanted to know the path up onto Toumba. They said they wanted to photograph some birds."

"And one of them had a camera that looked like a gun," said Yanni. He and Thanassi had gotten their story straight while walking down the mountain.

"But what about the one who was bleeding?" asked Spiro. "You know, when Yanni and I got there he was sitting..."

"We don't know," said Thanassi. "Maybe he fell and then went back up the cliff to join them later. Yanni was looking for me and I was over to the north, you know? Where some of the goats go in the winter? After a while we were worried and we went to look for them, but we lost the trail east on Toumba. It's dangerous over there!" And everyone murmured agreement.

"Maybe the Forestry Department can look for them with their helicopter," said the Mayor, thinking that a certain leadership was required here.

"That's a good idea!" "Yes, indeed!" "Of course. You should call immediately!" This was the general reaction, which meant that now the Mayor had to try to call the helicopter people. They were usually very busy this time of year because so many dumb people were starting fires in the dry brush by throwing away cigarettes. But the Forestry Department would always go out looking for four lost Germans. Thirty percent of the economy of Crete depended on tourists, it was said.

"But that doesn't explain where their van went," said Manoli. "Do you suppose one of them came back and decided to go for help?"

"What was the rental company?" someone asked.

"Kretatours," answered half a dozen townspeople.

"Well then, we should call tomorrow and find if the van was returned. Maybe they all came back and left without Thanassi seeing."

"That's possible," said Thanassi, and he and Yanni nodded

seriously to each other. Yes, yes, quite possible.

"But where were you two for so long?" a woman asked. "We thought you were dead, you and Yanni!"

"Me? What a *vlachas*, a dummy!" said Thanassi. I tripped on a dumb stone I've walked over twenty times. It hurt so bad I thought it was broken. Good thing Yanni was there. He brought me water, milked some goats, then I tried out the foot and found it was only sprained. So all this morning we've been walking down here!"

Fotis the butcher had been listening intently. Now he got up quietly and walked away, a big old man, but light on his feet. On his way he encountered the policeman, a portly man with a big grey mustache, whose look of pain betrayed a slow recovery from the excesses of the wedding party. Fotis clapped him on the shoulder with a hard and heavy hand, causing a sudden wince and a grimace.

"Well, doesn't look like it's our problem here, does it?" he asked.

"No, no. I'll tell the police in Chania there are some Germans missing. But with the rental car gone they won't worry too much up there. They'll think the Germans just drove somewhere else. They hate rounding up lost tourists anyway. And I'll tell them not to send them back here, that bastard hitting Yanni! If I'd been there I would have arrested him!"

But everyone else found the events too unusual just to drop and they stayed in the plateia for another hour, sitting around Manoli's, eating and drinking and sorting out every aspect of the strange German disappearance. Only Manoli gave Thanassi a searching look. Finally the only people left were those with medical advice for the sprained ankle. It should be hot, no—cold; well wrapped, no—leave it loose. And in the middle of the discussion an ancient lady had gone home and now returned with an old tomato sauce jar full of brown grease that smelled of rotting fish but also of bitter wild herbs and of sharp acids and spices. Without asking, she took Thanassi's ankle and smeared it with her unguent. Then she took a long, dirty length of cloth out of her pocket and gently wrapped up the ankle, finally looking up at Thanassi and giving him a triumphant, toothless grin.

"Leave it just like that," said an old man. "If old Voula put it on you're as good as cured."

Old Voula left but a great argument started over whether she was a true healer or just a crazy old lady, so Thanassi, with Yanni's help, went back into the taverna, up the stairs to his room, and went to sleep.

Chapter Fifteen
Los Angeles

In the late morning the fog had burned off the coast of southern California and the sun that would sear the inland valleys later today was still mild and pleasant here on San Vicente boulevard in Brentwood.

Ottie Shamus ordered his latté in the boutique coffee shop and took it outside to sit at a shaded table on the sidewalk where he could watch the Brentwood people going by on their way to everything but work, it seemed to him. He had on his usual dark suit, a white shirt, a tie with lots of little couples doing the tango, his wife had given it to him for Christmas. Everyone else was wearing shorts out here. Almost everyone had a ponytail, men and women, except that some of the women had shaven heads. He couldn't imagine, how are these people making the money to keep up the life style? Ottie kept a careful eye on the black attaché case he'd put by his feet, then began to read the sports section of the *Times*. An attractive woman in a business suit came out of the café with a croissant and a capuccino on her tray, clutching her briefcase under one arm. She looked around for a vacant table, found none, and then saw Ottie sitting alone with three empty chairs around him.

"Mind if I share this table? It gets crowded this time of morning."

"Nah. Help yourself." Ottie didn't even look at her, just kept reading his paper. His lip curled slightly in distaste as she lit a cigarette and he looked up but she blew the smoke out into the street so he hid behind his paper again. The woman made no attempt at conversation either, in fact turned away to make it obvious that she didn't expect any cheery repartee. Ottie finished his latté with a slurp, folded his paper, picked up the woman's briefcase, and walked off to the corner of San Vicente where he flagged down a cab and took off in the direction of downtown. The woman looked off into the distance, took another puff of her cigarette, then moved Ottie's attaché case with her foot so it was under her chair. The other side of the table was now taken by a pair of men in tennis togs, carrying their racquet cases, juggling espressos, chatting about yesterday's Dodger game. They could almost be actors in a commercial, both of them good looking, one white, the other one a light brown African American. They stopped talking long enough to take a quick sip at their espressos. Ouch, hot! They laughed about it.

"You put some sugar in, it cools off faster," said the African American.

"I know, but I never take sugar," said his friend.

"I know, I know, neither do I."

The young woman finished her cappuccino, left her croissant untouched, looked at her watch and began to reach for the black attache case at her feet.

"You know, it's such a nice day, and this is such a great place..." said one of the tennis players to her, getting her annoyed attention, "...that I really hate to say this, but here goes: *you have the right to remain silent, you have the right to an attorney, anything you say may be used as evidence against you..."* and he went on reading her the Miranda formula. "I'm sorry," he said at the end. "But you're a lawyer and I guess you know what's going on. I'm Detective Larsen, LA Sheriff's Department, and this here is Agent Longway, Justice Department."

His friend had picked up the black attaché case now and was sealing it with colored tape.

The young woman had been strangely silent, not voicing the expected protest or objecting in any other way. Now she shook her head in resigned disbelief.

"You've probably got all this on video, don't you."

"That's right Ms Aldrich, and we're all still on camera, as we speak, haven't tampered with your attaché case at all, or I should say, Mr. Shamus's case. We caught the switch, of course. Now we're filming it being sealed."

"And someone is arresting Mr. Shamus, I suppose?"

"Also as we speak. Now I think we have to get along."

Ms Aldrich made no attempt to get up. "You know, I'll make a statement right now. I'm not going down for this! My fucking boss sent me to exchange cases with Shamus. He didn't say what was in them but I can tell you, and I will testify in court, that he's dirty, that he's done this before, and I will give you names, places, and dates. Now, how's that for cooperation?"

Agent Longway put his racquet cover on the table. "The tape recorder's in there," he said. "In case you were wondering. And your boss is who, just for the record?"

"J. Jordon Roscommon," she replied promptly. "Vice Chair of the California State Coastal Commission. Former State Assemblyman from Orange County, former Orange County planning commissioner, former mayor of Mission Nuevo. And he's supposed to be deliberating the various permits for Malibu Horizons, coming up next week for final approval."

"Before we go any further, Ms Aldrich, I'd like you to state for the record that you are giving this information freely and completely of your own will."

"I am," she said. "Now let's go. I want to get this over with."

*

Goomba was on the phone to Thanassi, who'd been called from the restaurant to the public phone in the post office. He had a crowd around him, hanging on every word.

"They nailed Ottie Shamus for good this time," Goomba was saying. "He was doing the same old switcheroo, this time leaving an attaché case for some lady lawyer who worked for the Coastal Commission. She's telling everything. *Ottie's* telling everything, he's scared shitless 'cause they showed him some videos, they got him leaving the bag for two other politicians!"

"So what's that all mean—you know, for us?"

"George told me, both the Justice Department and the State Attorney General have a policy—they go after the public servant, the guy that took the oath, every time. So if Ottie goes state's evidence and if this lawyer testifies, they get off easy and all the politicians, the guys who took the bread, they're in the crapper! They're looking at significant time."

"Yeah. But Goomba! That's half of it. You know Ottie didn't give a shit! He was just the bag man for Jolly. And when I get a second I'll tell you about the people Jolly sent after me."

"Sent after you? What're you telling me, Danny? You okay?"

"Yeah, just. *Please! Excuse me! Could you all go gossip somewhere else!*" This he said angrily to the crowd around the phone. And then Thanassi told Goomba about the Germans, about the two strongarm guys and the even scarier woman who was probably going to torture him.

"Jesus! When'd this all happen?"

"Just a couple days ago. And Ottie got busted, when?"

"Yesterday. You sure Jolly sent them after you?"

"Come on, Goomba! You're the one who was warning me that anyone could find me, anywhere! They found me! It was smart, too, sending Germans. There're more Germans here than Greeks, the middle of summer. I was just lucky—had Yanni looking after me."

"So, where are these Germans now?"

Thanassi gave him the rundown. There was one guy splashed all over the rocks somewhere halfway down Toumba. The Germans' Greek friend had copped out, left for Sfakia, according to Yanni. The woman and the guy with crazy eyes were still missing, but they'd evidently taken the van. Or someone had.

"Anyway they might be coming back after you?"

"Not a chance! The police are looking for them now and the Forestry helicopter is out over the mountains, looking for anything moving. The word is out and everyone in western Crete is keeping an eye open. Yanni says in a couple of days, look for vultures, way up in the sky over Toumba, circling, that's where they'll be."

"I'll hold that thought," said Goomba, and they both laughed.

"Anyway," said Thanassi, "We're still talking about Jolly. Who's he going to send next time, that I won't even notice? I'm more scared now than I ever was!"

"This is the best part," said Goomba. "George says Jolly has disappeared. The word on the street is that his father-in-law, he's some gangster in New Orleans, he's taking over all Jolly's action because Jolly owes him so much money. So Jolly's out of the picture now."

Thanassi was thinking, now he had a New Orleans mobster after him, and he didn't even know who he was.

"So what's George's reaction to that?"

George says they got a good chance nailing the New Orleans guy, name of Charbon, on the whole Malibu Horizons deal. He says Charbon is going to be too busy."

"And we're going to have to testify in court, right in front of God and everyone?"

"George says no. They got the goods on Ottie, he's going to tell all the people he gave bribes to, he's going to implicate Jolly..."

"So, what do they need from us?'

"Turns out there's some Dead Philadelphians in some Congressman's Swiss account and they need us to tell the Grand Jury about Dead Philadelphians."

"Then we *do* have to testify!"

"But it's in secret and it's sealed, Danny. Federal Grand Jury and with immunity. All we have to do is make the connection."

Thanassi thought he might be right. But he'd had the advantage of talking to cons for four years, some of whom had been told they could testify in secret, no problem, they might get parole. Some of them were still in the joint, never did get parole, some had friends who'd testified and then disappeared.

He had a sudden unexpected thought about Elli for a second and that made his mind up. "Okay, I'm coming back for a while as long as George is going to guarantee we don't get arrested. And I guess you can tell Katina, my family...the hardest part of being here was them not knowing where I was, what I was doing..."

"Count on it!" said Goomba. "Also, you'll be glad to know, I found Costa too. And he's coming back."

Chapter Sixteen
The boat to Athens

THANASSI WAS STANDING ON THE STERN of the ferry in Souda Bay, the evening boat that returned every day from Chania to Athens. From the upper deck he was watching the usual chaos of cars and trucks lined up, coming on board one by one and being choreographed by the crew, who were expertly trying to cram every inch of the huge lower cargo compartment, directing this one hard right, that one hard left, making others back and fill, yelling with exasperation at their fellow Greeks, gesturing wildly but silently at hapless foreigners. A long line of pedestrian passengers was coming in the same gangway and dodging the vehicles on the way to the passenger stairways. Thanassi had tried to get a flight to Athens but this time of year the flights were all full...you needed a reservation at least three days in advance.

He'd decided to leave in a hurry. He'd told Manoli he had to go home, take care of urgent business, and he'd asked Yanni to go up to the farm every couple of days, water the goats and chickens and bring back the produce for the restaurant. Manoli had stared at him for a long time, then grabbed him by both arms.

"You're coming back? This isn't just some bullshit so

you can get out of here, leave us forever?"

"Manoli! You can count on it! How could I leave this place? Come on, man! It's just for a while. And I'm counting on you to tell everyone that I'm coming back!"

And Manoli had grinned and swatted him up alongside his head but still obviously didn't believe him. And that morning, when he drove out of Kali Vrisi, he caught a glimpse of Elli coming out of her house, seeing him in his Fiat on the way out of town, and her face collapsing into a tragic mask, her mouth open...saying *no, no, Thanassi! Where are you going?*

There was a commotion down on the dock where the crowds of passengers and vehicles were boarding. Two burly men were trying to wheel a wheelchair on board, over the corrugated gangway, and disputing the space with an enormous truck, whose driver obviously believed he had the right of way based on disparity of size. The frail little lady in the wheelchair was slumped in pain or fatigue, not paying attention to the angry shouts passing over her head, one hand up to keep her dark glasses from falling off from the bouncing over the ridges of the gangway. Thanassi looked out to the west where the sun was going down over Chania. A subtlety of the light suggested the coming fall instead of just the next hot day, which Cretans endured for a hundred days or more each year. A strong north wind had come up, catching his attention, and to the northeast past the point of Akrotiri he could see the white-caps building in the growing darkness. It would be a rough trip all night, plowing into the wind.

He stood at the rail until the ship was well out of the harbor, into the waves and the wind, enjoying the motion of the ship and the wetness on his face. Then as the sun disappeared he wandered into the first class lounge. There were already people looking half dead, some sprawled in the big armchairs, others leaning forward with their heads in their hands. He went to the bar, the only customer so far, ordered an ouzo, and discussed seasickness with the barman.

"Oh yes," said the bartender, a wiry middle-aged man with curly hair, what was left of it, and a big black mustache. "Yes. You see these people dying here you'd never believe we Greeks are the greatest sailors in history. Odysseus, Pytheas, who sailed around Britain, the ones who sailed to India, and later ones. You're an American?" He used the word *omoyénis*, meaning Greek American.

"Yes, but I'm living on Crete now."

"Good for you. When you get bored come to Athens. You'll like it. You live in a village in Greece? We all did. In the winter they're so bored they pick fights and quarrel just for something to do. You live in Athens? Fight with the taxi driver, get it out of your system, you know you'll never see him again, no poison sitting in your guts all winter. What I was saying about Greek sailors? You have a big strait there in America, I read once, called after Juan de Fuca?"

Thanassi had never been there but he knew about it.

"Yes. It's between the US and Canada, up near Seattle. But that's Spanish, De Fuca."

"Spanish, bullshit! I read lots of history. The Spaniards were imbeciles, only knew how to fight, they all hired pilots from somewhere else. Columbus, Italian, right? Portuguese, too! And De Fuca? His real name was Phokas... Ioannis Phokas, from Kephalonia. That's where I'm from," the bartender grinned. "Argostoli. There're still Phokases there. Three hundred years ago they tried to get money from the Spanish king, for discovering the strait. Good luck!" He laughed. "My name is Dimitri. Yours?"

Dimitri had an unending trove of stories about Greek

adventurers in history. Thanassi had two more ouzos and finally a sandwich with a tiny sliver of ham. He figured he needed something in his stomach but he didn't feel like sitting down to a full dinner in the dining room. After a while he decided to go down to his first class cabin and catch up on his sleep. He'd had nightmares the last two nights and he'd read, a long time ago back in the States, about tranquilizer drugs. They didn't just put you to sleep. They were dangerous, especially to humans, because the drug was akin to the street hallucinogenic, PCP, and had a worse effect on the complex minds of humans than on say, grizzlies.

So he was looking forward to his bunk when he wandered down the long corridor, found his cabin number, opened the door into the darkness, and was searching for a light when he felt the prick of the needle in his neck and the coldness and the awful helpless weakness and knew he'd been stuck with a tranquilizer again.

*

"...Had to go to much trouble. Didn't know you were leaving. Just guessed it. Hee hee! Hurt, hurt. Hurt my leg, other things, damned rocks!" The voice rambled on, sometimes in English, sometimes in German.

Thanassi was coming down through the circles in the water with the clanging, the metallic clanging in his eyes. The circles were all around them, he could hear their sound, but he could see the clanging, painful clanging in his eyes. His senses were all mixed up: he was hearing images and seeing sounds. And suddenly he felt a pain in his foot and it was if he could taste the pain and he fell out of the circles and found himself in a dim light looking at a nightmare. The nightmare was sitting in a wheelchair. A bundle of shapeless clothes with a thin face like an axe blade. She was grinning at him and waving a long needle, like an ice pick, but thinner.

"You see! I give you a little prick in the foot, you wake up! But I had to give you some amphetamine first. You were sleeping so hard, I thought I killed you!"

He tried to say something to her but realized his mouth was covered with something. The circles were still spinning and his eyes went in and out of them but in a moment of clarity he knew that his hands and feet were fastened, it didn't feel like rope, maybe duct tape, to the corners of the bunk. And from the feel of the air he knew he was naked. His first absurd thought was that he must tell her that he'd been shot with a tranquilizer only days ago, that the dose was too much, twice in a row, that he would die, but then she was leaning forward again, and he felt the pain in his foot, not sudden or shocking, but as if someone was phoning it in long distance, it arrived bit by bit, and then he went under again, through the circles, the circles swimming around him and he was on the slippery surface again, sliding too fast towards the mountains in the distance, going to crash..."

"Arrraggh!" It was a harsh noise and his eyes opened again. There was the same dim light, reddish in the small cabin. The figure in the wheelchair had changed. She had taken off the pants of her warmup suit and he was looking at mangled flesh.

"Ach, ach, ach! That hurt so much," she almost sobbed. "Your goddamned mountain moved, you know that?"

All he could do was stare at the ravaged flesh on her knee and lower leg, dark red, black, almost blue, brown in places It looked as if she'd been caught in a terrible machine. And it smelled of spoiled meat.

"The mountain...I was too high. I couldn't find the way around where you were...I was coming back and I jumped...and the mountain, your goddamned mountain, it moved.

"I fell," she sobbed, as if once more feeling the shock, the sharpness of the rocks carving into her flesh. "Ach! Those rocks like knives! Cutting, scraping! The pain, I couldn't stand it!" She showed him the palms of her hands. On the heels of her hands the skin had been torn off while she was trying to break her fall. The raw flesh shone with some kind of ointment. She grinned at his reaction, started to say something in English, then winced and switched to German, started crooning something comforting to herself. Then back into English.

"I walked the whole way back like this, you see? Took the Volks, drove all the way back, you hear..." He started hallucinating again, was back on the glass, sliding towards the mountains. Then the pain in his foot again.

"You must not sleep! I'm going to have some fun with you, you wait and see! And first you tell me, before the stupid goddamned money, first you tell me, what happened to my Jürgi? What I was going to do to him I do to you, now. Where is he?" And he saw her hand rise up with the needle above his genitals and thought, please let me go to sleep again. But for the moment he was buzzing awake and he saw her lower the needle, touch it to his testicles, push a little bit, then she put it under his penis and flopped it back on his stomach.

"Such a nice hard body. All hard except the one thing. But no problem, I have a little needle here..." And she was fumbling in her fanny pack. "A tiny shot of this and we will make you all hard, all over, hee hee! Maybe I'll have some fun first. You won't believe what I did to an Englishman once. Such idiots, they pretend to be spies... Uh, uh."

The ship had lurched, moving the wheelchair and she was grunting with pain from trying to keep her balance..

"Maybe I'll need some morphia first, just a little..." And she took another hypodermic out of her pack. Thanassi started swirling down the circles again and then felt a prick in his foot, an itch that wouldn't go away. When he came back she was poking his foot with the needle, cackling with laughter. He wondered idly what she'd done to the Englishman.

"You think I'm crazy! Laughing. No. I just was thinking what they did to me. You know they fired me? The Stasi? You say 'secret police' in English, if you didn't know. Dumb Americans! The Stasi fired me, you know for what? For *sadism*!" And she was cackling again and he saw she had a needle still sticking out of her arm, the inside of the elbow. Then she started babbling in German again and organizing her hypodermic needles on the tiny desk in the cabin, getting them all straight for the long night, the amphetamine, the drug to make him hard, the morphia for herself, the long needle for asking questions...and Thanassi went completely under, no circles, no sliding on the glass, just completely out.

A violent sound went crashing through his head, once, twice, again, slicing his brain to ribbons, startling his whole body into convulsions. His eyes flew open and saw instantly that faint light was coming in under the curtains on the portholes. He spontaneously tried to jerk erect, then realized he was still fastened to the bunk, remembered where he was, wondered what the sound had been.

Ilse Wilamowitz was still in her wheelchair, head thrown back, her savaged leg stuck straight out in front of her, still stinking. There was a hypodermic stuck in her arm. Thanassi realized he was lying in a pool of his own sweat, that he was soaked, his head sending a spray of sweat flying when he turned it from side to side. He strained against his bonds and could feel, suddenly, that his sweat had turned him slippery under the duct tape, that he might get out.

It wasn't easy, and finally he just concentrated on one wrist, turning it this way, that way, pulling, pushing back up on it, until the tape had curled into a sticky black rope and then finally with all his remaining strength he pulled steadily, slipping a little bit at a time, and his wrist came out. Then he just had to pick at the edge of the tape on the other wrist and finally he was out, sat up, and passed out completely again.

The horrible noise went through his head again and brought him to and he knew it was the ship's horn, sounding as if it was two feet from the cabin, and that they were coming into the port of Piraeus in Athens. He managed to get his feet free, managed to find the various pieces of his clothes and put them on, found his pack. Then finally, he dared look at the woman. She was dead, no doubt about it, no telling which drug she'd been giving herself did the job. And a sudden jolt of pain reminded Thanassi that she'd actually started to torment him, sticking the needle into the top of his foot. But he could walk, even though he sobbed from the pain of putting his shoe on his right foot, the one with the punctures in it, the one he'd sprained.

He got out of there, fighting off the dizziness, carrying his pack, joining the long, jostling line of passengers fighting their way down the companionways and the narrow halls, out of the ship, and he thought he'd pass out again when they were stopped interminably in a tiny passageway, the air stuffy, diesel fumes in his nose, but he stamped his damaged foot on the steel plates under him and the shock of the pain woke him up again.

On the dock he staggered to the first free taxi.

"I'm sick," he said. "You know a clinic?"

The man looked back, concerned, "A hospital? What's wrong, mister...?"

"No, no, no hospital. A private clinic? You know? I have some money, I can afford..." He struggled with his wallet and pulled out a five thousand drachma note and gave it to the driver.

Thanassi woke again, being helped out of the taxi by a man and two women in white smocks, all looking very concerned. They put him in a wheelchair and pushed him into a pink stucco building surrounded with trees and shrubbery, He could see the sea in the background and knew this must be an expensive private clinic somewhere around Glyfada, maybe. Just what he wanted. Inside he made himself stay awake long enough to give the doctor the right phony passport.

"I was at a crazy party! Someone was passing around drugs and I was stupid...I said okay. They said it was tran-quilizers...Does that help?"

The doctor didn't look happy, but she nodded. They wheeled him away and he went under again.

Chapter Seventeen
Zurich

The phone call woke Sun instantly. The predawn light was coming through his window there in the Zurich hotel.

It was Knoblauch on the phone and he was viciously angry.

"Werner is dead. They followed the birds with the helicopter, the Greek police. He fell two hundred meters, maybe more! And Ilse? They found her dead on a ferry boat, drug overdose they said! No trace of the man who had the cabin. The police there don't care, won't look for him, drug overdose makes it easy to close the books, especially with a German, they hate us anyway!"

Sun was struggling to wake up. "But the brother, Jürgen, and Mikali? What about them?"

"No trace! *Spurlos gesenkt!*" And it's been six days now when Ilse called me from the village and said it was all set up for the next day!"

"But...but how did you hear?"

"We had a Greek security service in Crete. They found this fucking Castle for us, his rental car. Strictly contract—they knew nothing else. Then three days ago they hear on the radio that Germans are missing, then Ilse showed up at their office in Chania, half dead, and insisted on going on a ferry back to Athens. They wanted to take her to the hospital but she said terrible things and threatened them with a needle, they said. Then the ferry comes to Athens and she is dead, of an overdose, the fucking police say! Then the radio says a German is found in the mountains, all smashed!"

Sun was trying to make sense of all this "But is there any word about Castle?"

"Castle, bullshit! You gave me bad intelligence! You said one man, alone, we're looking for! But this is an organization! One man, one puny civilian kills Werner Jaeger and Ilse Wilamowitz? Those two? Bullshit, bullshit! This is CIA, and you didn't tell me!"

"It's not CIA, I promise you..." Sun started to protest.

"It is an operation, no doubt about it, CIA, probably, maybe some other company. They go after one young man, all alone, just out of prison? It should have been like a simple field exercise! And somebody kills Werner and Ilse? Two experts like that? One in the mountains, one on a boat to Athens. And the other two disappear? You dare tell me you don't know?"

Sun was getting angry. "You must forgive me, but I insist that Castle was all alone, no backup. And our intelligence was that the American agencies were looking for him too, not backing him up. What would the point be! Just to eliminate gangsters who were trying to catch him?"

The other end of the line was silent for a moment.

"You may be right," Knoblauch conceded. "It doesn't make sense. I'm going to keep looking into this. And your Mr. Jolly, you can tell him that he's not getting a penny back! We don't operate that way!"

Sun was mystified when he got off the phone, but it didn't bother him. He felt that as all the various parts of this operation failed and dropped away that the burden on him became lighter and lighter, until only one duty remained before he could go to Hong Kong and work for his own people. He certainly had no regrets about Werner Jaeger and the Wilamowitz woman. In fact he hoped someone had taken care of the crazy brother at the same time. He had virtually no curiosity left about Castle, about the money, the bonds, about where they were, and he had to admit that he was secretly glad that Castle was not at this minute being tortured by a sadistic psychopath in the cellar of some villa in Chania. He called his travel agent in Zurich and made a reservation for the next flight to New York. Then he called the forwarding number for Jolly and let him know he was on his way.

Chapter Eighteen
Flying home

THANASSI WAS SITTING IN THE DOCTOR'S OFFICE. Through the window he could see windsurfers slicing across the coastal waters. He felt drained but also cleansed of whatever poisons had been coursing through his system. Last night he had slept for eleven hours and he was still groggy. The doctor was not looking happy. She was one of the three who had helped him into the clinic, when? It must have been three days ago now. She was a handsome woman, maybe early forties but looking younger in spite of her stern expression at the moment, and she was looking at him critically.

"I think we can let you go, Mr. Poulos. But you were very foolish."

He made an apologetic gesture. "I don't usually do things like this, but I met some people at a party, there was too much to drink, then some other people took me to another party...I have no idea where it was..."

"I don't care. I have no patience for people like...like that." Thanassi had the impression that she was about to say "people like you."

"And you, you should be ashamed. You are very healthy, you have a superb constitution, otherwise you might have been very, very sick, even dead."

"But these drugs...these are only tranquilizers, I thought..."

"You thought? Forgive me! I don't believe you were thinking at all, your brain was turned off! We had to pump your stomach, where the drug accumulates, then make you drink liters of water and vomit them up again. We had to give you some strong drugs that are themselves dangerous, diazepam and others, just to keep you from going under where we might not be able to bring you back again! And the tranquilizers are a great stress on the liver. In fact, I must insist you eat no meat or oil, or drink alcohol for the next two weeks, at least. Do you understand?"

"Yes, I have no problem with that..."

"Because when the liver is stressed too much it gives up and there is no cure, you will die."

Thanassi did his best to look ashamed of himself.

"And your foot! The nurse thought you had been trying to give yourself a shot of drugs or something in your left foot. But the holes were too big for a hypodermic. There was a slight infection but it is healing now. We almost thought you had gangrene because your ankle is a strange color and it smells. We tried to wash it off but you can still see the color. What was on your foot?"

Thanassi was thinking fast. "I live in a little town in Crete and I made the mistake of walking at night with only my sandals. I tripped and went off the path into the thorns. You know what they're like in Crete! And then an old woman put some kind of salve on it." His foot felt nearly healed and he wondered if Voula's ointment had a residual effect that could cure needle holes too.

She obviously didn't believe him. "Mr. Poulos, I don't know who you are or what you're doing these days but I think you have a dangerous life style. Do you have close friends or relatives in Athens who can look after you for a while?"

"No I don't. But I'll be alright, I'm sure."

"Well at least you will be poorer than you were!"

She handed him an itemized bill. Thanassi just glanced at the total and realized he had stayed two nights in a clinic, had received urgent care and treatment, for little more than an simple office visit to a doctor would have cost him back in California. He smiled. "Well, I really learned my lesson."

"I doubt it," she said. And after he had paid and as he was leaving she finally gave him a crooked smile, the first friendly expression he'd seen from her. "You know, Mr. Poulos, you, with a different name in your wallet, if you ever come back this way again and have some time, please come by and tell me what was going on. I'll buy you lunch. They have very good fish just down the road!"

From the clinic to Olympic Airlines was only a five minute taxi ride. Thanassi told himself that now he was Danny again. He looked at the forests of eucalyptus on one side, the villas, the coastal buildup of hotels and restaurants, with now and then a glimpse of sea between the buildings. He was leaving Greece but this didn't seem like Greece. There were four lanes of traffic on each side and they were packed solid and the cabs were honking, blaring at other cabs making outrageous lane changes. It could be Sunset Boulevard going through Hollywood except the signs were in Greek. There was a Marlboro billboard in English; underneath in prominent Greek letters it instructed him ΤΟ ΚΑΠΝΙΣΜΑ ΒΛΑΠΤΕΙ ΣΟΒΑΡΑ ΤΗΝ ΥΓΕΙΑ: *smoking harms your health severely.* The taxi had interior signs in both English and Greek saying *don't smoke, please!* The driver had been chain-smoking since he got in the cab.

Danny had phoned a travel agent and had been told

there was nothing back to the US for four, maybe five days and he had decided to try at the airport. He limped up to the international counter thinking at least his ankle sprain was almost well. Old Voula's ointment must have done the trick. He should have asked the doctor what could cure both sprains and flesh wounds. It took an age, standing in line at the ticket counter and several people had made a terrific hullaballoo at the agent, about what he had no idea, but it was standard practice here to make a lot of noise and fuss when you were feeling insecure. When it was his turn he smiled and rolled his eyes up, *what we all have to put up with*, he was saying with his expression, and when he spoke, he spoke in English. *"I know it's difficult, but I'm trying to get back home. It's very important, please!"* The dark, pretty woman looked at Danny, saw the urgency, saw the interesting hazel eyes and the warm smile, a real smile. He looked like a man who would stay awake after love, who would talk, who would listen, who would wake up early and feed the cat...

"There's no problem. There is a tour cancellation. I can get you on Olympic two hours from now, connecting with Air France in Paris for Los Angeles. There's a three hour layover there in Paris, are you sure that's alright?" She was smiling warmly and Danny had a sudden insane impulse, *what if I just asked her to come with me to Santorini for a week?* He stamped his right foot and the pain fixed his head again.

Twenty hours later Danny was coming down over the San Bernardino mountains into Los Angeles. There was a thick layer of smog he could see over the eastern suburbs. A marine layer had begun to drift onshore and shoved the smog away from the western Los Angeles basin. Danny had only flown into Los Angeles once before, many years ago, and now although he'd only been away three months it was almost like a foreign country. But now he could recognize the long straight lines of the freeways below, and there was Hollywood Park, the racetrack, there was the San Diego Freeway, and now the plane was much lower, coming down over hangers and freight warehouses and then the wheels hit and screeched and he knew that now he had to face reality. It was as if he was out of one movie, a crazy one, with crazy characters and settings and now he was back in real life, like waking up out of a dream. Or maybe just another movie. Coming back an orphan, no mother, relatives he knew well but with whom he was not really close. Coming back to the scene of a crime—they *had* committed a crime and he was only taking someone's word that they wouldn't go to jail for it. And then he thought about jail. Four years that he'd only been able to endure knowing that he would get out relatively soon. He didn't think he could go back to jail again and in a sudden panic he wondered, *what the hell am I doing here anyway?*

The big 747 taxied for a long time and then there was dumb American musak on the loudspeakers to listen to and it helped him think of being an American again. In a half hour he had cleared customs at LAX and came up the ramp at the Bradley terminal to find Goomba, Katina, and most of his nieces and nephews waiting for him. He couldn't help bursting into tears in the midst of all the hugs and kisses.

Goomba's eyes were shining too. "Danny! It's great! And wait till you hear the latest!"

Danny pointed a finger at him, like a pistol. "No, you wait, you won't believe where I've been."

Chapter Nineteen
Sun in New York

SUN LEFT ALL HIS LUGGAGE IN A LOCKER at JFK and took only a thick manila envelope into town with him in the taxi. In the lobby of the Times Square Marriot he was glad to see a horde of conventioneers. The crowd made it easier for him to wander about a little and make sure no one had picked him up at the entrance. There were some watchers out there for *someone*, he felt sure, just from instinct. The homeless guy with a watchcap and dark glasses over by the newsstand. The usual phone company van across Times Square. But no one came in after him and after a half hour he made his move. On the mezzanine there was a long table where people were picking up their name tags. As he passed by he happened to see one that said, "Hello, my name is TOM YAMAGUCHI."

"I am Mr. Yamaguchi," he said to the pleasant lady behind the table.

"Oh great!" she said, handing him the tag. "And do you want to take Mrs. Yamaguchi's name tag too?"

"Yes, that is most helpful," said Sun, hoping his caricature Japanese accent wasn't too over the top. He put the name tag on his lapel. At a no-host bar he picked up a drink, a double vodka, no ice, then loosened his tie as most of his fellow conventioneers seemed to have done and boarded an elevator for the fifty-fourth floor.

There was a crowd of name-tagged people on the elevator, all cheery, many of them carrying drinks too. His name tag was inspected.

"Yamaguchi...You're with the Omaha people, aren't you," stated a big red-haired man who was clutching an armful of convention literature.

"No, Los Angeles," Sun said, hoping that two obviously Japanese tourists on the elevator wouldn't start talking to him as well, or wonder why he was speaking English with an accent that didn't sound Japanese. He was trying to be inconspicuous and he didn't need any distractions. Luckily the mention of Omaha brought a response from a fluttery woman in a business suit and a very ruffled blouse who'd just moved from there and how glad she was to get out of there. The horrors of living in Omaha, loudly catalogued, enabled Sun to blend into the background until his floor came up.

He walked down the long hall composing himself, achieving the calmness of the inner spirit that was crucial just before sudden action. His only advantage was surprise—he was half an hour early. The time difference would have made no difference to the alertness of an intelligence professional waiting for him, but these were only gangsters, he reminded himself.

When he saw that the door he was looking for had the doorknob on the left side, he visualized the room and shifted the drink to his left hand. He knocked on the door. A large black man opened it almost immediately with puzzlement on his face, seeing the expected Asian face but also the confusing nametag and the drink. Sun instantly hurled the vodka into his eyes then slammed the door open the rest of the way as hard as he could and felt someone behind there. He took a quick step into the room and kicked the man who had been behind the door in the head, then whirled back and chopped the blinded black man across the throat, kneed him in the groin and finished with the heel of his hand under his nose. Whirling back he found the man behind the door bloodied and staggering but struggling to get out a pistol. He grabbed the gun hand, pivoted and spun the man over his hip into the middle of the room. In the middle of the throw he relieved him of the pistol, a 9 mm. automatic, reached behind him and slammed the door again

"Black guy's got the silencer!" he heard Herschel Jolly yell and he turned to see his boss getting out of an armchair. Across the table from him, also seated, was Eddie Charbon, who was just beginning to react. Sun held the automatic on him, then stooped and felt under the jacket of the black lying at his feet until he found the gun with the silencer. The man thrown into the middle of the room was starting to get up so Sun tried out the silenced gun. It worked perfectly. Just a little cough and the man lay down again. He looked back down at the black man but he wouldn't need the gun for him. The bone of his nose had gone up into his brain.

"Are you fucking nuts!!" Charbon was blustering. "We just needed to talk..."

"Talk, bullshit," Jolly shouted to Sun. "They were going to whack you the second you came in, then I was next. It's the same way I would've done it too. They just wanted what's in the envelope. What's in there, by the way?"

Still holding the silenced gun on Charbon, Sun opened the flap, looked in. "Let's see...you got your airline magazine, last week's *Time*, chart of airplane emergency exits, air sickness bag...that's it."

Charbon was stuttering with rage and wouldn't shut up so Sun shot him too. Finally the room was quiet enough to talk.

"You saved my ass, you know that, Sun?" Jolly was wiping his face. "I was sweating! I figured I was going to be aced the minute Eddie showed up with the muscle. But I guessed that anyway."

"That's what you said in your fax," said Sun. "So I had this outcome planned from the beginning, if you will forgive me. It was a little risky but it was the cleanest way to finish the thing, tie up loose ends. Will anyone come after you from his family?"

"Probably not, you know? First they all gotta fight it out, see who's gonna take over. Then they gotta find me. And where I'm going to be they're not going to chase me. So now, what's the bad news on the bonds?"

Sun told him about Zurich and then about the ruin of the Cretan operation: two dead, probably all of them, in those mountains. He mentioned Knoblauch's belief that the CIA was involved."

"CIA! I wish! They at least might've fucked it up. But this Castle, first he steals the bonds, then he wipes out an army of German gangsters. I'm not forgetting that kid!" Jolly had picked up his briefcase and was beginning to go around the room with his handkerchief, wiping the door, the table, the arms of his chair.

"I tried not to touch nothing, and I remembered everything I touched. Room's registered to Charbon. Now what's the story with the stiffs?"

Sun was deep in thought, considering scenarios. Then he made up his mind. "They start having a fight, the two shooters, they punch each other a bit, then the black guy pulls out the silenced piece, nails Charbon and the other guy. But before he's dead the guy on the floor pulls his piece out and shoots the black guy."

"Yeah, but that last part didn't happen yet. Nobody shot the black guy. What're we going to do about that?"

"No. You ready to get out of here, didn't leave anything?"

"Nothing. What you gonna do?"

Sun carefully picked up his envelope, tucked it under his arm. Then he went over to the television and turned it up loud.

"Okay, get over by the door, get ready to leave in a hurry." He pulled the black bodyguard so he was lying next to the other man on the floor. He wiped off the silenced pistol, put it in the black's hand then put the automatic in the other man's hand. He looked up at Jolly. "One, two..."

Holding the gun in the man's hand he pulled the trigger and fired a shot into the black's chest. The noise of the shot was fierce. Sun quickly stood up, picked up his vodka glass from the floor, and followed Jolly out the door. They walked casually to the banks of elevators and took the next one down. They didn't see any heads sticking out of doors on the way.

In the cab out to the airport Sun was explaining to Jolly. "Cops're going to think it's fishy right off the bat. But they do things by the numbers and they won't be sure it's a setup until they autopsy the black guy and find out he was killed twice, that he was already dead when he got shot. Then they'll check his hand and find out he never fired the gun. That will be maybe six hours from now. I'll be on the way to San Francisco, catch a plane for Hong Kong. And you...?"

"Sun, I'm not even telling you," Jolly chuckled. "You know I owe you more'n I can ever pay, saving my life like that. But I paid you what we agreed, right?"

"Yes. And you were very generous."

"Okay. I got one last request. If you can get a flight to Hong Kong out of LA instead of Frisco, spend an extra day, just check one last time for the Castle kid, see if he figured he's out of the woods and came home...can you do that?"

"Yes, but..."

"And then you can take this to Hong Kong. They can change it there just like Switzerland, maybe easier." Jolly reached into his briefcase, took out a beautifully engraved document and gave it to Sun. It had the figure $100,000 in one corner.

"Here's one of them fucking bonds. You know as well as I do, it's only worth about sixteen grand, maybe less, time you get it cashed in. But it's worth it to me at least to find out if that little prick is still alive, maybe I'll send somebody after him."

*

The big ugly detective from Homicide in Manhattan was in a filthy mood. Everyone who'd ever had to work with him knew about his hemorrhoids and they all sort of tiptoed around when in his presence. But they thought that there must be some magic connection between hemorrhoids and brain power because he was a fucking genius. Now when he started yelling they all quit what they were doing and listened hard.

"I got a guy here with his eyes full of vodka, down his face, in his collar. When I got a guy had a glass of vodka thrown in his face and there's no glass around with vodka in it, no fucking vodka in the whole room, I get very upset! Call every fucking agency in the country and find out, were they tailing somebody to this hotel, some crime celebrity we don't know about?"

His deputy had the FBI on the line in two minutes. Yes, they had lost a suspect in the lobby of the Marriot. Who was it? We can't reveal that information. The homicide detective said things over the phone none of his closest associates had ever heard before, ending with a calmer statement that he was about to tell the papers that they had a suspect in a triple homicide but the FBI wouldn't tell who it was. He found out who it was.

The police and the FBI got to JFK at the same time. Because of the fake passport and the different name the fugitive had been using it took them a while, showing around Herschel Jolly's photo. And the two agencies still weren't cooperating. They got to El Al an hour and fifty minutes after the plane left and they didn't have a warrant yet and really no grounds for one so they couldn't get the plane to come back.

That evening the US attorney in New York was called away from a Masterpiece Theatre drama he was watching with his wife. He listened patiently to the whole story. Then he asked, *is this big time drugs?* No? *Is this about terrorism?* No? *Just crime?* Then he looked in his schedule and said he should be able to look over the case sometime next week.

Chapter Twenty
Santa Monica

Danny and Costa had a great reunion, hugging, smacking each other around. It had been over four years, both of them thinking the other one might be dead, and they were both high with rambunctious good spirits even though they were in an anteroom in the Federal Building in downtown Los Angeles, waiting to go before the Grand Jury. Danny had told George Kiosoglou that maybe they should have a lawyer, they could afford one, but George had to tell them, this is the Grand Jury, the whole deal is that you *can't* have a lawyer. And there're no lawyers out there trying to get you. You're talking to your fellow citizens. So just tell the truth.

So they did, one after another, Goomba telling about the meeting where Jolly had arranged the transfer of the bonds, Danny explaining the plan they'd come up with, and finally Costa describing his disguise as a Latina stewardess. When he told the Grand Jury about trying to switch suitcases at the same time a pilot was feeling his ass the whole room broke up. The federal attorney let them laugh a bit, then she dug in, getting her hooks into the real culprits.

"So you see, jurors, that we have a complete chain of evidence: Herschel Jolly provides the bonds, transfers them to Mr. Arthur Shamus, who is then responsible for paying off various legislators. We could have come to you four years ago with our suspicions that this was taking place. Finally we were able to document the recurrence of a fund transfer and Arthur Shamus has testified that he was making the transfer on behalf of his employer Herschel Jolly and his partner, as we now know, Mr. Eduard Charbon, of New Orleans. Now we have the testimony of Mr. Scarlatta, Mr. Castle, and Mr. Arvanites that they intercepted the payment of a bribe. In both cases the financial instruments used for the bribe were revenue bonds from the lower Schuylkill sanitation district.

"The law of our country is and always should be most rigorous at punishing those public servants who have taken an oath to serve the public and have then allowed themselves to be corrupted in return for their vote."

She read off an impressive list of Congressmen, California state legislators, city councilmen, and the recent Vice Chair of the state coastal commission, whom she wished the Grand Jury to indict.

"These dishonest politicians must be punished most severely, as a lesson to all Americans that public office must not be perverted and corrupted by criminal bribery. Our second goal is to punish the criminal conspiracy behind the pleasant sounding name of Malibu Horizons. As we have all read or seen on television, there seems to have been a falling out among thieves. Eduard Charbon and two bodyguards were shot to death in a New York hotel room. We are pursuing leads in that case which are not relevant to the present case. Mr. Jolly and his mother have fled the country to Israel. We have presented the Israeli government with a strong case for extradition. But there is no need to wait upon what will certainly be a long drawn out extradition process. We believe we have presented you with sufficient evidence to establish a criminal conspiracy going back more than four years and we have plenty of criminals to indict without having to wait for Mr. Jolly."

During the question period Goomba, Danny, and Costa were taken back to the anteroom. George reported to them later that two, but no more, members of the Grand Jury were angry that the young men who had committed a robbery were going to go scot free. The rest of the jury seemed to be mildly amused. They were reminded that the witnesses had been promised immunity for their testimony. Since the bonds had been intended as a bribe and had been intercepted in mid-transfer there was even a metaphysical question as to who actually owned them at that particular point in time. There were questions about how much the young men had stolen but the federal attorney had said only that the face amount had been virtually wiped out in the S&L failures of the early nineties.

"Virtually wiped out!" said Costa. "One point eight mil ain't bad, old buddy. I never thought I'd see a cent. Shit! I never thought I'd ever get back to LA again! You sure we're okay?" He'd heard about the Germans and couldn't get himself to believe it just yet.

"The only mob interest left is the Charbon organization in New Orleans," said George. "We're monitoring them pretty good right now and it looks like it's heading for a rumble. Whoever winds up on top probably isn't going to come out to LA after what, a mil five, Danny?"

"That's what my man in San Francisco says," said Danny. "And he's one smart banker. He's been looking after the account since May. And that gets split up three ways."

"I been thinking about that," said Costa. "I never thought I'd have any dough so I'm not used to it now, so maybe this is a dumb idea, but I think we should give something to Johnny Z's family. I know them pretty good, you know, and they're not doing too well..."

Goomba and Danny looked at each other. "Well," said Goomba, "First we subtract that Dead Philadelphian he was busted with, four years ago, that we told him not to try to cash. Then we should charge something for the four years Danny's in the joint cause Johnny ratted him out. Then..."

Danny held up his hand. "Okay, okay. I got no problems with that, we'll work it out later. Right now we're supposed to be getting ready for dinner at the restaurant. Katina closed the place tonight so it's just for family and friends. And friendly feebs who happen to be Greek." He cocked an imaginary gun at George. "Goomba, can I change at your place?"

*

Danny was silent almost all the way out on the Santa Monica freeway. Goomba monopolized what little conversation there was, interrupting himself now and then to curse the rush hour traffic staggering its way west in the late day.

Danny was thinking of his life and what he should do with it. In little more than a week he'd suddenly been confronted with the possibility of the end of his exile. Then he'd almost been killed, not once but twice. Now, it seemed, the threats had vanished and for the first time he was actually in charge of his own life.

A pickup swerved in front of them and Goomba had to stomp on the brakes. Danny laughed suddenly, thinking of how many ways you could get killed anywhere. *Let's get real!* And suddenly a web of clanging circles filled his eyes. He shook his head, swatted himself on the forehead. He knew he'd be getting flashbacks for days, maybe weeks...

He'd have to think. The choices he had were overwhelming. Should he go back to college, to grad school? He knew that he'd have to take lots of course work, and be able to read French and German. Could he do that? He thought, *if I had to do that to be an archaeologist, don't worry about it, I can do it!* He thought of himself in an actual classroom. He'd been a lazy jerk before, the one year he'd actually been to a real college. But up there in the camp, at San Luis Opispo he'd learned to study and had liked it. Reading the books for Barbara and ready to talk about them the next day. Writing essays on the reading he had done, and Barbara telling him over and over, don't use big words! Write simple sentences, like talking! And he'd gotten good at it. And memorizing the Greek poetry for Sam Papadakis, maybe even more fun! Danny knew he could do college, knowing secretly how much more he really knew than the kids sitting around him. But then, on the other hand, should he go into finance, as Sam Papadakis wanted him to do? What would that kind of life be like, dealing the whole time with people whose basic motivation was greed? He didn't think he could put up with that, not as a career.

And then he couldn't help thinking about the women in the places he'd been, and he could see the faces swimming in front of him. Since being tranquilized not once but twice he'd had almost halucinatory visual recall; in fact the doctor had told him he might halucinate and that he should avoid driving for a few weeks. Oddly the first face that came clearly to mind was the woman at the Olympic ticket counter, her dark beauty and inviting eyes, he couldn't even remember the name on the tag above her breast, a sweet swelling breast. And other breasts...he could see them bouncing in the darkness, Elli, tragically waiting back in Kali Vrisi, and how would he deal with her. He could convince himself that that night had all been a dream, but even thinking about it he remembered everything they'd done, in sequence, every detail, and he was getting horny again. And he knew Elli wasn't thinking of it as a dream. The doctor at the clinic came to mind and he realized that in his deep memory there were more images of her than just those few moments when he left the clinic. He now remembered her face, anxious and curiously tender, looking down at him as he fought off the terrors of the drugs he'd been given. And the face turned to that of Fiona, also looking down at him but with a far different expression, and then Barbara, just up the coast, and he knew he'd been avoiding thinking about Barbara, should he go see her, and if he didn't and she found out he'd been right here in Los Angeles, wouldn't she be hurt, insulted even? Of course. How could he not at least call Barbara. He could now tell her what he'd been through these last weeks. Let's take it one at a time, he thought. Let's get through the dinner at the restaurant, then sit down and make up my mind. Okay, where do I go next?

*

Sun came out of the terminal feeling anonymous. He'd been worried about watchers but the terminal at LAX seemed to be three quarters full of people like him, medium height Asians in dark suits, white shirts, conservative ties, always a slightly worried expression as they rounded up luggage, looked for the next means of transportation. He tried to disguise the fact that he was alone, moving along with families, nodding and grinning at them, whether they were Japanese, Chinese, Filippino, Thai, Indonesian, all the ones who looked completely alike to American intelligence professionals. He even saw a man he figured for a police spotter of some kind, a tall guy with a cowboy hat standing at a snack bar near the entrance where the phones for the hotels were. The guy looked normal and casual but any professional could recognize how his eyes made the sweeps back and forth, far distance, middle distance, close, catching anybody who stood out in any way. Sun was just waiting until the cowboy's eyes came by and focussed on him. And then suddenly a man in one family spoke to him.

"You are Korean?"

"Yes, how did you know?"

"You look like my grandfather. Are you a Kim?"

"No. I'm a...another family. But I have Kim relatives. What brings you to Los Angeles?"

"My son has a company here. He's doing well." Sun saw the spotter's eyes pass over the group of Asians all talking together and then go on, looking for something more out of the ordinary.

So he arranged for a taxi for all of them and if anyone else had been watching they would only have seen a medium large Korean family getting into a taxi and taking off for the Sunset strip.

Once there, and having said profusive goodbyes to his countrymen, Sun got another taxi. It dropped him at a garage next to a dry cleaners in Koreatown. The owner gave him a big smile.

"You never saw me here," said Sun.

"I never see anyone in this business," said the owner.

"You got a car I can borrow?"

"You can have your own, the Sonata...it's all fixed up. Different color, Arizona plates. Just don't get stopped. The plates won't hold up."

Kim drove all the way west on Sunset to the Barrington left turn and then made a loop around a block while he watched to see if he was being followed. But no one came after him and he felt relaxed making his way by side streets to Scarlatta's address in Santa Monica. If he couldn't find out anything about Castle from Scarlatta he'd try the restaurant. But he just had a hunch about Castle. Based on timing, if the young man had in fact decided to come back to Los Angeles, Sun thought he would be with Scarlatta. Everything in his instinct told him so. If he located Castle there, what would he do? He didn't know yet. Jolly had said he *might* send someone after him. But he hadn't specifically asked Sun to take care of it, and the bond wouldn't be enough anyway, maybe sixteen thousand. Sun hadn't taken a final contract on anyone for less than a hundred K for twenty years or more, and he'd always insisted on approving the hit. What did he think about Danny Castle? Would he take a contract on him? He realized that he'd gone to Germany to arrange exactly that and that the promised money had been mid-six figures. But it was contingent on a successful mission. The mission was a complete failure so he didn't get paid the six figures. But he could deal with that. It was the nature of the profession. He felt no ill will to Danny Castle. He would, if the opportunity ever arose, be delighted to sit down with Castle over drinks and hear how he had wiped out the deadly Germans. He was approaching Main Street in Santa Monica now and Sun forced his mind to empty itself of all thought. He was now the hunter, looking for people, for information.

Four blocks away from Goomba's house Sun parked in the lot of a mini mall. He then walked two blocks north, one west, one north, two west again, and one block south, keeping an eye out for a tail. No one. And now he was there.

Sun took a deep breath and walked up the driveway. There was a Ford Aspire parked there. He rang the doorbell.

A young man answered. "Hi! How ya doin'?"

"You are Mr. Castle?"

"Nah. I'm Costa. Danny's in the garage with Goomba."

Sun paused for a second. "Whose car is that?"

"The little Ford? That's Goomba's. I think it's a piece of shit, the money he makes, he could have a Porsche, you know, something like that?'

"No, no! It's a good car, not really a Ford. It's made in Korea, you know."

"Yeah? Well. Anyway, you want Danny go on through that door there. I think they're lifting weights."

Sun walked through the door from the kitchen to the garage and down two little stairs. He was facing two men, both looking startled at his presence. One was very big, one was tall but not fat, had a very good tan. That would be Castle, in the Greek sun all summer. Just in back of them Sun could see two weight benches. One had a big Olympic style barbell on a rack above the bench, maybe a hundred kilos. A great burst of light filled Sun's brain. Seeing the bar, the heavy bar on its posts, poised above the bench, it was all shockingly clear to Sun, after all these months. That bar, that huge weight...the strange way Moon had been smashed across his chest...and he knew what had happened that day.

A strangled cry burst from his throat, he took four steps across the garage and launched himself feet first in the kick of death, directly at Danny Castle's throat, with the agony of his cry still echoing in the closed garage.

Goomba had been nervous, just seeing another Korean in his garage and he was on his toes. When Sun launched himself, faster than anything he'd ever seen in his life, he was just able to move forward and fling up a massive forearm. Sun's leading foot was heading for Danny. His trailing foot snapped forward and hit Goomba's forearm, cracking the bones. But the movement gave Danny just enough time to duck. The hard black street shoe on Sun's foot glanced off the side of Danny's head, went driving past and into the wall in back of him. Sun's foot went smashing through the dry wall, stuck, his ankle broke and Sun fell back down and hung, upside down with his foot trapped inside the wall. The pain was enormous and he lost consciousness.

*

Danny got Goomba to an old armchair in the garage. The big man was holding his arm to his body, moaning but he relaxed once he was sitting down. Then Danny turned to Sun. The Korean was hanging upside down from the hole in the wall, he was unconscious and his breath was ragged. So Danny went over to the wall, grabbed Sun around the middle of his body, and managed to lift him up enough to pull his foot out of the wall. He put him gently down on the dirty rug that covered the concrete slab of the garage and then he pulled up a deck chair himself and collapsed into it. He couldn't think what to do. If the police came, would they find something new that would put him and Goomba in jail? He went over to the garage phone extension and tried to call George. No one there, of course. George had left the office and was on the way to Katina's restaurant. He saw Costa nervously looking through the kitchen door into the garage and motioned him in.

Goomba called him. "Danny, Danny! The guy's coming to!" He whirled around, expecting a threat, but saw only that the Korean on the floor had his eyes open, trying to focus. Danny found an old sofa cushion in the corner of the garage and propped it behind the Korean's head. Danny loosened his tie. The man was in bad shape, sweating, no doubt from the pain of the broken ankle, but he was trying to talk.

"Moon. What happened to Moon," he said. "Please tell me!"

Danny started to answer, but Goomba spoke first, his own voice contorted with pain.

"Moon? The big guy? Yeah. He was here. He tried to kill us, Danny anyway, maybe me too. We didn't do anything to him. It was a big fight, we were crashing around the place, we all fell down, the big bar fell on him. God! It must have killed him in a second. I didn't mean to. Nobody tried to kill him. We took him down to the docks that night, thought it'd look like a gang killing. Did you know him?"

Sun took a long breath. "He was my son."

The three strong men were silent in the garage. Goomba, sunk in his chair, Danny, sitting with his head propped in his hands, Sun lying on the floor. They were there for a long time.

"How's the arm?" asked Danny, finally.

"Busted, one bone, anyway," said Goomba. "How's your head?" Danny hadn't realized that there was a long corrugation on his right temple and that blood was drying all the way down into his shirt. He put a hand up, winced.

"It feels like it's drying. No problem."

No one spoke for a moment.

"Uh...how's the leg feel?" Goomba asked Sun.

"Not good."

More silence.

"What happens now?" asked Danny. "Are you going to be trying to kill me the rest of my life? And why should I believe anything you say?"

Sun didn't answer right away. And when he did he wasn't really answering the question.

"My boy. Moon was my youngest son. The only one left. My son was always one tough kid. He was ten when I brought him to this country. His mother was dead, his brother too. I always worked for hard people, all I knew, so he did too. He was good, very cruel, very hard. I loved him. We...we have very strong families in Korea. When I lost my son I had no one left. So you can do me now if you want, take me down to the docks too. That was smart, you know, what you did with Moon. Even I believed it."

"We're not going to kill you," said Danny. He'd gotten up and was standing over Sun. "But I don't trust anyone. You sent those Germans after me, didn't you!"

"It was my job. I was in Zurich, waiting for the bonds." Sun laughed, then cringed from the pain in his ankle.

"I found out about the bonds," Sun went on. "How little they were worth. And then he called, the German boss back in Berlin. All the Germans were dead, he said."

"You know what they tried to do to me?" said Danny, his voice rising. "They chased me most of the way across a mountain, they shot me with a tranquilizer dart, I'd have rotted there if my friend hadn't been there. And then the woman got me again on the boat..." He couldn't go on for a moment. "That woman, crazy, with her needles! She was going to torture me to death!"

Sun chuckled. "Yes. You are American. You don't believe these things can happen. And they never will! You people are so lucky! Because your life is on a different side of the great balance, the peaceful side. You can live your whole life without monsters like those Germans chasing you. But then one day you steal the money. You go from one life to another and you don't even realize that you have changed the point of the balance. And now you're in another world. In this world there are criminals who will torture you, kill you. Now you are in my world and you are playing my game. Mr. Castle, don't blame me for these things. Blame the day you decided to change the balance!" He sighed.

"And now I think I am leaving you, because my ankle has a compound fracture, I have been losing blood and I am dying. So we are even, we are in balance, you and I. Now I give you one small piece of advice. Get out of my life and go back to yours, back to the other side of the balance."

Danny got up quickly and saw the pool of blood under Sun's ankle. It wasn't large.

"You're not dying. You're probably in shock." He kneeled down and loosened Sun's tie and collar some more. Then he took the pillow from beneath his head and lowered his head to the floor.

"Should keep your head low, get more blood to your brain. And I'll put your other leg up on a stool." Very carefully he lifted Sun's left leg, the one not broken.

"Now I guess I got to call an ambulance."

"You sure I'm not bleeding fast? It feels like..."

"No, in fact it's stopped dripping."

"Okay then. No ambulance, unless you want one for your friend. You have a phone?"

Danny handed him the cordless from the workbench of the garage. Sun punched in a number, waited, then spoke rapidly in Korean. He looked up at Danny.

"I called the dry cleaners. They'll come in a truck, take care of me." He looked at Goomba.

"You're a good man. Very fast. I'm sorry I broke your arm. I lost control. Not..." he was searching for a word.

"It was not businesslike."

Danny helped Goomba into the Aspire and made the short drive to the small hospital that normally ministered to the City College football team. Goomba knew everyone there and was in good hands. Costa was going to wait at the house until Sun was picked up, then he'd lock up, go to the party at the restaurant and tell everyone that Goomba'd had a weight-lifting accident and that Danny would be late.

*

Danny got to the restaurant an hour later. Goomba's arm had been set and the big man was sedated, staying at the hospital overnight. Danny had a bandage across his forehead where Sun's shoe had struck him but it didn't look serious. Katina and her husband smothered him in hugs and kisses and he had to stand up and be applauded by all there.

"So, Danny, where you been?" asked an elderly aunt. And that set off the crowd.

"Yeah! Danny! What's the story?" and it went on for over a minute until Danny held his hand up, getting his story straight.

"What happened, when I got out of the prison up there, San Luis Obispo, because of the securities I got framed with, the ones Johnny gave me, there was a bunch of mobsters here in LA, wanted to find where the securities all came from. Me? I didn't know anything, and my friend George, here, with the uh...Justice Department, he said if I could, I should get lost for a few months. So I've been in Greece, can't tell you where yet, but in the meantime the feds have nailed all the bad guys, is that right, George?"

George Kiosoglou made a little hand gesture, yeah we got them all.

"So he tells me I can come back, talk a little to the Grand Jury, and I'm home safe. Only thing is, I can't say much more because of on-going prosecution. But boy, am I glad to be home!"

There was lots of cheering and one of Katina's children put on the tape of Theodorakis' *Stróse to stróma sou yia dyo*, "Make up your bed for two" and the crowd started yelling, "Dance, Thanassi, dance." but he pointed to his forehead, to the bandage and was able to sit down and eat.

Later George got him and Costa aside.

"Alright, what the fuck was that all about? And where's Goomba?" And they told him about Sun, about the lethal attack in the garage, and how they'd let Sun go.

"Jesus! You let the guy go? He could have tied the whole thing together! Do you realize New York PD has already ID'd the Charbon killing at the Marriot as a kung fu operation? One guy has his whole nose up in his brain, the other guy has massive damage to the head done by, get this, a foot wearing a black street shoe..." and George was pointing to Danny's forehead, "They actually got a make on the polish because, this guy comes through an airport, he gets a shoeshine! Is this guy a snappy dresser or what?"

Danny was grinning. "Hey George, maybe Sun took care of our whole problem. And he said he was all through with us, with this operation."

"And you believed him?"

"Some people you believe, others you don't" Danny shrugged.

Chapter Twenty-One
San Francisco

So WHAT ARE YOU GOING TO DO, I mean right now?"
asked Sam Papadakis. "You got a brokerage account up
there in Pocatello, Idaho, those creeps could never have figured out how to access it! Can you imagine a bunch of
Nazis showing up there, going to your brokerage, trying to
tell those Mormons you'd authorized a transfer? It was a
good plan. Anyway, what you're going to do?"

"Right now?" answered Danny. He was looking out the
window of the fortieth floor, seeing Berkeley across the bay,
still shining in the sun as the late afternoon fog began to
close down San Francisco. Sam had moved his banking
operations here several months ago. Danny took a tiny sip
of the champagne Sam had just insisted on pouring. He
thought his liver might be back in shape. They had been
talking all afternoon and he was thirsty.

"I'm going back to Kali Vrisi, tie up loose ends. First
thing, I'm going to buy the farm from Manoli, I owe it to
the guy, then put Yanni on it to run the garden, the goats,
the chickens. After that, maybe I'll stay a month or two, see
what it's like in the winter. Then I'll come back. I've already
been accepted for Winter quarter at UCLA in Classical
Archaeology. They liked my grades up at Cal Poly and they

were interested that I lived in Crete part of the year. So. Now tell me, can you come visit next month? I swear to God you'll love it, Sam!"

Sam was smiling. "You make it sound good, pal. But what I want to know, what're you going to do eventually, with the archaeology, with the women, with the restaurant you own there in Santa Monica? Come on, tell me!"

"I don't know," said Danny. "But it's going to be interesting to find out."